Moonthorne

Pasqua DiNicola

Contents

Chapter One

CHAPTER ONE

DUNHARRA

Everything suffered in misery on that sticky, humid night.

Dunharra glistened with sweat. After hours of tossing and turning, sleep still eluded her. She blew a sigh through her lips and sat on the side of the bed, peeling her damp cotton sleeping shift away from where it clung to her body. Dunharra sighed again, rose, and walked barefoot across the well-worn stone floor to the open window.

Dunharra excised a flat, circular space of about twenty yards across from the dense, deep Thunder Hill forest. The excision let the moonlight shine, and it spilled forward from the abode's front and sides. The ancient forest stood as a guardian at the cottage's flank. She loved the idyllic view from her cottage, on the gentle slopes of a small meadow in the forest at the base of the Silver Haven Mountains. The forest kept quiet in the thick summer humidity. The silence is what she sought when she had moved there. The Wheel of the Year kept turning, and Litha recently passed.

Dunharra adjusted the damp black ringlets that hung down her back as her grass green eyes gazed out the window at her glade. Resting her head on her forearms, she leaned fully on the thick oak windowsill and hoped to catch a stray refreshing breeze. The moonlight silhouetted her diminutive, thin frame inside her delicate sleeping shift. The clear night sky glittered with countless stars and galaxies. The full Triplet Sister Moons illuminated the forest with an ethereal glow. Three Sisters—Jyotsna, Jey and Jhokomis—rose and set as a trio, never leaving each other's side.

Tonight, they danced far above the heat, which strangled those bound to the mortal bonds of Mantua. Even the night fauna gave up on being up and about. They languished in the warm moonlight while hoping for a cool breeze to ease their suffering.

No creature stirred. The forest kept completely still.

Dunharra's small cottage seemed more like an apothecary than a home. A healer lived there. Her eyes scanned the sturdy wooden shelves that lined the walls and housed countless glass jars and containers with various roots, leaves, and powders; all placed there by her careful hand. Dunharra's collections of herbs and flowers, gathered by their stems and bound with string, hung everywhere in various states of dryness. She took a deep breath of the fragrances that married and wafted through the humid air, giving the cottage a light and welcoming aroma.

Her wooden table sat under the room's largest window. The slick and smooth top, well-worn by unknown ages of work, long before coming into Dunharra's possession. It stood sentry with its time-worn chairs under the unshuttered portal. She watched the Triplet Sister Moons' light spill in, bathing the room and all its contents in a rich glow. Her ancient mortar and pestle sat centrally on the tabletop, ready for the coming morning's work.

Dunharra envied her black and white cat, Mercy. It curled up in a shadowy corner near the hearth with its tail tucked neatly around its body, sleeping. The only thing able to sleep in the forest.

A small gift from the Mother arrived as the cool gentle wind, which Dunharra had been waiting for. It blew gently across the glade, rustling the grass, and into the open window. She inhaled deeply, delighting in the moment as the airy respite cooled her skin. Then the refreshing breeze departed as stealthily as it had come, returning Dunharra and everything around her to the night's hot and humid grip.

Dunharra noticed something seemed off. It had been quiet in the forest before, but now it was too quiet. And too quiet brought no good. The hair on her arms and the back of her neck prickled, and she could sense something went sideways somewhere and about to go very wrong.

Dunharra's training taught her to trust her instincts. If she tried, she could still hear the words of her first teacher, Brea, in the old woman's gravelly voice.

"Lessons learned will either exact their toll or pay royal dividends," Brea said. "Just as every student knows that there has never been one who became poorer by paying attention, they must decide how much attention to invest into each situation."

Brea also taught Dunharra various uses for magick. "Only the Mother gave the gift of magick. Simple magic, barely above simple parlor tricks, illusions, and sleights of hand; people used this to entertain children at parties with tricks that were easy to learn and required minimal natural talent. To make and use magick, however, humans and others alike needed the imprinting of sacred ink to connect them to the Mother. Without the ink, there no one could make magick."

Dunharra's musings broke when a figure burst from the forest line a scant five yards away with their sword in hand. Surprised by the sudden commotion, the sweltering fauna skittered away, seeking shelter deeper in the humid shadows. They chittered and hooted in complaint as they fled, unhappy about being forced to move on such a warm and sticky night.

The solitary figure half limped, half ran directly toward Dunharra's cottage. If it were not looking over its shoulder and back into the trees, it might have locked eyes with Dunharra and perhaps seen the obstacle ahead. The lithe shadow tripped over a gnarled tree root and fell to the grass with an ungraceful thud. Its short sword twisted from its hand and slid forward in the dirt. The figure made one feeble attempt to rise, rolled onto its back, then fell motionless.

The shadowed Elf lay still before her window. Dunharra could see that the once ice-blue silken travel tunic, trimmed with familiar silver Elvish embroidery, became torn and bloodied. Mud and debris caked the elegant boots, unable to hide the cuts and bruises covering their legs.

Dunharra held her breath and gripped the windowsill tightly as she resisted the urge to run to the prone figure and provide aid. She knew what it took to unsettle an elf, but someone, or something, unsettled this elf to the degree that she would take flight. Whatever gave chase she knew must be fearsome, lethal and close by.

Instinct kicked in and Dunharra connected with the Mother and asked for camouflage. As she spoke, her cottage shimmered in the moonlight. As she finished her magick, the abode gave off a slight sparkle, then disappeared completely against the forest's background. Dunharra and all within became invisible to the naked eye. If Dunharra remained inside, she and her home remained unseen. Whatever tromped through her woods, unbidden and out of control, no longer had the upper hand.

In the same instant her words faded into the silence, five orcs, large by even orc standards, stomped through the forest directly toward her and the prone Elf. The near six and a half foot tall orcs dwarfed the Dunharra and the vulnerable Elf; they were bigger and more muscular than they were. The orcs outsized them by a foot and a half and outweighed them by several hundred pounds. They had greenish grey skin and tufts of black hair on their heads. They were heavily armed, as if they were fighting mercenaries, not one small Elf. The orcs had two teeth that jutted out of their mouths on either side, making their countenance ferocious. They smashed a trail of destruction through the flora, shoving limbs and branches aside and tearing bushes from their roots.

Dunharra intently watched the largest of the orcs, who happened to be the ugliest, grunt and gestured to the remaining four to help themselves to anything of value on the injured elf. He bent down and checked the elf for signs of life.

The orcs tore through the Elf's belongings. They took pouches out of her backpack and opened them. It seemed to Dunharra that they were looking for something specific, but she could not be certain. The more they searched without finding what they were looking for, the angrier they became. Sniffing the contents of the pouches, they crinkled their misshapen noses and then tossed the pouches away, carelessly spilling the contents onto the forest floor. The orcs took her short sword and coin pouch to divide among them, with a quarrel. The orc captain settled the dispute, pushing them away and grabbing the sword for himself. He delivered a devastating punch to the elf's face, and cobalt blood flowed out of her nose and mouth. Dunharra winced at the scene but stayed in the cottage's safety.

"Find the brownie," the largest orc snarled. "It must have the Moonthorne."

Brownie? What brownie? And why do orcs want Moonthorne?

Dunharra met a brownie before, when she still studied under Brea, in her younger years. She remembered Misha the brownie, who bonded to a snow elf named Kiiral of Manasquan. Even in the magical world, people often gave them a casual stare, but nothing more, because they were an unusual pairing. Dunharra remembered learning from Misha how they freely chose who they bonded with and when. Brownies ranged from thin to stocky and usually no more than eighteen inches tall. Misha stood tall for a brownie at twenty inches. All Brownies came with attitudes twice their size, and so did Misha.

Moonthorne treated the Cough, an illness that caused violent coughing followed by an expectoration of blood. If left untreated, death followed quickly. Long since eradicated a thousand years ago by the Lycaena after it ravaged their nation, it hadn't resurfaced until recently in Innesfrees. The Lycaena, a reclusive race that lived in the Silver Haven Mountains, developed the cure: Moonthorne. Dunharra knew the flower and the disease well in their own respects. She possessed a few doses of Moonthorne herself, carefully stored away in small brown bottles with cork stoppers.

Once satisfied, each orc took turns giving painful and destructive kicks to the elf's thin frame, then left it for dead to look for the brownie.

Finally, the forest returned to its normal, peaceful quiet.

Dunharra undid the latch and pushed the wooden door aside silently on its well-oiled hinges. She scanned the front meadow once again cautiously. Seeing nothing, she stepped forward. As her foot crossed the threshold, breaking the magick camouflaging her home, the cottage shimmered and became visible once again. Dunharra tiptoed to the fallen elf and crouched by her side, her pulse slow and weak. Dunharra checked once more for the orcs. Seeing none, she threw the elf's limp arm around her own neck and half carried, half dragged the elf into her cottage.

"By the Mother, you're heavier than you look," Dunharra said as she laid the broken elf gently on her bed. Whispered words re-enchanted the cloak to hide them from prying eyes. Dunharra surveyed her new charge and inventoried the damage done by orcish hands and feet.

The elf bled from her mouth and her broken nose. She still breathed, although rough and ragged. When she coughed, she coughed up blood from broken ribs piercing her lungs, causing internal bleeding. Darkening bruises covered most of her exposed skin. The beating this elf endured left no part of her untouched, and death hovered nearby to claim her.

Dunharra worked purposefully. She had the situation under full control. Her eyes shifted from grass green to iridescent. She hovered her hand over the elf's mouth and nose. The flow of blood slowed and then stopped. She checked the elf's body for other injuries and found many. The elf suffered broken and bruised ribs, a crushed pelvis, a broken eye socket, and a shattered jaw. One rib pierced her lung, filling it with blood.

The healer patiently worked her magick to stem internal bleeding and repair the broken bones. The bluish skin above each of the fractures shimmered and glowed in Dunharra's iridescent light, while the broken ends of bone beneath them found each other and fused into their proper place. She drained the lung of blood, and the elf took a deep, cleansing breath. Lastly, Dunharra healed the concussion she suffered from the orcs' devastating blows.

Slowly, the elf's complexion returned to her cheeks. Her breathing became even and regular. What the orcs and their violence had done, Dunharra had undone. She sighed, spent from the healing effort.

The Elf awoke as if nothing had happened. Dunharra estimated that the tiny framed elf might be about one hundred eighty years, although no one could discern an elf's true age with any accuracy. She had silvery blue hair with smooth and pale skin. A sleeve of intertwined filigree and flowered inks ran the length of both arms, from shoulder to fingertip. Beyond an initiate, but she still had some way to go before she would be called a master.

The curious black and white tuxedo cat woke and left its shadowy corner. She sniffed carefully around at the torn and bloodstained tunic to step around the elf. Dunharra's magick had a familiar scent, but the not the scent of her patient did not. The cat's tail twitched with a curiosity she could not contain.

"That is my cat, Mercy. She won't hurt you."

The elf relaxed with a quizzical, if not weary, look.

Dunharra asked, "What's your name?"

The elf paused a moment but then answered, "Iseabail Allora."

"Nice to meet you, Iseabail. I'm Dunharra Tor. I'm a healer. Your journey ended right outside my door. The orcs robbed you and left you with a wicked beating." She walked to the hearth and spooned some savory broth into a smooth wooden bowl.

After a pause, the elf exclaimed, "Calyx! I have to find Calyx! She has the bag." She looked around with her eyes wide and her breaths coming in ragged bursts. Iseabail tried to get out of bed.

Dunharra brought the fragrant, steaming broth and sat on the side of the bed with Iseabail. "Tell me about Calyx and the bag."

"Calyx is my brownie. My familiar. My friend," she explained. She sat up with her eyes pained knowing Calyx endured the forest alone.

"You're remembering, which is good," Dunharra said with a soothing tone. "You took some serious blows to the head. What else do you remember?"

"The orcs," Iseabail said as her lip curled and her nose wrinkled. "I couldn't get away, and there were six of them."

Dunharra frowned. She counted only five. Orcs unaccounted for could only mean trouble. "Are you certain?"

"I killed one," Iseabail said. "I gave Calyx the bag and told her to hide."

"What's in the bag?"

"Moonthorne. I need to bring it to Innesfrees."

"I'll go look for Calyx and the Moonthorne. For now, you stay here," Dunharra said as she stood and walked out of the cottage.

Dunharra walked through the Thunder Hill Forest, looking up at the treetops for a Brownie and a leather bag. She heard the orc too late, which surprised her, but she turned around in time to see him charging. She raised her hands and brought magick to her lips, but he jumped upon her and knocked her to the ground before she could connect with the Mother. He pawed at her with his filthy hands, trying to rip at her clothes. He licked her neck with a slimy, odorous tongue. Smaller than the orc they both knew who had the upper hand. She kicked and fought back as she connected with the Mother. She connected with the Mother and her eyes turned iridescent.

A blue bolt of lightning shot out of her fingers, knocking the orc backward. He landed at the base of a nearby tree, smoke rising from his mottled skin. Startled birds flew from the tree in protest, squawking loudly as they went. The orc roared a guttural rumble.

Dunharra scrambled to stand, and took a few steps backward.

"I have no quarrel with you," Dunharra warned. "Be on your way."

He snarled and charged her again with a sword in hand.

Dunharra swore. Shorter, thinner, and lighter than the massive orc bearing down on her, she narrowed her eyes, readied more magick. She ducked when he swung his heavy sword at her head. Losing her balance, she landed flat on her back; the dew and humidity on the mossy forest floor made everything slippery.

The orc grinned as she struggled to regain footing. "This will be fun, human. For me."

Dunharra finished her magick, and another sizzling bolt hit its mark. The orc's scream of pain distracted it, allowing Dunharra to put several yards between them. Nostrils flaring, the orc's lips pulled back, exposing his yellow, misshapen teeth. He took off at a run toward Dunharra. She took a step forward and sent a foot wide flaming orb into his chest with both hands. It slammed him into a small nearby tree, shaking it violently.

From the boughs above, a brownie and a deerskin bag came tumbling down, hitting the forest floor with a dull thump.

The orc finally took its last breath, dropping its sword to the forest floor. Dunharra sighed and wiped dirt and sweat from her face.

The brownie peeked out from behind the tree. She regarded the smoking, dead orc and carefully stepped out into the open. She asked, "Where's Iseabail?"

"You must be Calyx. I'll take you to her. She's eager to see you," Dunharra said, and thanked the Mother for her aid and for finding the wayward brownie.

Dunharra watched the reunion in her cottage, and her eyes teared up. She wiped her eyes and couldn't help but smile as she watched Calyx run to Iseabail. Her heart danced as Calyx held Iseabail tightly.

"Thank the Mother you are alive, Calyx," Iseabail said as she hugged her.

"Who knows you carry Moonthorne?" Dunharra asked after the moment passed.

"I thought only the Lycaena and her father. Who benefits? Who gains if the Cough goes untreated in Innesfrees?" Calyx asked.

"We are to deliver this to the Queen first," Iseabail said. "Someone in the royal family must also be ill. Now, we have targets on our backs."

Dunharra frowned. "Those orcs nearly killed you. I bet whoever sent them also thinks you're dead. What you need is someone to make sure you travel there in one piece, and I know the perfect couple."

The next morning, on their way to Innesfrees, they made a short but necessary stop in Rhyl.

Chapter Two

CHAPTER TWO

AOIFE

Princesses do not cry over skinned knees.

Speeding across the cobblestone pathway in her blue linen dress, Aoife's bare foot slid on an errant rock. She tumbled headfirst to the ground, badly skinning her right knee and tearing her dress. The shock of the severe, stinging pain brought tears to her eyes. Fighting back the tears, she stood with blood flowing down her knee and slowly walked back to the castle. She needed to see Iain, her tutor, and Innesfrees' lead healer, for a bandage.

Aoife knew Iain would scold her.

When she arrived at his office, he sat her down on a functional, rustic wooden chair and bandaged her avulsed and bloodied knee with an aromatic poultice for the pain and a thick salve for the broken skin. "I will be gone in a few days."

Aoife gave him a doubtful look. "Thank you, Master Iain," she said, looking down at the bandage. "And thank you for not scolding me."

"That will come from your mother when she sees you've torn another new dress. Let's not be late for tomorrow's lesson, Aoife?"

Aoife nodded solemnly as she turned to go. Iain watched her walk away slowly as he absently rubbed his right knee.

Aoife returned, late, as usual, for her actual lesson. She usually kept her tutor waiting. "Sorry, Master Iain."

"Changed behavior is the sincerest apology, Aoife. Let's begin."

Aoife sighed as the hours of lessons on maths, the geography of Mantua, and conversational Elvish passed. She knew how being a princess and future queen of Innesfrees, a small Southern Kingdom, that this was all necessary, but it was mind-numbing to her. She wanted to learn international relations, not maths. Master Iain kept sending deep frowns her way until she went back to her work.

How much longer? She asked him using mind-speak, an exciting new thing she figured out how to do with her mother. Maybe it would work with the Master, too? She wanted to try.

Master Iain looked up suddenly at her, sitting back slowly in his creaky, wooden chair. She watched as he slowly closed his eyes and let out a slow breath. Unsure if her new trick worked, she decided to try again.

Master Iain? Aoife asked, focused on ringing clear in his mind.

"Courtesy dictates you use verbal communication. However, you may leave for the day, Aoife," Iain whispered, cowed by a shocking thought.

He had heard her! Aoife wondered why he appeared ill out of the blue. She hoped he would not get sick before the grand feast later. If he got sick, he would miss the best part.

"So you did hear me?" This time Aoife asked her question out loud.

"Yes, but I suggest you not speak to others about this."

"But why?" His grave tone perplexed her.

"Usually, only certain people can communicate this way." He paused briefly before continuing, "I remember being able to speak like this with my brother." A slight smile relaxed the Master's face. "We got ourselves into a lot of trouble this way."

Leaning forward, serious again, "But Aoife, do not speak of this. I will take care of it. I will talk to your mother after the Summit. Do you understand?"

Aoife nodded. Master Iain seemed concerned and she did not want to bother her parents with this now.

"Ok, away with you then, enough lessons for today." Master Iain dismissed her with a wave of his hand, his lips and brows pinched in thought.

Aoife scampered through the corridors with almost reckless abandon, dodging castle staff and villagers. Her poultice-treated and bandaged knee from a few days ago had been long forgotten. People were slowing her down, and that frustrated her ten-year-old self. She found the first internal, hidden corridor behind the walls and slipped inside. She breathed a huge sigh of relief. Here, she could run free or take her time as she wished.

She emerged in a deep, dark corner of the frantically busy kitchen, bathed in cool shadow. The secret entrance to the kitchen, rarely used by anyone but her, hummed with activity. The upcoming summit would keep this corridor very busy.

The kitchen staff frantically worked to prepare the food for the Summit. All the other cooks worked double duty since Mathéo's devastating murder last week. Mathéo had been her favorite cook and her favorite target from whom to get pilfered treats. The cooks whispered among themselves while chopping onions. The smell made Aoife wrinkle her nose. She wanted to see if she could sample the dessert. She walked over to Noemie, her chosen substitute since Mathéo's tragic death, who focused on the custard and puff pastry.

"Hi, Noemie!"

Noemie jumped and squeezed too much custard, so it exploded out the top. "Aoife, you made me ruin the pastry!"

"Well, since it's ruined, can I have it?" Aoife asked wide eyed and smiling.

Noemie rolled her eyes. She gave it to Aoife with a heavy sigh. "Off with you! We have work to do down here." Noemie waved her away with frustrated hands, then picked up the next pastry to try again.

"Thank you, Noemie," Aoife said, as she walked away.

Giggling, Aoife took the pastry and ran off to her room, where she could savor it in peace.

Aoife loved her room. She loved the feel of the rich Elven sheets and warm wool blankets against her skin when she climbed into bed at night. Reaching out, she pet her black cat, Dubh, as it lay sleeping at the foot of her bed. In the corner sat a book nook; with a large, comfortable chair and a warm woolen throw. Her full bookshelves held many books about the far off places she might see for herself one day. She pulled out a book and brought it to her bed. Aoife petted Dubh as she lost herself in the battles of knights and dragons.

Outside her door, the castle buzzed with preparations for the Buckhaven visit. Aoife put her book down and peered out her window. Blue and red Buckhaven banners fluttered in the hot summer breeze as they drew near. Dozens of horses and knights rode ahead of the enemy royal family. Finally at the rear, she saw the carriage of the Buckhaven royals in all its famous extravagant splendor. Gilded wheels pulled by two pure white chargers, and led by a driver in full formal regalia, replete with shining medals from faraway wars, rumbled through the castle gate.

Unfortunately, that meant the time came for Aoife to don her emerald gown and join her parents in welcoming Buckhaven to Innesfrees. She stared at the dress and it looked stiff with responsibility.

Responsibility she didn't want yet. With a heavy sigh, she did as her responsibility dictated and allowed her two maidens to help her into it. She didn't fuss or fight getting dressed; that would not be fair to Coira or Dalles. So she stood there as they fastened the many buttons and fussed over her until they deemed her perfect. She didn't like this part of being a princess.

Aoife walked purposefully and carefully to join her parents. Prince Regent Kieron stood tall at six feet with curly deep brown hair and brilliant blue eyes. Queen Maebh, a strong willed woman with flaming red curls that hung in ringlets to each side of her face stood by his side. Not willing to risk a single stitch or hair out of place, Aoife walked rather than ran to stand at her parents' side. Every eye in the courtyard watched the actions of the royal family today.

Aoife's father looked down on his daughter and smiled. "You look beautiful, Aoife. I know this isn't your favorite thing, but I'm glad you're here and on time. Your presence here matters."

The Buckhaven delegation dripped in gilt and the stiffest formality. To Aoife, it appeared like they spared no expense for this performative arrival. King Darragh O' Dochartaigh and Queen Aelwen stepped out of the carriage first, assisted by the driver. King Darragh's slightly pronounced belly showed though his finest clothing. He stood shorter than Kieron. He fancied himself a warrior king. He carried a sharp looking battle worn sword at his side. Queen Aelwen braided her light brown hair elegantly around her plump face. Prince Ronan, resolute and grim for his early twenties, with a head of curly brown hair, not unlike his father's, emerged from the carriage with his young brother. Donal, only five years old.

"It is my great honor and joy to welcome you to Innesfrees, King Darragh and Queen Aelwen," Queen Maebh said.

Aoife watched as the King wrinkled his nose and sniffed a few times, his brow raised as he surveyed the assembly. Disdain apparent, he maintained a thin veneer of courtesy. "Thank you, Queen Maebh. I look forward to the Summit."

Queen Aelwen signaled to her attendants. Aoife watched them bring a muscular woman with callused hands to the Queen. "This is Kielly. It wounded us deeply to hear of the terrible and senseless tragedy of your cook. It would honor us if you accepted our loan of a cook..." Aelwen paused for effect. "As a token of goodwill."

Aoife looked at her parents, who kept their faces stoic and their thoughts to themselves. She could tell that they did not expect any overtures of goodwill from Buckhaven, and they did not appreciate this one.

Maebh cleared her throat, taking control of the awkward and uncomfortable situation. "Of course," she said as she gestured for a guard to step forward. "Please take her to the cooks' quarters and see to it she is comfortable and settled in."

Before being excused, Aoife watched as Innesfrees knights showed the Buckhaven coalition to the guests' quarters so they could wash off several days of travel before the official state activities began. She helped her mother set up the luxurious and extravagant quarters where Buckhaven would stay during the summit. They bordered on gaudy, purposefully accommodated to their expectations. Tapestries detailing the history of Innesfrees hung on the walls, and the furnishings were gold and sparkling. While she loved the tapestries, when she ascended to queen, she would never put up such gaudy furnishings only to make visitors happy.

The sun hung high in the summer sky when they were called to the celebration. Knights escorted King Darragh, accompanied by Queen Aelwen, Prince Ronan and Ambassador Pytor Tymoshenko to the intimate meeting room where the talks would take place. There were sconces of gold, lit with aromatic twigs of sandalwood and cedar to give the small room a fresh and fragrant aroma. Light shades, tied back fashionably with linen, dressed the windows and let fresh air in. In those tiebacks rested sunflowers celebrating the coming Litha.

King Darragh looked around but nodded his assent to the ambience. He let out a disgruntled snort. "It'll do, I suppose."

Prince Regent Kieron, and Queen Maebh soon after arrived and took their places at the round table.

And so, the Summit began. Aoife silently slid into her seat, thrilled that her age finally allowed her to be a silent observer. She didn't know what to expect from today, and she hoped her face didn't show it.

"Thank you for attending," Kieron began. "It's our hope that the summit will be productive and beneficial for both Innesfrees and Buckhaven." Darragh, Aelwen, and Ronan nodded their appreciation. The kitchen staff ensured the room overflowed with creature comforts such as spiced nuts, and bread with cheese and honey. Mugs of ale sat at each person's place, with the exception of Aoife who drank sparkling fruited water imported from Manasquan. They shifted in their seats and made themselves comfortable.

"First on the itinerary is the Disputed Lands. Innesfrees is prepared to cede lands to give access to the west bank of the Bannockburn River. In return, Buckhaven will drop its current and future claim of contested lands for the entire mouth of the Bannockburn," Maebh continued.

Darragh bristled. "The entire mouth of the Bannockburn are ancestral lands of Buckhaven. Access to the river is critical. Transportation and trade count on having access to the entirety of the river."

"You will have access from the west side," Maebh said. "We will make the center of the river a demilitarized zone, where no one will travel, fish, or troll for oysters. This agreement grants you access to the river and restores the eastern bank to the rightful Innesfrees."

"Rightful? Who says rightful?" Ronan snarled, slamming his fist on the table.

Darragh shot Ronan a look that could sour milk but did not disagree with his hot-headed son. Ronan cowed and returned to his attentive silence.

"All the ancestral maps chart Innesfrees as having ownership of the entire mouth of the Bannockburn River. This is a more than fair compromise," Kieron replied.

The Summit's attendees spent the next three hours hotly debating the accuracy and authority of the ancestral maps before breaking for lunch.

They took their meals privately, so both Buckhaven and Innesfrees could refresh and regroup. The talks were going nowhere.

After lunch and a sufficient cooling off, they returned to the table.

Buckhaven doubled down and became more obstinate than before.

Day one ended in an impasse.

The Triplet Sister Moons danced together among the stars in the summer's late night sky. Crickets chirped, and Aoife had trouble sleeping. The stress of being on her best behavior and wearing the itchy, formal dresses took their toll. She tossed and turned in her bed, but sleep would not come, no matter how she arranged her pillows. Dubh meowed at her for disturbing her slumber, and Aoife's fitful attempts at comfort and sleep annoyed the normally snuggly feline. Dubh abandoned Aoife's bed to curl up on the chair to sleep.

Aoife rose from her bed and took a walk around the inner tunnels. She knew the tunnels inside and out, and the light of the moons shining in the arrow slits partially lit her way. The tunnels were cool and dark with deep shadows in the corners. The shadowy corners reminded her of scary tales she read in books near Samhain and Yule. They were like a secret only she knew, and she kept that to herself. She walked through the tunnels until she heard voices and stopped. Visiting dignitaries were also awake and deep in conversation.

Aelwen, Darragh, and Ronan sat in their room talking about the negotiations. Aoife pushed herself flat against the wall to eavesdrop.

"Is there any suspicion about our murder of the cook?" Darragh asked.

"There seems to be none," Ronan answered. "It's an unfortunate, unsolved crime."

"And what of the Dark Elf Lands?" Darragh continued.

"The Cough is rampant and unchecked in the Dark Elf Lands," Darragh said. "They were more than happy to exchange a sick slave for a well one. Her symptoms will be easily mistaken for the common cold. The Cough will be rampant both in the castle and the countryside within two weeks." Darragh laughed and it sent shivers up her spine.

"It's all going as planned," Aelwen said.

She grasped the importance of the summit-related information she overheard, and shock overwhelmed her. She turned to walk back to her room, but she tripped over her own feet and thumped against the wall. Terror seized her; she froze, fearing discovery. She held her breath. Immediately, the conversation stopped between Darragh, Aelwen, and Ronan. They were quiet for a moment, listening.

"Rats," Aoife heard Ronan sneer.

Aoife relaxed, and she exhaled silently, relieved. She crept carefully to her room, intending to talk with her parents before the second day of negotiations.

Early the next morning, Aoife met her parents in her father's private quarters to have breakfast before day two of the negotiations. The intimate apartment, decorated with tapestries of the glories of Innesfrees long ago, accommodated them well. They sat together at a table large enough for three and had her mother's favorite pancakes with a strawberry compote.

"Mum, what are the Dark Elf Lands?" Aoife asked between bites of pancake and strawberries.

Her parents stopped. Her mother asked, incredulous, "Where did you hear that?"

Aoife squirmed in her seat. Could she admit she eavesdropped on the Buckhaven royal family last night? Could she tell her parents she crept around the castle's hidden corridors late at night when she needed to be in bed asleep?

"Aoife?" Her father encouraged her to answer with a firm tone. "We have not told you about such things yet. How did you learn about the Dark Elf Lands?"

"I heard the Buckhaven coalition discuss them. They were talking about cooks and the Dark Elf lands. What is it?"

Her parents exchanged looks. Things were making sense. Her mother nodded.

"The Dark Elf Lands is an underground realm where the Dark Elves—"

"—the corrupted elves," her mother interjected.

"—live. They raid cities and towns on the surface for slaves and human sacrifices. They are a dangerous, ruthless people not to be trusted."

Somber, Aoife pushed her breakfast around her plate until she got permission to leave.

Chapter Three

CHAPTER THREE

DUNHARRA

Dunharra knew Anaïs didn't like getting up in the morning, but she hoped at least Zauvadok would be awake.

On their way to Innesfrees, they stopped in Rhyl. Dunharra remembered meeting Anaïs and Zauvadok about a year ago. He introduced himself, full of nervousness and self consciousness and asked her if she would heal someone. He wouldn't say whom or what from, but she couldn't say no to the desperate look in his steely grey eyes. She followed the stranger to the Fat Nun, an inn on the far outskirts of Rhyl. On the way, Zauvadok told her about the frightened serving girl who found a Dark Elf hiding in the cool, dark corners of the wine cellar. As the bouncer and leading member of the brute squad, they sent him to kill her. Zauvadok took one look at the suffering Dark Elf and decided he couldn't do it. He carried her upstairs to a room and went to find a healer. Finally he found a healer. Dunharra readily said yes.

Dunharra put a hand over her mouth as she saw the intense sunburn suffered by the Dark Elf, somehow out of the Dark Elf Lands during the day. The sun even burned her eyes.

She immediately set upon healing the Dark Elf. Her eyes shifted to iridescent, and she lightly touched her face and eyes with her iridescent hands. Immediately the blisters and swelling went down quickly and painlessly.

Dunharra watched carefully as Anaïs slowly opened her eyes and felt her pristine black skin.

"Pain? Dunharra asked.

"No," Anaïs said. "Who are you? How can I thank you?"

Dunharra smiled and sat back. "I'm Dunharra Tor and rumors of my healing must remain a strict secret. Why are you above ground during the day?"

"I ran into trouble on the overnight raid last night," Anaïs haltingly began. "I didn't bring back a slave. It's wrong, and I am tired of pretending. I escaped and ran to the surface. I didn't know what to do or where to go. I searched for a place where I could get out of the unforgiving sun. I found this inn and hid in the wine cellar. The perfect place to hide and regroup." Anaïs' eyes were wet, and tears threatened to spill onto her cheeks.

"You're safe now," Zauvadok said. "I won't let anyone hurt you. Ever."

Dunharra smiled at the memory, allowing herself a brief moment of reverie.

She knocked on the door to their cottage and waited.

Moments later, a seven foot half orc ripped open the door with a snarl. He wore fitted leather pants with a white shirt and a matching leather vest. His black hair formed a wild mess, and his perfectly kept teeth showed through when his mouth made a hideous snarl. His eyes were a steely grey and not the least bit happy at the interruption.

And that snarl melted away when he saw Dunharra.

"Dun!" Zauvadok reached down and picked up Dunharra and hugged her. "Oh, Dun, it's been too long!"

Dunharra laughed, and it sounded like tinkling bells to his ears.

Anaïs emerged from the bedroom and squealed. "Dun!" She gave Dunharra a tight hug. Anaïs, thin but appropriately strong for her size wore her long white hair up in a topknot. Her brown eyes complimented her perfect black skin. She wore black leather and a keen eye could see the hint of black filigree ink on her skin.

"Who are your friends?" Anaïs asked.

Dunharra introduced Iseabail and Calyx and told them about the orcs, the Cough and the Moonthorne.

"We need to get to Innesfrees. We need your help to get there. Will you come with us?"

Anaïs regarded Zauvadok, who turned to Dunharra.

"When do we leave?" they asked in unison.

Chapter Four

CHAPTER FOUR

AOIFE

The healers kept the sickroom cool and dark. Aoife saw a row of white candles that danced to mingle with slivers of morning light shining through the closed drapes. Even on the warmest days deep inside the castle, which sat at the top of the Star Wall cliff on the edge of the Bay of Charms, offshore breezes always kept the castle cool.

Aoife lay in a large, soft bed in the sickroom. She lay between fresh cotton sheets that were the traditional healer's white with a warm, brilliant green comforter with intricate silver stitching. A young healer doted on her lovingly, and she tried to smile. Her mother told her to be brave, and she tried. The abundant seriousness of everyone around her inspired a nagging sense of doom.

Aoife watched the healer's face wrinkle, and then bite her lip. She didn't feel very well. The herbs and medications they used to control her temperature worked only moderately well but did nothing to soothe her cough. After she coughed again, the healer frowned. She coughed with such intensity that her whole body shook. After each spasm, she moaned as her little body ached with the effort. Her hair, a brilliant red, lay in sweaty ringlets on her forehead. Fever ravaged her tiny body. The young healer dabbed Aoife's forehead and reddened cheeks with cool water to keep her comfortable.

She knew that the royal healers eventually discerned that the Cough appeared with the new cook, the goodwill loan from Buckhaven, and spread through the servants like wildfire. Within two weeks, the castle functioned with a skeleton crew. Dedicated and loyal staff worked day and night to complete the basic tasks.

Aoife overheard the healers talk of a cure. The Lycaena found the Moonthorne flower and its other ingredients at the peaks of the Silver Haven Mountains long ago when the Cough afflicted them. It needed to be reconstituted into a tea for effectiveness.

Would it come in time?

***

IAIN

Iain knew the Queen and the Prince Regent well. A guest at their wedding, he saw Maebh through a rough pregnancy, painful labor, and delivery of a baby girl. He oversaw the healing of scores of people throughout Innesfrees but never came face to face with something he, and nature, could not cure. Not until the Cough ravaged Innesfrees.

He wondered if he should have learned more healing magick instead of only herbalism, botany, and medication. Iain heard the reports from his associate herbalist healers of what feats those healers with the magick performed. Although he had a magical healer on his team, he did not think very highly of her talents. He recalled one instance in particular where he embarrassed a magickal healer when he said that he would take herbs over magick any day. He later came to regret saying that and tried to apologize to the healer, who of course, demurred and said nothing. Iain thought that the Mother gave everything needed as herbs to cure all ailments, when applied early enough. Now he knew otherwise.

He walked down a long, candlelit hallway hung with tapestries detailing the glories of Innesfrees of long, long ago. Cobwebbed candelabras with many cream-colored candles stood sentry, illuminating the beautiful pieces. He stopped by his favorite tapestry depicting a legendary healer.

It is too bad that the Prophecy of the Healer is simply an old fairy tale.

A fairy tale told ages ago, the Prophesied Healer could heal any injury, illness or disease. Even death would cower at their touch. What a frightening responsibility to put on one person. He imagined that the disclosure of their ability would lead to constant hounding to heal anything and everything. Iain wondered if the Prophesied Healer had come and gone and no one noticed. Maybe they had come but were in hiding.

Once at the Queen's private rooms, he paused, took a breath to steady himself, and knocked on the door. In the foyer, Beit She'an guards watched over the Queen. The guards dressed in full regalia. Iain thought this unnecessarily extravagant. They stood sentry to protect the Queen from any attack. They were soldiers from the island of Beit Shemesh, and were ready for anyone and anything.

Once past the guards, Iain saw Maebh sitting with her three ladies in waiting. He saw the Queen looked tired and tense. Deep concern etched her pale, freckled face. Dressed casually in her sitting room, her curly red hair lay unbound about her head and shoulders. When Iain entered, the women glanced over at him in unison, surprised by the intrusion, and their secret conversation halted. His heart skipped a beat, as Maebh would forever hold a special place there.

"Your Majesty," Iain said respectfully with a deep bow.

"Iain," the Queen replied. Her eyes were red-rimmed and watery. "How is Aoife?"

Maebh sat with her shoulders hunched, and nervously picked at her fingernails.

As the lead healer in Innesfrees, Iain quarantined Aoife away from her parents to keep the Cough from spreading to them. While the wisest decision, the toll became much for Maebh to bear.

"For now, she only coughs," he replied. "She burns with fever, but we care for her night and day. We are doing everything we can."

The Queen looked crestfallen at the news, and it made Iain's heart ache to deliver it to her. Her brow arched, and she swallowed hard against the reality of Aoife's condition. The ladies in waiting laid loving hands on her and stood behind her in unanimous support.

The lady of the bedchamber, the oldest, wisest, most informed, and leader of the ladies in waiting, shot Iain a dour and dark look. "I'm assuming you have some good news to report, Iain?" the lady asked, her words sharp and her tone threatening.

"Yes, there is a treatment. Moonthorne," Iain continued quickly, stumbling over his words, feeling the sting of their rebuke. "The Lycaena perfected it hundreds of years ago. We can ask them for assistance."

"Iain, go to the Lycaena," Queen Maebh ordered, and her voice held the spark of hope that her daughter would live. "Whatever they ask, pay it. Accept any price. Any price."

"Yes, Your Majesty," Iain replied. He bowed and left the Queen and her ladies, who resumed their hushed conversation.

Iain gathered two knights, Duncan and Fergus, and a promising young magickal healer, Mhari, to take the trip. Iain had the fastest horses tacked and ready. Dressed in full diplomatic regalia, the four of them mounted and rode off to the Silver Haven Mountains at the break of dawn. They rode hard all morning, intending to go straight through to Dhangadi, the capital city of the Lycaena.

Iain did not notice that Mhari tried all morning to engage him in conversation. He thought about Aoife, Maebh, and the questions that swirled around him now. He didn't realize anyone wanted to talk to him. Iain did not notice when Mhari ceased speaking to him at all.

At midday, they stopped and dismounted at the Bannockburn River to rest the horses. The deep and narrow river boasted a deadly undertow. Many unwise riders tried to traverse it only to be swept away by the current. Iain planned they would skirt the river until they reached the Thunder Hill Forest at the base of the Silver Haven Mountains.

"Look over there." Duncan noticed a group of three men on horseback flanking them about two hundred yards off to the west. The three men, who looked like mercenaries, seemed to be trained in battle. They carried swords and daggers and handled their horses like professional soldiers. They kept pace with the group all day, shadowing them like lionesses stalking prey. The three men rode quarter horses, the kind people take when they are chasing others. The men looked in their direction and talked among themselves.

"This can only mean one thing," Duncan observed.

"Trouble," Fergus agreed.

They saddled up and rode toward the Silver Haven Mountains. The group of men kept up with them for most of the day, which made everyone in the group uncomfortably edgy. As the sun crept lower on the horizon, it cast long shadows as day passed into twilight. When twilight dwindled into near darkness, the men raised their swords and spurred their horses into a dead run toward them.

Duncan and Fergus charged in a counterattack to parry and thrust against their enemy. Iain and Mhari reined in their horses. They stayed far enough off that they could gain a head start in case the mercenaries overtook the knights.

Sparks flew, and the sound of steel on steel pierced the night with neither side giving way. Grunting with effort, the men raised their swords against each other a final time. The trained knights were enough to keep three mercenaries occupied, but not to the point of advantage.

“Stay here,” Iain ordered Mhari. “If this goes sideways, you must ride on to Dhangadhi alone.”

Mhari tried to protest, but Iain spurred his horse onward into the skirmish. He drew his ceremonial sword into battle, hoping that his engagement would be the tactic the knights needed to turn the tide. Iain waited for an opening and he sliced with all his might, only for the pristine sword to bounce off the studded leather armor and ricochet back. He barely dodged in time, but his intrusion gave the knights the benefit of surprise. Fergus could disarm and disable his opponent in the confusion. Duncan fought on with the mercenary, unmoved by Iain’s comedic intrusion at first, but eventually gained his win.

The third mercenary broke away and disarmed Iain with one swift move of his sword. Unarmed and outmanned, Iain had to think fast. Without magick, he had a shallow well from which to draw to defend himself.

Iain spoke the words of one of the few parlor tricks he knew, Light, and cast it on the enemy’s helmet. It glowed a bright white, temporarily blinding the mercenary. He dropped the reins of his horse, which almost threw its rider. The mercenary screamed, simultaneously trying to yank his helmet off and regain control of his horse.

Iain watched as Duncan and Fergus disarmed the remaining mercenaries in moments. Faced with defeat, they regrouped and then fled toward Innesfrees.

After the mercenaries fled, Iain received a terse scolding from Duncan. "What the hell were you thinking? You could have gotten yourself killed!"

Iain retorted. "I am not completely defenseless." He crossed his arms.

Fergus laughed. "Yes, you are. You got lucky."

"Desperate times call for desperate measures," Iain said defensively.

The sun slipped below the horizon, and they needed to make up time. They set out at a full-on gallop to Dhangadi. Iain and the others arrived late at night, but the heat of the summer still laid like a thick blanket on Mantua.

They rode straight through the drawbridge and into the courtyard. The dim moonlight divulged enough to reveal a city of sparkling white granite with elegant, flowing architecture. Tired stableboys took the spent horses for an overdue rubdown and rest.

The Lycaena had full heads of white hair, cobalt skin, and tall, muscular bodies. Circular silver tattoos of various sizes graced their elegant faces and frames. Some had full sleeves of silver and black ink that extended all the way to their fingers. Consistent with the other cultures in Mantua, ink showed status among the Lycaena as well as magickal prowess.

A tired looking ambassador greeted Iain. The ambassador rubbed his eyes and bowed with flair, despite his fatigue. Iain gazed, fascinated, at the Lycaena's complexion of rich cobalt accented by silver inked concentric rings that framed his long, thin face. His pure white hair, amazingly impeccable even at this late hour. He sported short hair, cut in the customary Lycaenan style with a side part on the left. He did not have a hair out of place. Two sleeves of silver and black filigree ink flowed down his arms, covering every inch of cobalt skin from shoulder to fingertip. A master, but also a man of rank and status.

Iain never saw a Lycaenan before, and it he tried not to stare. He blinked and held his hand out in the human way for the ambassador to shake.

"It is my distinct pleasure to welcome you," the ambassador said with a flourish. "I am Bibek, and I will see you to your quarters."

Mhari, Duncan, and Fergus gratefully accepted, but Iain demurred politely. "Is there any way I can see your healers before retiring?

"Are you injured?" Bibek asked, concerned. "Are you ill?"

"No," Iain said, but he told Bibek about how the Cough tore through Innesfrees, leaving bloody death in its wake. He left out no details and told of the sad tragedy of Aoife falling ill.

Iain held his breath as Bibek softened and reconsidered. With a sigh, he acquiesced. "We will gladly supply the aid you seek to the best of our abilities."

Instead of the guest quarters where Mhari, Duncan, and Fergus retired, Bibek led Iain to a magickally lit sitting room and provided him with a cool drink, Lycaenan black tea. Light magic illuminated various stones that were strategically placed in the room to provide ambient light. Soft cushions and intricate carvings adorned the mahogany chair where Iain waited.

Bibek left him for the better part of an hour, but Iain, like most healers, knew how to be patient. Upon his return, a tall and fit Lycaenan woman accompanied Bibek. Graceful silver and black ink adorned most of her body, and she wore her long hair neatly tied in a ponytail. Her eyes were a striking pale blue that contrasted with her rich, smooth cobalt skin. She wore a white silk dress that rustled softly when she moved.

Bibek stepped forward. "Iain, this is Azra, the chief healer of the Lycaena."

Iain rose from his comfortable chair and greeted Azra with a deep bow.

"Please forgive me for disturbing your sleep, Wise One," Iain said with reverence and respect. "It's important, or else we would all be at least trying to sleep on this dreadfully humid night."

Azra took Iain's hand and shook it in the human way. "Please sit. Tell me about your plight and travels."

Iain relayed again the plight of Innesfrees, with particular attention to Aoife and her suffering. Azra listened politely, taking in every detail, asking questions where appropriate.

"So, the Cough returns," she said with a distant, empty stare. "It's been eradicated for centuries. However, why should we help you? When the Chernushka destroyed our herbarium and ransacked our library, we called for aid. Only the Mountain Elves answered."

"Wise One, I cannot speak for the inaction of my people before my lifetime. Please accept my apology on behalf of Innesfrees, the late King Nathair, and their majesties Queen Maebh and Prince Regent Kieron," Iain said. He needed to be exceedingly careful.

Azra pounded the table with her fist. "Not enough! Humans ignored our cries for help, and you come with tears in your eyes, begging for the same from the Lycaena. Did you think we would forget? Do you have any idea what we lost to the Chernushka?"

"The Lycaena are a wise and noble race. We would like to be on better terms with you. What can I offer you that you do not already have to right this past wrongdoing?"

"There are three things, Iain of Innesfrees."

"Innesfrees is at your mercy and command, Wise One," Iain said, trembling.

"Yes. Yes, you are." An uncomfortable silence weighed down the room. Azra spoke, breaking the pregnant pause. "The Lycaena will provide the treatment, but at a price." She leaned forward looking directly into Iain's eyes.

"Whatever you desire, Innesfrees will see to it. Our queen said that any price is acceptable for your much-appreciated aid with our gratitude," Iain replied.

Azra held up an inked hand. "There is no gold or silver that can cover this cost."

If not money, then what? What could Innesfrees offer that the Lycaena did not already have? Iain's heart sank. He feared not being able to meet the Lycaena's terms. "What do you require?"

"We are strict isolationists, and that will remain so. Also, we require a complete copy of your herbalist and botanist's tomes. Finally, we want our library back from the Chernushka."

Iain gaze went from Bibek to Azra. Iain could hardly breathe, and his mouth went dry. How could he promise this? Would Maebh approve? Her words, "Accept any price," pierced his memory.

Bibek broke his reverie and the silence. "Do you agree, Iain of Innesfrees?"

Iain reluctantly nodded. "Agreed."

"Excellent," Azra said. "Please enjoy our hospitality for the night. Then, you will ride for Innesfrees in the morning. To meet your needs, it will take one day to prepare. After we prepare the Moonthorne, a special envoy will take it from here, planning to meet you in Innesfrees by day three. That gives you ample time to save Aoife and your people."

Stunned, Iain nodded. Returning to Innesfrees empty-handed is not what he envisioned when he began this journey. However, the promise of gathering aid and transporting the Moonthorne to them would need to suffice.

Bibek called a page boy to escort Iain to his quarters. As he left, Iain heard Azra whisper to Bibek, “Send word to the Mountain Elves. We will need their services again.

Chapter Five

CHAPTER FIVE

IAIN

The uneventful return trip to Innesfrees suited Iain fine. He needed time to figure out how to explain the Lycaenan terms and his lack of Moonthorne to Queen Maebh. Iain wondered about Aoife. He had a lot of questions, and no answers.

They rode through the castle gates to be met by young stable boys, who took the tired horses for a good rubdown and rest. Iain noticed that Ambassador Pyotr seemed annoyed that they returned. Puzzled, Iain made a note to look in on him later. However, he delivered the expected pleasantries with Pyotr and headed toward the Queen's quarters, traveling down the same tapestry-laden hallway.

When Iain reached the Queen's quarters, there were no Beit She'an guards posted outside her door. The Queen left her private rooms. He knocked anyway. The youngest lady informed him she went for a walk.

"She mentioned Aoife," the youngest lady whispered. "She may be in the sickroom."

Iain sighed and wearily rubbed his eyes. The whole point of the quarantine and the sickroom were to keep the Cough from the Queen and Prince Regent. Maebh would not be controlled, and she often kept her own counsel. She could be immensely headstrong with an iron backbone.

Iain made his way to the sickroom, where he found Maebh and Kieron doting on Aoife. The scene of parental love moved him. Maebh wiped Aoife's brow and gently patted her cheeks with a damp cloth to stave off her fever. Kieron smoothed her sweat laden hair and straightened the wrinkles in her blankets. Iain stood there for a few moments, unwilling to interrupt them as they consoled their sick daughter. His heart broke for them.

After quite some time, he cleared his throat. His hands trembled at the thought of relaying the news. He did not know if they would meet the messenger with understanding or anger.

Maebh looked up, and gently patted the sleeping girl on the chest. They both stood and approached Iain, so they could talk without disturbing their daughter.

"Iain," Maebh whispered. "You have returned quickly. Where is the Moonthorne?" Her voice strained, she looked eager and anticipated his response.

Iain dreaded this moment. He stammered, unsure of how to begin.

"My Queen," he said. "I did not get the Moonthorne. Yet."

The blood drained from Maebh's face, and she took a deep breath. "You had one job, Iain."

"A courier will deliver the Moonthorne," Iain said. "The Lycaena readily agreed to give us the Moonthorne but at a cost of peace, privacy, a complete copy of all our herbalist and botany collection and Innesfrees retrieving its library stolen by the Chernushka. It will take three days for the Moonthorne to be delivered, and they were not content for us to wait. They assured me that it would arrive in time to treat Aoife."

The Queen went silent. She gazed at Iain directly into his eyes, as though she were looking into his very soul. He shifted his weight on his feet and sweat glistened on his forehead.

"You are excused, Iain," the Queen said, voice firm and her eyes set like stone. He had only once ever seen her like this before. He felt the blame then too.

Iain protested. "Your Majesty–"

"You heard your Queen," Kieron thundered from behind Maebh, hands clenched and jaw tight. "Get out." Kieron took a threatening step toward Iain.

As Iain backed out of the sickroom, he watched as Kieron stood tall despite the worry that weighed him down.

Iain heard Kieron's cough echo off the walls of the sickroom as he left.

Chapter Six

CHAPTER SIX

DARRAGH

Darragh remembered it keenly. Innesfrees' then Princess Maebh would ascend to the throne when her father, King Faolán, went to the Summerlands. Convention held that she needed a husband, although Maebh held she needed nothing of the sort. Her father didn't care what she needed, ignoring her protests as he set about making her a political match. Everyone wondered who the king would pick to be the lucky bridegroom. Kieron of Sterling. His best friend. He should have been happy for him–but he couldn't be.

It should have been me, Darragh thought. I am best for Maebh and Innesfrees, not Kieron.

Jealousy rather than offense consumed Darragh, but that did not stop him from aiming his fury and his saber rattling at his best friend. More than once it came to blows between them. Even once, Darragh drunkenly threatened to overthrow Innesfrees to get Maebh and get back at Kieron. Only he could be the best Prince Regent for Innesfrees and for Maebh. From that day forward, he treated Kieron with disdain and envy. The kingdoms of Innesfrees and Buckhaven were more compatible, and Maebh would give Darragh strong sons.

So many friends talked to and cajoled him that summer. There are other women, Darragh, they scolded him. As if he could find someone as perfect as Maebh. No. He blamed only one person for his unhappiness. Kieron. His best friend had contrived this somehow. How could he forgive this betrayal? How could he forgive his alleged friend stealing the one woman he wanted for himself?

How could Kieron not see I am the better match? How could Kieron do this to me? Did all our years of friendship, all our years of brotherhood, mean nothing to him? No, this could not stand, Darragh thought, days before Maebh and Kieron's wedding. He could not endure this humiliation. Innesfrees needed him, and so did Maebh.

On the evening before the nuptials, Darragh slipped from his guest room at Innesfrees Castle and found himself in front of Maebh's door. He smelled of ill intent and wine, clearly inebriated and willing to be reckless. There were guards at her door, but not the Beit She'an.

"Guards! There is a ruckus in the main hall. Prince Regent Kieron needs all his men!"

When they rounded the corner, he pounded on the door.

A young lady-in-waiting answered the knock, surprised and nonplussed that any man would dare to seek the bride on her wedding eve. He craned his neck to look past the lady to catch a glimpse of Maebh. His breath caught in his throat as she investigated the commotion.

"Darragh?"

"Maebh, please reconsider your actions," he begged. His head swam with drink, but he continued, "Choose me instead. I am a better man for you than he is."

He pushed past the young lady to gasps of shock from Maebh's ladies-in-waiting. They formed a protective circle around her, denouncing him and demanding he leave. The youngest of the ladies slipped out of the door for a Beit She'an guard.

Darragh would not stop. The resistance merely fueled his intoxicated lust, and he lunged toward Maebh, grasping her shift and tearing it to expose her breast. Outnumbered by the women, they forced him toward the door as he pleaded for Maebh, while reiterating how Buckhaven, and he would be the better match for her.

Two Beit She'an guards appeared and grabbed Darragh, getting him under their control with admirable ease. Their training subdued his body instantly, but they could not restrain his words.

"You will regret this, Maebh!" he shouted. "Not today, not tomorrow, but in time. You will regret this."

They brought Darragh to his guest chambers, a courtesy of a distinguished visitor, rather than throwing him in jail and letting him sleep it off.

The wedding went above everyone's expectations. Maebh shined with incomparable beauty that day than Darragh had ever seen, and he seethed. It did not escape his notice that Kieron beamed happiness, seemingly oblivious to Darragh's rage. He continued to drink, and it only fueled his rage.

Kieron tasked Pyotr with the dubious honor of returning Darragh to his room. He half walked and half carried Darragh to his room for the night. He drunkenly tripped over his own feet. After wildly careening into a wall, Pyotr dismissed the guards. Along the way, Darragh talked about Kieron, Maebh, and his thirst for revenge. He won Pyotr's ear.

"Why pine over a woman who does not love you?" Pyotr asked. "Why not console yourself with her crown instead? Unite all of the

Southern Kingdoms under your crown. It will be the ultimate in humiliation and revenge."

Darragh's bibulous mind raced. A thoughtful, albeit boozy, gaze replaced his scowl. Pyotr saw reason, Darragh's righteousness, so he agreed. In his drunken state, this treason seemed a most excellent idea. In the guest quarters, they hatched the plan. Innesfrees deserved better. It deserved Darragh.

Now, Darragh rode into Innesfrees accompanied by a full complement of knights. He couldn't wait for what the night would bring. Darragh watched as Ambassador Pyotr made his way to the courtyard of the castle, coming straight to him.

He shook Pyotr's hand and exchanged pleasantries with him.

"Ambassador Pyotr, How fares the princess?" Darragh asked.

"She suffers nobly," Pyotr replied evenly. "We expect the blood within days. The Moonthorne will not arrive in time, and her dear father will die of a broken heart."

"If not from a broken heart, then most assuredly from the Cough," Darragh said. "It's all going according to plan."

"Indeed," Pyotr replied with a grin.

"The orcs? Have they dealt with the Mountain Elf Ambassador?" Darragh inquired.

"Beaten, robbed and murdered," Pyotr said. "Such a shame, a young elf cut off before her prime. Her loyal brownie dead by her side. The vultures are sure to be taking care of them now. The Moonthorne is nowhere to be found. And it all looks like an unfortunate robbery gone horribly wrong. It will be an international incident. The murder of their ambassador on a mission of mercy will outrage the Mountain Elves. Are you prepared?"

"Always, Pyotr, always," Darragh said darkly. "After I am crowned, I will smooth it over by charm or by force."

"Come, Darragh," Pyotr said. "The Prince Regent is preparing a feast in your honor."

"If he only knew," Darragh said and laughed. "If he only knew."

Darragh watched the Great Hall that glowed with the light of hundreds of candles. He could hear the murmur of servants as they prepared for the unexpected guests. The aroma of smoked meats wafted into the Hall, coupled with the scent of baking bread. Capons and venison, with small bread loaves and sweet puddings, were on every table. Summer fruits and fresh sunflowers adorned the center of the tables. The Wheel of the Year kept turning, and Lughnasadh, the first harvest, approached, only days away.

Visiting knights of Buckhaven took their place near the few remaining knights from Innesfrees. Their uniforms of blue and red stood out among the sparse green and silver of Innesfrees. As they mingled, the knights exchanged pleasantries and introductions. Darragh, dressed in his most formal attire, watched from behind the curtain and waited for his cue to enter.

Darragh heard the quiet murmurs of a dozen conversations cease as trumpeters emerged from a door near the head table to announce Maebh and Kieron.

Pyotr and Darragh engaged in sparse banter as quiet lute music rambled its lilt over the soft sounds of conversations. Topics centered on the sweltering heat that had Innesfrees locked in its grip. They spoke of when the summer would break, and autumn descended with its crisp air.

Dinner gave way to more lively conversations, as the flowing wine loosened demeanors and tongues. Knights relaxed and mingled for the first time since the feast began. At long last, the dinner ended. Maebh and Kieron took the first opportunity to retire, entrusting the remaining knights and honored guests to Pyotr.

Once the Queen and the Prince Regent left the Great Hall and were safely out of earshot, King Darragh and Ambassador Pyotr stood. With one nod of Darragh's head, his knights raised arms against the last few knights loyal to the Queen. In an instant, swords unsheathed, and a battle for the sanctity of Innesfrees ensued. Steel met steel, and the knights of Innesfrees heartily stood their ground. In the end, three knights fell, and their captors took the remaining six to jail.

They were the first casualties and prisoners of a war no one knew existed.

"Yes," Darragh said. "All is going according to plan."

Chapter Seven

CHAPTER SEVEN

ISEABAIL

Iseabail kept quiet and to herself at the beginning of the journey. Keeping her horse far enough apart from the others to be separate but not on her own. She talked to Calyx using their mental link.

I need to be doing this myself. How else can I show my father that I am capable?

Calyx noticed Iseabail's pensiveness. *Why do you think that, Iseabail?*

It's nothing of consequence. She sadly gazed over at Dunharra, Anaïs, and Zauvadok, who were deep in their own conversation.

Don't give me that 'nothing of consequence' bullshit, Iseabail.

Iseabail sighed. *How can I prove to Papa that I can handle anything if I don't take on challenges myself?*

There is wisdom in knowing when to ask for help, Iseabail. I don't think he thinks less of you. On the contrary, I think he holds you in the highest regard.

Iseabail looked at Calyx, head cocked to the side and eyebrow raised. *I wish I could believe that.*

The hilly forest slowly gave way to flat plains. Tall golden grass grew between large, sprawling meadows of colorful wildflowers. The occasional grove of trees gifted them shade from the unforgiving summer sun. They traveled all morning and part of the afternoon, when storm clouds formed far off on the horizon. It painted the sky a moody gray. Thunder rolled ominously in the distance.

Iseabail felt Calyx tense at the rumble of thunder. She knew how Calyx felt about thunderstorms and expected her to climb in her lap any time now.

"Why are you afraid of thunderstorms, Calyx? It's only light and noise," Zauvadok asked.

"Lightning can kill you," Calyx replied, carefully eyeing the sky. Through their link, Iseabail felt Calyx's tension rise.

"Maybe you haven't had the right experience in a thunderstorm." Anaïs quipped with an impish grin.

"Are you offering?" Calyx said, not missing a beat.

"No, but we need to find you a brownie man after this is all over," Anaïs said.

"Or woman," Calyx replied. "Remember I like blondes."

Lightning snaked across the sky, illuminating the clouds from within. With the first flash of lightning, Calyx jumped into Iseabail's lap, her body trembling and eyes wide. She rested her hand on the brownie, who leaned into her palm, burrowing as close as possible.

Iseabail smelled the air, thick with the oncoming rain. She needed to disentangle from the frazzled brownie and make camp for the night. She watched, impressed, when Anaïs cast wyverns to watch over the campsite. They flew in a circle above them, silent sentries to anything approaching. To her relief, no one needed to take watch. Her tent went up as the thick droplets of rain fell. She went in with Calyx to ride out the storm.

***

DARRAGH

Darragh roared when he heard from Buckhaven scouts near Innesfrees that Iseabail and Calyx survived. He stomped around Pyotr's office like a caged animal. Parchment and scrolls flew across the room as he released his pique on Pyotr's formerly tidy, sturdy oak desk.

"The vultures are taking care of her!" Darragh mocked Pyotr. "Take care of them, Pyotr, or I'll hang you out on a pig pole!"

"The Cough has decimated Kieron's knights," Pyotr reminded Darragh, who thought he heard a slight patronizing tone. "As we planned, not one Innesfrees knight is fit to ride. Can't you spare knights to intercept them?"

Darragh spent his ire and slowly regained his composure. He stood and watched as Pyotr collected the papers that were strewn across the office with a heavy sigh.

"Send four," Darragh commanded. "They should be easy enough to find. But I want the Mountain Elf alive."

Darragh turned and left, slamming the heavy oak door.

***

DUNHARRA

Another day of traveling. If they kept up this pace, they would arrive in Innesfrees in two hours. Dunharra noticed seabirds flying overhead and could smell the salty ocean air. They were close.

"How did you get to be a healer, Dunharra?" Iseabail asked.

"I don't know," Dunharra replied, unsure of herself or even her answer. She did not like being the topic of this conversation. The conversation came too close for comfort for her. She shifted uncomfortably in her saddle, looking down, anywhere but at Iseabail.

"How do you not know?" Calyx asked. "Who can forget getting inked?"

"I ... always...," Dunharra said. She wanted this conversation to end.

Zauvadok interrupted Dunharra as she tried to avoid answering. He held his large hand out and asked for quiet.

"Look," he said, pointing toward the horizon. Four armed riders lingered to the east and watched them intently.

"I don't like that one bit," Zauvadok said with a low growl.

"Aren't those—" Dunharra asked, confused why Buckhaven knights watched them.

"Go!" Anaïs shouted.

They pushed the horses as fast as they could, for as long as they could, but the knights overtook them.

Zauvadok pulled his two-handed sword and engaged the nearest knight. The man suffered an ugly chest wound and fell from his horse. Zauvadok easily overpowered him, and the knight lay on the ground, dead.

Anaïs' eyes and ink glowed blood red as she readied magick that tripped the second rider's horse to send him flying. The rider fell hard and rolled to a stop. He stumbled as he stood.

Dunharra called tendrils of fire that knocked a third knight from his horse. He hit the ground, motionless and burning.

Iseabail and Calyx readied magick that sent a wall of fire, which caused the horse to rear up and throw its rider. He also fell to the ground with a grunt.

Before Anaïs could prepare more magick, the knight delivered a punishing blow to her head, with a bleeding gash across her face. She crumpled to the ground, limp but living. The knight picked her up and laid her wilted body across the front of his horse, then rode toward Innesfrees.

Zauvadok ran to another knight towering over Iseabail as he swung a sword toward her. He intervened, sliding between the soldier and Iseabail, sword ready.

"Why are you here?" Iseabail shouted at the knight, incredulous.

The knight laughed. "To take you dead or alive, Mountain Elf. Preferably alive, but dead is fine with me."

"Not today," Zauvadok said. The knight drew first blood with a slash at his chest. It cut deep, but not deep enough to deter him. Deep green blood ran down his chest.

Zauvadok blocked and answered with a slice of his own. He plunged the blade into the surprised knight's chest. Zauvadok looked around for his wife. He couldn't find her.

"Anaïs!" he called out.

Dunharra helplessly watched the rider gallop away with Anaïs toward Innesfrees.

"Zau, I need to take care of that wound," Dunharra said, turning to Zauvadok.

Zauvadok, unwilling to wait, initially declined. He started walking back to his horse.

"To have Anaïs back, you can't go in there all banged up," Dunharra scolded him. "Now hold still."

Dunharra's eyes shifted from grass green to iridescent as she healed Zauvadok.. The edges of his skin glowed softly as she held her hands above the gaping wound. The bleeding slowed and then stopped altogether. She traced the scar with her finger, and it vanished under her touch.

They were ready to ride.

Chapter Eight

CHAPTER EIGHT

DARRAGH

Darragh strode into the jail, his mouth turned up in a smirk, followed closely by Pyotr. Darragh saw Anaïs, as she lay on the straw mat under a barred window. Her hands were bound with a coarse rope that cut into her skin. Dried silver blood matted her white hair and she tried to shield her eyes from the sun.

He snorted at Anaïs, then sneered. He didn't want her. He wanted the Mountain Elf.

Darragh turned to the knight guarding Anaïs, pointed to her, and said, "Does this look like a Mountain Elf to you? I wanted the Mountain Elf, you idiot!"

He watched Anaïs stand on wobbly legs. Their eyes locked.

"My, aren't you a feisty one," he said with a dark chuckle. "Is she your friend? Where is the Moonthorne?" His hard and edgy voice growled as he regarded the injured Dark Elf.

Silence.

Darragh regarded the silent Dark Elf.

"You'll find your words, eventually. And you'll beg to tell me all you know," Darragh said, his dark, piercing eyes regarding her. He turned to Pyotr and said, "Send more knights to greet her friends. Maybe companionship will loosen her tongue."

Darragh ordered the cell open, and stood behind his knight.

Anaïs formed the beginning of magick, and her eyes and the ink on her arms glowed blood red.

"Time to talk, Dark Elf," Darragh sneered.

Anaïs' finished the spell, which shocked the guard. He screamed and fell backward into the corner.

Darragh glared at Anaïs, who regarded him with a satisfied grin.

"Take her to the chamber."

***

DARRAGH

Darragh opened the door roughly, banging it against the wall with such force that it startled Kieron, who sat at his desk. He didn't hear them coming, distracted by the news that Aoife new coughed blood. Worry etched his face, and he regarded his ill-willed cousin with disdain.

Behind Darragh, Pyotr and two Buckhaven knights followed close behind.

He admired the working office of the Prince Regent. He appreciated the large room comfortably furnished with carved chairs, a warm fireplace, and walls covered with tapestries depicting the magnificent feats of the Warrior Kings. He could get used to this.

"So, this is how it begins," Kieron said, his eyes dark and cold as he coughed.

Darragh laughed. "It began when Faolán chose you for Maebh. This is the culmination of years of planning."

"And you, Pyotr. I trusted you," Kieron spat, the veins on his neck bulging.

"Pity," Pyotr replied, his face bathed in the sun streaming in the open windows. "The Moonthorne will not make it in time for Aoife. Or you."

With a nod from Darragh, the knight's rough hands grabbed Kieron from his desk and locked him in the cells with the last of his remaining knights.

***

DUNHARRA

Zauvadok, Iseabail, and Dunharra pushed the horses to their limit. Innesfrees Castle loomed on the horizon, along with a line of Buckhaven knights speeding toward them.

"Is that what I think it is?" Iseabail asked.

"More knights," Dunharra said. She could hardly believe her eyes.

"Ten," Zauvadok said grimly. "What kind of magick do you have that can even these odds?"

Dunharra smiled grimly. "Leave it to us."

Dunharra waited until the knights were close enough, then called down lightning, which threw off two of their horses. They laid on the ground, lifeless. Iseabail and Calyx created a wall of fire that startled the horses. Two of them reared up and threw their riders to the ground. The knights sprang up quickly and headed toward Iseabail and Calyx.

Both Dunharra and Iseabail dismounted, readied magick, and sent a volley of fire into the remaining knights on foot. Two fell to the ground, dead.

Zauvadok engaged two knights.

Iseabail could keep the knights at arm's length distance. She could fight better defensively rather than offensively. One soldier exploited an opening she left and delivered a devastating blow to Iseabail's face. She fell, unconscious. Calyx stepped in front of the unconscious Iseabail ready to defend her. The soldiers laughed and kicked the brownie out of the way. She flew about three yards before landing in a heap. Calyx steadied herself to defend Iseabail despite the pain slowing her, readying magick as she went.

She grasped the nearest knight's ankle, finished speaking the magick, then bit down on his bony flesh. The magick successfully shocked the soldier, who lost his balance and fell to the ground.

Seeing Iseabail fall, Zauvadok plunged his sword into the abdomen of one knight, who fell to the ground. He then took his sword and swung it with all his might, cleaving the head from the body of the second knight. With a heaving chest, he ran to help Dunharra.

Dunharra threw fire at the two knights, hitting one while the other dodged out of the way. One knight fell to the ground, smoking as the acrid smell of burning flesh filled the air. The other knight delivered a crushing slash with his sword. She fell to the ground with a cry of pain; she sustained a muscle-splitting, diagonal gash from her left arm to her chest.

The soldier raised his sword to deliver the death blow as Zauvadok killed him from behind. His sword penetrated his enemy's back clean through. Zauvadok engaged the last-standing soldier, who left himself open to attack by laughing at the ankle-biting brownie. Zauvadok got a disabling blow, knocking the soldier unconscious.

Zauvadok worried Dunharra when he didn't want to take the time for her to heal him.

After Dunharra's gentle insistence, Zauvadok eventually acquiesced, and she laid her hands on him. Her eyes shifted to iridescent as his cuts and bruises glowed with the same ethereal light. They shimmered as the cuts knitted neatly back together. The bruises soon vanished. Not only were his wounds healed, but he also no longer felt tired or spent from all the fighting.

Calyx had bruised and broken ribs from being kicked by the soldier. She breathed painfully. Deep inside, the break tingled as Dunharra brought healing to her ribs. Calyx took a deep breath without and exhaled slowly, a small smile lifting their lips as they gazed at Dunharra.

Dunharra concentrated and held a hand over the gash suffered by Iseabail, eyes still iridescent. The wound responded in kind, and the blood flow slowed to a stop. A moment went by, and Iseabail's eyes fluttered open.

"Good morning," Dunharra said.

"Hi," Iseabail said. Her eyes were still glassy. Dunharra continued on to heal the concussion Iseabail suffered.

Dunharra, now focused on her own wound, her eyes iridescent. The wound's edges glowed with the same iridescent light as her eyes. Quickly, the wound closed and left no scar behind. Her eyes shifted back to grass green.

"Let's go," she said.

***

ISEABAIL

Dunharra, Zauvadok, Iseabail, and Calyx galloped to Innesfrees Castle. Dunharra knew Iseabail would be relieved that this would soon be over. She would deliver the Moonthorne, heal Aoife, and update diplomatic relations. She could shine in her father's eyes.

They crossed the gate and rode into the courtyard. Stable hands ran up to secure the horses. Iseabail's eyes narrowed as Ambassador Pyotr met them in the courtyard.

"What do we have here? I am Ambassador Pyotr."

"I am here for my wife," Zauvadok growled.

Pyotr didn't blink. "And you are?"

"Where is my wife?" Zauvadok demanded, taking a threatening step forward toward Pyotr.

Iseabail quickly interrupted them. "I am Ambassador Iseabail Allora of the Mountain Elves. I am here to deliver Moonthorne directly to Queen Maebh. I ask for an audience with her and the Prince Regent."

"It is my distinct pleasure to welcome you to Innesfrees. You may start with me," Pyotr said coldly. "I will take the Moonthorne."

Iseabail handed the leather bag hanging over her shoulder to Zauvadok. "No, you won't. I am to deliver this to Queen Maebh. Personally."

"Follow me," Pyotr said and looked down his nose at them.

He led Iseabail, Calyx, Dunharra, and Zauvadok to a comfortable sitting room meant for visiting dignitaries. Intricately carved mahogany chairs surrounded a long, polished table. Pyotr invited them to wait there.

Pyotr returned to the room after a brief wait. Iseabail saw King Darragh walk in behind Pyotr and take a seat at the head of the table, which shocked her. "Welcome to Innesfrees."

"You're King Darragh," Iseabail said, incredulous.

"In the flesh," he said as he extended his arms in a conceited flourish.

"All this...you?," Iseabail said, the enormity of it all slowly dawning on her. "Why?"

"Kieron never deserved Innesfrees. I should have been the one to court and marry Maebh. Unfortunately for them, they were well matched. Maebh may have survived the Cough and remained queen. Eventually, I will unite the Southern Kingdoms under my crown."

"Where is the Queen?" Iseabail demanded.

"Mourning her daughter in the sickroom," Pyotr answered with a roll of his eyes. "One down, two to go."

"Complicit!" Iseabail accused.

"Guilty," Darragh retorted with no remorse.

"Where is my wife?" Zauvadok demanded.

"Who?" Pyotr asked, feigning ignorance. "Oh! The Dark Elf. She's a bit busy at the moment."

Darragh stood at the head of the table. "Who carries the Moonthorne?"

"The half orc holds it, Your Majesty," Pyotr said.

Zauvadok let out a low rumble from his throat. "Come and take it."

With a word, Darragh called knights into the room. Zauvadok drew his sword. Iseabail and Dunharra readied magick.

"So it seems we are at an impasse," Darragh said with a conceited sneer.

"No impasse if you let us through with the Moonthorne," Iseabail said, eyes glowing icy blue and ready at a hair trigger to throw magick.

"Where's my wife?" Zauvadok demanded with a snarl, pointing his sword at Pyotr.

The small room would make using swords to fight difficult.

Iseabail threw shards of razor sharp ice at the knights who blocked them with their shields.

Dunharra threw small balls of fire, striking three of the six knights. They dropped their swords with screams of pain as they tried to put out the flames licking at their clothes.

The remaining three looked to Darragh and Pyotr for orders.

"What are you waiting for? Get the goddamn Moonthorne!" Darragh bellowed.

The three remaining soldiers rushed them before they could ready more magick, placing threatening swords on Iseabail's and Dunharra's necks.

Zauvadok observed Dunharra, being held from behind with a sword threateningly close to her neck. He growled a deep, guttural growl.

"No, Zau, don't do it!" Dunharra said before the knight pressed his sword into her neck, nicking her and drawing blood. "Don't give up the Moonthorne!"

"Don't hurt her!" Zauvadok said, defeated. He lowered his sword.

Darragh walked up to Zauvadok and relieved him of the large deerskin bag that held the fragrant Moonthorne. Satisfied, Darragh took enough for Pyotr and himself and poured the remaining powdered herbs onto the fire.

"No!" Iseabail shouted. With a sword at her throat, she could only watch the Moonthorne burn.

"Take them to the jail," Darragh ordered. "I have someone to see."

Chapter Nine

CHAPTER NINE

ISEABAIL

Dunharra met Zauvadok's eyes, and they nodded in mutual agreement as guards led them away. When they arrived, they saw the remaining knights of Innesfrees, and the Prince Regent, jailed in their own cells. They seemed miserable and ill.

Dunharra eyed Zauvadok. He inhaled a deep breath and then shouted, "Now!"

He immediately punched the knight to his right and slammed him into the knight on the left. They both fell to the ground, unconscious but alive.

The knights collectively pointed to a heap of skeleton keys on a large steel ring hanging on a peg near the far corner. Calyx couldn't reach them on her own.

Zauvadok threw a third knight into the wall to stun him, and the knight slumped against a cell door.

Dunharra tried to push away the knight holding her, but he grabbed her hands and held tight. She pulled hard, hoping to throw him off balance. Larger and stronger than her, he pulled her back toward him. She rewarded him with a crushing knee to his crotch, and he crumpled to the floor.

Iseabail grabbed the keys hanging on the wall. There were so many on the ring, Iseabail fumbled the keys as she tried to sort through them all. She tried one key, and it did not open the lock. She moved on with another key and another. Iseabail continued trying each key, until she found the one that unlocked the cells. The knights poured out. They grabbed the remaining knight fighting with Zauvadok. Iseabail then unlocked the last cell and freed Kieron.

"Thank you," he said, grateful. "Are you the Mountain Elf I am expecting?"

"I am, Your Majesty, but the Moonthorne—" she said trying to keep her voice from cracking, "Darragh and Pyotr burned all but two doses."

"Two doses will do," he replied between coughs. "That will save Aoife. She is a youngling and will not need a full dose."

"You need the other one," Iseabail said.

"Let's get it," Dunharra said.

Zauvadok, Iseabail, Calyx, Dunharra, Kieron, and his knights ran to the sitting room. They broke through the door to find Darragh and Pyotr sitting by the fireplace.

Pyotr's eyes went wide when he saw them. He tried to run out of the room, but an Innesfrees knight blocked him from leaving.

"Pyotr," Kieron said between coughs. "It's over. Give me the Moonthorne."

"It's over for Aoife. She is coughing blood. It's too late and you know it," Pyotr gloated. "Soon you will be, too. And Darragh will have Maebh and the crown, uniting the Southern Kingdoms."

"Over my dead body," Kieron growled.

"As you wish," Pyotr said as he stood at the fireplace ready to burn the last remaining Moonthorne. Zauvadok lunged at him and stopped him from throwing the remaining Moonthorne into the fire. He grabbed Pyotr roughly by his neck, lifting him easily off the ground. Iseabail took the Moonthorne safely away from the flames.

"Take me to Aoife," she said, and a knight whisked her and Calyx away to the sickroom.

Iseabail and Calyx joined Maebh as she dutifully wiped Aoife's face and mouth of blood each time a coughing spasm wracked her body. Each coughing fit came with a slower recovery to normal breathing. Now, Aoife could only wheeze and rattle.

"I am Iseabail Allora from the Mountain Elves," she announced as she entered the sickroom. "I have the Moonthorne."

Iain reconstituted the last two remaining doses. He cast a worried glance to Iseabail and Calyx, expecting much more. "Is this all?"

"Yes, Darragh burned the rest," Iseabail said, crestfallen.

Iain's eyes grew wide, and his dry mouth fell open. Within an hour of administering the Moonthorne, Aoife's breathing eased. She did not cough.

Iseabail brought the Moonthorne in time. Aoife needed time to recover, but she would live.

Chapter Ten

CHAPTER TEN

DARRAGH

When Darragh discovered that Innesfrees had a secret dungeon, he smiled. The dark, and wide room lay at the very bottom of Innesfrees castle. The smell of old blood permeated the air, and it hung like a pall over the room. He watched as Buckhaven soldiers strapped Anaïs to a table with wide, bloodstained straps. She fought to avoid being strapped down, kicking and biting, but with a soldier on each limb, she could not resist. He enjoyed watching her struggle.

An inquisitor sat in a shadowy corner, biding his time. He stared at Anaïs, studying her. She took a deep breath to steady herself.

"This is your chance, Dark Elf," Darragh snarled.

"For what?" Anaïs answered.

Darragh backhanded her.

"Tell me how the Mountain Elf survived," Darragh demanded as he paced around the table.

"No," Anaïs replied, keeping her control.

"Do as you will," Darragh said to the inquisitor, gesturing to Anaïs.

The inquisitor laughed as he began his work.

Darragh stood near the inquisitor who grinned showing his unbrushed, dirty teeth. “I’ve never broken a Dark Elf before.” He reached out to touch her smooth, white hair.

Anaïs turned her head and tried to bite his finger. “Back off.”

The inquisitor cackled. “Feisty. I love it. You can end this now. Tell me all about the Mountain Elf. Where did she get the Moonthorne?”

“My husband will come for me,” Anaïs said, defiant. “Don’t do anything you’ll regret.”

“Oh, my dear,” the inquisitor began. “Regret is not something I ever feel.”

Darragh watched, fascinated, as the inquisitor slid a long, flat blade across Anaïs’ face, tracing the cold steel along her cheekbones. He flicked the knife and cut her cheek, a promise of things to come. A drop of silver blood rolled down her face. The inquisitor slowly dragged the knife down her neck, occasionally nicking her skin. Anaïs flinched at the nicks but said nothing.

“Here’s your chance, Dark Elf,” Darragh said. “Tell me where she got the Moonthorne.”

Anaïs met his question with silence. Undeterred, the inquisitor plunged the knife into her right shoulder and then cut off the right sleeve of her shirt, exposing more of her skin.

“Where did the Mountain Elf get the Moonthorne?” the inquisitor asked patiently. He really did not want her to answer, so he could continue his work.

Anaïs silently breathed heavily through a set jaw. Darragh thought she would not break. Fascinated, he could watch this for hours.

“Alright. Let’s continue.”

He plunged the bloody knife into her left shoulder.

The inquisitor impressed Darragh. He sliced muscles with precision to make any movement excruciating. When he thought he finished, he returned with new torture, all calmly applied as if he did this every day.

"Things are about to get serious," the inquisitor said, rubbing his bloody hands, eager to continue. "Tell me where she got the Moonthorne."

Darragh saw that Anaïs barely reacted to her torture now. She breathed in quick, ragged breaths. The inquisitor broke ribs in between questioning her, and each breath brought new, searing pain. Sliced open muscles in her limbs left her limp, making even the slightest movement excruciating.

"Tell me, Dark Elf, is it all worth it? Is the pain worth it?" the inquisitor asked with a slow, calm, and creepy patience. "They will come and find you dead. They will not make it in time to save you. Why not tell me what you know, and all the pain will stop. It will be over."

"No," is all she could manage. Darragh could barely hear her. Anaïs' soft and weak voice barely carried through the chamber and her strength ebbed as her lifeblood flowed out of her.

The inquisitor stood. "Then it is as you want it."

He walked over to the fire and pulled out a white-hot poker from the flames. He returned and held the glowing rod right up to her face. Darragh could see her lack of a reaction to the poker and knew she would soon be dead.

"For your eyes, my dear," the inquisitor said with a sinister grin.

Darragh looked upon Anais' broken body, watched her lungs struggle to take in air, her body instinctively flinching away from the searing heat. Too weak to do any more. Powerless. He smiled. He loved seeing her this way.

The inquisitor stated, "Your pain will end soon, but not before this."

"Anaïs!" Zau shouted, and he pushed past everyone and ran to his wife lying on the table.

"Stop!" Kieron shouted at the inquisitor. "It's over."

Zauvadok disarmed the shocked inquisitor and threw the poker safely away from Anaïs. A solid punch to the inquisitor's face left him unconscious on the chamber floor.

Kieron and his knights surrounded Darragh, as he tried to slink away unnoticed. "It's over Darragh. You failed."

***

DUNHARRA

Dunharra gasped at the sight of Anaïs.

"Oh, by the Mother, Anaïs," Zauvadok cried as he took in the sight of his bloody, broken wife.

"Zau? Is it you?"

"It's me, my darling," he said. "You're safe now. I'm here."

He sliced the leather straps and cradled his wife, feeling her broken bones underneath his hands. Tears welled in his eyes.

Dunharra ran over and assessed Anaïs. Her stomach knotted, and it broke her heart to tell him, "She's dying, Zau."

"No, Dun, please, no!" he pleaded. "I can't –Please, please don't let her go! You can heal her. I know you can. Please!"

Dunharra locked eyes with Zauvadok. The love he felt for Anaïs shone through, and her heart broke for him as his wife lay dying in his arms. Anaïs' silver blood dripped onto the floor and mixed with his tears.

Dunharra could not bear the thought of Anaïs being ripped away from Zauvadok when she could do something about it. She could heal her.

But healing Anaïs in front of other people, including the Prince Regent, could betray her secret. The thought made her breath catch in her throat. If discovered, she could never go back to her simple, quiet life in her cottage with her cat; the one place where she felt at peace.

But Anaïs? Dunharra's life would never be the same without her. She could not forgive herself if she let fear rule her and let Anaïs die.

Healing Anaïs now, here, in front of everyone, would change Dunharra's life forever.

She knew what she needed to do.

Dunharra took a deep breath and pursed her lips. "Hold her still, Zau."

She placed her hands on Anaïs' chest and focused. Zauvadok held Anaïs gently. Dunharra's eyes glowed iridescent. Anaïs stopped breathing and lay limp in his arms. Zauvadok quietly sobbed. Anaïs died in his arms.

"No!" Zauvadok cried as he gently cradled the limp Anaïs in his arms.

Calyx and Iseabail held hands as Zauvadok grieved the loss of his wife.

Dunharra inhaled and exhaled deeply again. She would not die on her watch. Anaïs gasped, breath still ragged, but she breathed. She lived.

"Hold on, Anaïs. Let Dun help you," Zauvadok whispered as he cradled her body in his arms, tears falling on her bloody face.

Dunharra saw considerable damage to internal organs and many were bleeding out. She focused on stemming the bleeding first, then repairing the damaged organs.

Dunharra healed her broken bones next. Brokenhearted, Dunharra saw every bone broken or shattered. Bit by bit, her bones knit together. Anaïs breathed easier but still needed to wake up. Dunharra took her finger and traced every scar along Anaïs' supple skin. They disappeared underneath her touch. Anaïs' eyes fluttered open, and she gazed up at Zauvadok with her dark brown eyes.

"Zau," Anaïs said. "Is it really you? I thought I'd never see you again."

"Thank you," Zau mouthed to Dunharra through happy tears as he held her.

Anaïs reached up and wrapped her bloody arms around his neck. Zauvadok held her gently as if she would break.

"Iseabail, what did I just see...?" Calyx asked, eyes wide, mouth open and looking up at Iseabail. "Anaïs died. We saw it. How...?"

Dunharra smiled, content. Her eyes shifted back to grass green and belied the intense fatigue that gripped her body. She stood slowly, covered in grime and Anaïs' silver blood, when the world spun. Kieron caught her before she fell, and her world went black.

Chapter Eleven

CHAPTER ELEVEN

ISEABAIL

Iseabail and Calyx made a return trip to Dhangadi to request more Moonthorne from the Lycaena. The Lycaena expressed annoyance over their burned Moonthorne, but they consented to produce more for the ailing Innesfrees. This time no interference came from Daragh, Pyotr or Buckhaven. Iseabail, Calyx, Zauvadok, Anaïs and Dunharra safely ferried enough Moonthorne to cure all of Innesfrees and the villages surrounding the castle.

After they delivered the Moonthorne, Iseabail and Calyx returned home to Ayr. Her father ran to them and greeted them with open arms.

"Iseabail!" he cried. He pulled her close to him, squeezing her tight, not letting go. After the moment passed, he pulled back and looked her up an down, eyes welling with tears. "They told me you were dead! Oh, how I mourned you!"

"Rumors of my demise are premature," Iseabail replied with a shy grin.

"I am so proud of you," he continued holding her tightly. "I never doubted you."

The news floored Iseabail. She covered her mouth with her hand. "Proud of me?"

Iseabail looked up at Padraig to confirm it.

Padraig insisted, "I always knew you could do it."

Told you, Calyx said through their link.

Iseabail hugged her father and felt her soul exhale after a week of holding its breath. All this time, after being fraught with worry and apprehension about being good enough, he really believed in her.

***

DUNHARRA

Queen Maebh and Prince Regent Kieron held a celebration of life for Aoife the next month in honor of her recovery and her eleventh birthday. She received her first, royal ink on her right shoulder. Queen Maebh rewarded Iseabail, Calyx, Anaïs, Zauvadok, and Dunharra with elevation to the Noble Order of the Dragon.

The ceremonial ink of the Noble Order of the Dragon kept them in Innesfrees for a little longer than they expected. The green dragon had four legs and breathed fire. Laurels supported his rear claws, and his wings remained fully unfurled. It denoted an elevated status among those in the Southern Kingdoms. It did have a secret function that only its wearers knew. It allowed you to summon a dragon from the remote mountains of Kara Dağlar Mountains, where they hibernated and remained unheard from for the last eight hundred years.

Dunharra stared at Anaïs and Zauvadok, her eyes wide. "No one can know," Dunharra whispered, her heart beating against her chest. She feared being discovered and it consumed her.

To decline the ink would insult the crown. Accepting the ink would expose Dunharra's skin and her secret. Anaïs, Zauvadok, accepted privately, avoiding a public ceremony.

"We need no crowds to honor us," Zauvadok explained.

"It will be as you wish," Kieron replied. "Get the ink in private. Then we celebrate."

Mhari met Anaïs, Zauvadok, and Dunharra in the healing wing of Innesfrees Castle. Anaïs bared her left shoulder, exposing radiant black skin. It only took a moment for Mhari to see the black ink. She applied the numbing agent and went to work. Anaïs stopped her and stayed Mhari's hand. "Can you make it all black?"

"However you want," Mhari said.

Dunharra's heart beat hard against her chest. She felt as if it would burst. What would she do? How could she explain this away?

Mhari applied the ink to Anaïs' skin swiftly. The magick came next. The magick applied through the final ink application made the ink tingle and burn.

Next, Zauvadok bared his left shoulder. Mhari could see the edges of ink on his back.

"What's that ink for, Zauvadok? Why do you hide it under your shirt?" Mhari asked.

"It enhances my strength," he replied. "It's hidden, so it's assumed I don't have any. I am, however, not as creative as my wife, and I rarely remove my shirt for anyone but her."

"That's rather clever, Zauvadok," Mhari said.

Mhari did her work swiftly and easily.

Before long, she stared at Dunharra through narrowed eyes and said, "Lady, what is wrong with you? Don't you want to call dragons?"

Dunharra pursed her lips and said nothing. Her hands shook and clearly she tried to focus on staying calm.

"Long story," Zauvadok interjected. "Let's go."

"I have one more to do," Mhari retorted.

"No, you don't," Anaïs said.

"What's wrong with her?" Mhari demanded.

"What will it take not to do it, and say you did?" Dunharra whispered quickly.

"You telling me what's wrong with you," Mhari replied.

Dunharra remained silent. She dreaded this moment.

"Look, she doesn't want the ink," Zauvadok interjected.

Zauvadok and Anaïs formed a protective line in front of Dunharra. Mhari furrowed her brow and looked at them through squinted eyes. She crossed her arms, fully invested in sorting this out.

"Looks like we are at an impasse," Anaïs said, softening. "Let's try this a different way. Dunharra is not getting ink."

"I can't," Dunharra blurted out.

"You're a healer," Mhari stated with an unbelieving glare, shaking her head. "You're a healer," she said slowly, thinking.

Mhari pushed past Anaïs and lifted Dunharra's sleeve, exposing her clean, uninked skin. "You did the healing without the ink! You saved Anaïs without the ink!"

"Enough," Zauvadok said, standing at his full, imposing height. "You need to keep this to yourself. No buts. Not a word."

"I knew this would happen," Dunharra repeated to herself. Her heart raced and she had trouble controlling her breathing. Mhari knew her secret, and soon, she thought, so would the world.

Anaïs put a consoling arm around Dunharra. "Not. A. Word."

"How can I not talk about this?" Mhari asked. "This is the news of the century!"

"I'm sure you'll find a way," Anaïs said.

Zauvadok bent down to look Mhari in her eyes. He let a not so low growl emanate from his throat and grabbed her by her neck. He lifted her off the ground enough so her feet were no longer touching the floor. "Not. A. Word."

After a long moment of staring each other down, Mhari eventually cast her gaze to the floor.

"We appreciate your silence," Anaïs said.

Mhari watched them walk away together, protectively flanking Dun on each side. She smiled a knowing, sly smile.

***

DUNHARRA

Dunharra lay in the grass watching the sun rise. The clouds were on fire with reds, golds and oranges as the sun began its journey across the sky. The Triplet Sister Moons were slightly above the horizon, ready to surrender the dominance of the night to the sun and as the new day began.

She brushed the errant blades of grass from her leather pants and went to join the others in the Great Hall. Dunharra saw it alive with activity, people running around as Queen Maebh set upon having the botany and herbalism tomes copied for the Lycaena. Maebh and Kieron called Dunharra, Zauvadok, Anaïs, Iseabail, and Calyx to an audience. Dunharra's curiosity piqued as to what she had to say.

"There is still one last promise to be met," Maebh announced. "Iain made an agreement, as instructed on my behalf. Four hundred years ago, during the reign of Nathair the Snake, the Lycaena called to Innesfrees for aid, and we left them unassisted. To right this wrong, Innesfrees needs to go to the Chernushka people, retrieve the stolen books, and bring them back to the Lycaena. There is one problem, though."

"What is that, Your Majesty?" Dunharra asked.

"We don't know what we're looking for. I am not versed in either Lycaenan or Chernushkaian culture and would not know what belonged with whom. I am asking you if you will prevent an international incident. Please seek guidance from the Lycaena to see what they are missing, so we can return it to the rightful owners."

Dunharra impishly glanced at Iseabail, Calyx, Anaïs, and Zauvadok. They all grinned back at her. "We would need someone to accompany us," Dunharra answered for them.

"You will take two of our knights with you," Maebh insisted. Iseabail opened her mouth to protest when Calyx kicked her.

They broke the trip up into two nights and traveled without incident. Upon arrival at Dhangadi, stable hands took their horses and tended to them. The white marble buildings gleamed in the sun, accentuating their spiraling architecture.

Bibek officially greeted them. "I am Bibek, Ambassador for the Lycaena. With whom do I have the pleasure?"

Dunharra stood by Iseabail as she made introductions and exchanged pleasantries. Afterward, she said, "I request an audience with King Miraç and Queen Farya. Queen Maebh and Prince Regent Kieron sent us to reclaim and restore the missing books to your library."

Bibek's face blanched. Though he looked surprised, he recovered quickly. "You're what?"

Iseabail repeated herself, nodding for emphasis.

"Come with me," Bibek said.

They followed him to a large meeting room lit both magickally and naturally. Complex and beautiful sculptures glowed in the early morning sunlight streaming in from many open windows. Dunharra thanked the Mother for the cool, mountain air. The Lycaena were mostly immune to the late summer humidity gripping most of Mantua. In the middle of the room sat a large table with ten chairs. Each of them sat down and waited.

Thirty minutes passed, and they received refreshments of white wine, bread, and several cheeses served on chilled marble slabs. They all gratefully partook. An hour later, servants led them to a large vaulted room with two thrones.

A tall man with cobalt skin and bright white short hair sat on a throne. He had many silver circles gracing his cheekbones and small circles above his eyes. He wore black leather. By his side, in the next throne, sat a slender Lycaenan woman with long white hair neatly tied in a topknot. Silver circles adorned her graceful high cheekbones and the area above her eyes. She wore a velvet dress that laced up the front. Her ice-blue eyes could see into souls.

Bibek spoke first and introduced the visiting guests individually. Turning to the group, he said, "King Miraç and Queen Farya."

"Your Majesties," Dunharra began. "We are here to retrieve the stolen books from your library. There is only one problem." Her voice echoed off the cold marble walls.

Dunharra cautiously watched as the Queen rolled her eyes, crossed her arms and looked away. "And that is?" She needed to speak carefully.

"We lack the expertise in Chernushka and Lycaenan cultures to identify the stolen materials. We need someone to guide us," Dunharra explained.

The Queen, looked over at the King.

He nodded once. "We will select a Lycaenan well versed in our culture. We categorized and listed the stolen items. If the books still exist, and the Chernushka did not destroy them, our representative will identify them," Miraç stated.

Farya continued, "Please enjoy our hospitality; we'll choose the librarian and have them prepare. We will bring them to you."

With a nod from Miraç, Bibek led them out of the throne room, past the large meeting room where they waited previously, and to a well-apportioned sitting room. Zauvadok saw a loveseat large enough to accommodate him. He sat and Anaïs settled in next to him. Zauvadok put his arm around her, and she leaned her head on his shoulder. Dunharra found a chaise lounge and settled in for a long wait. Iseabail and Calyx nestled into a high-sided settee bench.

They waited a long time.

Several hours passed. By then, only Zauvadok remained awake and he occasionally dozed. The sun journeyed across the sky, and the shadows grew long. At last, a soft knock came at the door. Immediately after, the door opened, and Bibek entered with a Lycaena of medium height and build. She wore brown leather pants and a white traveling shirt with a brown leather stay. She wore a cloak light enough to protect her from the elements, and knee-high black leather boots. Silver circles adorned her face on her cheekbones and above her eyes. She wore her short white hair to the right side of her face.

Bibek introduced her. "Please meet Beyza Yilmaz, resident librarian."

He then introduced the group individually, and they all exchanged pleasantries. Beyza's eyes lingered a bit too long on Zauvadok, and Anaïs noticed. Her back stiffened and her eyes narrowed as she regarded Beyza.

Dunharra noticed Beyza's gaze as well but said nothing. Yet.

"Right," Iseabail interjected. "Shall we be off?"

Duncan and Fergus, the knights accompanying them from Innesfrees, previously partaking of kind company, rejoined them. They left Dhangadi with a planned trajectory for the Chernushka lands.

Beyza kept her eye on Zauvadok, much to the consternation of Anaïs and the curiosity of Dunharra. Dunharra's hackles went up.

Dunharra walked next to Beyza and engaged her in some light conversation. "So, I see you looking at Zauvadok."

"I don't mean to be rude. I have never seen a half orc in person. He's rather... muscular," Beyza said, casting another glance at him.

Dunharra sighed. "That he is. Beyza, I like you. You seem very educated and like a good person. I don't recommend that you pursue him. He's not that kind of man."

"Hadn't thought of it," Beyza said. "By that, you mean he's taken?"

"Very," Dunharra said, crossing her arms.

"Oh, I see. By you?"

"No. By Anaïs. They're solid."

Beyza sighed, a dreamy look crossed her eyes. "That he is."

"Beyza," Dunharra warned. "I'm not joking. Don't pursue him. Put that thought out of your mind."

"Message received, Dunharra. I won't," Beyza said again.

Chapter Twelve

CHAPTER TWELVE

DUNHARRA

They set out on horses and a wagon to hopefully bring back the stolen books. Duncan took point, followed by Iseabail and Calyx. Anaïs and Zau held the middle, followed by Beyza, while Dunharra and Fergus brought up the rear. They traveled down the treacherous western path down the mountain. They took extreme care, going slowly along the narrow, craggy paths. Even though their riders seemed nervous, the Lycaenan horses, specifically trained for mountain traveling, had sure footing. Their only company of mountain goats and lions watched them from a distance.

Zauvadok and Anaïs kept a sharp eye on the mountain lions. Dunharra watched as Beyza kept a sharp eye on Zauvadok and Anaïs. Riding behind them, she had a front row seat to their interactions. Beyza made Dunharra uneasy, but she could not put her finger on why.

She couldn't let herself trust Beyza. Something about her would not let her put her guard down.

The strong shadows of the late afternoon gave way to the dim light of twilight. Time to stop for the night. Duncan and Fergus attended to the horses, while the rest set up camp. Crickets chirped, and stars sprawled across the night sky as, one by one, they entered their tents. Beyza offered first watch. Dunharra carefully watched as Anaïs sized her up.

"No need," Anaïs said as her eyes glowed blood red, and she made the wyvern magick. With a word, the three large wyverns circled above the camp.

Anaïs' eyes narrowed as she met Beyza's gaze. "So, do I need to explain, or do you get it?"

Dunharra could tell that Anaïs also noticed Beyza's longing gazes at Zauvadok and wanted nothing to do with her.

"Be sure you do," Anaïs said with a hard edge to her voice. She went into her and Zauvadok's tent. One by one they all entered their tents, leaving Beyza standing outside, alone.

The night passed uneventfully. Wyverns circled overhead in their silent watch. The sun rose over the Thunder Hill Forest to the east and bathed everything with the light and potential of a new day. Everyone emerged from their tents, awake and getting ready to travel.

Zauvadok broke camp for Duncan and Fergus as they readied the horses. They were quiet and kept to themselves. Beyza seized this opportunity to speak with Zauvadok alone.

What's Beyza doing? She watched, incredulous, as she sauntered over to him; she assumed to help him break camp. When he reached for the tent poles, so did Beyza, and her hand touched his. She let it linger for a moment before Zauvadok pulled it away. A low growl emanated from his throat.

"Beyza," he said, his tone a warning. She stood her ground. Zauvadok silently finished breaking down the tents and walked away. He left Beyza standing alone.

Beyza walked over to Dunharra as she packed her gear. She asked, "Dunharra, have you heard the Prophecy of the Healer?"

Dunharra froze. Her blood ran cold and her mouth went dry. She felt as though she couldn't breathe. "Of course. Who in the Southern Kingdoms hasn't?" Dunharra asked, tying her bedroll to her saddle, trying to look bored with the conversation.

"Anaïs made magick without ink."

Dunharra could breathe again. "Beyza, I think you are playing with a hornet's nest. Leave well enough alone." She turned to walk away.

"It's true, isn't it," Beyza stated more than asked as she stepped in front of Dunharra, blocking her way. "The healer has finally come?"

"You do not know what you're talking about. None. Leave Anaïs and Zauvadok alone." Dunharra pushed past Beyza with her jaw clenched.

The Chernushka lands were a half-day's ride to the west. Iseabail called them together.

"We need to be in complete agreement," Iseabail said. "The first group we should encounter is the Oryol. Beyza, if they have any artifacts, I will negotiate seeing them. Then, on the off chance they permit us to examine their objects, you may do so. It will be like this for all seven tribes."

There were unanimous nods of agreement, including Beyza. Dunharra doubted it would be that easy.

They recreated their traveling formation, and the hilly forest eventually gave way to challenging rocky steppes. The morning brought a respite from the sweltering heat, a break that everyone relished. Perhaps the cool breezes distracted them. They didn't realize eyes watched them from vantage points above. Then, an arrow buried deep in the ground next to Zauvadok. The horse startled and nearly threw him.

Two more arrows flew, which also impaled safely in the dirt.

"Warning shots," Duncan said, finally seeing the Oryols. "If they wanted to hurt us, they wouldn't miss."

Iseabail and Calyx rode to the front of the party and stopped alongside Duncan. "We seek the wisdom of your elders."

One Oryol stood up. "What wisdom do you seek?"

"We seek the wisdom of your elders regarding Lycaenan objects," Iseabail replied.

"The Oryol has no Lycaenan objects."

"We trust your word, but we must verify."

"The Oryol has no Lycaenan objects," he repeated slowly and pointedly.

"We want to clear Oryol name from suspicion of having these items," Iseabail said, taking a different tactic. "We wish to talk about the Lycaenan objects."

The soldiers conferred among themselves.

"I am Pavel. We will take you," Pavel said as the two others stood proudly. "Follow me."

They followed at a close but safe distance to Pavel and the two other Oryols. Twenty minutes later, they found themselves in the middle of a settlement. They saw many yurts and at least fifty men, women, and children, who all stopped to look at the strangers on horseback. The weight of their stares bore down heavy on them, and they shifted in their saddles.

The Oryol dressed in the traditional Chernushka black pants and skirts, with colorful stitching on white shirts. Pavel directed them to dismount and leave their horses at a young oak tree. Duncan and Fergus stayed with the horses and basked in the rare shade.

Pavel led them to a yurt, where they found two older men and a middle-aged woman. Pavel introduced the tanned and wrinkled tribal elders, Tomek, Luka, and the elder healer, Katiya. He invited the delegation to sit. Iseabail introduced them, and they exchanged pleasantries.

“The Lycaena of the Silver Haven Mountains sent us,” Iseabail began. “Four hundred years ago, raiders from a Chernushka tribe plundered their library and destroyed the herbarium. I came to negotiate the return of the missing items.”

“We are a peaceful and honorable people,” Tomek began. “We were not a part of the raids that stole from the Lycaena.”

“Then who—” Iseabail began.

Beyza stood up and shouted at the tribal elders, her voice cracking with emotion, “You should be ashamed, liars!”

Dunharra and Zauvadok grabbed Beyza and took her, kicking and screaming, out of the yurt. She squirmed futilely against them, yelling about a Chernushka conspiracy to keep the books. They carried her to the stable, where Duncan and Fergus waited. Dunharra let go of Beyza’s legs, and Zauvadok dropped her on the ground. Duncan and Fergus watched, wide-eyed and slack-jawed that Beyza carried on this way.

“What are you doing?” Zauvadok roared. “You are putting this whole search in jeopardy!”

“They are lying! All the Chernushka were involved. All the groups.” She grabbed Zau’s hand and held it over her heart. “Feel my heartbeat, and tell me you don’t feel it, too?”

Dunharra's eyes were wide. She could not believe what Beyza did.

Zauvadok, stunned at her brazen action, roughly pulled his hand away. “By the Mother, you are a crazy woman.” Dunharra watched him walk away, furious.

Duncan asked, "You know he's married, right?"

"Such a funny thing, Duncan. He's never mentioned it," Beyza said with a smirk.

"By the Mother, help me not to kill that woman," Iseabail said as she, Calyx and Anąïs walked to the horses to wait. Once there, they found Beyza and Duncan sitting apart from each other and not speaking. Dunharra stood near the stables with Zauvadok.

"Beyza," Iseabail began, trying to keep her voice even through clenched teeth. "What in the name of the Mother are you thinking? This is not off to a good start, and it's all because of you. You! The one who has the most to lose here."

Dunharra, shocked, watched Beyza feign innocence and rolled her eyes. "Like they would have let us examine anything anyway, Iseabail."

"They might have until your outburst! Have you lost your mind?"

The shouting drew a crowd. Curious Oryol onlookers watched the scene unfold. Children stared at first, then adults congregated near them.

Iseabail stopped and looked around as she drew a breath in through her nose and out her mouth. "Now, we wait."

Dunharra walked up to Beyza. "Let's take a walk."

She pulled Beyza along with her. Dunharra waited until they were out of earshot to talk.

"Beyza, what are you doing? You are chasing a married man, and you threw this search into confusion and jeopardy. You have more invested in getting the library back than anyone. What's going on?"

Dunharra thought she saw a shadow overcast Beyza's eyes as if she were thinking about something unpleasant. Something she hid from everyone.

"Dunharra, I'm sorry about my outburst. I want to see the library back more than anyone. I...acted poorly. I will control myself from now on."

Her face, no longer petulant, stared down at the ground.

Dunharra pressed, "And Zauvadok?"

"What about him?"

"You know damn well what."

"He's worth fighting for."

"Beyza, he's married."

"He handfasted nine months ago. That gives him three months until the marriage is binding under Mantua law. He can choose as he wishes with no repercussions. He can leave, and it would be as if the marriage never existed. So, you see, he is still free to choose me."

"How do you know all this?" Dunharra frowned and gave Beyza the side eye.

"I'm a librarian. It's my job to know and catalog information."

Dunharra shook her head. "Know this, Beyza. I handfasted them. I will not, *will not*, let you tear apart what I and the Mother have brought together."

Beyza rolled her eyes. "It's Zauvadok's choice. I am smarter, better-educated, and better-looking than Anaïs. If he chooses me, which he will, it will show their unbound marriage for the sham it is."

Dunharra thought back to the desperation in his voice and eyes when Anaïs lay dying in the Innesfrees Chamber. She saw his tears mix with Anaïs' silver blood as he wept over her broken body. Zauvadok deeply loved Anaïs and would never leave her. "You don't know as much as you think."

"I know Anaïs is the Prophesied Healer."

Dunharra drew in a sharp breath, and her heart beat against her chest. This quickly got too close for comfort. "That's not true, Beyza, and you know it."

"Oh, is that right?" Beyza asked, a satisfied grin splashed across her face.

"That's right. Don't belittle the Prophecy by making false accusations. You're making enemies here. I advise against that."

Dunharra and Beyza locked eyes for a long moment, until Beyza blinked.

"Watch your step, Beyza. We are the wrong enemies to make." Dunharra walked away.

***

DUNHARRA

After some time, Tomek, Luka, and Katiya returned.

Tomek spoke first. "We discussed the issue at length. We know we have nothing that does not already belong to us."

"Yet, we also have nothing to hide. We will let you view our sacred artifacts," Luka said. "But not before a test of strength and character."

"A what?" Beyza asked.

Luka repeated himself slowly and stared at Beyza as if she had something wrong with her. "Follow us."

In a clearing behind the yurts stood a square, scaffold about six feet tall with crossbeams for sturdiness. It appeared rugged but solid. Tomek met each person's eye, as if he were burrowing into their soul. He pointed to Dunharra. "Her."

Two soldiers grabbed Dunharra by each arm. They half-carried and half-dragged her to the scaffold. Confused, Dunharra screamed and tried to fight them when they tied her hands and feet to a pair of the crossbeams with leather strips. Her heart pounded in her chest when they blindfolded her.

Shouts filled the air in furious protest. Zauvadok and Anaïs drew their swords to prevent the protesters from attaching Dunharra to the scaffold. Six Oryol warriors armed with swords stood between them and Dunharra.

From one of the yurts, a soldier brought out a small target made of well-worn oak. He placed it in front of Dunharra. Tomek looked very pleased. Another soldier came out of the same yurt, this time with six axes designed for throwing.

"You will each take turns throwing your axe at the target," Tomek announced. "If she lives, we may discuss our artifacts."

"You son of a bitch!" Zauvadok shouted, his hands balled into fists.

"You can't be serious!" Iseabail yelled, her voice rough with emotion. "You are making sport of her life! I'm not a soldier. I've never even held an axe before and certainly have never thrown one."

"Those are the terms," Tomek said stoically. "The choice is yours."

Zauvadok growled; a deep and guttural sound. "Dun! It's going to be alright."

Dunharra swallowed hard and tried to control her racing heart. She couldn't make sense of any of this.

Zauvadok clenched his fists until his fingernails dug into his palms. He fought to control a guttural roar. He took his axe and threw it as hard as he could, venting his impotent anger and frustration. It hit dead center.

Duncan took a deep breath and let his axe fly. It hit the target, but not in the center.

Fergus's eyes were dark with concern. Sweat rolled down his forehead. He threw the axe. It missed the target completely and it landed safely in the grass.

Iseabail took her axe gingerly. Calyx put a reassuring hand on her leg.

"Hold it high, then let it fly, Iseabail," Zauvadok coached her. "It will be alright."

Iseabail steeled her resolve and threw it. It flew, wobbly, but it flew. The handle hit the target, and the axe bounced safely onto the rocky grass.

Anaïs stepped up next. She watched Dunharra and then focused on the target. She let her axe fly. The axe impaled the target directly to the right of Zauvadok's axe. She sighed heavily and walked back to stand next to Zauvadok.

All eyes fell on Beyza. She held the last axe to throw. She played with it absently and tested the razor-sharp edge, toying with time.

"Beyza, this is not the time to dawdle," Iseabail warned.

Beyza appeared more annoyed than concerned, as if this were an inconvenience; a means to an end to seeing the Oryol artifacts. She pompously huffed, drew back, and threw her axe. She would miss the target completely. Beyza aimed too high.

The backside of the axe head hit directly into the left side of Dunharra's head. Only sheer luck or the divine intervention of the Mother saved her from more serious injury. She slumped against the leather straps that held her to the scaffold, unconscious and bleeding from her left temple.

Zauvadok roared, muscles tight and clenched, and he ran to see how much damage Beyza had done. Everyone else followed except Beyza, who simply shrugged. She felt no responsibility or remorse. She walked to Tomek and asked when she could see the artifacts. Zauvadok started to cut Dunharra down when the soldiers stopped him.

"Keep the woman bound on the scaffold where she is until you finish viewing our artifacts," Tomek commanded.

"She's bleeding!" Anaïs said.

"Get your healer," Katiya replied with a shrug.

"She *is* our healer!" Anaïs snarled and wrinkled her brow as worry overtook rage. She inspected the gash on Dunharra's temple. Head wounds were dangerous.

"What?" Beyza asked, trying to look innocent.

"You know goddamn well what, Beyza," Anaïs said, jaw tight and set. "You are on thin ice here. Watch your step."

"I can't believe you did that," Iseabail said as she walked by. "You threw it right at her head. Dunharra's been nothing but nice to you. She's our healer."

An Oryol warrior walked up to Iseabail and said, "Our elders have decided to show you the artifacts. Follow me."

Calyx, the only one willing to speak to Beyza, retrieved her, and they followed the tribesman across the settlement. Once they reached the far northeast corner, they met Tomek, Luka, and Katiya.

Iseabail, Calyx, and Beyza followed the Oryol wise men and healing elder to another yurt; secluded from all others. Their sacred space. They opened the yurt and let sunlight bathe the objects inside. Tomek stepped in, followed by Luka and Katiya. After a moment of prayer, they invited Beyza in.

She inspected each item. There were no books to be found, only sacred objects, and those fell under her close scrutiny. Small statues, chest plates decorated with what Beyza could only guess were semi-precious stones, and sacred knives laid out, all arranged neatly on a blanket on the ground. They were all beautiful and well-made, resulting from careful craftsmanship.

Beyza emerged from the yurt empty-handed.

"There are no Lycaenan objects here," she said with disdain.

Without hesitation upon hearing the news, Zauvadok cut Dunharra down and carefully cradled her head in his lap. He patted her face, and Anaïs found a rag wet with water. She gently cleaned the jagged gash, patting it at first, and then wiping the dried blood from Dunharra's black ringlets. The steady bleeding stemmed to a trickle.

Dunharra squinted in the afternoon sun. "What happened?"

Everyone replied in unison, "Beyza."

"My head," Dunharra said as she reached up to touch the gash. She drew away a smear of blood on her fingers. She rubbed her eyes. Dunharra tried to sit up, but the world spun, and Zauvadok eased her back in his lap.

"Beyza hit you with the blunt side of a throwing axe, giving you a nasty cut on your temple," Anaïs said.

Without a word, Dunharra took a deep, cleansing breath as her eyes turned iridescent. Moments later, the gash closed, and the scar vanished.

Zauvadok and Anaïs helped Dunharra up. She felt fine and steady on her feet. Wordlessly, they walked to the horses. They had no desire to interact further with the Oryol people.

"The Oryol are an honorable people. We have only what is ours. You will find that not all Chernushka are so forthcoming," Luka said.

Then, the elders turned and left. Katiya escorted them back to the horses to meet with the others. They rode out of camp silently, keeping their thoughts to themselves.

Chapter Thirteen

CHAPTER THIRTEEN

DUNHARRA

They broke camp after lunch and headed directly for the Topki people.

Duncan again took point with Iseabail, Calyx, and Beyza behind him. Next were Anaïs and Zau, with Dunharra following them, and Fergus bringing up the rear. Dunharra kept Beyza distracted with conversation, which left Anaïs and Zau unbothered.

Shadows became longer and deeper on the rocky ground as the sun moved across the sky. At the border of the Topki lands, Dunharra saw two soldiers waiting on horseback.

"Good news travels fast," Dunharra said. "We have a welcoming committee."

Iseabail and Calyx rode up to the soldiers, and Iseabail spoke first. "The Lycaena sent us. I seek to discuss missing Lycaenan objects with your elders."

"We know why you are here. We will take you to the elders. Follow us."

Iseabail and Calyx thanked them, and they followed the two soldiers into a small encampment of about forty people. The Topki were the smallest of the Chernushka and, clearly, the most creative. Fascinated, Dunharra admired the beautiful artwork. The elder's yurt appeared the most beautiful.

They dismounted. Duncan and Fergus stayed with their horses again, while the rest of them waited for the elders to be ready and available for visitors. They did not wait long.

A beautiful woman met them, who brought them to the elder's yurt. She stood short for her people group with a muscular body proportional to her height. The woman wore black pants with an embroidered red shirt and had a bow slung on her back with a quiver of arrows. She opened the flap of the yurt and gestured for them to enter.

They decorated the inside in the same elaborate way as the exterior. There were two elders: an ancient and wizened man, and an equally old and wizened woman with long gray hair in a neat bun. They wore red and white shirts with intricately stitched sleeves. Their skirts were black, red, and gold; also intricately stitched. They gestured for the travelers to sit.

The man spoke first. "I am Konstantin, and this is my wife, Nasia. We are the elders of the Topki. We heard from the Oryol that your group is traveling the Chernushka lands, looking for artifacts from the Lycaenan library that suffered devastating raids hundreds of years ago. Is this true?"

Iseabail addressed the Topki elders. "That is true. The Lycaena sent us, and we have a librarian expert in Lycaenan artifacts. I would like to talk to you about seeing your objects. We wish no harm or dishonor to you and your people, only to make the Lycaenan library whole again."

"The Topki appreciate your desire to achieve such a goal. We hope to show you our sacred objects to clear the Topki name from suspicion. Other tribes will not be as forthcoming or forgiving," Nasia warned.

"We are thankful for your forthrightness and information. It will help us as we visit the other tribes," Iseabail replied.

Konstantin held up a hand. "There is a price to view these items."

"What price?" Iseabail asked.

Dunharra's heart beat quickened as she remembered the price the Oryol's exacted from them.

"Every group that travels on a quest such as yours has a healer with them. My granddaughter has been burning with fever since giving birth to our great-granddaughter. Your healer must aid her. Only then will you see our sacred objects."

Beyza's eyes shot to Anaïs, but everyone else looked at Dunharra, who stood and nodded. "I can heal her with magick or herbs, whichever is the elder's preference."

The elders nodded. "Our herbs have not helped. Any means will do. Magick is acceptable."

Dunharra knew this type of fever well. She had encountered it often when while studying under Benazir the Midwife. She recognized this as the deadly Younglingbed Fever. It usually came about when less educated birth attendants did not have clean hands when they assisted with the labor. Many women died when help arrived too late or not at all.

Nasia stood up and led Dunharra to a nearby yurt, where their granddaughter rested in fitful sleep. The inside of the yurt smelled of urine and sickness. In the deep darkness a young, brown-haired woman slept under woven cotton blankets. Sweat soaked her clothes. She looked like death had its grip on her.

"How old is the child?"

"Five days," answered Nasia.

Dunharra knelt beside the sick girl. The woman's breasts were leaking. Her milk came in, but she could not nurse her baby. A foul odor and purulent discharge emanated from her vagina, that mixed with dark red blood. Dunharra palpated the young woman's uterus to find it enlarged and displaced to the right because of her full bladder. A Topki wet nurse who held the sleeping baby at the back of the yurt looked both sad and terrified.

Dunharra's eyes glowed iridescent, and she laid hands on the woman's abdomen and pelvis. She took a deep breath. Dunharra could sense the infection deep within the woman's uterus and blood. She would not have survived another day. Her magick weaved into the woman's body, cleansing the infection. Her forehead no longer glistened with sickly sweat, and her eyes fluttered open.

Nasia went to the young mother and carefully knelt by her side. She felt the sick woman's forehead and stroked her hair. Nasia spoke in Topki to her. She hugged Nasia, and a tear escaped her eye.

Nasia spoke the intricate Topki, in words that sounded like a prayer of gratitude. She held her hands up toward the sky and muttered words of thanks.

"The Mother sent you to us," Nasia said. She hugged Dunharra and said more words of thanks in Topki. "You have saved Oksana. We thank the Mother that you are here.

Before Nasia and Dunharra returned, the hunter who escorted them in gestured for them to follow her. She guided them to a meadow and displayed the items on an intricately woven blanket. There were not as many items as the Oryol people possessed, but these items were sacred to the Topki. These were ritualistic, blessed vessels. No books.

Beyza stepped forward and inspected the objects. As before, she held them to the sun, examining the script on the ritual vessels. With a sigh, she declared, "There are no Lycaenan items here."

Dunharra returned after Beyza finished inspecting the Topki items. She stayed behind to help Oksana and her baby breastfeed. They gratefully attended a celebratory feast held for Oksana's healing and recovery. There were plenty of flatbreads, hummus, and a smoking pit of meat for everyone.

Twilight subtly fell, and darkness approached. The Triplet Sister Moons rose in the sky when they took their leave, and the celebration ended. They thanked Konstantin and Nasia for their hospitality.

They rode to a lush green meadow, where they camped for the night. No one wanted to socialize. They laid out their bedrolls, and then eagerly sought the relative comfort of their tents.

Dunharra woke before the Triplet Sister Moons fully reached the horizon. She left her tent and lay in the grassy meadow, relishing the coolness of the dew on her skin. She connected with the Mother as she watched the sun take its place in the cloudless sky. Nature soothed and calmed her when life got tense.

Sunrise woke everyone, Anaïs last as usual. Dunharra watched as Beyza seized the opportunity and offered breakfast to Zauvadok. "A handsome man like you needs a good first meal of the day."

"Thank you, but no." Zauvadok walked over to Anaïs. He kissed her forehead gently and stayed at her side until they broke camp and left.

Dunharra watched as Beyza got a visible flush to her cheeks and a pinched expression on her face. She could only imagine what Beyza's true intentions were, and none of them were good.

It would be an hour ride through rocky, craggy land, and they wasted no time riding to the Abakan people in their usual formation. The Abakan lands were in sight a few hours later, when two warriors once more rode up to them on horseback. The woman of the pair asked, “Who approaches the Abakan lands? Do you arrive in peace?”

Iseabail answered, “We approach in peace, desiring to only to talk to the Abakan people about missing items from the Lycaena.”

The female warrior said, “We were expecting you. Please follow us.”

Beyza leaned over to Iseabail and Calyx. “All the Chernushka must know about us. Do you think they took this opportunity to hide the artifacts?”

“That’s always a possibility,” Iseabail replied. “It is something to keep in mind, although there may be another reason. How would it feel if strange people from a strange land wanted unfettered access to your sacred objects? Wouldn’t you spread the word?”

"You should be prepared for the possibility of these artifacts being lost to time or destroyed." Four hundred years is a long time,” Dunharra said.

Dunharra could tell this unsettled Beyza. “Let’s hope that is not the case. I will not go home empty-handed.” Her eyes were cold and hard.

“You might have to,” Calyx said, saying what everyone else thought.

The warriors led them to the Abakan elders, a group of five men and women sitting on horseback. They seemed strong despite their age, and sat proudly in their saddles. A younger-looking healer stood beside the five elders.

The elder healer spoke. “We of the Abakan welcome you to our lands. Please, come and enjoy some food with us.”

She gestured to a large yurt, with the door left open for the aroma of fresh breads and smoked meats to waft out to tease the delegation’s noses. Duncan and Fergus gathered the horses after they dismounted and corralled them near the yurt.

Once all were inside, a familiar and calm sequence of events unfolded as the oldest elder spoke. "I am Dmitri. I have seen much in my time. During my grandfather's grandfather's grandfather's life the Chernushka people raided the Lycaenan library. Everyone present at the raid has long since passed to the Summerlands. Our history preserves that sad time. We would like to tell you the story from our perspectives."

They settled in for the story. Dunharra said, "Please, continue."

"Hundreds of years ago, a young king from the south contacted us to request a meeting with all the Chernushka elders," Dmitri began. "The Abakan attended this meeting. This brazen young king asked the honorable Chernushka people to attack the Lycaena and raid their library. He didn't tell us what he searched for."

"Where did this king hail from?" Iseabail asked.

"Buckhaven."

The yurt went silent. They did not expect this. They sat completely still, hanging on every word Dmitri said.

"King Teague paid us handsomely in grain, meat, and water during a great famine among the Chernushka. We reluctantly accepted. Our younglings were dying for want of food and water. Mother's breasts were dry, and our hunters brought home nothing. Buckhaven came to our aid in tangible ways to stop the deaths and aid in our recovery from this famine. So, to our shame, we assembled and raided the Lycaenan Library."

"What did King Teague want?" Dunharra asked.

"He wanted information about a Frozen Crown. But no Chernushka could read the Lycaenan script. So, we took all the books and scrolls, and we delivered them to King Teague of Buckhaven."

"A conspiracy!" Beyza interjected. "The one who can wear this crown would be King or Queen of all Mantua. Someone can only wear it if they are magickally protected from its effects, or else it will freeze the wearer alive."

"The Frozen Crown remains unclaimed," Dunharra added. "King Teague's attempts were unsuccessful. The question is, are those artifacts still in Buckhaven?"

"We do not know," Dmitri replied. "Our knowledge of them ended when we placed them in the hands of King Teague."

"This does not look good for Buckhaven," Iseabail said.

"The House of Buckhaven is devious," Dmitri said and shook his head.

The Abakan showed the delegation all of their sacred objects. As before, Beyza certified she could not locate the missing artifacts. Iseabail thanked the Abakan elders and exited their company.

Rejoining Duncan, Fergus, and the horses, they rode out of the village to find a place for making camp. After setting up camp, Iseabail called everyone to the center.

Beyza sat directly to the left of and within arm's reach of Zauvadok. Anaïs sat on his right.

"We heard the Abakan tell us what happened four hundred years ago. I don't think we will find any Lycaenan artifacts or books in any of the Chernushka tribes," Iseabail said.

"Do we believe the word of one to represent all the Chernushka?" Beyza asked.

"Why shouldn't we?" Dunharra asked. "This wrong is far enough removed that many of the Chernushka no longer have anything at stake. Why would they lie?"

"Because they are loyal to Buckhaven for their help during the famine," Beyza said, incredulous. "Are you suggesting we stop searching?"

"That is exactly what I am suggesting," Dunharra answered, crossing her arms.

Beyza put her hand on Zauvadok's shoulder. "Do you think we should stop?"

"This is becoming a fool's errand," Zauvadok snarled. "Get your hand off me. Don't touch me. Ever."

Beyza slowly removed her hand, but her eyes lingered on him.

"The Chernushka, while they were the ones to do the deed, were not the driving force behind it. We uncovered the true enemy and their motive, Dunharra said. "Further intrusion into the Chernushka is unnecessary. You should take this information back to your people for consideration."

"So, it's over then? The Lycaena are supposed to swallow our loss forever?"

"No, not at all," Iseabail said. "Looking for the artifacts and books where they clearly are not is a waste of time and resources. We should look in Buckhaven, not with the Chernushka. However, like with the Chernushka, we need diplomacy to gain access to the artifacts and books from Buckhaven. Go in talking and negotiate seeing the objects."

"More delays!"

"Yes," Dunharra interjected. "Delays but not denials. "The wrong approach could mean the permanent and irretrievable loss of the library's items. All that is being asked of you is patience on behalf of your people."

"Four hundred years is long enough!" Beyza shouted, standing.

"Are you suggesting we actually go to Buckhaven and demand to see their archives? Now?" Dunharra asked.

"Yes! That's exactly what I'm saying. What makes Buckhaven so special? Why should we treat them any differently than the Chernushka people?" Beyza asked.

"It's getting late," Dunharra said. "Let's sleep on this and talk about it in the morning. Agreed?"

All but Beyza agreed. Her disdain clearly evident, she could not stop the end of the meeting. She walked to Anaïs, intent on venting her frustration. "Enjoy him now, Anaïs. Soon he will belong to me."

Anaïs didn't flinch. "I know my marriage is strong. It will survive you." She pushed Beyza back and clearly off balance. Beyza nearly fell. "Bitch! You don't deserve him. He will see he belongs with me."

"Bitch? Oh, it's on, whore." Anaïs' eyes shifted to blood red and the ink on her shoulders beat in sync with her heart. Before she could unleash her magic, Iseabail and Dunharra intervened, separating them, and led them to their tents.

"Are you insane?" Iseabail yelled at Beyza from her tent.

Gaining her self-control, Beyza held up her hands in surrender. "I'm alright. I'm alright."

"You better get a hold of yourself. We should take you back to the Lycaena in the morning. You're more trouble than you're worth," Calyx said.

***

DUNHARRA

Dunharra put an arm around Anaïs and held her. "I'm going to kill that whore."

"No, you're not," Dunharra said. "Take a breath. She's not worth it."

Anaïs closed her eyes, took a deep breath, and shook her hands as she let her magick flow away. Her skin glistened with sweat. "She's not worth it. You're right."

"Stay here," Dunharra said. "I need to have a talk with someone."

Dunharra walked up to Zauvadok and said, "We need to talk."

They walked toward the horses, where they were out of earshot.

"What can I do for you?" Zauvadok asked.

"More like what you can do for all of us. Zauvadok, you have a problem." Dunharra crossed her arms over her chest and sighed.

"I don't know what to do. This has never happened to me before," he paused and pointed to himself. "I mean, look at me. I'm not the type to have this sort of problem. I have only been cordial to Beyza. There isn't a reason for her to want to be with me other than wrecking what makes another woman happy. I cannot and will not do that to Anaïs."

"Beyza is upping her game," Dunharra said. "You need to put a stop to it. Someone is going to get hurt, like Anaïs. Beyza will not listen to anyone but you."

"What do I say at this point?"

"You need to make a statement that Beyza will understand. I know you've never told her yourself that you're married. You've left that up to other people. You need to put a stop to all this."

"Do you really think that will help?" Zauvadok asked, eyes searching Dunharra for a sign.

"It's a start. Can't you see how much this is hurting Anaïs?"

"Anaïs should know that I love her," Zauvadok said, looking at the ground. Feelings he didn't understand swirled in his heart and it confused him more as to what to do.

"You know what you have to do," Dunharra said. "Do it."

Anaïs called the wyverns to watch over the camp in their silent vigil overhead. The camp grew quiet, but the tension remained thick.

***

DUNHARRA

The Triplet Sister Moons were spinning their last dance with the stars. The sun peeked over the horizon ready to rise spilling its early morning light across the land. Dunharra made sure she was awake to see it.

Slowly, they shook off sleep and emerged from their tents. No one spoke; they only went about their morning under the blanket of tension that filled the air.

Iseabail cleared her throat once most of them finished with their routines for the morning. "Alright. Let's get this meeting started. There are three choices. We continue to interview the remaining four tribes of the Chernushka people; we change course to Buckhaven to see their library; or we return to the Lycaena to report what we know."

Zauvadok spoke for himself and Anaïs. "We should return to the Lycaena and report this trip's full events, including their librarian's poor behavior as a representative of their people. Buckhaven is preparing a defense for King Darragh and his crimes against Innesfrees. Their preoccupation could cause further delays, or they could draw us into their conflict.

"Which is why it's a perfect time to go," Beyza argued, half ignoring him. "Their distraction will prevent them from hiding anything."

"If they are not already hiding it. Who's to say that the Lycaenan library isn't languishing in a dark storeroom far away from the Buckhaven library? Why would anyone, even Buckhaven, display stolen items?" Dunharra asked. "Haven't we done enough damage already? Stomping in where we don't belong, demanding to snoop around for something that may or may not be there?"

"You underestimate the audacity of Buckhaven, Dunharra," Beyza retorted. "They tried to assassinate the entire royal family of Innesfrees."

"I'm aware of that, thank you. I was there," Dunharra snapped.

"While I agree we need to move diplomatically," Fergus interjected. "The fact that they would hide away whatever they have with enough advanced notice of our arrival decreases our chance of finding anything."

Dunharra watched as Beyza smiled smugly. Beyza had people on her side and split the group into factions. Dunharra wondered what her motives were. Clearly tearing them apart made her top three.

"So, it's time to vote," Iseabail said. "All for going back to the Lycaena to report what we know?"

Dunharra, Anaïs, and Zau raised their hands.

"All for going forward to Buckhaven?"

Duncan, Fergus, and Beyza raised their hands.

"I shall call the tied vote," Iseabail said. "We go to Buckhaven."

Dunharra sighed. Beyza clapped her hands and smiled at Anaïs.

In a matter of hours, they skirted the Lukoyanov Plains and headed south toward Buckhaven. They kept the Bannockburn River to the east as they traveled. The sun hung high overhead when Zauvadok noted a group of four men set on a course to follow them out of the southern end of the Chernushka lands. They made no threatening moves, only followed from a distance.

They rode for hours when Duncan suggested they break to let the horses rest. About an hour later, they were ready to move again. When

Zauvadok went to check the horses alone, Beyza followed close behind him.

Zauvadok glanced at her, grunted, and continued to check the horse's tack.

Beyza rested her hand on his chest, over his heart. Zau stared down at it, then glared at Beyza. However, he did not remove her hand.

"I know about your handfasting," Beyza began. "I know you have three more months until it's binding under Mantuan law. You have time, Zau. Your commitment isn't complete yet."

Dumharra could hardly believe her eyes. She couldn't understand why Beyza persisted in doing this.

He looked down at Beyza's hand on his chest again and swallowed hard. Time to handle this.

Chapter Fourteen

CHAPTER FOURTEEN

DARRAGH

Darragh heard hammering in the Innesfrees courtyard. He heard the scaffolding being built. He knew his fate.

Prince Ronan and Queen Aelwen were charged with conspiracy to commit murder and aiding a coup. Should they ever be unwise enough to come near Innesfrees, they would meet the same fate.

Knights roughly dragged Darragh and Pyotr from the jail to an old, foul-smelling hay cart, pulled by a ghostly old horse. An angry crowd gathered to witness their execution. On the bumpy cobblestone road, it seemed like they hit every hump, hole, and curb that existed between the castle and the square. The uneven travel jostled them about the cart, adding indignity to the scene.

As they forced them up the scaffold, Pyotr begged for mercy. Darragh felt no pity as tears streamed down Pyotr's face as the executioner pulled the hood over his head and tightened the noose around his neck. Darragh stood regally, scanning the crowd for any friendly faces and a sliver of hope that he would survive. He could see no one.

The executioner placed a hood over Darragh's head, and secured the noose tightly around his neck. The executioner waited for the signal to pull the lever that would drop the floor and send them to their deaths.

Darragh heard the signal and braced himself. What he could not hear were two arrows sailing through the air from the back of the crowd. One arrow severed the rope connected to Darragh, who dropped helplessly to the ground. The other arrow buried itself deep in Pyotr's chest.

The crowd, stunned into silence, stared with mouths open and eyes wide. Then, with shocked gasps and screams, they shouted their disbelief and demands for justice. Disguised in the front row of onlookers, three Buckhaven loyalists ran toward Darragh. They picked him up, hood and all, and ran from the town square. The crowd rushed the scaffold, creating a great mob of chaos.

The three men who carried Darragh ran through the courtyard and the castle gate. Innesfrees knights picked up the pursuit, sprinting after them. The foot race began.

Darragh's habit of overindulgence in food, and wine made him a heavy burden. This slowed the Buckhaven loyalists, and the knights were gaining ground. Ahead of them a rowboat floated on the bay, which they meant to use to make their escape.

The men threw Darragh so roughly into the rowboat it threatened to capsize. They climbed in and began rowing out to sea, heading toward a clipper that slipped into view from behind the Star Wall. The timing could not be more perfect. Blue and red flags gleamed in the noon sun, fluttering in the bay breezes.

Darragh stood and waved at the Innesfrees knights with his execution hood. They could only watch as the tiny rowboat met the Buckhaven clipper.

Once on the clipper, Darragh breathed easier. His sore neck proved he lived to tell the tale, and finally heading home to Buckhaven he could relax. For a long while, he enjoyed the bay breeze and the salty spray on his face. Halfway to Buckhaven, Darragh went below deck to be met by his older son, Ronan.

"Your Majesty," Ronan said, before giving his father a one-armed hug.

"Took you long enough," Darragh said, only half joking.

"That archer is a rare one, Father. I could barely find someone of his talent, or someone who could mingle through the crowd so well without being seen."

King Darragh sat, followed closely by Ronan. "Pyotr?"

"Dead, father. If the noose didn't kill him, then the arrow to his chest did. He will cause no treachery or repercussions, and I have purchased your liberty."

"Excellent. Well done, son. Well done."

***

DUNHARRA

A threatening growl emanated from the depths of Zauvadok's soul. Dunharra stared at Zauvadok and Beyza with wide eyes.

"You never call me Zau. To you, I am Zauvadok. Never Zau." He leaned down and put himself face-to-face with Beyza. "There will never be an 'us'. If you claim to feel about me the way that you do, then you will respect my answer and leave me alone. This is the last time we will have this conversation where I am polite."

Before he could stop her, she kissed him. Not any kiss. She drowned him with her tongue by force and not by choice. His eyes were wide with shock.

Dunharra could hardly believe her eyes. She stood next to Anaïs, watching the scene unfold, her hand covering her shocked, open mouth. A lone tear slipped down Anaïs' cheek.

Breaking the kiss, Beyza peered up at him. Dunharra saw the look in her eyes; pure, unadulterated satisfaction.

Zauvadok's face contorted into a snarl and he wordlessly backhanded Beyza. She fell to the ground. Everyone looked at him and he shrank back from the attention. He stepped over her limp body and walked to Dunharra and Anaïs. "Beyza needs you, Dun."

Zauvadok lifted Anaïs' face up to his and kissed her tear away. "I don't need three months, Anaïs. I knew then. I know now. It's you. It's always been you."

"About time," Dunharra sighed as she knelt to inspect Beyza's face. A bruise formed on her cheek, under her eye. Dunharra began her healing magick on Beyza until she stirred. With iridescent eyes, she healed the bruise.

"A concussion, too. Way to go, Zau," Dunharra said with a smile, continuing to heal Beyza. Beyza's eyes fluttered open after a moment, and Dunharra's iridescent eyes shifted back to grass green.

"Good morning. I think you got your answer from Zau. We will not tell you again. Leave. Them. Alone."

The tension of the previous days finally shattered. Beyza's face took on a pinched look, and she stayed in her tent until the morning.

They broke camp and headed for Buckhaven. They traveled most of the day until the sun slipped under the horizon. The Buckhaven city of Iron Gate stood within an hour's ride and seemed like a good place to stop for the night.

In the Weeping Witch in, only three rooms were available, and Dunharra immediately took them. Anaïs and Zauvadok shared a room, and Iseabail, Calyx, Beyza, and Dunharra took another. Duncan and Fergus took the third and slipped down to care for the horses before heading into the tavern to eat.

Downstairs, Dunharra watched as people filled the tavern room. The murmur of dozens of different conversations made the place hum. Scattered through the growing audience were men wearing Buckhaven blue and red military garb. Mostly, the room seemed full of travelers.

A serving woman approached the table. "Whaddaya have, loves?"

"Seems like a busy night," Dunharra observed, raising her voice above the noise.

"Oh, yeah. There's live music tonight. Random's back. You should stick around, uh huh. So whaddaya have?"

"Random?" Duncan asked. "Is that a person?"

"Oh, yeah, hun! She's a regular here. A Selenite bard. She puts on an amazing show. Full house every time she comes. Standing room only. You're lucky to have seats."

The group placed their orders and had their first meal in a while in relative peace, ease, and calm. Beyza kept to herself and spoke only when spoken to, which no one did. As they finished eating, a petite, human-looking woman entered and stood on the small stage at the front of the tavern. She carried only a lute. Random, dressed in wildly colorful, glittering clothing and seemed completely at ease as she surveyed the crowd.

She licked her lips and smiled a devilish smile. Without a word, she strummed the lute, and the crowd immediately hushed. Another strum, and the lights in the room dimmed. Whoops and hollers began in anticipation.

Random held one hand up, and colorful lights burst from her fingers like fireworks. She played the lute and sang as the lights danced around her to the music and as she continued to sing. Some lights exploded into glittery flames, while some flowed around the room like illuminated mist. Mesmerizing and sweet, her angelic voice filled the inn. She sang ballads, bawdy tavern shanties, and almost everything in between.

Iseabail, Calyx, Dunharra, and Anaïs sensed powerful magic, and they looked around the room. They had never seen a tavern singer like Random, and they were not surprised to see a full inn. No one seemed to know anything but Random. Patrons ignored their drinks, and food grew cold on their tables.

Dunharra noticed that Fergus and Duncan were as riveted as the rest of the crowd from the moment they came in from the stables. She poked Duncan and received only a minimal response. He became enthralled.

After each song, came wild cheering and applause. Dunharra could not get Duncan's or Fergus' attention until the very last note of the very last song. When Random finished, they blinked and smiled.

"I never saw anything like that before," Fergus said, eyes wide.

"I can see," Dunharra said, noticing the affected crowd shaking off the illusions, cantrips, and reverie after Random finished. Conversations resumed, and more orders for food and drink kept the serving women busy for the rest of the night.

Chapter Fifteen

CHAPTER FIFTEEN

IAIN

Iain, relieved to see Aoife fully recovered from the Cough, smiled as he watched her run around the castle grounds. The mental link between Iain and Aoife grew to where he could know her location in the castle at any time. Iain never got the chance to talk to Maebh about what burned within him most. Official duties after the attempted coup kept her and Prince Regent Kieron busy; communications were formal and work-related. And so it remained until Iain crossed paths with Maebh in the Tapestry Hall.

"Your Majesty," Iain said as he bowed.

"Iain, hello," Maebh replied.

"Can you spare a moment of your time? After all that's happened, I would like to clarify a few things." Iain's voice trailed off, and he lost his nerve.

"You seem troubled, Iain. What is it?"

"A personal matter, best discussed in private."

Maebh nodded slightly. "Meet me in the rose garden in one hour, Iain. We can speak freely there."

The hour dragged by, and Iain busied himself with checking on the progress of copying the herbalists' tomes for the Lycaena. Soon, Iain headed to the rose garden. On his way, Mhari caught his eye, and he exchanged pleasantries with her. She just left the rose garden.

Mhari did not seem somber, but at the same time, not happy.

"What's wrong, Mhari?"

"Nothing, Iain."

If having sisters taught Iain anything, 'nothing' absolutely meant something, and to be ignored at your own great peril. "Mhari? Nothing?"

"Nothing, Iain. It can only be nothing between us." She left without a word. Iain watched her walk away, his heart beat faster. Now he didn't have the time to pursue her. More important matters required his attention. He vowed to catch up with her later.

In the rose garden, Maebh sat alone. She admired the roses and indulged in their fragrance while she waited. When he arrived, she stood with a smile.

"Your Majesty," he said as he bowed to his queen.

"Iain, what troubles you?"

Iain did not know how to begin. He imagined a hundred different ways he would ask her, but in this moment, he could remember none of them. His forehead glistened with sweat.

"Iain?"

He could bear it no more. "I have had some curious interactions with Aoife."

Iain had Maebh's full attention. "Tell me."

"Are you aware of the mental link that is shared by mages and their familiars?"

Maebh's brow furrowed. "Casually," Maebh answered.

"It allows free communication without the use of audible words. They can literally hear each other talk, with no one else able to hear. A telepathy."

Aoife had told her about this. "Understood. And?"

"It can happen among close family members, like siblings, or parents and children."

"What are you getting at, Iain? Isn't she learning magick?"

"Yes, my lady. But I have heard her speak. In my mind."

All the color left Maebh's face. "Please tell me this is some kind of joke. This can't be happening."

"It is. And it is getting stronger and more frequent as time passes."

Maebh closed her eyes, bowed her head, and sat back down on the bench surrounded by roses.

Iain asked, "Your Majesty, is there something I need to know?"

Iain stood back as Maebh sighed heavily. "I thought we could raise her as our own, and that no one needed to know."

His mind raced back to the time when he threw caution to the wind and followed his heart straight into Maebh's arms. Many days of flirting by day and passion by night lasted for more than a year. The intimacy they shared grew deep and wide, far from the shallows of a passing fling. He told her his hopes and dreams. He never knew happiness like this and feared he never would again.

Then came the arranged marriage to Kieron, and things between him and Maebh turned complicated. There were duties of a wife that needed her attention. They had heated arguments about loyalty. The words they exchanged hurt his heart to this day.

You can't be serious, Iain! I am not some backstreet harlot you can order around. And what choice do you think I have? What options do you see for me? The queen rejecting her husband? Absolutely out of the question, and you know it. I love you. I did not choose this marriage. My father arranged it for the good of Innesfrees, not for me! No one ever gave me a choice. My needs and wants were not then and are not now considered. I have a duty.

It broke Iain's heart when she chose duty over love. Maebh whispered, "Two days later the midwife told me about my pregnancy," Maebh said, wiping a tear from her eye.

"I did the only thing a woman in my position could do. I slept with the Prince Regent. The dates were close enough not to arouse too much suspicion, and I could have the last remaining scrap of happiness from the dreadful situation. I could not bear to take poison to lose our baby, Iain. Aoife is your daughter."

"A priest of Qo cursed Kieron to be infertile," Maebh continued, tucking an errant red ringlet behind her ear. "He would welcome any child born to us, but I couldn't bring myself to tell him the truth." He believes Aoife is his, and that the curse failed."

Iain reached out his hands and clasped hers gently. "I will ask you the question I should have asked you eleven years ago, my sweet Maebh. What do you want to do?"

"Eleven years is a long time, Iain. I am on good terms with Kieron. I do love him. Not like I loved you. Our wild and passionate love will always be the love of my life. Kieron's love is quieter. But it's there. I want things to continue as they are."

Iain paused to let that sink in. "Do we tell Aoife?"

"In time."

"She will figure it out eventually, Maebh. The link will continue to grow stronger, and she will have questions. What shall I say to her?"

"When that time comes, we will tell her. Together."

Chapter Sixteen

CHAPTER SIXTEEN

DUNHARRA

Dunharra and Iseabail dragged Duncan and Fergus to their room, where they spent an uneventful night, until they heard a scuffle in the hallway, outside their doors. It grew more intense. They heard shouting, barked curses and the unmistakable thud of someone falling to the floor.

Dunharra cracked the door to look at the commotion. Three men were fighting against one Wild One. The ringleader snarled, "You can come quietly, or you can come unconscious. The choice is yours."

"Be on your way! I am no one to be trifled with," the Wild One said.

Dunharra watched in horror as one man approached the Wild One and tried to grab her arm. She rewarded him with a humiliating kick to the crotch. He unleashed a howl and fell to the floor in the fetal position while holding his battered manhood. The remaining two rushed the Wild One and knocked her to the ground.

Dunharra flung open the door. “Leave her alone!”

The ringleader eyes shot up. “No witnesses!”

Dunharra slammed the door and locked it. The mercenary pounded on the door and wrestled with the doorknob. When he couldn’t open it, he pounded on the door again, shouting, “Open this damn door, bitch!”

Zauvadok threw his door open and asked angrily, “Who are you calling a bitch?”

The men surveyed all seven feet of Zauvadok. The ringleader stood up and held his hands out. “Hold on here. This is of no concern to you. It’s a private matter that needs to stay private.”

Zauvadok growled. “Too late. Wild One, do you want to go with them?”

“No, sir,” she said, eyes wide.

Zauvadok locked eyes with the mercenaries. “Leave.”

“Now wait a goddamn minute,” the ringleader stammered.

“I said leave!” Zauvadok shouted.

The ringleader drew a small knife from his boot. “This says I don’t.”

Zauvadok rolled his eyes at the tiny knife. He pulled back and hit the ringleader with a massive right hook. He fell to the floor, limp but alive. “Who’s next?”

The remaining two mercenaries scrambled away, dragging their ringleader with them.

Dunharra opened the door again to see Zauvadok standing with the Wild One. Duncan swung his head around his door, and Fergus yawned as he peered into the hall. Zauvadok offered his hand to help her up. “What’s your name?”

The Wild One replied, “Tupuxura Olynatothra. My friends call me Tup.”

Tup dressed in a snug-fitting black leather shirt and pants with black leather boots. She wore a cloak, even in the sweltering weather. She resembled a Wild One but did not dress the part.

"Do you need a safe place to stay for the night?" Dunharra asked.

Tup shook her head. "My room is up the hall. They found on my way there."

Zauvadok asked, "Would you like to join us for breakfast?"

"Sounds good. Thank you," Tup replied as she went down the hall and safely to her room.

The night passed quietly. Duncan and Fergus meandered downstairs for breakfast, followed closely by Dunharra, Zauvadok, Anaïs, Iseabail, Calyx, and Beyza. They found a table large enough for one more and made themselves comfortable.

Tup joined them with a smile. Dunharra noticed her blush, suddenly shy, and slid into a chair. "Hello."

They exchanged morning pleasantries and then ordered breakfast. Duncan asked the question on everyone's minds: "So, Tup. Why were those men after you?"

Tup sighed and closed her eyes. "I have been running from men like them for about a month, after I saw something I shouldn't have."

"What did you see?" Iseabail asked, horrified but too curious to let it go.

"King Darragh of Buckhaven conspiring with a mage to wear the Frozen Crown."

"Wait, what? The Frozen Crown? The one that will freeze you to death? Isn't that a tale told to younglings at campfires or bedtime?" Fergus asked with a chuckle under his words.

"The one and only, and no. It's very real," Tup said. "The mage said he knew of a spell that would keep Darragh from being frozen, but at price."

"What price?" Duncan asked, giving his fellow knight a warning glance.

"The Lycaenan library."

The pregnant pause broke when Beyza interjected, "So, he has it. It still exists."

"It would seem so," Dunharra replied.

Tup continued, "And not only access. Giving him the whole damn thing."

"This changes things," Iseabail said, bewildered. This diplomatic mission took on a more serious tone.

After they finished breakfast, they sat, unmoving.

Dunharra observed everyone getting lost in their own thoughts.

"That bastard almost killed Anaïs. Let's take him down," Zauvadok growled.

A shadow fell over Beyza's face. "Agreed."

"On to Buckhaven," Iseabail and Calyx said at the same time.

"So, are you in, Tup?" Dunharra asked.

"Oh, you bet I'm in."

***

ISEABAIL

Travel to Buckhaven castle proved uneventful on the first day. The group skirted the Bannockburn River and avoided the Great Northern Road. Adding at least a day's travel did not sit well with Beyza, but they deemed this the safer, less public route. Exactly what they needed.

The Disputed Lands lay over the horizon. Zauvadok, Fergus, and Duncan found a suitable place to rest for the night, away from the main road. Duncan and Fergus tended the horses while the others put up their tents. Tup who recently gained a tent of her own, struggled to build hers. When her third try didn't work, Iseabail walked over. "Need a hand?"

"I'd be grateful, thank you," Tup replied, stepping aside for Iseabail.

Iseabail and Tup worked together to put up the tent and it went up quickly. Iseabail smiled, and met Tup's eyes. "Thanks again," Tup managed to say after a moment.

Iseabail's fingers tangled with Tup's as they checked the last tent tie. Tup's hand lingered, her eyes lifting to Iseabail. Heat pricked the back of her neck and she knew her cheeks must be flushed, but Iseabail could not look away. Feeling silly, she shook her head, and stood abruptly, brushing her palms against her thighs as if to clean them. "Well, this looks set. Um..."

"Yes," Tup said, brushing her hands against her shirt. "Thank you, Iseabail."

***

DUNHARRA

Dunharra relished the cooler air. The summer, with its record heat, proved a difficult one. The cold and long sleeves so far protected her deepest secret, keeping her inkless skin from prying eyes. No one could know she had no ink. She considered getting ink to hide the fact that she could use magick, especially the healing, without it. Zauvadok talked her out of it, telling her she should not hide her true identity with a simple lie on her skin. That one day, she would regret getting the ink, one day when she would tell the world. She doubted him as much today as she did then, yet she remained inkless. She still felt the need to keep her skin out of sight.

So, she hid behind those long sleeves.

A sudden, deafening silence broke Dunharra from her reverie. She rushed to open the flap of her tent and saw red eyes piercing the night like hot coals. Dunharra held her breath as she waited to see if something, or someone, approaching would heed the glowing eyes and stay away.

Ear-splitting wails from the wyverns penetrated the night. Zauvadok came out of the tent first, followed closely by Anaïs and the others. Tup poked her head out, taking in the scene. One last, loud cry came from the wyverns, and they vanished.

Ten yards from the perimeter of the camp were three heavily armed men. The men stopped, ready to take up arms against the wyverns, when they faded away.

"Be on your way; we have no quarrel with you," Zauvadok warned.

The oldest-looking and most grizzled man looked Zauvadok up and down, then considered his course of action. After a moment's pondering, he spoke. "We will be the judge of that. We're looking for a Wild One. I think you have her. You can give her up and live another day or die hiding her. Your choice."

Tup tried to make herself as small as possible in her tent.

"Who wants to know?" Beyza asked as she stepped out of her tent.

The lead man stared at her Lycaenan skin and replied, "None of your concern, freak."

"I know who you're looking for," Beyza retorted, earning glares from the rest of the group. Their collective pulses were speeding, and their bodies tensed at the situation. Anaïs' hands balled into fists as her eyes drilled into Beyza.

"I'm listening, freak."

"I saw her. She is alive and well, last seen in the Iron Gate and traveling north."

Zauvadok growled, and everyone else unleashed the collective breath they were holding.

"There. You have your information. Be on your way."

"I'll be the judge of that. I see one more tent that's occupied. You are hiding the Wild One. Give her to us, and there will be no trouble."

Two men jumped down from their horses and drew their swords. They were large, muscular, and heavily armed. They walked toward the camp in a formation, showing their military training.

"You sealed your fate," Zauvadok snarled and charged toward the men, followed closely by Anaïs as the group divided to deal with the other one. Zau drew his sword, and Anaïs readied her staff. Sparks flew as their swords met, and Anaïs took advantage of the opening to bring her staff down on the back of the enemy's knee. Throwing him off balance and sending that knee buckling to the ground gifted Zauvadok the killing blow.

***

ISEABAIL

Iseabail heard them overcome their enemies as the second man leered at her. He spoke with an evil grin. "I haven't had an elf before. Get ready to have the time of your life."

Iseabail had magick ready. Her eyes glowed an icy blue, and her ink pulsed to the beat of her heart. She spoke the final word and sent icy missiles to blast him directly in the chest. He staggered back, momentarily stunned by the blow. This only angered him, and he dashed toward her, sword drawn. Before she could speak the last word of magick, he grabbed her and knocked her to the ground. He pinned her down by her shoulders and laughed.

Iseabail screamed.

"Shut it, bitch," the attacker snarled as he ripped at her clothes, but the Elven silk did not tear easily. This frustrated and angered him further.

Calyx ran to her defense, only to be kicked out of the way.

Desperate, Iseabail cried out as she clawed at his face. It slowed him down. She needed help. As if answering her prayer, Dunharra arrived, forcing her body in between. Iseabail heard the magick Dunharra uttered and her attacker's stunned face. In a blink, lightning arced to the ground, striking her attacker's chest. Dunharra saved her.

The last remaining man turned his horse and set off at a full gallop away.

"What the fuck, Beyza?" Anaïs asked. "Do you really think they would accept that and leave us be?"

"What difference would it make? You were only going to kill them anyway," Beyza retorted. "What does it matter that one of them got away to report back on us and our location."

"We are not mindless killers. If we were, you would have been dead a long time ago, Beyza. Remember, we defended you, too." Anaïs warned. "Don't. Do. It. Again."

***

DARRAGH

Darragh paced in his room. The poison hadn't arrived yet but could be minutes if not hours from his hands. A dark shadow blocked the sun shining in the window. He glanced up and saw a syrinx, a mix of man and bird, perched on the windowsill.

"Darragh of Buckhaven?"

"Who wants to know?"

"I have a delivery for you."

Darragh stopped, and raced toward the window. "I am Darragh."

The syrinx held out a clawed hand and dropped a scarlet silk pouch into Darragh's hand. It spread its wings and Darragh opened the pouch to find a glass jar with a cork stopper holding clear liquid. He held it up to the light, and he could barely see an oily substance swirl inside when he shook it. Satisfied, he smiled an evil grin. "Who do I test this on?"

Strong thunderheads crept up the horizon with noise to match, muting the sun and casting an eerie pall over Buckhaven Castle. Servants rushed to close shutters. The wind picked up, and the smell of rain permeated the air. More thunder rumbled, much closer than before. Rain fell in large droplets that smacked the side of the castle.

Deep inside Buckhaven Castle, they could only hear the faint tapping of rain. Darragh looked over missives by candlelight as the storm blew in overhead. He couldn't quite bring his attention to bear as he watched the rain fall.

"Maebh. If I can't have you, no one can." His eyes became cold and hard. He had a murder to plan.

"Bring me the Queen."

An hour later, Queen Aelwen arrived at Darragh's private quarters.

"You requested my presence, Darragh?" Aelwen's voice became thin and fraught with worry. Her forehead glistened with nervous sweat.

"Not to worry. I wanted to share a drink with you and hear how you are." Darragh had two glass goblets of wine sitting on an elegantly set table in his room. There were two small cakes sitting on plates. He showed Aelwen to her seat and made sure she felt comfortable. Darragh played the role of manners and courtly love. He held her chair out for her. He took his seat at the other end of the intimate mahogany table.

Darragh raised his goblet in a toast, and Aelwen mirrored the same motion as he spoke, "To us, my queen."

They clinked goblets, and Aelwen drank a mouthful of white wine, carefully chosen for its compatibility with the sweet dessert in addition to its strong taste.

She replied, "To us."

Darragh cut into his small cake, and strawberry filling flowed out. He ate the dessert, carefully watching his wife do the same. "Are you well?"

She replied, "This is an unexpected treat, Darragh. I have longed for time with you."

Aelwen suddenly felt the back of her mouth go dry. A sharp pain ratcheted through her abdomen, and no matter how hard she tried not to, she felt like she must vomit. When the sensation unleashed, foamy bile cascaded up her throat. She tried to scream for help as the bile flooded her mouth and nose.

Darragh remained calm and cool. "What is it, my dearest?"

Aelwen clawed at her throat and stumbled to standing. When she could not scream as she gagged on her own blood, she sent all the dishes flying from the table. Stumbling more, she knocked every item off every nearby surface until the guards rushed into the room, and Darragh stood abruptly. "Get the healers! The Queen has fallen ill. Someone from the kitchen may have poisoned her. Hurry!"

Darragh knelt by her side as Aelwen's face contorted with pain and confusion. He smoothed her hair to comfort her. "Shhhh, now. It will all be over soon."

Aelwen's last vision became the crude smile on her husband's mouth as he said, "One queen down, one to go."

Chapter Seventeen

CHAPTER SEVENTEEN

ISEABAIL

Iseabail went to see Tup, who packed her tent, and asked, "How are you?"

Tup smiled. "I am well. What's up with Beyza? What made you travel with a woman like that?

Iseabail sighed. "No one wanted to travel with Beyza, but the Lycaena forced her on us. We had no choice in the matter."

"She's not behaving like your average Lycaena. They are usually aloof but kind. Beyza has some growing up to do." Iseabail placed a reassuring hand on Tup's shoulder. "We will protect you. From her and from whatever comes our way."

Tup and Iseabail looked into each other's eyes. Tup cleared her throat, and Iseabail removed her hand from her shoulder. They smiled awkwardly at each other and finished getting ready for the day.

They set out toward the Disputed Lands, making their way to Buckhaven. It would be at least a day's travel until they got into Buckhaven, and things got more dangerous by the hour. Both Buckhaven and Innesfrees claimed the Disputed Lands. There were soldiers from each kingdom in the area, along with many thieves and mercenaries.

They could keep their distance from all parties until late in the afternoon, when a squad of Buckhaven knights stopped them. A tired captain in their ranks asked, "Who travels to Buckhaven?"

"The Lycaena sent us," Iseabail said. "We seek an audience with King Darragh and Queen Aelwen."

The soldiers observed them with suspicion until one of them whispered with reverence, "Queen Aelwen is dead."

The news flowed like shock waves through the group. Iseabail recovered first.

"We are very sad to hear this news. Please accept our condolences for the loss of your Queen," Iseabail said quietly.

The squad leader nodded and allowed them to pass with a warning.

"The news of our queen makes people view us as weak," he said. "The Disputed Lands are full of mercenaries and thieves. Be careful, as there is no official protection from either Buckhaven or Innesfrees here, either. Be on your way."

With that, the captain and his detail turned their horses and rode toward the border.

"What the hell?" Anaïs said, tightening her grip on the reins.

"A young queen gone in her prime," Zauvadok remarked.

They rode on unmolested for most of the day. The sun lay low on the horizon, and the Triplet Sister Moons were about to rise. The waning daylight peeked through the spattering of trees lining the road, making a pattern of light and shadow on a lone traveler's black cloak as he approached at a slow trot.

"Alms for the poor?" the man asked, extending a rough and calloused hand. A glint of steel peeked out from deep in his sleeve.

Zauvadok growled, yet pulled two silver pieces from his pouch and tossed them to the beggar. "We have little to spare."

The man caught the coins and grinned from underneath the hood, revealing perfect white teeth. "Peace be with you. Beware of those who promise safe passage, for they do not have good intentions."

"Blessed be," Zauvadok replied as he watched the man ride away. "It is getting late. We should rest for the night."

Before long, they found a clearing to the west of the road that seemed suitable. Far enough off the road not to be tempting for those with ill intentions but close enough to it to make a stand or a hasty retreat if necessary. Less than half a day's ride separated them from Buckhaven Castle, and its spires were faint on the horizon.

The tiny group settled into their typical evening routines. Once completed with her tasks, Tup emerged from her tent and saw Iseabail with Calyx sharing Elven bread. She walked over and asked if she could sit with them. Iseabail and Calyx smiled and invited her to sit.

"So," Tup said awkwardly. "What's going on?" The question tumbled out of Tup's mouth before she could stop it. "I mean, you know about me, and I know barely anything about you."

Iseabail went about describing their group, and Calyx chimed in with her own additions over the course of an hour. Eventually, Iseabail said, "Dunharra's different. Not like any other human I've ever met. She is unassuming, and content wherever she is. There is something about her I can't quite put my finger on."

Iseabail felt butterflies in her stomach when Tup asked, "Are the two of you together?"

"What? Dunharra and me? No, she's not my type. She likes men, you know," Iseabail said with a wink.

***

DARRAGH

Darragh sat in his private chambers and reveled in his success. The potent poison made her death a quick one. Aelwen didn't suffer long. With a contented sigh, he leaned back to ponder his next move. Maebh.

Before his eyes appeared a red, swirling, oblong light. Black sinews extended beyond the edges like tentacles. Out of the darkness stepped a man in a red cloak with the hood pulled over his face. He stood before Darragh and revealed a handsome face, shiny brown hair, and captivating blue eyes. Fit, muscular, and conventionally attractive, Hagan raised an eyebrow and regarded Darragh skeptically.

"Do you always need to make such an entrance?"

"Did you need to test the poison on your wife? Tsk. And you think I'm extravagant?"

"Are you spying on me?" Darragh asked, incredulous. "What do you want, Hagan?"

"I want what you want, Darragh," Hagan replied with a mock bow. "You in the Frozen Crown, and a deposit. A down payment of sorts."

"You're getting an entire library when we finish."

"And I don't believe you have the artifacts you claim to possess."

"Buckhaven has hidden the Lycaenans' lost items for centuries. I am not your lapdog, Hagan. You will not order me around."

"Oh, but I think you are, and I believe I have leverage to order you around alongside the power to keep you alive while you wear that crown. You need me more than I need you. Don't forget that."

Darragh rolled his eyes. "What kind of deposit do you want?

"A book, of course," Hagan said, crossing his arms.

Darragh met his eyes. "No shit. Which book?"

"Oh, I thought you'd never ask," Hagan said, tapping his chin.

Darragh sighed heavily. He grew tired of Hagan's games. He said through clenched teeth, "What book?"

"The Rud Eskimiş."

"Now see here—" Darragh stood, hands balled into fists.

"You don't have it, do you?"

"I do," Darragh said defensively.

"Then what's the problem?"

"That is the most important book in the entire library. It's worth more than all the other books combined, and you know it."

"Always the best, you know," Hagan said in a mocking tone and shrugged.

"Fine. When and where?"

"You mean it's not hiding in plain sight on your bookshelf?"

Darragh clenched his teeth again. "When and where?"

"Oh, alright. You have it hidden. I get it. The next new moons. A time for new beginnings, don't you think?"

The new moons symbolized starting new projects, new intentions, and new beginnings. It would be a fitting time. "Where?"

"I'll be back." Hagan spun back to the glowing red and black portal, stepped in, and vanished.

Darragh rubbed his forehead and called for Sylvestre. "I need a courier. One who can keep a secret."

***

DUNHARRA

"We have no trouble with you, let us by!" Duncan shouted.

"We offer you safe passage," the man replied. "For a price."

"We know these lands better than anyone, and we can guarantee your travels to your destination will remain uneventful," the woman traveling the highway with him said.

"We do not need your services, thank you. Move aside and let us pass," Fergus said.

"Or what?" the woman asked.

Duncan drew a deep breath to keep his temper. "This is your last chance. Let us pass."

"No, no, no. This is your last chance," the woman threatened and drew a vicious-looking scimitar. She leapt from her sleek black horse. Duncan and Fergus drew their swords and climbed down from their horses. The woman immediately engaged Fergus with a slash.

Zauvadok and Anaïs dismounted, ready to join the fight. The woman held her blade ready and spoke words of magick that made Fergus drop his sword. He stood there, staring at her.

"Fergus!" Zauvadok cried. "What did you do to him?"

"Tsk. Temper, temper. He's fine. He's admiring my beauty," she mocked him.

"Undo your magick."

"Make me," she dared him. She brought her blade ready and spoke words of magick again. Anaïs had enough. She spoke magick of her own and shielded the others from the woman's charm. The woman said, still mocking Duncan. "Finally, a worthy opponent."

"Playtime is over," Anaïs said, determination in her voice.

"Bitch, please. I control this road. You pass when I say."

Duncan demanded, "What do you want?"

"Gold. All of it."

"Come and take it," Zauvadok challenged them.

The woman whispered more words of magick, and shards of ice flew from her hand. Anaïs easily blocked them, and they fell, impotent, to the ground. "Is that all you got?"

"You don't know your place, Dark Elf. Go crawl into that hole in the Dark Elf Lands. You shouldn't even be out in the daylight, you fat cow."

Anaïs answered with fire, singeing her, leaving her clothes scorched and smoking.

The man slowly pulled a throwing blade from his sleeve. With a flick of his wrist, the blade flew.

"Watch out!" Beyza ran toward Anaïs, pushing her to the ground, only to be struck in the chest with the throwing dagger. Beyza toppled on top of Anaïs, bleeding profusely and struggling for air.

"Beyza!" Anaïs shouted when she realized what had happened.

Dunharra, saw the situation spinning out of control, connected with the Mother and quietly said, "Bees."

A moment passed, and from the trees flew a large cloud of angry bees. They dove for the man and woman blocking the path. They both screamed and began flailing their arms to fight off the attacking bees. The woman jumped into her saddle, and they rode off with the angry, stinging bees in tow.

"Bees?" Tup asked, incredulously. "You can call bees?"

Dunharra sheepishly shrugged.

"Dun, Beyza needs you!" Anaïs shouted and cradled Beyza's head in her lap.

Dunharra ran over to Anaïs and Beyza. The blade buried deep in Beyza's chest up to the hilt. Dunharra tried to pull the blade out, but couildn't. "Zau? Can you pull this out?"

Zauvadok settled to Anaïs' side making sure she made it out of the scuffle unscathed, he quickly and easily pulled the blade from Beyza's chest. Dunharra's eyes shifted from grass green to iridescent as she mended the lung pierced by the blade and closed the wound. She emptied the lung of blood that prevented Beyza from getting the air she needed. Dunharra traced her finger across the scar, and it vanished under her touch.

The group held their breath until the bleeding ceased, and Beyza coughed for air. She looked straight at Dunharra, then to Anaïs.

"Are you alright?" Dunharra asked.

"Thank you, Dunharra," Beyza said, her eyes moist. "Anaïs, Zauvadok. I'm sorry for trying to come between you and making your lives miserable. I hope you can forgive me. But there is something else you need to know. They sent me to break you up. Not Zauvadok and Anaïs, but all of you. To keep you from finding the books before Darragh could use them."

"What? Why?" Zauvadok asked.

"My sister sits in the Buckhaven jail. If I broke you up, she would go free."

"But—the books," Iseabail said.

"Were supposed to be returned to the Lycaena after Darragh's use. But Tup showed me what he planned on using it for. And that he never intended to give it back."

"Who sent you?"

"Buckhaven," Beyza said, eyes cast downward.

"What? How? The Lycaena are so reclusive," Iseabail said.

"His spies are everywhere. Library politics can be deadly."

"That is incredible," Duncan spoke up. "But can we do something about Fergus?"

Fergus remained standing, staring at nothing, with a little drool coming from his mouth.

"Allow me," Tup said as she walked over to Fergus. She whispered words to dispel the magick and her eyes shifted to a deep indigo. Then she gently touched his temples. Fergus jumped back and looked around anxiously.

"They're gone?"

"Gone," Tup assured him.

Chapter Eighteen

CHAPTER EIGHTEEN

IAIN

The black and green ink sank into Aoife's skin, finalizing her first rite of passage into magick. Pride swelled in Iain's chest. He longed to let her know. Hand clenched at his side, he smiled at his student, the not so little girl who suddenly became his daughter. Instead, he cherished these weeks of bonding, teaching her, and being with her in this moment.

Aoife grew with grace and elegance. Since receiving her first ink, she transitioned into a remarkable young lady. She still ran about the castle barefoot, but with more sophisticated poise. She held the promise of womanhood, the changes delicate but apparent.

He walked to the healers' quarters, expecting to find it bustling with activity. To his pleasant surprise, he found only Aoife and Mhari. Aoife recently received more ink, which explained the tingle in his shoulder a short while ago. He had been meaning to catch up with

Mhari. He got a curious feeling in the pit of his stomach when he was around her.

"Where is everyone?" Iain asked.

"The Beit She'an are giving combat training to the knights," Aoife said excitedly. "The other healers are all down there patching the knights up."

Aoife turned to Mhari. "Can I go now? I want to see the knights fight," she pleaded.

Mhari nodded, and Aoife scrambled out to the courtyard. After they were alone a moment, Mhari stood and whispered, "Excuse me."

"Mhari," Iain began and sat a gentle hand on her arm. She looked up at him, eyes filled with woeful sadness, but she did not remove his hand. "You've been avoiding me."

"You have been very busy," Mhari replied as she tried to excuse herself again.

"I'm not busy now," Iain said. "It has come to my attention—" Iain cleared his throat. "I mean, I may have noticed that you keep your distance even when I am not busy."

"I have many things to do. Have a good day, Iain." Mhari sidled past without another word.

He silently cursed himself as he watched her walk away. Then, he felt something he hadn't allowed himself to feel in eleven years. His heart ached.

***

ISEABAIL

Castle Buckhaven loomed large in the sky as they approached the city walls. Midday shadows cast foreboding pools of darkness on the ground. The outer courtyard smelled of chicken droppings and horse dung. The city gate recently lumbered open and people milled around. Iseabail searched for someone official.

"I am Iseabail Allora of the Mountain Elves, ambassador to the Southern Kingdoms of Innesfrees, Buckhaven, Stirling, and Cobh. I request an audience with the King."

"You will go to the ambassador of Buckhaven. You need to request your audience with King Darragh through him," the low-level official said offhandedly. He glanced at a small man who appeared at the snap of fingers. "Take them to Sylvestre."

Knights escorted them through the castle, not as emissaries, but like suspects. One guard escorted Anaïs, another Zauvadok, and a third led the rest of them to the reception room where they waited. Iseabail watched as Zauvadok went from chair to chair, trying to fit. At last, he managed to wiggle into one. She wondered if he might permanently wedge himself there. The two knights who watched them remained. Iseabail bristled at their handling of her friends and asked, "Would you kind knights mind leaving?"

"We will remain at the door to give you privacy when you speak with Ambassador Sylvestre."

Iseabail sighed, disgusted. Roughly an hour passed before the door opened and a man appeared. Dressed in the usual elaborate style of Buckhaven, he took a seat at the head of the table. "So, you are the Ambassador from the Mountain Elves. I am Sylvestre, Ambassador of Buckhaven to all. Who are your companions?"

Everyone introduced themselves and exchanged pleasantries. Sylvestre did not hide his contempt for Anaïs and Zauvadok, and it caused tension in the room. Iseabail picked up on Sylvestre's attitude and stated, "Where I go, they go."

Sylvestre became indignant. “I will not expose the king to those creatures.”

“They’re not contagious, and they’re not creatures, Sylvestre. They are living beings with thoughts and feelings.”

“Well, they can have those thoughts and feelings elsewhere. Not in front of the king. You want the audience, and those are my rules. Take it or leave it.”

Iseabail sighed. Before she could say anything, Zauvadok spoke. “Anaïs and I will remain here.”

“And so will I,” everyone else chorused.

Anaïs and Zauvadok could not help but smile. Anaïs whispered, “I don’t know what to say. Thank you.”

“Fine. Have it your way,” Sylvestre said, rolling his eyes dramatically. “I will take you to the king.”

Sylvestre stood and gestured for Iseabail and Calyx to follow. Decorations in the Buckhaven style adorned the long and narrow throne room. Sylvestre pounded the floor three times with his staff to announce their arrival.

“Presenting Iseabail Allora of the Mountain Elves,” Sylvestre shouted pompously. His words echoed off the walls.

King Darragh waved Iseabail onward. Conflict clashed within her. This man weaponized the Cough and tried to kill the royal family of Innesfrees and her. And now she stood before him to ask about the Lycaenan library.

Iseabail curtseyed as manners dictated and approached the throne. “Your Majesty, the Lycaena sent me to inquire after the whereabouts of books and scrolls missing from their library.”

Darragh looked her up and down, swallowed hard and pinched his lips shut. He spat, “You! I should have you drawn and quartered!”

Iseabail fought to keep her composure. She gritted her teeth and clenched her jaw but kept a smile as she remembered the Cough, the coup, and the relentless attacks from mercenaries and orcs. She would never forget the orcs. "I wonder how you escaped being hanged."

Darragh snorted. "You think I'm opening my library for a tiny Mountain Elf? You better think again."

"I am sent directly from the Lycaena. We know from the Abakan Chernushka that Buckhaven instigated the raid on the library four hundred years ago. It's time to make amends," Iseabail said, keeping a cool head.

"There are no amends to be made, ambassador. I deny all involvement in the Lycaenan raid. Find someone else to apologize. Buckhaven will have none of it," Darragh sneered.

"Is that your final answer?" Iseabail inquired.

"Final. Sylvestre, we're finished here.

Sylvestre escorted Iseabail back to the reception room.

"What did he say?" Beyza asked, barely able to contain herself.

"He denied knowing anything about the library, of course," Iseabail said.

Beyza groaned and rolled her eyes but held her tongue.

"So, what now?" Tup asked.

"How about we ask for a tour?" Dunharra asked.

All eyes fell on her, and she shrugged at the sudden attention. "What?"

Iseabail called the ambassador. "Sylvestre!"

Sylvestre rolled his eyes as he addressed the visiting delegation. He asked, "A tour? Very well. Remain here, and your tour guide will be with you shortly."

Sylvestre walked away to summon a short woman dressed in Buckhaven regalia. She flashed a devilish smile with her hips swaying.

"It is my pleasure to meet you," the guide said. "I am happy to bring you around the honorable Buckhaven Castle. Follow me."

The guide made sure they saw all parts of the castle. An hour into her droning on, Beyza redirected focus by asking, "We are particularly interested in the library. Can we see it?"

The tour guide paused, and she stared at Beyza as if she asked for the world on a platter. After a pregnant pause, she reluctantly agreed, "Certainly. Follow me."

The heavy oak door, bound with iron, swung open smoothly, revealing a comfortably ornate room with soft chairs and long tables for extended reading. They filed in and saw stacks and stacks of books. The aroma of ink and paper permeated the room. Beyza inhaled deeply, taking in the ambiance.

Iseabail pulled Beyza aside and asked, "How long do you need?"

"Give me an hour," Beyza said. "If anything is here, I'll find it."

The tour guide smiled a fake smile, as this tour went sideways. She excused herself, no doubt going to find Sylvestre and inform him of the situation.

"You have however long it takes for her to get back. Go!" Iseabail urged.

Three short minutes elapsed before Sylvestre arrived, stomping and with a head full of steam.

"Iseabail Allora, this is an outrage!" Sylvestre shouted and ushered everyone out of the library and back into the formal waiting area. Once in there, Sylvestre loosed his ire further, "You have no right to be skulking about the library without our express permission."

"What are you hiding?" Iseabail asked.

"How dare you suggest we are hiding Lycaenan property!" Sylvestre roared.

"I didn't mention Lycaenan property," Iseabail retorted. "An inconvenient slip, don't you think?"

"Well, I never—" Sylvestre protested, but stopped when he realized Iseabail made a fool of him. He blinked for a moment, smiled evilly, and then said calmly, "I will take you to the parlor, where you will find refreshments before your departure."

The tour guide returned and escorted them to an appropriately sized parlor, large enough for all of them to be comfortable. They found an amenable amount of comfortable chairs, and even an extended love seat ample enough for Zauvadok and Anaïs to sit together. Everyone made themselves comfortable and settled in for another wait.

After about half an hour, they received trays of wine, several types of cheese, bread, and a vinaigrette for dipping. The elegantly arranged food on pure silver platters made their mouths water. It had been a while since any of them had eaten. The cheese filled the room with a savory aroma, and a slight hint of bitter almonds.

Calyx, having a lower line of sight, saw a folded piece of paper under the plate of bread. "Iseabail. There's a note under the platter. Look at this."

Calyx reached up and pulled it out from underneath the platter. Iseabail scanned the note, and her eyes grew wide as saucers. She read aloud, "The Lycaenan Library is in the ruins of Therson's Light. You won't live to see it."

Tup motioned for the group to wait, but not before Zauvadok took a handful of food and eaten three pieces of cheese.

"It tastes fine, Tup," Zauvadok said. "Have some."

Tup shook her head. She didn't know Zauvadok well enough to take food out of his hand. "Don't you smell the bitter almonds?"

"No," Iseabail answered.

Tup frowned and inspected the food closer. She smelled the cheese but did not touch it. Her nose wrinkled as she sniffed the cheese. The odor of bitter almonds wafted profoundly to her nose. Next, smelled the wine. "Stop, please! I think someone tampered with the food."

Zauvadok swallowed hard and smacked his lips. He noticed a subtle taste of almonds. He looked to Dunharra, "Goddammit!"

Tup held her hands over the trays and drinks as the ink on the back of her hands glowed an intense, deep indigo. Her eyes followed suit.

"There is poison in the food. A lot of it," Tup said.

The magic faded, and Tup cast a worried look at Zauvadok. "Cyanide."

At that moment, Zauvadok's mouth frothed, and he wheezed. The poison took effect. Iseabail screamed and backed away from the poisoned food.

Dunharra raced to Zauvadok and placed her hand on his chest. Cyanide worked by interfering with how the body used oxygen, and she wasted no time. She concentrated and took a large breath in through her nose and out of her mouth. In an instant, she could feel the poison working through him as her eyes glowed iridescent.

A tear fell from Anaïs' eye. "Hold on Zau, focus on breathing."

Zauvadok felt the air hunger ebb. In moments, he could breathe normally again. Dunharra's eyes slowly returned to her usual grass green and compassionate color. "That is some potent poison," she said.

Anaïs grabbed Zauvadok and hugged him tightly.

Iseabail asked, fascinated but puzzled, "How did you know they poisoned the food, Tup?"

Tup shrugged. "I smelled bitter almonds. Whenever there is the smell of almonds without seeing them in the food or knowing them to be in the dish, you should worry."

"But how did you know about what the smell of almonds meant?" Iseabail pressed.

Tup blushed at the attention from Iseabail. "Well, I, um...I'm an assassin, or used to be. A lifetime ago."

The room fell silent with Tup's revelation. Dunharra asked, "That's it?"

Tup nodded, and Zau asked, "Were you sent to kill any of us?"

Tup shook her head. "No. I left that life."

Anaïs said, "We all have past lives that we've left behind."

Tup visibly relaxed at the acceptance. "Thank you."

"You're welcome. With that sorted, we have a bigger issue," Iseabail said.

"Sylvestre thinks we're poisoned," Dunharra said. "We have to sneak out of here undiscovered, or we really will be dead."

Calyx cracked the door and looked in the hallway. Empty.

They left the deadly parlor quietly and retraced their steps to find the quickest way out of the castle and into the stable to collect their horses. After finding a few dead ends and corridors with footsteps and voices, they tried a worn wooden door. They found it locked. Behind it they smelled horse dung and freedom.

"Should I break it?" Zauvadok asked.

"Too noisy," Dunharra said. "Does anyone know how to pick a lock?"

All eyes fell on Tup. Again. She shrank back but nodded.

Iseabail pulled her up to the door. "Time is of the essence. If we're discovered, we're dead."

"But no pressure, though," Tup retorted. Her hands found a pick in one of her many pockets and went to work. She knelt in front of the door.

"How many pockets do you have?" Beyza asked, incredulous.

"A lot," Tup said, not looking up.

After what seemed like forever, the lock clicked, and she opened the door to poke her head inside. With a wave of her hand, they spilled out into the stable. Stable boys rushed up to them.

"Horses, sir?" one of them asked Zauvadok.

He nodded, and the stable boys brought the horses without question or suspicion.

"Where's the cart?" he asked.

"What cart?" the stable boy replied, confused.

They heard footsteps behind them. Shouts of 'Stop!' and 'Where are they?' echoed through the hallway they had left. They saddled up quickly and rode out of Castle Buckhaven. As they rode into the countryside's safety, a man rode by them at breakneck speed, barely sparing his horse. Tup noted he vanished quickly in the opposite direction.

Chapter Nineteen

CHAPTER NINETEEN

DARRAGH

Darragh watched out his window for any hint of his courier. Frustrated with the lack of time, he turned toward his desk to busy himself with other matters. In a fit of pique, he threw his arm across the desk, sending papers flying about the room. He walked back to his window, watching for his courier.

Darragh roared with rage as he watched Dunharra and the others escape Buckhaven. He snarled and called for Sylvestre, fuming and swearing. "They were supposed to be dead! How many lives do they have?"

Then, out of the corner of his eye, he saw something. His unbridled rage nearly blinded him to the courier's return. This tempered his mood, but not by much. Sylvestre entered Darragh's private chamber, familiar with the results of his anger.

"Sylvestre, they are very much alive, aren't they?" Darragh shouted.

"I put in enough poison to kill three times as many," Sylvestre cowed.

"Apparently not."

"They must have a healer."

"Find them, and make sure they are dead this time. They cannot make it to Therson's Light."

Sylvestre nodded in acquiescence. He backed away to leave when he said, "The courier has arrived."

"Make sure you bring him only to me. At least carry out one part of my orders correctly for once."

Darragh did not have to wait long. The courier sneered with great satisfaction and walked into Darragh's chambers.

Without hesitation, he said, "I am King Darragh. Who are you?"

"No one of consequence," the courier said. "Merely your courier."

Darragh could not tell from the tone of his voice whether this man meant trouble.

"I have The Rud Eskimiş," the courier said. "You know my price."

"Indeed, I do."

Darragh walked to a table with two goblets and what appeared to be pure Keaauan rum. The liquor's aroma filled the air. Darragh poured the drinks and handed one goblet to Vaclav. They savored the rum in silence for a moment before Darragh said, "Let's see it. There better not be a sapphire out of place."

The courier removed the priceless, jewel-encrusted book and handed it to Darragh. His eyes glittered at the sight as he caressed the book and grinned.

"You may leave."

"Your Majesty forgets the price," the courier said, deadly serious.

"Oh, I haven't forgotten. I'm not paying you," Darragh said.

The courier frowned. Then, he coughed, and his mouth foamed. He fell to his knees and managed to squeak out, “You bastard.”

“And that’s why I’m still alive,” Darragh sneered.

The courier succumbed to the poison and fell lifeless onto the floor.

***

IAIN

Iain and Aoife’s bond grew daily. It would not be long before he could see through her eyes. Her focus on learning new magic occupied her for most of each day.

“Iain?” Aoife asked through their link.

“Yes, Aoife?”

“Why is it we can talk this way? Everyone else uses their voice around you. Not me, though. I can talk to you in my mind.”

Iain dreaded this moment. She deserved to know; would there ever be a better time? A thin sheen of sweat formed on his forehead, and he said, “Let’s go see your mother. I think it is time the three of us had a conversation.”

Every step seemed like an eternity. The Beit She’an guards stood outside of the Queen’s private quarters, and Iain allowed a sigh of relief. He didn’t have to wander through the castle looking for Maebh.

“I am here to see my mother,” Aoife stated, with all the seriousness her eleven-year-old self could muster.

The Beit She’an soldiers allowed them through to find Maebh studying reports of spouse-on-spouse violence. Learning that someone who promised to love, cherish, and protect would commit such evil acts horrified her. Her weary countenance lit up when she saw her daughter. Maebh cried and held her arms out for a hug. "Aoife!"

Aoife hugged her tightly, then Maebh smoothed her daughter's wildly curly red hair and said, "This is a surprise! To what do I owe the honor of a visit from you and Master Iain? Do you have new ink?"

"I have a question that he wants me to ask you. Why can I talk to Master Iain without using my voice?"

Maebh froze. Her heart dropped, and fear tingled in the pit of her stomach. She looked at Iain, searching for any help he could provide. Words failed her.

"Let's sit, Aoife," Maebh said.

Maebh excused her ladies-in-waiting, and they all walked to the antechamber where she handled less formal matters.

"Eleven years ago, I married your father..." Maebh paused as she took a long, slow breath. "However, before the wedding, I loved another man. Right before the wedding, the midwife told me about the pregnancy."

Aoife's eyes grew wide, and her mouth fell open.

Iain knelt beside Aoife and looked her in the eye. His voice quivered as he admitted, "Aoife, I am that other man. I am your father."

"Excuse me, what?" a voice came from behind them.

Their eyes shot up to see Kieron standing in the doorway.

"Kieron," Iain began. "How much did you hear?"

"Enough," Kieron said, glaring.

"Aoife, go wait in Iain's office," Maebh said. "It's time for your lessons."

"It's not–" Aoife began but stopped short when she saw the look on her mother's face. "Yes, mum."

"Now, Kieron," Iain began. His mouth went dry and his forehead glistened with sweat. He didn't know what to say or where to begin.

"Are you still–" Kieron asked.

"No!" Iain and Maebh answered in unison.

"So the curse is true," Kieron said quietly.

"I have been faithful to you since my father matched us," Maebh said, trying to salvage the situation.

"Have you though? Really?" Kieron asked.

"It's true," Iain said, instinctively stepping between Maebh and Kieron. "She ended our relationship the day her father matched you."

"Hmmm," Kieron said as he turned and walked away.

Chapter Twenty

CHAPTER TWENTY

DARRAGH

Darragh's fingers trailed over the silver lock of the Rud Eskimis. Magnificent. Palm splayed he traced the iskender and the inlaid diamonds and sapphires that adorned the cover. A true work of art. He ached with desire to open it. Unable to resist, he turned the key in the lock—his stomach turning with excitement ...and fear.

Darragh's fingers caressed the cover and danced over the locking mechanism, flirting with the idea of opening it. As he turned the lock, a gnawing feeling in the pit of his stomach interrupted him.

Directly in front of him appeared a small black oval that grew exponentially. Red tendrils emerged, flailing like an angry octopus. Smoke erupted from the black oval and Hagan stepped from the dark.

Darragh grumbled, "You could knock, you know."

"But what fun would that be?" Hagan replied. "What is that?"

"The Rud Eskimiş," Darragh said through clenched teeth.

"I hate to tell you—no, wait—I love to tell you that you have the wrong book," Hagan teased.

"The wrong book?" Darragh said.

"I guess you don't know anyone who knows what it looks like," Hagan mocked Darragh.

Darragh shouted obscenities and dropped the book on his desk.

"My dear boy, 'Rud' means red," Hagan mocked him again. "You'd think a king would know that. Didn't your father teach you anything?"

Darragh could no longer hold his temper. He threw the book at Hagan, who waved his hand as it fell harmlessly to the floor.

"Tsk tsk," Hagan said. "Such a temper won't get you anywhere with me. Send someone who knows what they're looking for, and then I'll be back."

Hagan stepped back into the portal and vanished.

***

DUNHARRA

They stopped before reaching the Royal Western Road to rest the horses and regroup. There were occasional groups of travelers crossing their paths. They stopped at an inn called One Eyed Willy's. They hitched their horses to the post and walked inside. Small tables scattered the room, but they found one long table in the back that could seat them all. Soon, a woman took their food and drink orders before disappearing into the kitchen.

"Alright," Beyza said. "The library still exists."

Iseabail watched as Beyza's face became alight with unbridled joy.

"Yeah, but they hid it in the ruins of Therson's Light," Iseabail said.

"It's haunted," Dunharra finished her thought.

"We need to go," Beyza replied, undeterred, as she took a full swig from her wine and signaled the serving woman for a second.

"How are we going to reclaim the books and other artifacts to take them back to the Lycaena?" Iseabail asked. "We left the cart in Buckhaven."

"One book," Dunharra compromised, holding up one finger to Beyza for emphasis. "One book, any book, that you can bring back home should be enough for your people to come here."

Their food arrived as the sun slid toward the horizon, and the Triplet Sister Moons were on the rise. They asked for rooms for the night, but there were only two. Zau, Anaïs, Dunharra, and Fergus shared one, so Iseabail, Calyx, Beyza, Tup, and Duncan could share the other.

***

ISEABAIL

Iseabail's bladder woke her in the middle of the night. She attempted to tiptoe to take care of her needs. Iseabail had her eye on the door when she tripped over Tup's bedroll with an enormous thump as she hit the floor. She fell and slid into the wall with a thump. Tup and the others sat up with a start.

"Sorry," Iseabail whispered, sheepish.

She took a step toward Iseabail and knelt down to her.

The new moons lent barely any light, but Iseabail could see Tup's eyes glitter. Iseabail settled into butterflies again. She reached out to touch Tup's shoulder but misjudged in the low light. Her hand brushed Tup's cheek. Iseabail drew in a sharp breath and froze. Seconds felt like hours, and they sat there, unmoving. Tup reached up and held Iseabail's hand. Iseabail's butterflies returned to her stomach and her breath caught in her throat.

Iseabail didn't think; she acted. She leaned in and brushed her lips against Tup's . It made her heart flutter. She cupped Tup's face and gently brushed her lips with hers. The gentle touch of their lips together made Tup give a slight gasp of joy, her whole body electric with the moment and she squeezed Iseabail's hand. The slight pressure gave way to a more wanting kiss, which Tup readily returned. When she broke the kiss, Iseabail sat back and rested in the moment.

"It's about time you two kissed," Calyx said as she propped up her head with her hand.

The sound of Calyx's voice startled both Tup and Iseabail. They turned around to look at her.

Calyx waved. "Weren't you on your way somewhere? The necessary?" Calyx reminded Tup.

"Oh! Yeah, the necessary," Tup said as she stood and left the room to find it.

"You two are cute," Calyx said with a chuckle.

***

IAIN

Iain finished the lesson with Aoife, and the sun slipped below the western horizon. Aoife's success with her new studies distracted her. Two sets of ink, two separate magicks to protect herself, if needed. He liked how Aoife progressed.

Iain roamed around the castle, not paying attention to where his feet led him. He thought about Maebh, Aoife, and Kieron's reaction when he learned he about Aoife's true parentage. He seemed to have taken it well. No yelling or carrying on. He simply turned and left.

Iain wondered how this would change his life. What role would he take with Aoife? What would Kieron do? Would he disavow Aoife and make her illegitimate? That would throw the line of succession into chaos.

So many questions. He looked up and saw Mhari too late. He collided with her, sending her falling to the ground.

"Iain!" Mhari shouted. "What are you doing? You need to watch where you're going!"

"I'm sorry, Mhari." He offered a hand to help her up, which she accepted. Her hand in his electrified him. He helped her up and brought her face to face with him. His eyes locked with hers. His mouth ran dry, and he fought for the right words to say.

"Mhari..."

"Iain," she replied. To him, her voice reminded him of the wind rustling in the trees.

"I missed you," were the only words he could string together.

"Missed me?" Mhari asked, doubting she could trust her ears. "Me? Ha! That's a lie."

Iain leaned down and kissed her with a pent-up passion even he didn't know he had.

Iain could tell that the kiss shocked Mhari. At first, she could only breathe. Then, she threw her arms around Iain and returned his kiss, meeting his passion with her own.

"Was that a lie?" Iain asked.

Mhari smiled and Iain kissed her again.

Iain looked deep into Mhari's eyes. "I didn't know. All this time?"

"Yeah, well, you're stupid. I always knew you were stupid. Since before Dhangadi."

Iain's mind raced back to that desperate time. He recalled how she tried to make small talk, but he ignored her, his mind full of a cure for Aoife. He flushed, crimson climbing up his neck to his face. How could he have missed that? What other signs did he miss?

Not willing to miss anymore with Mhari, he bent down and kissed her again.

***

DUNHARRA

Morning broke through the window and lit the room with beams of sunlight. They all met downstairs for breakfast, joining each other one by one at the largest table in One Eyed Willy's. Tup and Iseabail were the last to arrive, and they walked to the table holding each other's hands.

Side eyes gave way to giggles and approving hugs. They ordered breakfast, and the conversation turned to the library.

"Let's go, get one book, and bring that back to the Lycaena," Dunharra suggested.

"Agreed," Beyza said.

Everyone turned to look at her.

"What?" Beyza said, indignant. She sat straight in her chair.

"What do you mean, 'what'?" Zauvadok asked. "No arguing? No demands?"

"No stirring the pot?" Anaïs asked.

"Did you want me to–" Beyza began.

"No!" they said unanimously.

"Who are you, and what have you done with Beyza?" Iseabail asked.

Therson's light would take a day's ride from One Eyed Willy's directly to the west, and they could follow the Royal Western Road all the way there. They reached Therson's Light as twilight descended. In its day, it had been a beautiful and regal lighthouse. Tall, with a large light and red and white spirals. It watched over the Wicked Shoals, guiding ships as they negotiated the strait.

Now, it lay in ruins. The paint, once bright, became weathered, pale, and chipped over time. Overgrown grass surrounded the ruins, and the light turned off long ago. The appearance suggested years of abandonment and neglect.

The closer they came to the lighthouse, the more they thought that the note in the parlor only meant to send the off on a wild goose chase. Their hearts sank as they rode up in time to see the old, weathered door sag under the hinges and knock it out of alignment with the doorframe.

Beyza looked defeated. "The library must be here. Somewhere."

"Well," Iseabail started. "Let's go inside and see. Maybe it's in this abandoned lighthouse. Stranger things have happened."

Duncan and Fergus dismounted and approached the door. Its paint flaked off in several places, and the doorknob dull doorknob suffered from disuse. Duncan put his hand on it and turned. The door fell off its hinges and onto the ground when he put some muscle into it.

"Well, it looks like no one's home," Dunharra said as she dismounted her horse and peeked inside. "Hello?"

Silence encouraged them to join her. Fergus hitched the horses about ten yards away and stayed with them.

Dunharra went inside first, and her eyes adjusted to the profound darkness. The new Triplet Sister Moons rose in the sky, they provided only a little light; enough to show spider webs with enormous spiders.

She ducked to avoid a low-hanging web as the rest of them filed in; she did not like the thought of a spider in her hair. Zauvadok lit a torch, and it bathed the lighthouse in flickering light. A rickety metal spiral staircase led up to the light, and a stone spiral staircase went underground.

"We know what's up there," Dunharra said. "Shall we go downstairs?"

They heard shuffling. It had an ethereal quality that suggested a ghost-like creature, but from this high up, no one could tell.

"Do you believe in ghosts?" Beyza asked as she peered into the darkness. "Seems like we have one."

Lycaenan culture had many myths and legends about ghostly creatures who haunted abandoned structures like this one. Some were harmless, and some were rather malevolent.

Zauvadok led them down the stone stairs, since he had the torch. Anaïs followed behind him, and the rest of them fell in line.

The stairs were sturdy but narrow. The dirt walls rubbed Zauvadok's shoulders, so tiny rocks fell onto the stairs, making each step treacherous. More than once, someone lost their footing and grabbed onto the person in front of them to steady themselves, threatening to send all of them tumbling to the bottom.

The stairs led them deep underground, at least fifty stairs before they reached the landing. Once there, Zauvadok held up his torch, and the room glittered with books covered with gold, silver, and iskender. There were eight large bookshelves, each with four rows of books.

Beyza stared, mouth wide open. "It's here! The library!"

The books were valuable for the housings they were in, but priceless for the words inside. Lost history, tales of heroes, lore of gods and goddesses, and tomes of magick. All in one place.

Tup wrinkled her nose. "Do you all smell that?"

Duncan and Zauvadok walked toward the back of the room, following a growing stench. They didn't have to go far to find the source. Between the bookshelves lay a middle-aged woman, recently deceased. She did not look like a victim of foul play. They guessed she died of natural causes.

However, they heard footsteps walking down the stairs.

Anaïs and Iseabail went to see. They found no one. The stairs were empty. But the footfalls continued. They both readied magick. The footsteps stopped, and silence filled the room. Before their eyes materialized a female mage, who stood at the bottom of the stairs and stared at them.

"Hello?" Dunharra asked hesitantly.

"Who are you?" the spirit asked. "How did you find this place?" It's beautiful face with fierce looking eyes looked at each of them, daring them to speak.

Beyza stared at the spirit. She recognized it as a maajida, a Lycaenan guardian spirit that could be called to protect places or things. "I am here to return the library to its rightful owners," she said.

"And who is that?"

"The Lycaena."

"You may pass," the spirit said and vanished before them.

Zauvadok walked back to them in time to see her vanish. "We found her body."

"Beyza," Dunharra began. "Which book are you bringing back?"

Beyza seemed overwhelmed at her choices, as if she never thought she would have this chance. Dunharra watched her walk up to the back corner of the room and reach high for a thick book. The book housed iskender with rubies and garnets embedded into it. Carnelian edges adorned its corners. She easily flipped the lock open and read the title inside.

The Rud Eskimiş.

"This one," Beyza said. "It's the most powerful book of magick the Lycaena possessed."

They carefully climbed the narrow stone stairwell and came to the broken door. Stepping outside they saw night fell, and the Triplet Sister Moons were dark, still in their new phase.

Fergus ran up to them as they emerged from the lighthouse. "Did you find it? Is it there?"

"It's there. All of it. That's what matters," Dunharra said.

***

DARRAGH

Darragh sat at his desk, his head in his hands. What could he do now? Who would know what to look for? Then, he had a devious thought. Who actively sought it? Who probably had it by now?

Iseabail and her group of traveling trouble would not escape him this time. Darragh called ten of his best knights and set out on horseback with them to find them. They rode from the castle, carefully eyeing everyone on the Royal Western Road without a sign of the Mountain Elf or her companions. They pushed through the oncoming twilight toward Therson's Light.

"Spread out," Darragh ordered. "They have to be here somewhere."

A specter of a woman appeared in front of the lighthouse door. "Who disturbs me?"

The maajida, blocking the way of anyone trying to enter. The frightened horses reared up as the knights struggled to regain control.

"King Darragh," he said, stiffening and sitting at his full height.

"What do you want here?"

"I want The Rud Eskimiş," Darragh said.

The maajida screeched and wailed. "You are not worthy!"

She transformed from a beautiful maiden mage to an ugly, frightening demon. Her face shifted to a decomposing skull with thin, insect-filled hair. Inside the empty eye sockets emanated sickening green light. Her robe, once intact and stunning, became tattered and torn. The horses, no longer willing to submit to their riders, reared up again. Some threw their riders and galloped back to Buckhaven without them. When the thrown knights saw the maajida, they scrambled, turned, and ran.

Darragh's horse reared up, and he could not stay mounted. The horse followed all the knights back to Buckhaven, despite Darragh's attempts to control it.

The demon maajida followed them for about three hundred yards, ensuring the horses stayed their course and did not return. The few travelers still on the road ran out of their way to keep from being trampled by the wild horses. When they saw what made the horses race, they screamed and searched for something, anything, to hide behind. The maajida paid the travelers no mind and focused on Darragh and his knights until they were far out of sight.

***

The screeching caught Dunharra's attention and woke everyone else. They scrambled out of their tents, expecting trouble, and instead found a demon chasing Darragh and his knights away. Awestruck, they could do little more than watch as the horses reared and fought their riders.

"There's something you don't see every day," Tup said.

When they knew Darragh fled, they slept easily.

Morning broke over a partly cloudy sky, casting brilliant colors over the clouds. Fiery reds, oranges, and golds crept softly over the horizon and announced a new day. They emerged from their tents, still amazed by last night's spectral appearance.

"If he's giving the whole library to that mage Tup saw, then what does Darragh want with The Rud Eskimiş?" Iseabail asked.

"What's in it?" Tup asked.

"It's an ancient book," Beyza began. "It contains the ancient spells that the Lycaena used to shield the mountains from curious colonizers. We called the maajida to frighten away anyone who thought of going to the Silver Haven Mountains—or the Dağ Harika, as the Lycaena call them."

"That's a big book for one spell," Zauvadok said.

"It's more than that," Beyza continued. "It contains specific instructions on calling and controlling demons, spells of both protection and mass destruction."

"So, if you want something or someone protected?" Dunharra asked.

"The Rud Eskimiş is the ultimate book to do so," Beyza finished.

"We need to get this back to the Lycaena where it belongs," Dunharra said.

Chapter Twenty-One

CHAPTER TWENTY ONE

DARRAGH

Darragh seethed. How did the library come to be guarded by a demon? Did the last human guardian pass? That had to be it.

Through his window, he noted the moons beginning to rise over the horizon. Before he could ruminate any longer on the Triplet Sister Moons and Samhain arriving, a spot of darkness appeared in front of him. It enlarged to a man-sized oval, red tendrils writhed with a hiss, and Hagan stepped out of the portal.

"Darragh."

"Hagan," he replied. He had no time for this.

"Oh, you poor boy. You don't have it, do you? Pity. Tsk tsk tsk," Hagan utterly enjoyed teasing him.

Darragh slammed his fist onto his desk, and his face grew red. “There is a demon guarding the library. How am I to get past that?”

Hagan rolled his eyes. “Kings. They want everyone to do their work for them.”

“How can I get past it?” Darragh asked again, grinding his teeth.

“You can’t,” Hagan said with a shrug. “It’s a maajida. You need a Lycaena. Too bad you tried to poison the only one around. Not playing nice yesterday? I don’t think she’ll want to perform on your behalf so readily.”

Darragh boiled inside. His forehead glistened with sweat, and his eyes narrowed as he looked at Hagan. “You aren’t suggesting what I think you are?”

“Any Lycaena will do.” Hagan left the rest hanging, letting Darragh come to his own conclusions. Hagan stepped back into the portal, but before it closed around him, he turned and said, “Tick tock, tick tock, Darragh. Don’t keep me waiting.”

The veins in Darragh’s temples were near bursting. His heart pounded against his chest, and his breath came in ragged snarls. There had to be a way to get that book.

Darragh spent the next hour ruminating on how to get the book. He went through several scenarios and came up with nothing.

When Sylvestre announced a man before the throne, the man startled him out of his reverie.

“You sent for me, Your Majesty,” the blond man asked, kneeling before Darragh.

“Yes. I’m looking for a book,” Darragh began. “It’s a good-sized book with rubies and garnets. All encrusted with iskender. Red carnelian marks the corners.

“What kind of book is it?” the blond man asked. “What’s in it?”

“You don’t need to know that.”

"I need to know if it's cursed or not. Cursed items are double."

Darragh rolled his eyes. He had no time for such details. "No, it's not cursed. Someone took it from Therson's Light, possibly to the Lycaenan Kingdom. The only clue I can give you is that it went by the Great Northern Road."

The blond man nodded. "Who may have the book now?"

Darragh couldn't help but seethe. "A Lycaena. They're easy to spot. She has with her a Mountain elf and a brownie, a gigantic half-orc, a Dark Elf, a Wild One, and a human.

"They must draw a crowd."

"Indeed," Darragh answered. "Half now, half when you give me the book," he said as he tossed a pouch of coins at the blond man, who caught it without looking up. "I want this book, even if you have to kill to get it."

"It will be as you wish it."

***

DUNHARRA

As the sun rose high overhead, the road became thick with travelers. Beyza carried the Rud Eskimiş in a leather bag which she held in her arms. Dunharra noticed that Beyza did not pay attention to her surroundings. She daydreamed about something. Probably the recognition she would get when she returned to Dhangadi, Dunharra thought.

"Beyza," Dunharra warned. "Pay attention. There are thieves and pickpockets everywhere here."

Beyza nodded, absentmindedly.

Then, a tall boy hit her like a ton of bricks, grabbed the bag with the Rud Eskimiş. She could see only his feet as he vanished into the growing crowd.

"The book!" Beyza shrieked. "Thief! That boy has the book!"

She got off her horse and chased him.

Dunharra watched him zigzag through the crowded street and spotted another young boy watching him. She sprinted toward the second boy.

The boy with the book rounded the Pretty Horse Pub and ran to the back. By the time Beyza, Duncan, and Fergus got there, the boy, and the book were gone. The bag lay empty on the dirty back street. Duncan and Fergus helplessly watched as Beyza knelt by the empty bag, defeated. "No!"

Zauvadok, Anaïs and Tup rounded the corner to find Beyza sobbing on her knees, clutching the empty bag with Duncan and Fergus standing impotently with her.

Dunharra grabbed the second boy before he could run.

"Hey! Ow! Knock it off, lady! Ow! It ain't me, lady! You got nothin' on me!"

"I know," Dunharra said, keeping her voice quiet, so he had to concentrate to listen. "But your buddy stole something important. Where's he selling it?"

The boy yanked himself away from Dunharra. "I'll never tell you, lady."

Dunharra wondered about his age. He appeared barely eight years old. "Do you have a family?"

"Not since the Cough," he said, an ever-so-slight crack in his crusty, dirty exterior. "What's it to you?"

"When's the last time you ate?" Dunharra asked.

"You're strange, lady," the boy said.

Dunharra pulled out a handful of coins from a pouch in her pocket. "Go, get food."

His eyes grew wide as he looked at the small pile of copper in his hand. "You're still weird, lady. Nice. But odd."

He put the coins in a hidden pocket and ran away.

Dunharra watched him run until she lost him in the crowd. "Yeah. You have no idea."

***

AOIFE

Aoife gently knocked on her father's office door. She last spoke to him yesterday, and she only half understood the tension that laced that day. She missed his company.

"Come." Aoife heard his voice from the other side of the door.

She quietly opened the door and peeked in.

"Aoife," her father said softly. "Come in. I've missed you." He leaned back in his chair and waved to her to enter.

She entered his office and stood close to him.

"You seem tense, father," Aoife said, looking at the deep frown lines etched into his face.

Aoife thought back to when Iain and her mother told her Iain about Iain being her biological father. How her father reacted to the news bothered her. He said nothing. He walked out.

Today he seemed distant. Preoccupied. Like something weighed heavily on his mind that he didn't want to talk about.

"Nothing for you to worry about," Kieron said, reaching out to hug her, which she gratefully reciprocated. "I had to do something to protect you and your mother."

"Like what, Father?" Aoife asked with curious wide eyes. She wondered what she needed protection from.

"Never you mind, my sweet child," Kieron replied.

"Tell me about your studies," Kieron asked, changing the subject. "What new things are you learning with Iain and Mhari?"

Aoife's lessons were now in tandem with Mhari and Iain. It did not escape her that they were sweet on each other. She took every opportunity to gently tease them, calling them love birds and making faces at them. She wholeheartedly approved of them together. Also, she would never admit it, but she noticed boys weren't as gross as they used to be. Some boys, anyway.

Some things never changed, however. The sun rose in the sky as the Three Sisters sleepily slipped below the horizon. Aoife raced through the corridors, careened around corners, and narrowly avoided a collision to arrive for her daily lessons with her favorite tutors on time. Yet, it amounted to nothing.

She ran around the last corner and skidded to a stop in front of Iain's door. She caught her breath and knocked.

"Late again, Aoife," Iain scolded from behind the door. "Please join us."

Aoife opened the door a crack and peered in. No kissy-face, just disappointed, stone-faced mentors waiting on their charge. They each tapped their feet, impatiently waiting for her.

Aoife cast her eyes downward. Her face burned with embarrassment as she took her appointed seat.

Aoife pouted at the supposed unfairness of her situation. They promised new ink, if she were on time. The ink she longed for. To enable her to read any language. No book would deny her access to its contents and knowledge via a language barrier ever again. They knew she cut it close on the best of days. She monitored the sky, but somehow, time always slipped away from her.

"No ink today," Mhari sighed.

Aoife let loose an overly sarcastic, dramatic moan, letting all her eleven-year-old angst fly.

"Aoife," Iain warned. He walked a delicate line.

She rolled her eyes and sat straight in her chair. 'Yes, Master Iain."

Calling Iain father felt strange when Kieron raised her. In the end, she left things as they were, and he remained Master Iain.

Mhari added, "There might be ink tomorrow, if you are on time."

Aoife exclaimed, "Finally!", earning disapproving looks.

"Let's get started, shall we?" Mhari said, eager to move past the awkwardness.

After a long morning lesson, Iain suggested they break for lunch, much to her surprise and joy. An elated, "Thank you," echoed from the hall as she sprinted toward freedom.

Iain looked at Mhari, eyes clouded with frustration. "This is going to be difficult."

"She's still young, Iain. Wait until she's a teenager," Mhari said softly. "You will both adjust as she grows older."

His face took on a pinched, downcast expression.

"I know something that will cheer you up," she said, and took Iain by the hand. "Let's go look at the tapestries. I have a secret."

After the break in her lessons, Aoife went for a visit with her mother.

A soft knock came on the door.

Without waiting, her father entered and smiled a tight lipped smile. She knew that look. He had something he wanted to talk about.

"Kieron?" Her mother asked, her voice fraught with tension.

"Maebh," Kieron said, sitting next to her and putting her arm around her.

Aoife watched as her mother visibly relaxed at his touch. She felt better when her mother felt better. She put her hand on the door to leave.

"Aoife, it's good you're here," Kieron began. "I'm here to talk about you. Stay."

"Me?"

"Yes, you," Kieron said. "Yesterday challenged all of us in ways we never imagined we'd be. We all learned something."

Aoife swallowed hard. She didn't know what her father thought about the whole situation. She didn't know what could happen. So many possibilities roiled in her mind, she got a sick feeling in her stomach.

"What about Aoife?" Maebh said, guarded.

"I've thought a lot about it," Kieron said. "Things will remain how they are. I will continue to officially be her father, and she will still inherit the throne from you. I will not make her illegitimate. Born while we were married, she should remain mine."

Aoife watched her mother as it seemed the weight of the world lifted from her shoulders.

Maebh turned to Kieron with tears in her eyes. "Are you sure?"

"Curse or no curse, she is mine," Kieron said. "Mine."

"You forgive me?" Maebh asked, eyes wet and hopeful.

"There is nothing to forgive," Kieron said, holding her close. He lifted her tense face by her chin and looked directly in her eyes. "I love you."

Chapter Twenty-Two

CHAPTER TWENTY TWO

DUNHARRA

Dunharra sat at the table at the Pretty Horse Pub between Zauvadok and Iseabail. She couldn't stop thinking about the boy she gave the copper pieces to. There had to be a fence here somewhere. The Rud Eskimiş had to be close by. She needed to figure out where.

The Pretty Horse Pub, a normal-looking watering hole for passing travelers, came replete with hitches for horses, necessaries on the sides, and the aroma of ale wafting out the open windows. Travelers came and went, some relieved of their coin by the local boy gang.

Dunharra went up to the bar to get more wine for everyone. As the serving girl fetched a new bottle, she overheard the barkeep talking about the rooms downstairs.

Downstairs? There's a downstairs?

She kept listening, trying to look impatient waiting for her wine. The barkeep went on about a fence and how they could get anything they wanted down there.

The book could be downstairs.

She needed to find this fence.

Dunharra brought the wine back to the table and shared the news.

"I'm going to find this fence," Dunharra said.

Zauvadok growled. "You should take Tup with you."

"I'll be alright. If I'm not back in half an hour, come looking for me," Dunharra said.

Dunharra turned the corner to the back of the pub when she noticed a man with shaggy blonde hair walk by. The local boy gang, who were loitering there, scattered when the man approached. They left nothing behind but dust.

She flattened herself against the side of the building, trying to melt into the afternoon shadows. She waited until she knew he entered and gone down the stairs and then entered herself.

The back door led down a flight of stairs. The smell of hookah smoke hit her like a brick as she descended the well-worn stairs. She paused at the bottom to let her eyes adjust to the darkness. A casual glance around showed no ostentatious books on proud display. She watched and waited.

Dunharra feigned interest in the loose diamonds as a blonde man walked up to a woman behind the counter. She listened to their conversation as she pretended to admire the gems.

"Whatcha need, buddy?" a scantily clad woman approached him and leaned on the counter, giving him a good show of her cleavage.

He admired her breasts and with an approving nod, he said, "Rubies."

"Ya sweet on a lady, are ya?" she asked, making her own conclusion.

"A lady in high places," the blonde man continued the charade. The woman brought out several flats of rubies in various cuts and carats. Some rings and some pendants rounded out the collection. He appreciated the selection and found a large, loose, pillow-cut ruby that caught his eye.

"Excellent choice, sir," she said.

"I'll take this, but I need something with more—" he paused to think.

"More of a statement?" she guessed. "Is there something she likes to do? Stitching?"

"No," the blonde man began. "She likes to read."

The woman teased gently, showing a little more skin. "Fancy! She must be in a very high place, you lucky man! Come with me."

The blonde man followed her back to a heavy oak door with iron hinges and a sturdy lock. She jostled her keys until she found the one she wanted. The woman unlocked the door and invited him in after her. She did, however, leave the door open.

Dunharra wandered her way close to the open door. She wanted to hear every word.

A casual glance inside the room showed that they kept the higher-end items in there. Exquisite jewelry, tiaras, rings, everything the blonde man's supposed woman of means would probably already have. The entire room sparkled.

She watched as the blonde man made a show of examining several of the higher-end pieces until he looked up.

Dunharra followed his gaze and her eyes grew wide, and she covered her open mouth with her hand.

The Rud Eskimiş sat up on a perch above the display cases.

She collected herself and continued to listen to the blonde man and the sales woman converse.

"That's not for sale, sweetie."

"I am a man of means," the blonde man said. "I can make it for sale."

"Not this one, hun," she said. "Off limits."

"Pity. My gold means nothing in here?"

"Oh, it's fine in here, mister," the woman smiled and sidled up to him, giving his arm a not-so-accidental brush with her ample breasts. "In here, you can have anything you want."

"Just not the book."

"Anything," she repeated, and gave her lips a sultry lick. "Just not the book."

He leaned his face close and gently brushed her lips with his own. She returned his kiss, heightening the passion. Without a word, she shut the door and locked it from the inside.

Dunharra swore as she shut the door and heard the lock click. She needed to come back.

***

Having heard the news, they got rooms and stayed at the pub that night.

Dunharra waited for hours in the dark shadows outside the rear of the Pretty Horse Pub. The night grew long. The blonde man should be back any time now.

Then she saw him.

He kept to the shadows, skulking slowly to the door of the pub's basement. He found the door locked, which he dealt with deftly. The harder part would be the charm on the doorjamb, which would sound an alarm if the door moved so much as half an inch. Ink on his fingers pulsed and glowed as he concentrated. He traced his fingers across the doorjamb. The magick fell away.

The blonde man opened the door.

Dunharra waited for a few minutes and followed the blonde man into the basement.

She let her eyes adjust to the dark. Dunharra remembered the layout from her visit earlier today. Dunharra flattened herself against the wall, hiding in the shadows in the corner when a man with a spiked club snuck up on the blonde man. She didn't want to be anywhere near that. She crouched in the shadows and watched.

The blonde man crouched and tackled his assailant to the ground. Punching and kicking, they vied for dominance, neither succeeding. The attacker got in a lucky punch that landed the blonde man flat on his back. He drew his dagger, and leapt to his feet. He lunged with the dagger and stabbed his enemy below his navel. Blood flowed, and intestines fell to the floor.

Dunharra resisted the overwhelming urge to help the stabbed man. To render aid now would lead to her discovery.

The blonde man stood there until the man breathed his last breath. He tried the door and found it locked. He pulled out what Dunharra thought were lock picks and knelt in front of the door.

The smell of blood and entrails permeated the air. The lock clicked open, releasing the door and inviting him in. He did not linger. He grabbed the book and shoved it into his leather backpack.

Dunharra watched in horror as the blonde man gathered papers and lit them on fire. He casually tossed them on top of his dead assailant and left The Pretty Horse Pub to burn.

She stifled a gasp when he lit the papers on fire. She couldn't leave right behind him; he would discover her. And discovery would be fatal. So, she waited, terrified, as the pub burned.

When she felt that the blonde man would be long gone, she ran up the stairs, coughing from the smoke. She flew out the door and ran into the front of the pub. She ran up the stairs and banged on every door she saw.

"Fire!" Dunharra shouted.

Smoke flooded the building. It burned her eyes and throat as she ran door to door. She pounded on Anaïs and Zauvadok's door. When she heard nothing, she pounded on the door harder, shouting, "Anaïs! Zau!"

Getting no response, Dunharra tried the door and found it locked. She tried kicking in the door. It took her several tries before the door gave way.

She ran into the room and shook them awake. They woke up coughing.

"By the Mother," Anaïs cried as she saw the entire main room of the pub engulfed in flames.

"Fetch the ladies. I'll get Duncan and Fergus. We have to jump," Zauvadok said. "We have to be quick. Go!"

Zauvadok pounded on Duncan and Fergus' door. When he didn't get a response, he kicked it in. He found them asleep in the smoke-filled room. He shook them both awake, and they woke up coughing. "The pub is on fire! The fire has fully engulfed the downstairs. We have to jump."

Fergus tied two sheets together and then tied that to the bed. They climbed down the bed sheet and landed on the ground with an inglorious thump.

It took three kicks to the door before Anaïs could get it open. Iseabail, Calyx, Beyza and Tup were unconscious, sprawled in their beds.

"Zau! I can't wake them," Dunahrra shouted over the roaring flames.

"Drag them here if you have to!" he shouted as he ran up the hallway and past a few of the others. "I'm going to toss them out the window to Duncan and Fergus."

Zauvadok gathered up Calyx and Iseabail in his arms and lumbered toward Duncan and Fergus' room. Anaïs dragged Tup and Dunharra dragged Beyza to Duncan and Fergus' room. They were waiting on the ground, looking up.

"I'm tossing the ladies down!" Zauvadok shouted. "Get ready!"

They caught Calyx easily. Together, Duncan and Fergus caught Iseabail and laid her on the ground. When he tossed Beyza, they caught her and laid her on the ground next to Iseabail. When Zauvadok tossed Tup, Fergus and Duncan dropped her. She hit her head on the hard ground.

This woke Tup, and holding her head, she shouted, "Goddamit!"

Next, Zauvadok gently hoisted Dunharra up and out the window. Anaïs shouted down to them, "Don't you dare drop her!"

Zau put his strong and loving arms around Anaïs. He hugged her tightly. The roar of the flames couldn't hide the sound of creaking beams and falling wood. "Never doubt that I loved you from the first moment I saw you, Anaïs."

Dunharra watched in horror as the pub listed to the right, threatening collapse. She watched as Zauvadok kissed Anaïs and tossed her out the window. "Don't drop her, either!"

As Zauvadok looked down to make sure Anaïs landed safely, he grabbed the bedsheet to climb down. He tugged on it to make sure it would hold his weight. It could. "Zau, hurry!" Dunharra shouted. "The pub–"

The pub let out a hideous groan. The sound of wood beams giving way made Zauvadok's blood run cold. He tried to hold on while trying to get out of the window. The pub listed again and collapsed, with Zauvadok still inside.

Dunharra could not believe her eyes. She blinked, staring with her mouth open, not wanting to believe what just happened.

"Zau!" Anaïs leapt to her feet and climbed on the burning wreckage. She dug through the burning timbers frantically as they splintered in her hands.

Fergus and Dunharra jumped in with Anaïs' efforts and helped her move the heavier beams.

Fergus yelled, "Zauvadok! Can you hear me?"

A crowd collected on the street side of what remained of The Pretty Horse Pub. Some stared, but a few people climbed on and started searching when they heard someone remained trapped inside. Anaïs dug down until she reached what she thought would be the ground floor. She heard a murmur, then a moan.

Zauvadok. She redoubled her efforts to dig down.

Anaïs, Dunharra and Fergus continued to dig deeper, toward the moaning. It seemed like they went through another floor. Down on the bottom floor of the pub Zauvadok lay under burning timbers, unmoving.

Fergus yelled, "Zauvadok! Can you hear me?" Getting no response, he and Anaïs kept slinging beams aside.

Anaïs and Fergus continued to dig deeper, toward the moaning. It seemed like they went through another floor. Her focus on finding Zau prevented her from realizing the structure had a basement. Down on the bottom floor of the pub lay Zau under burning timbers unmoving but breathing.

"He's alive!" Anaïs shouted.

Zauvadok lay on broken glass from what seemed like glass display cases, bleeding, smoldering, and moaning. Fergus almost reached him when more of the burning structure gave way. Fergus fell onto some of the broken glass on the floor and swore loudly.

Most of the fire burned above them. It almost burned itself out on this level. Pieces of burning wood fell around them. The smell of burning flesh wrinkled their noses. To Dunharra, it looked like hell in Mantua.

"Don't move him," Dunharra instructed as she navigated the rubble and joined them. Fallen debris burned and blistered Zauvadok's face, smoldered his tunic, and actively burned across his legs. "Can you move those?"

Fergus and Anaïs worked together to move the flaming beams from Zauvadok. Slowly, the beams lifted and fell harmlessly off to the side. Dunharra knelt next to him, cutting her knees on the broken glass. Blood dripped into the case as she examined Zauvadok.

A burning piece of wood impaled him. He had second and third degree burns over most of his body. The fire singed his hair. The fall broke his left leg and pelvis, and he profusely bled internally.

"Anaïs," Zau moaned.

"Pull that wood out, please, Anaïs," Dunharra said. When she pulled it out, blood spurted as the ripped artery bled free.

Dunharra's eyes glowed with an iridescent light. She placed her hands on the bleeding artery. She had to work fast. Quickly, the bleeding stopped.

Dunharra knit together his leg and pelvis so he could walk, then stemmed the internal bleeding.

The remains of the pub were burning out of control and falling down around them. If they did not leave soon, the fire would trap them all inside.

She gently laid her hands on his skin and concentrated. The blackened third-degree burns and the blistered second-degree burns vanished under her touch. Zauvadok opened his eyes and looked around.

"Anaïs? What–" Zauvadok began.

"This building is about to give out completely right above our heads," Dunharra said, crouching to avoid fallen, burning beams. "How do we get out of here?"

Zauvadok searched around for options. He pointed, seeing a door barred by smouldering timbers. "There."

Zauvadok and Fergus worked together to move the two timbers that blocked the door. Zauvadok kicked the door open, and they emerged out into the night. Anaïs led them to Duncan and the ladies. When they dropped Tup, it jolted her awake, but Iseabail, Calyx, and Beyza were still unconscious.

"Smoke inhalation," Dunharra said. She knelt next to Iseabail and laid her hands on her chest. Her eyes shifted to iridescent as she focused on healing her. A few seconds went by, and she sat up while coughing smoke. Dunharra did the same for Calyx and Beyza.

"What happened?" Iseabail asked, awestruck at the destroyed pub.

"We would have all burned to death if it weren't for Dun," Anaïs said.

Dunharra's world spun. Zauvadok barely caught her before she fell as the world went black.

Chapter Twenty-Three

CHAPTER TWENTY THREE

IAIN

Mhari and Iain walked hand in hand to the tapestry hall. Neglect afflicted the hangings while Innesfrees suffered from the Cough, but they received proper care weeks later. Now their colors burst from the tapestries and they looked better than new. Iain stopped at the Prophecy of the Healer tapestry. It had long been his favorite, not only for the artistry, but for the story it told.

"What are you thinking, Iain?" Mhari asked.

"If I will ever live to see the Prophesied Healer."

"Well, I have something to tell you that may lift your spirits," she began.

He looked at her, intrigued.

"Do you remember Dunharra?" Mhari began.

"Of course. She helped thwart the coup and saved the kingdom." Iain gave her the side eye.

"Well, she's –" Mhari began.

"Master Iain!" An Innesfrees squire came running towards Iain and Mhari. "There's a woman in labor and she's ready to deliver! It's twins! You're needed in the infirmary, now!"

"Hold that thought, Mhari," Iain said, taking her hand. Together, they ran to the infirmary.

***

DUNHARRA

The Blushing Dragon overflowed with people since the Pretty Horse Pub burned, and the serving ladies could barely keep up. The smell of smoke clung to them, and their clothes had various burns. Dunharra found a table large enough for them all to sit together. Then she noticed the glittering of the book before she saw who held it.

"Zau," Dunharra whispered. "The blonde man sitting in the far corner."

"Yes? So?"

"Look at his left hand," Dunharra said.

"I'll be a son of a bitch," Zauvadok said as he crossed his arms. The blonde man held the Rud Eskimiş right out in the open.

"So, what do we do?"

"We kill him and take it home," Beyza hissed.

Dunharra watched as the blonde man's reverie broke when he felt the weight of eyes on him. He placed the book in his bag and left the inn.

"That's a thought," Zauvadok began. "Or we can follow him and see who wants this book besides the Lycaena."

"Oh, be logical, why don't you?" Beyza said, glaring at the blonde man as he retreated out of the inn.

"Tup, let's follow him," Dunharra said.

"And we'll trail behind and watch your back," Zauvadok said.

Tup nodded. She and Dunharra left with the rest of them following behind them. They slipped through the main gate and skulked around the outside of the castle until they found the kitchen's entrance. They argued about the size of a dinner party. The ink on Tup's fingers glowed a deep indigo, and her eyes followed suit. Though they were not invisible, and people could see them, the kitchen staff did not pay them any attention. They slipped through the kitchen and into the main hallway.

***

DARAGH

The blonde man walked through the door to King Darragh's private chamber without knocking. Darragh stood with a dagger in his hand and said, "You impudent little bastard!"

"This impudent little bastard has The Rud Eskimiş," he retorted.

"Let's see it," Darragh said and took a step toward the blonde man.

He stepped back and held up the book. "Money talks, Your Majesty."

Darragh tossed him a pouch heavy with coins, which the blonde man caught with one gloved hand. He then laid the book on Darragh's desk. He watched as the king marveled over the book. Darragh noticed a white powder on the first few pages of the Rud Eskimiş, which he sniffed but smelled nothing. He partially wiped it away with his hands.

"Are you still here?" Darragh asked with a sneer and a side-eye.

"Yes. I have never before witnessed the death of a king, Your Majesty."

"What?" Darragh said, eyes bulging and hand balled into fists. "What have you done?" Darragh shouted, then doubled over in pain as his mouth frothed.

"Kieron of Innesfrees sends his regards."

Darragh fell to the floor, convulsing and drooling.

***

DUNHARRA

Tup and Dunharra found the empty throne room easily. Their footsteps echoed off the high marble ceiling as they walked back behind the dais and found a door. They heard Darragh and someone talking about a book, and Dunharra presumed the blonde man who had the Rud Eskimiş stood in the room with him. Dunharra saw that the gurgling noises made Tup suspicious, and it made her nervous. She held up her hand for Dunharra to stay still. She paused, and her breath caught in her throat. Could the blonde man have killed Darragh?

At that moment, one of the two men inside audibly slumped to the floor. Tup peeked through the door only to be rewarded with a dagger flying at her and impaling itself in the doorjamb next to her head.

"Too late, Tup," the blonde man said. "I got here first."

"That's the same man with the book!" Dunharra said, shocked. "How does he know your name?"

The blonde man grabbed The Rud Eskimiş and hastily shoved it in his backpack. He waved his pouch of coins and darted from the room, laughing.

Tup looked at Darragh, convulsing on the floor. She grabbed Dunharra and they darted out the way they came. They did not need to be around when this got out. Her eyes flashed deep indigo as she dashed through the castle, through the kitchen, and out into the courtyard. As they neared the gate, someone sounded an alarm.

"Murder! Murder! Close the gate! Close the gate! The King is dead!"

Tup and Dunharra had to run fast, as the gate had already started to lumber closed. They dove to make it under the gate before it came down on them. They tumbled out as it slammed shut. Dunharra and Tup did not stop running until she reached where Zauvadok and the others were waiting for her.

"Run! We need to get out of here!" she shouted, and ran straight for the Royal Western Road, without stopping to see if they were following her.

Dunharra and Tup didn't slow down until Iseabail caught up with them. "What happened?"

"The blonde man assassinated Darragh," Tup said between ragged breaths. "He has the book! I don't know if he got out before the gate closed, but if he's still there, he'll find his way out, eventually."

"Then we'll be here to greet him," Beyza said.

***

DUNHARRA

Dunharra, Tup and Zauvadok stood by the castle wall, watching and waiting for the blonde man to make his escape while the others waited a short ways away. Dunharra heard that the Buckhaven knights were trying to restore order on the other side of the wall. They all heard a loud bang and then chaos.

"We're under attack!" someone screamed, and any sort of order the knights had gained shattered. People shouted and ran everywhere.

"He should come over this wall any time now," Dunharra said. She thought this would be an excellent opportunity for the blonde man to make his escape.

They didn't have to wait long.

The blonde man emerged on top of the wall and jumped down with ease.

"Hello," Zauvadok said, pushing him up against the outer wall of the castle courtyard.

"Excuse me," the blonde man said. "You must have me mistaken for someone else."

"Nope." Zauvadok pinned him to the wall..

"I'm not the person you're looking for," the blonde man said as he tried to push past him.

"Yes. Yes, you are," Tup said, moving out from Zauvadok's shadow and into the light.

"Tup."

"Lars."

"Do you two know each other? Zauvadok asked, confused. Confusion evident on their faces, Dunharra and Zauvadok looked at each other. How did Tup and Lars know each other?

Zauvadok grabbed shoulders. "Let's talk."

"Let's not," Lars sneered as he pulled a dagger from one of his uncountable pockets.

"Look, we only want the book," Tup said, crossing her arms.

"It'll cost you. I don't think you can afford me, Tup," Lars said, still holding the dagger.

"What do you want?" Zauvadok asked.

"Gold."

"I have five hundred right here, right now," Tup said, holding out a large pouch filled with coins.

Zauvadok gave Tup the side eye, who looked up at him and shrugged. "What?"

"Sold." Lars handed over the bag with The Rud Eskimiş to Tup. "Good luck, Tup. You'll need it."

Lars turned and vanished into the crowd.

"That was easy," Zauvadok said as he watched Lars vanish into the crowd.

"Too easy," Tup replied.

"How do you know him?" Dunharra asked, frowning. She could see that they shared a past and couldn't let it go.

"Glorious results of a misspent youth. It's a long story for a later time," Tup said sadly, as she started walking toward where the Iseabail, Calyx and Anaïs waited for them.

***

IAIN

Iain and Mhari were sharing a private lunch on a beautiful harvest day. Samhain finally arrived, and there would be a celebration. Iain took this opportunity to woo Mhari. He brought her the last rose of the season and placed it in her braided hair. She smiled, and her eyes danced. Her whole countenance glowed. The soft pink of the rose set off her complexion. Iain wanted to remember this moment for a long time.

Mhari blushed at the attention and turned away.

"Mhari, the last time we were together, you had something to tell me. Can you tell me now?"

"How sweet! You remembered," Mhari said, blushing and smiling.

"Everything you have to say is important to me."

"That means so much to me, Iain." Saying his name, her voice sounded like angels singing. He could listen to her forever.

"You know the prophecy of the Healer?" Mhari asked.

"I know it well," Iain replied. "I wish every day that the Healer will come in my lifetime."

"The Mother granted your wish, Iain. The Healer has come."

Iain trembled. "What? Such a thing cannot be true."

"It's true! I talked to her myself." Mhari beamed.

"Who?" Iain asked, breathless.

"Dunharra Tor," Mhari said, immensely proud of herself, ignoring her promise.

"How do you know?" Iain asked, stunned.

"During the inking ceremony for Aoife's recovery and eleventh birthday, everyone else took the ink, but Dunharra wouldn't. When I looked at her, she didn't have any ink on her skin. None.

Iain's eyes grew wide as saucers. He couldn't believe his ears.

"All that healing and no ink," Iain said, mesmerized by the prospect that the Healer had finally come. "It must be true. Dunharra is the Healer! We must tell Kieron."

Iain saw a dark look of regret pass over Mhari's face as he stood. He frowned, but the news preoccupied him too much for him to pay it much attention. He focused on the Healer and the need to tell Kieron. Iain thought he would ask Mhari later about it.

Chapter Twenty-Four

CHAPTER TWENTY FOUR

DUNHARRA

News of King Darragh's assassination by poison spread like wildfire. Dunharra heard people whisper rumors in back corners and taverns. Many of them pointed their fingers at Innesfrees.

King Ronan's first order after he ascended to the throne, having everyone in the castle searched for the one thing his father desired most: the Rud Eskimiş made Buckhaven erupt in fury. When his knights came up empty-handed, he expanded the search to everyone in Buckhaven all the way through to the Garrison Line.

Word of the search spread like wildfire, and Dunharra saw people react poorly. She heard a lot of complaining and grumbling from those being searched. Authorities quickly suppressed any resistance. Scuffles broke out between the King's guard and passing travelers.

People threw hands and drew weapons. There were many travelers who stayed in the Buckhaven jail.

Dunharra heard that Ronan seethed as he sat in his castle. Rumor had it that the Rud Eskimiş traveled on its way to Innesfrees. From the travelers, she heard Ronan would consider extreme measures to get what he wanted.

"Tup, I know you can make yourself ignorable," Dunharra said. "Can you do that on the book?"

"I can."

Tup took the book in her hands. She closed her eyes, and when she opened them, they were a deep indigo. The ink on her fingers also glowed and pulsed with her heartbeat.

"You there!" a guard shouted. "Stay where you are. Prepare to be searched."

Tup quickly shoved the book into the bag.

"Hey!" Zauvadok said. "We've done nothing wrong."

"Likely story," another guard said as he approached. "Hands on your heads."

"Don't you get too handsy with my wife," Zauvadok said.

"Pipe down, pig man," the guard said. "All we're looking for is a book. I don't think the likes of you will have it, but we must search everyone, see?"

"Who are you calling a pig man?" Zauvadok growled. He stood every inch of his seven feet tall.

The guard looked up at him and said, "I guess that would be you, bitch!"

Zauvadok landed a right hook directly to the guard's chin. He fell to the ground, limp but alive.

"You take a punch like a bitch," Zauvadok spat, and took a warning step toward the other guard. The other guard took a step back and called for backup.

"So, why did you have me charm the book?" Tup teased Dunharra.

"Time to go!" Duncan shouted.

They mounted their horses and took off at a full gallop toward the Royal Western Road, and they did not stop until they reached the Disputed Lands. There, they stopped to rest the horses and regroup.

"So we're all on the same page, we are going to Dhangadi, correct?" Iseabail asked.

"That's a good idea, but we have nothing," Beyza replied. "No food, no supplies, no money. It all burned in the fire."

Zauvadok gave Tup the side eye, who shrugged. "Not all of it."

"The nearest town is Innesfrees," Dunharra said. "We can stop there."

People left Buckhaven in droves. The usual mercenaries and thieves were thick among the crowd, pickpocketing and robbing travelers. This made everyone on edge. Travelers exchanged sharp words, but they avoided scuffles.

"What's going on?" Dunharra asked a passing man with his two boys.

"We are leaving Buckhaven because King Ronan has threatened a draft," the father said. "I'm moving my boys to Cobh so King Ronan can't draft them into a pointless war."

"War?" Dunharra gasped. She could not believe her ears. "Between who?"

"King Ronan intends to declare war on Innesfrees," the father said and went on his way.

Dunharra could not believe what she heard. When they paid closer attention to the travelers, they saw that they were mostly men and boys. Fleeing for their lives. Leaving their wives and daughters at home to hold out as best they could. This only set fire to their urgency to get to Innesfrees. If they hurried through the Disputed Lands, they could make it to Innesfrees in a day.

***

ISEABAIL

Iseabail visibly relaxed when they rode through the Innesfrees gate. The darkness of night overtook the twilight and the Samhain festivities were over. Bonfires were burning low and the townspeople wandered the courtyard, heading toward the gate to go back to their village.

"Welcome to Innesfrees," the Innesfrees ambassador began. "I am Noam, and I will see to your comfort during your stay." Iseabail noticed that his dark brown hair matched his dark brown eyes. His smile came easily.

They introduced themselves, and exchanged pleasantries. Iseabail clearly happy that their reputation preceded them, followed him inside the castle, through the Great Hall, and to the guest quarters.

Noam said, "There are enough rooms for you individually."

"I'm staying with Anaïs," Zauvadok said.

"I understand the Samhain festivities are over," Iseabail began. "But is it possible to have an audience with Queen Maebh before she retires?"

"I regret Her Majesty has already retired for the evening," Noam said in his smooth baritone voice. "I will see that she knows you are here. Please rest well tonight."

Early in the morning, not long after the sun beamed through their windows, knocks at their doors woke them. A polite young girl, no more than eleven years old, stood waiting. She had the same message for each of them.

"Queen Maebh and Prince Regent Kieron request the honor of your presence in the reception parlor for lunch." With that, she nodded, curtsied, and walked away.

When they arrived at the reception parlor, Iseabail noticed they had arranged fresh flowers to decorate for lunch. The serving staff brought in a large rectangular table to accommodate everyone. Festive colored napkins complemented crystal goblets and fine plates. They threw open the windows to admit the sunshine and crisp autumn breezes. Servants put away the Samhain decorations, and hints of Yule were springing up. Sprigs of holly, evergreens, pinecones and candles of red, green and gold adorned the table. Mistletoe hung in the doorway to the Great Hall.

About thirty minutes after the visitors arrived, Maebh and Kieron entered the room. They sat at the head of the table, politely conversing until lunch concluded and a dessert of apples baked in dough appeared on each plate.

"One of our cooks, Noemie, calls this an apple crumble," Maebh said, delighted. "It's delicious. Please enjoy!"

"So, what brings you here to see us?" Kieron asked.

"We are the bearers of mixed news," Iseabail began. "First, we have evidence of the Lycaenan Library. It still exists and is intact."

"That's excellent news!" Maebh exclaimed.

Beyza took great delight in retelling the story of finding the library in Therson's Light, the maajida, and how it appeared as if every book in the library still existed.

"You said your reports painted a mixed picture," Kieron said.

Iseabail told them about The Rud Eskimiş, and how King Darragh had an agreement with a powerful mage to wear the Frozen Crown. At the mention of Darragh, Kieron's countenance clouded, but he kept his composure.

"We have it on good word that King Ronan now wants the book for himself," Dunharra added.

"And will do anything to get it," Iseabail interjected. She told them about the massive search of travelers for the book, and the mass exodus of men and boys to Cobh to avoid the draft.

"Draft?" Maebh asked. "That means—"

"War," Kieron finished.

***

IAIN

Iain and Mhari were having lunch outside in the rose garden, all smiles and flirting, until they heard Zauvadok's voice through the open window of the reception parlor. They stared at each other, with eyes wide as saucers. They knew that voice.

Zauvadok.

And where Zauvadok went, Dunharra might be close by.

They sprang up from their lunch and walked over to the parlor windows. The windows were too high to look through, so they had to satisfy themselves with eavesdropping.

"When?" Maebh asked.

"Soon," Dunharra said. "I expect that it would be imminent."

Iain and Mhari were ecstatic to hear Dunharra's voice. They hugged each other under the windows. Their mood directly contrasted with the mood in the parlor.

"So, Your Majesties, are we free to take The Rud Eskimiş to Dhangadi?" Dunharra asked.

"By all means," Maebh replied. "The farther away it is from here when Ronan comes, the better."

"I will send word to Stirling," Kieron added. "We have a mutual defense agreement."

***

IAIN

A short time later, Iain knocked on the door to Kieron's private rooms. He waited for an answer, which came softly after a moment.

Iain and Mhari entered. They bowed to Kieron, and Iain said, "We have information that we think you should know, Your Majesty."

"You sound a tad cheery about this information," said Kieron. He appeared tired and worn down to Iain, as ran his fingers through his hair and rubbed his eyes. "What have you learned?"

"The Prophesied Healer has come," Mhari and Iain said in unison.

"The Prophesied Healer?" Kieron asked, looking at them with a side eye.

Iain could tell that he did not fully understand what they were saying.

"Yes," Iain said. "The tapestries in the hall outside of Maebh's private quarters? The last tapestry is of the Prophesied Healer, prophesied by Good Witch Eibhlin hundreds of years ago. And now the Healer is here."

Iain watched as Kieron's eyes were dark and stony as he processed the news. "Who is this Healer?"

"Dunharra Tor," Iain said.

"Dunharra!" Kieron exclaimed. "She said nothing."

"I don't think she's ready," Mhari said, looking down and away. "I think we should wait for her to be ready."

Kieron and Iain both looked at her. Kieron asked, "What are you saying? You come to me with this information and then ask me not to act on this? With war looming?"

"War?" Iain asked.

"Buckhaven blames Innesfrees for the assassination of Darragh. Ronan has ascended to the throne, and declared war on Innesfrees," Kieron said, standing. "I must see the Queen."

Kieron walked down the tapestry-laden hallway to Maebh's private quarters. He stopped in front of the Prophesied Healer tapestry and examined it. Indeed, it predicted a healer who could heal all wounds that were brought to them.

Iain heard about Dunharra healing Anaïs after Darragh had her tortured in the Chamber. Did she get to Anaïs in time, or did she really steal her from death? Now he knew.

The Beit She'an guards allowed him to pass to Maebh's room without a word. She sat, reading a report from Cobh about the influx of refugees from Buckhaven fleeing the draft. She gazed up at him and smiled.

"To what do I owe the honor, Kieron?" Maebh asked as he kissed her lovingly.

"I have news of the indeterminate sort, my love," Kieron began as Iain and Mhari filed in behind him. "It seems the Prophesied Healer has come."

Maebh's face went from one of confusion to joy. "Oh, by the Mother! The Healer has come! The prophecy is true! Who is it?"

Chapter Twenty-Five

CHAPTER TWENTY FIVE

DUNHARRA

Dunharra sat in the sun, enjoying its warmth. She gave thanks to the Mother for the changing seasons. Soon, it would be Yule, and there would be snow on the ground. The sun soon would not be as strong as today. She drank in the sunlight as if it were both her first and last day to see it.

Eager to travel to Dhangadi, they retrieved their horses from the stable boys and rode out of the gate. They stopped in the village for some additional supplies when they saw the colors of Buckhaven fluttering in the wind. Ronan and his army marched on Innesfrees.

Dunharra saw that Ronan's army on the Great Northern Road made travel impossible. The Buckhaven forces blocked the road, and they found themselves trapped in Innesfrees. They hurried back to the castle with news of the assembled army on the horizon.

Two agonizing days passed with the shadow of Buckhaven hanging over them before Dunharra heard the call for the siege from the infirmary. Stirling would arrive the next day. They only needed to survive that long.

While Dunharra watched from the infirmary, she saw Ronan lead his forces from behind, leaving his general to take point with his men. She heard swords clash and the sound of metal on metal. Maebh and Kieron led from the front, choosing to meet the enemy shoulder to shoulder with their men. She heard bodies hit the ground with the groans and cries of the dead and dying. The battle raged for what seemed like hours. Each side held and refused to yield. Kieron raised his bloody sword to lead one last push. With his sword raised and his head turned, an arrow struck him in the shoulder. Another struck him in his chest. The third dropped him from his horse.

Dunharra saw his men carrying him behind the fighting lines to assess his wounds. Iain and Mhari rushed to his side to see what could be done. Kieron breathed raggedly. His face turned pale and he bled profusely. Blood spurted from the wounds when they pulled out the arrows. Kieron's breath gurgled, and he coughed up blood.

"Find Dunharra," Mhari said. "I'll do everything I can to keep him alive until she arrives."

A thick, dripping sweat formed on Mhari's brow, and all her ink glowed and beat in sync with her heart. She poured all of her magick into Kieron but she barely kept him alive.

"Kieron," Maebh said as she knelt down to him. "Hold on. Don't leave me."

Iain came running with Dunharra. She knelt down, ripped his armor off and assessed Kieron's injuries. She glanced at Maebh, whose worried eyes were wet and red rimmed.

Dunharra placed her hands on Kieron's chest. Her eyes shifted to iridescent. Dunharra could feel his heart beating slowly; without intervention he would not be alive for long. She took a deep breath and fixed the arteries that the arrows severed. Dunharra repaired his left lung after an arrow punctured it and filled it with blood. She drained the blood from his lung so he could breathe. Dunharra repaired the tissue around the arrow wounds and knit muscles back together. The arrow wounds closed, but he still needed blood. She drew a deep breath and concentrated on coaxing his pelvis and femurs to make more blood, which they did. But they couldn't comply fast enough. She helped his body make more blood. Satisfied he had enough blood to survive, she traced the arrow entry wounds, and the scars vanished.

Dunharra felt it coming, the inevitable fainting from so much healing exertion. For now, she fought it off to ensure the safety of her patient.

Kieron sat up, amazed. He felt fine, no residual pain, no lasting impairment. He sat up and stared at Dunharra.

"You are the Healer," Kieron said. "You are the one Mantua has been waiting for. The one I need. You must stay here in Innesfrees."

"What? How do—? Why, Mhari? How could you?" She looked directly at Mhari, who averted her gaze.

Dunharra's blood ran cold.

Her heart pounded.

Her mind raced.

She could barely breathe.

She climbed to her feet, meaning to run off, to anywhere but there, but it then all went black and she fell to the bloody ground. Kieron had Dunharra brought to the castle where she could recover off the battlefield.

Dunharra's eyes opened with a start, and she found herself in bed. She lay there dirty and bloody from healing Kieron on the battlefield. She frowned. Dunharra felt dirty and wanted to get clean. Once clean and in a new shirt, she noticed she ruined the bed linen. She left her room and went in search of fresh ones.

As she roamed the halls looking for linen, or Noam, or both, she saw Mhari on a collision course straight to her. Dunharra looked around and finding no way to elude her. She pushed her lips into a thin line and tried to control her heart that beat against her chest.

"Dunharra!" Mhari called to her. "Wait!"

She paused and inwardly cringed. She could not avoid her.

"Mhari," Dunharra sighed. "What can I do for you?"

"Why do you want to hide who you are?" Mhari asked pointedly.

"Wouldn't you?" As Dunharra spoke, emotion welled up inside and threatened to overwhelm her. All the air left her and she felt like she couldn't breathe. "How can I go back to my cottage now? You heard Kieron. He said I need to stay here. What if he keeps me here by force? I'll be a prisoner."

"He would never," Mhari said. "Kieron's not like that."

"How can you know that? Dunharra asked. "Whose to say he won't keep me locked up here for when he thinks he needs me? It's war out there."

"Regardless, you should embrace your gift," Mhari shot back. "You shouldn't hide behind those long sleeves and be who you were meant to be."

Dunharra shrank back. "You have no idea what it's like. What the fear is like. Wondering if today is the last day you walk free. When they discover me, and they will, I will no longer walk free. They will hunt me."

"You're being dramatic," Mhari said, crossing her arms.

"Am I?" Dunharra's eyes met Mhari's. She stared at her and didn't blink until Mhari looked away.

"That's what I thought," Dunharra said grimly. "You had no right to tell my secret, to Iain or to anyone."

Dunharra pushed past her and ran down the hall.

Chapter Twenty-Six

CHAPTER TWENTY SIX

ISEABAIL

Iseabail watched with stony eyes as Ronan commanded his troops to fall back as twilight faded to night. Campfires were lit, and the men rested and tended to their weapons. The sound of crackling fires and the sharpening of blades pierced the night. Knights burned the dead, and healers tended to the injured.

She knew he expected capitulation at sunrise. Iseabail also knew he thought the wounds to Kieron were fatal. He sat in his warm tent, sheltered from the cool autumn breezes blowing through the night. Those breezes hinted at the promise of the coming winter.

The camp remained calm all night.

As dawn broke over Innesfrees, the late autumn sun lit up the countryside, its light giving scant warmth in the frigid morning hour. Campfires slowly died as soldiers emerged from their tents. Their breaths came out in plumes of steam.

Maebh and Iseabail rode out to the border of their army to meet with Ronan. She hoped they cold fool him into believing Kieron died.

"Maebh, Iseabail, " Ronan said.

"Ronan," Maebh said.

"This is your last chance," Ronan said, gripping the reins tightly. "Surrender now."

"No," Maebh began. "This is yours, Ronan. Think of your knights and spare them this foolish and unwarranted loss of life."

"Think of your husband, and what you could have spared him," Ronan snarled.

Maebh, unmoved, her eyes like stone as she regarded him. As she turned her horse back to Innesfrees, she said, "Then we will meet on the battlefield."

Kieron rode out into the ranks of his soldiers, alive and well and uninjured.

Ronan sneered. He raised his sword and declared the battle on. The two sides ran toward each other and met in the middle. The metallic clang of swords meeting swords and axes hitting shields filled the morning. Shouts of men fighting and dying rose above the sharp sound of metal hitting metal.

Bloody but emboldened, Ronan held up his sword and shouted at Kieron and Maebh. "I have won the day! Look around you. Will you yield?"

Iseabail looked on as Maebh rode out to capitulate the battle. They rode out to meet Ronan when they heard someone ride near them. They saw King Lennox of Stirling.

"No!" King Lennox, father to Prince Kieron, shouted above all the noise. The man, strong for all of his sixtyish years, with short blonde hair and a trimmed beard, raised his sword.

“Stirling comes to the defense of Innesfrees,” Lennox said directly to Ronan. “I have fresh troops of ten thousand men ready to decimate you. The question is, Ronan, will you yield?”

Ronan visibility paled as the Stirling troops amassed on the battle's border, she didn't feel sorry for him. He turned and reassessed his battle-weary army. A sour look crossed his face as he said, “This is not over, Maebh! I will have Innesfrees and The Rud Eskimiş!”

·He angrily called his troops to retreat and leave the battlefield.

Maebh turned to Lennox and hugged him. “You have the best timing, Your Majesty.”

“And what are these rumors of Kieron’s demise?” Lennox asked as he eyed Kieron up and down. “You seem fine to me.”

“I received mortal wounds,” Kieron replied. “The skill of a visiting healer saved me.”

“Who is this healer?” Lennox asked. “I need to thank them.”

Maebh and Kieron looked at each other and nodded. “She is reclusive, Father. Let’s celebrate, and I will invite her and her companions for you to meet,” Kieron said.

***

DUNHARRA

Early in the morning, a young woman knocked on their doors and invited them to lunch with the Queen, Prince Regent Kieron, and King Lennox of Stirling in the reception parlor. Dunharra had no desire to leave her room, no matter how much Anais sought to convince her. But Anais found her weak spot, and how could she resist the prospect of shopping for a new tunic and trousers. Since it did not look like Kieron's knights planned to restrain her and make her a permanent resident of Innesfrees, she could wander the city freely.

When the appointed hour arrived, they took their places at the table and waited for Kieron, Maebh, and Lennox. They didn't wait long.

Similar to the previous lunch, they engaged in small talk throughout the meal, until the dessert arrived. This time, Noemie treated them to a cream cheesecake.

"Dunharra," King Lennox began, "I want to thank you for your talents. You saved my son. Thank you."

Dunharra's blood ran cold and her breath hitched when Lennox called her out, but she breathed again when he made no mention of her being the Prophesied Healer.

"There is no ink that could do you justice, and no monetary reward that could convey the depth of my gratitude," Lennox said. "Although I will certainly compensate you for your actions. Name your deepest desire, and it's yours."

"Your Majesty," Dunharra began. "I am not ready for the tales of my talents to be known. It is my solemn wish for it to remain secret."

"That's an odd wish, my dear, but so be it," Lennox said. "It will not leave this room."

Maebh and Kieron readily agreed. Dunharra sighed, relieved.

"Although, I have a son who needs to be married. He would take good care of you as his princess, and one day, his queen," Lennox inquired.

Dunharra demurred. "I am sure you will find him a suitable wife, Your Majesty."

"Can't fault an old man for trying," Lennox winked.

The Buckhaven hostility now over, Ronan and his army left Innesfrees. Dunharra, happy that Kieron showed no sign of keeping her against her will, felt free to go.

Chapter Twenty-Seven

CHAPTER TWENTY SEVEN

AOIFE

Aoife arrived on time for the first time in her life. She made it without running, careening around corners, or dodging people who had the misfortune to be in her path. She knocked on Iain's door and patiently waited for an answer. Iain and Mhari seemed shocked to see Aoife on time, and not a haggard mess.

"What?" Aoife asked, defensively. "I can come back."

"No," Iain and Mhari said in unison. Iain ushered her in.

"Congratulations, Aoife; you get the new ink today," Mhari informed her.

Aoife's heart leapt with delight. "When?"

"Now," Mhari answered.

"Now is good," Aoife said, smiling from ear to ear.

Mhari brought Aoife to the inking room, which sat adjacent to the healer's sickroom. She got her comfortable on the table.

"This is large ink for strong magick. After getting this ink, you will read any written language known to Mantua." Mhari said. "Where do you want it?"

"How large is it?" Aoife asked.

"It's red, shaped like a dahlia and is about ten inches round," Mhari said, holding up her hands in a circle.

Aoife thought for a moment. "My back, Mhari. That way, I choose who sees it and who knows I have it."

"Alright," Mhari said. "The back it is."

Mhari placed the numbing cream and then worked the ink's magick. The entire inking took about five hours to complete. The numbing wore off at the end, making it hard for Aoife to lay still. Mhari applied more numbing and finished the ink. Mhari gave Aoife a mirror and held another mirror at her back, so she could see her new ink. Aoife squealed like a youngling given sugar candy. She pulled her dress back over her shoulders and thanked Mhari for the new ink.

Eager to test the new ink and the strength of the magick, Aoife ran straight toward the castle library and found the oldest, dustiest, and most mysterious book she could reach. She pulled it out of its place on the shelf and blew the dust off it. And promptly sneezed.

The Unnamed City and The Darkness. Aoife, not sure what the title meant, took the book back to her room and settled into her comfy chair and read. Dubh meowed and jumped up and lay down on the top edge of the comfortable chair.

The book described a race of people called the Mauu, who were shapeshifters from human to jaguar. Their most common form took a cat-like, humanoid shape with the facial features and fur of the feline. Shifting to a quadrupedal jaguar or a full human did not happen often, although it did occasionally. They were long-lived, like the Lycaena, or the Elves.

Aoife looked at the cover again, trying to gauge the age of the book. It seemed ancient, and the parchment proved delicate. If she turned a page too roughly, the parchment threatened to break off in her hand. The paint decorating the pages hadn't faded. It seemed no one had opened this book for hundreds of years. The book detailed the lineage of the Mauu leaders for a thousand years, dating back to the book's creation. Those names and events were unfamiliar to Aoife, and she skimmed over them.

The book described how humans and the Mauu interacted, including a Mauu genocide perpetrated by humans. It went into great detail about the manner in which the Mauu perished. Tears streamed down her face as she read the last page.

After reading the book's horrors, she dried her eyes and went back to Mhari and Iain, with the book in hand. She told them how she went to find the oldest, dustiest book she could reach and found *The Unnamed City and The Darkness*. She relayed what she read, including a Mauu genocide.

"What do you know about this, Iain?" Aoife asked. "You omitted this part of Mantuan history. Why?"

"You're the first one to read the history in several hundred years, Aoife," he said, not pleased with her attitude. "The information is new to us and you know it."

Aoife rolled her eyes, but his words hit the mark. She felt the sting of the rebuke.

"I am dismissing you for the day, Aoife," he said. "Have a better attitude when you arrive tomorrow. On time."

***

RONAN

Ronan stormed around his private quarters like a caged animal. He could not fathom how Kieron survived three arrows to the chest. He fell from his horse. Kieron lay dying, everyone around him knew it and Ronan could see it. Yet, he lived. What healers did Innesfrees have? Were they Wild Ones? From Beit Shemesh? He must know.

Ronan called two of his best spies to his private chamber.

"At your service, Your Majesty."

"Yes," Ronan began. "I need you to find out what type of healers they have in Innesfrees. I want names, ethnicities, any information you can learn. Anything. I must know how they saved Kieron. Understand?"

The two spies nodded in agreement. "Yes, Your Majesty."

They needed to look hurt, like they were in a fight. The spies went to the knights who were glad to practice on them. Soon they looked like they had narrowly survived a battle.

They were ready to go to Innesfrees.

Late the next day, the spies returned to Ronan

"They immediately took us in and cared for us, without asking if we could pay for their services," the second spy said.

"Their charity knows no bounds," Ronan said, rolling his eyes. "What did you find out?"

"A visiting healer saved Kieron. One who does not stay at Innesfrees," the first spy said. "After removing the arrows, she used magic." The Prince Regent lay literally moments from his demise when the healer saved him."

"The healers at Innesfrees are of all races but Lycaena, and mostly female," the second spy said. "They have a separate area in the castle proper, where they care for the sick and do healing. They offer you a choice of herbalist or magickal healing. Ink covers the arms of the healers, and they are highly skilled. However, the healer who healed the prince regent is a human woman with long black curly hair. Her name is Dunharra Tor."

"Sylvestre," Ronan hissed. "I want a manhunt for this healer. Find her and bring her to me, alive and unharmed.

"Yes, Your Majesty," Sylvestre said. "And what about the book? Do you wish the search for it to continue as well?"

"Yes. We must still search every man, woman, and child until its found.

"If I may, Your Majesty," Sylvestre began, "I believe the book may be far from here now. Do you think it's reasonable to surmise that wherever she is, the book is close to her?"

This gave Ronan pause. His brow furrowed and his eyes got a faraway glaze to them. "You're saying get the healer and The Rud Eskimiş will come with her?"

"It's entirely possible," Sylvestre hinted. "And if she does not have it, we can offer a trade: the woman for the book."

"You're assuming I want to let her go, Sylvestre," Ronan said.

***

AOIFE

Aoife formed a plan.

She stepped past the Beit She'an guards and knocked on her mother's. However, her mother, busy over political missives asked her to return later. Aoife politely asked her mother for ten minutes of her time with her father.

"Come back after lunch, Aoife," Maebh said. "I'll have the time and the attention for what you need to talk about then."

Aoife hugged her mother tightly and left her to her business. As she left her mother's private chambers, she met her father on his way to her mother. She said in passing, "I need ten minutes of your time after lunch, Father."

Kieron grinned. "You are welcome to it."

Despite speaking with her father, Aoife made it on time for her lessons with Iain and Mhari, making it two days in a row. She had a streak going. Instead of Iain's lesson plan, she had a plan of her own. She asked, "Can we talk about how to initiate diplomatic relations with a nation?"

Iain demurred. "Is this about the Mauu?"

"Yes," Aoife began. "I think we should extend a hand of humanity."

"I thought you read that the hand of humanity caused them to go into hiding," Iain replied.

"I think it's time for the hand of humanity to evolve into something better," Aoife replied.

"Have we, though?" Mhari asked. "We are still technically at war with Buckhaven."

"It might come across as searching for help with the war," Iain added.

Heat crawled up her neck. Aoife hadn't thought about it that way. She only wanted to heal this breach with the Mauu. She'd been ignorant.

"Your instinct is good," Mhari said. "I like where you are going with this. Our question for you is, is this the right time?"

"Is there ever a wrong time to reach out the hand of peace?" Aoife asked.

Mhari glanced at Iain, who returned her gaze.

"Let's begin with introductions," Iain said.

Lessons on international affairs began.

***

DUNHARRA

The sun started its slide below the horizon, but they could barely see it through the clouds that threatened rain. The next inn remained about an hour away. They urged their horses on as they dodged tiny, misty raindrops. The travelers on the Great Northern Road thinned out considerably as the rain increased in intensity. Upon reaching The Fox's Fang, they entered, leaving a trail of dripping cloak drops behind them, drenched to the bone. Judging by the wet entryway, they were not the first and probably would not be the last drenched travelers to visit.

A tired innkeeper wiping down the bar met them. "What can I fetch you?"

"Rooms," Dunharra said. "Four if you have them."

"I have two left," the innkeeper said. "Take 'em or leave 'em."

"We'll take them," Iseabail said.

Zauvadok, Anaïs, Dunharra, and Duncan took one room, and Iseabail, Calyx, Tup, Beyza, and Fergus took the other. They settled in for a rainy night. The rain pelted the windowpanes; the constant tapping of the rain made a soothing sound for sleeping. The rain lasted through the night and into the early morning. As the sun rose, they saw a rainbow on the horizon.

The Great Northern Road became slippery with mud from last night's rain, making travel slow and difficult. They were approaching the Mother's Temple on the small island of Valide in the Bannockburn

River. There were many pilgrims going to worship or make requests of the Mother. A flock of shoebill storks lingered on the rocky shore. This left the Great Northern Road mostly empty, and they could travel with more space.

Dunharra rode in the center and the rest of them spread out in their typical formation. They traveled most of the morning, lost in their own thoughts. Worry lined Dunharra's face. Though Kieron and his people released her, she did not know if her freedom would last. She did more healing in front of more people than she should have. Rumors were starting. Mhari told Iain, who told Kieron, who told Maebh, and Dunharra felt on the cusp of being found out. It would all be her own doing.

How could I let them die? Their time hadn't come. Or had it? I healed young people with a whole life ahead of them. People with a premature death. I wonder if I am ready to take on this role, or if I am going to spend my whole life hiding. Running. Outrunning. But what good is having this gift if I am always going to hide it? But what kind of life would I have when it got out? Would people use me, or could I still be the person I am?

The whole thing terrified her.

When they came across The Ram, they were more than ready for a break. They wearily tied their horses to the hitch and went inside. The décor certainly had a ram theme. There were comfortable leather chairs with sheepskin throws and taxidermied rams' heads over the bar and the staircase leading up to the inn's rooms.

The barkeep bid them with a happy hello.

"You look rather awful. Why are you so sad?"

"It's been a long journey, and it's not even half over yet," Duncan said.

"Well, I have a Selenite bard playing tonight," the barkeep began. "You stay here; I'll ask her to play for you. Hey, Hope! You need to come downstairs!"

After a few moments, a very drowsy elven-looking woman with very long blonde hair slowly descended the stairs. Hope wore a sparkling red gown that hugged her hourglass figure. She tossed her hair and smiled. She had a mouth full of perfect white teeth. Hope pulled up a barstool and sat next to them.

With a flick of her hand, the aroma of cantrips and musky-smelling incense filled the room. With a flick of her other hand, soft inspirational music played. Hope sang happy, uplifting songs for about an hour. As with Random and Euphoria before her, Duncan and Fergus fell rapt to her charm.

Soon, they were feeling hopeful again. They paid their tabs and tipped Hope heavily for her well-timed and much-needed inspiration.

Renewed and refreshed, they unhitched their horses from the post and set off.

Chapter Twenty-Eight

CHAPTER TWENTY EIGHT

DUNHARRA

The night sky. full of stars, Dunharra stayed awake to see the Triplet Sister Moons slip below the horizon to make way for the sunrise, which painted the sky in hues of copper, gold and pink.

Dunharra observed Beyza smile about going home, but her eyes told her something different. Sad, perhaps? Anxious?

They rode the entire morning and most of the afternoon before resting the horses when they were at the top of the Thunder Hill Forest. The cool breezes that blew down from the Silver Haven Mountains were crisp and refreshing. They were close. They could see the glittering white spires of Dhangadi from where they were.

After resting the horses, they moved on and rode straight into the city. A messenger announced Beyza and the delegation's return, and

Bibek greeted them at the city gate. He remembered Duncan and Fergus from their previous meeting, and he greeted them warmly. They made introductions and exchanged pleasantries. The delegation sent their horses with several Lycaenan stable boys and followed Bibek into the city proper.

"We must speak with King Miraç and Queen Farya," Beyza bubbled. "We have great news of the library."

Attendants brought them into a large reception room and quickly supplied them with an assortment of foods, cheeses, wines, and water. After about four hours, the King and Queen of the Lycaena were available to see them. Another attendant brought them into the long and wide grand throne room. They paid their respects and waited for the invitation to speak.

"Your Majesties," Iseabail began. "We have found proof that the Lycaenan library is whole and in good condition."

"Where did they hide it?" King Miraç asked, leaning forward and eyeing each of them individually.

"The ruins of Theron's Light, down by the coast of the Wicked Shoals," Iseabail said.

"How did someone keep it intact in a ruined lighthouse?" Queen Farya asked.

"They kept it deep underground, away from the salty sea air," Iseabail explained. "A maajida also protected it."

"A maajida?" King Miraç asked, incredulous.

"Yes, Your Majesty," Iseabail continued. "The last of the family of guardians had passed. We saw her body in the library. She summoned a maajida to take over as the watchful eye over the library."

"Clever on her part," Miraç said. "She left the library protected when she could not."

"There is, however, interest in the library other than ours, Your Majesty," Beyza spoke up. She relayed the fact that King Darragh hid the library to use for his own personal gain. Specifically, he wanted The Rud Eskimiş so he could wear the Frozen Crown to rule over all Mantua. She continued, saying that someone assassinated King Darragh, Ronan seized the throne of Buckhaven, and he, too, desired the Frozen Crown.

"He searches every man, woman, and child for it," Iseabail said.

"Where is the Rud Eskimiş?"

"I have it here, Your Majesty," Beyza said and offered the book for her to see.

"So, it's true. The library exists and is intact," King Miraç said. "Beyza, return the Rud Eskimiş to our library."

"I must confess," Beyza began cautiously. "I had been in contact with Buckhaven prior to leaving on this trip."

"What communications did you have?" Farya asked, concerned.

"My sister languishes in a Buckhaven jail. If I broke up this group and foiled the return of the library, my sister would go free."

Farya's eyebrows raised, but she showed no other emotion.

"I failed, as you see, and ultimately returned the library to its rightful owners," Beyza said.

"So Buckhaven sent you to thwart the search," Miraç said.

"By Darragh himself. But I chose the library over my sister, and here we are," Beyza said.

Farya looked at Miraç who nodded.

"For your part in delaying the return of the library, I should demote you to acolyte librarian," Farya said angrily.

"No..." Beyza whispered.

"But you brought us the Rud Eskimiş, and the promise of the library returned. For that,I will only demote you to graduate librarian," Farya said.

"Thank you," Beyza said. "It is far more than I deserve."

"And," Miraç continued, "We will secure the release of your sister from the Buckhaven jail."

"By the Mother, I am forever in your debt," Beyza said, bowing to her King and Queen.

"You are free to go," Farya said.

Beyza quietly backed out of the throne room.

***

DUNHARRA

The assignment, now complete, Duncan and Fergus, the knights sent to protect them, left for Innesfrees to see their families.

Zauvadok and Anaïs turned to Iseabail and Calyx, who they expected would be the next to leave.

"I brought the Moonthorne to Innesfrees, and we found the Lycaenan library but I still need to set up diplomatic relations with the Southern Nations," Iseabail said. "So, if you'll have us, I'd love to travel back south with you."

Tup took hold of Iseabail's hand.

"So, I guess it's decided," Dunharra said. "Let's go back to the Southern Kingdoms."

They were unbothered through the Belanore Forest. They encountered the occasional bugbear and pack of wolves, but nothing unusual for the territory.

The pleasant journey ended when they encountered the first inn, The Swan. They tied their horses to the hitching post. That's when Dunharra saw it.

A wanted poster.

Her own face stared back at her. Ronan sought her, and wanted her alive, preferable to wanting her dead, but not much better. The reward made her worth a small fortune. Five thousand gold pieces for her in alive and in good condition.

Dunharra stood in front of the poster, stunned. She did not know why Ronan, who could want any number of people in Mantua, had decided on her, although she could hazard a guess. Zauvadok ripped the poster down and tore it into pieces.

They stepped over the threshold to see another wanted poster in the inn proper. The inn did not give the others a second look when they entered The Swan, but when Dunharra entered, the whole inn stopped and stared. Everyone's eye were on Dunharra, and they looked like they were deciding how to spend their reward money.

"There's another inn down the road," Zauvadok muttered.

They left The Swan for the next inn only to find more wanted posters for Dunharra.

"They're everywhere," Dunharra said, bewildered. She looked over her shoulder to make sure no one saw her next to the poster.

Zauvadok put a reassuring hand on Dunharra's shoulder. "We're here, Dun. We've got your back."

"People are recognizing me," Dunharra said. Her voice quivered, and she shook.

Anaïs put a reassuring arm around Dunharra. "Who's going to mess with a seven-foot half orc and his Dark Elf wife?"

"Or an assassin?" Tup added.

"Reformed assassin?" Iseabail asked pointedly.

"Mostly," Tup replied. "You might need my services now," Tup said.

Iseabail rolled her eyes but said, "And you have friends in high places too, dear."

"Let's try changing how you look," Tup suggested.

"How?" Dunharra asked.

"We could cut your hair," Tup said. "They're looking for a long-haired and, might I say, beautiful woman. Having short hair is one way to make a change. Throw them off the scent."

Dunharra instinctively reached up and touched her hair "How short?"

"As short as possible," Tup said. Tup reached into her boot and pulled out a razor-sharp knife. She took a handful of hair and sliced it off. And then another, then another until Dunharra's hair became pixie short.

As the hair fell onto the ground, a single tear fell from Dunharra's grass green eyes. She closed her eyes, and a tear fell to the ground, onto her hair.

"How do I look?" Dunharra asked after Tup finished.

"You look great, and I usually go for blondes," Calyx said, to nods of agreement.

Dunharra ran her fingers through her now short hair and tried to smile.

"Alright, let's go," Dunharra said, and they headed off to the next inn to rest the horses.

The Ram, an inn they visited before, on the way to Dhangadi came up next. It seemed like the perfect spot, so they hitched their horses to the post and went inside.

"You guys!" the innkeeper shouted. "You guys are back!"

"We're back," Zauvadok said. "I've seen wanted posters in other inns, but none here. Why?"

"Because I remember you guys," he said. "You caused me no trouble before. I threw them in the fire."

The innkeeper leaned closer to them and winked. "I was like you when I was a young man. Short hair looks good," he said to Dunharra. "Very different."

Relieved, they sat at the bar and ordered food and ale. They shared stories leisurely with Bruno, the innkeeper.

"I no see you," Bruno said. "You are always welcome here at Ram, but I no see you."

Chapter Twenty-Nine

CHAPTER TWENTY NINE

DUNHARRA

Dunharra eyed the Wild One who held a wanted poster in his hand. He looked around the outside of The Jolly Pecker and watched the comings and goings of the patrons. The Wild One leaned on a nearby tree and studied the women, looking for one in particular. Her.

She studied her would-be hunter. Straight brown hair pulled back into long ponytail, his sides shaved close. No shortage of weapons on him, she counted an axe, two short swords on his back and another sword at his side. Studded leather armor covered a lean, fit body, visible even through the thick cloak he wore. His breath steamed in front of his face as he breathed in the crisp air, not enough to hide the scars marring him, including the savage one running from his eye to lip. She didn't want him searching for her. Not today.

She watched him study every woman, not finding the one on the poster.

Twilight stretched along the Great Northern Road and long, deep shadows fell onto the ground. People were heading to their destinations for the night. She evaded him tonight, but she feared he would find her soon.

The Wild One bounty hunter took one last look around and entered The Jolly Pecker to get a room.

Dunharra, Zauvadok and Anaïs watched carefully until most of the stragglers were in for the night. They were concerned about a few people here and there, but one person stood out among the growing crowd of bounty hunters looking for a quick payday. Satisfied that everyone of consequence went to their rooms, they signaled Dunharra to emerge from the shadows and follow.

Tup and Iseabail watched from a manageable distance when Zauvadok and Anaïs brought Dunharra across to The Jolly Pecker. The rest of their group followed close behind. Instead of going inside The Jolly Pecker, they slipped into The Flaming Gnome. They kept Dunharra in the center to lessen the chances of being seen. Dunharra sat at a table in the corner with Anaïs and Zauvadok while Iseabail and Tup got rooms for the night. Out of caution, Dunharra would stay with Anaïs and Zauvadok, while Iseabail, Tup, and Calyx would have their own adjoining room.

"There were several people loitering and lurking outside the inns to see if you would surface," Iseabail said. "Most seem easily evaded, but one could give us trouble."

"The Wild One?" Dunharra asked.

"One and the same," Tup answered.

"Should we travel at night?" Anaïs asked.

"I don't think it will matter," Zauvadok said. "Five thousand gold is a fortune. People will search day and night. We need to stay vigilant."

Morning came much too early. The sun peeked in and out from behind clouds, making temporary passing shadows on the streets. New frost formed on the last few leaves hanging bravely on to their trees and in the grass below. The early risers crunched the frost as they walked outside, betraying their presence. Even at this early hour, there were many people about. Dunharra paced in the room while Anaïs, Zauvadok, and Tup surveyed the area. Iseabail went downstairs, ordered breakfast, and secured a table for them. Only when they knew the area was secure would Dunharra come downstairs.

Dunharra put on a brave face but jumped and startled at every noise. She felt like every eye fell on her. She ate little of her breakfast and ended up picking at it as the conversation got started.

"Where should we go?" Iseabail asked.

"We could go to Innesfrees. They would protect us," Tup said.

"Mantua is our oyster," Anaïs said. "We could go anywhere. Y'fe. Keaau."

"Ayr," Iseabail chimed in.

Dunharra's eyes darted to the door as another bounty hunter entered. He surveyed the room, then checked the portrait again. Dunharra couldn't fathom a reason why Ronan wanted her, of all people. She held her breath and tried to look as bored as possible. She tried to tamp down her rising terror, but the longer the bounty hunter lingered, the harder it became. Her skin turned clammy, her mouth went dry, and her heart raced as he compared the faces in the room to the one on the poster in his hand. She closed her eyes and asked the Mother to send him away.

His eyes lingered on Dunharra, but with her eyes closed and her pixie short hair, he decided to look elsewhere. He turned and left.

Dunharra finally exhaled. Anaïs and Iseabail each put an arm around Dunharra, and Tup offered a comforting hand.

"All this will be over soon," Iseabail said. "Let's go to Ayr. It's close to the Thunder Hill Forest, and you'll have asylum."

Dunharra walked with Anaïs and Zauvadok along the Great Northern Road, willing herself to be calm. She wanted to run. She wanted to go home. Dunharra wanted all of this to be over. Her heart beat out of her chest, and everyone looked like a threat to her.

It's like you're going home, she told herself. Although she headed somewhere else and she doubted she's ever see Mercy again. She missed her cat. That's the thought that broke her heart. Tears fell freely down her face.

Dunharra traveled with Anaïs and Zauvadok for most of the day. The sun set, and twilight fell. The Triplet Sister Moons were rising. Iseabail, Calyx, and Tup already arrived at Dunkeld and were waiting for Dunharra, Zauvadok, and Anaïs to catch up.

Zauvadok and Anaïs stopped at Dunkeld at twilight. Tears still reddened her eyes and tracked her face. Anaïs hugged her tightly and reassured her it would all turn out all right. Iseabail and Tup appeared seemingly out of nowhere and offered comforting words too.

In Dunkeld, the Wild One got a good look at Dunharra. Her hair, though cut pixie short, remained curly and black. He made no mistake. He found her.

The Wild One bounty hunter tried to pick up their trail heading north and found them getting onto the Aberdeen Trail.

The travelers were fewer on the Aberdeen Trail, and it took more stealth to blend in without arousing suspicion. Twilight moved to full-on night, so they looked for a place to camp. Now he trailed them to seize the best opportunity to take Dunharra when it arose.

***

DUNHARRA

Dunharra's eyes widened. She'd heard a noise, something he couldn't identify. It woke her out of a sound sleep and made her body scream *danger*.

She sat up, her eyes clouded with sleepy confusion as she looked around to see what caused the disturbance. It did not take her long to snap to attention and ready some magic. Her hands glowed iridescent as she tried to see in the dark.

"Hold on, lady," the bounty hunter said, trying to sound calm. "I'm not going to hurt you."

"But I'm going to hurt you," a voice from behind him said. Tup crept up behind him with a knife in each hand. "Leave. Her. Alone."

Tup swung a knife at the bounty hunter, who dodged but not quickly enough. He got a slice on his cheek that bled openly. "Goddammit!"

Zauvadok said. "I know what you want, and you can't have her."

"Why?" the Wild One asked. "Think of it, we can split the five thousand gold! We can take her in together."

Zauvadok reared back to punch The Wild One bounty hunter, but he dodged in time.

Dunharra surprised the bounty hunter, put her hands over his eyes from behind, then shocked him. He screamed then lay there unconscious. Zauvadok dragged him far from camp.

"Don't worry, Dun," Anaïs said. "We've got you."

"You're safe with us," Zauvadok said.

"I don't want any harm to come to you because of me," Dunharra said.

"Don't worry about us," Tup said.

"You're family," Anaïs said.

Following their trail would not be a problem. The wyverns that flew over them at night would pose a problem for the bounty hunter. The wyverns screeched at anything that got too close to the camp. Watching them over three nights, the Wild One estimated he had about thirty seconds from alert to ass-beating to get his job done. Thirty short seconds. He needed to break into camp, find her tent, dose her with Belleterel, tie her up, and carry her back to his horse. All in thirty seconds.

No time like the present. The bounty hunter broke the perimeter.

The wyverns started screeching.

The seconds began ticking.

The first ones out of the tent were the half orc and the dark elf. Next came the Wild One, and then Dunharra.

He dove and tackled Dunharra holding the Belleterel rag to her face until she stopped screaming and fighting. He quickly tied her hands and hoisted her over his shoulder.

"Dun!" Zauvadok growled.

"Stop!" Tup shouted in the Wild One dialect, which surprised him enough that he stopped and turned around. He winked and ran to his horse with Zauvadok, Anaïs, Iseabail, and Tup close behind him. He threw the unconscious Dunharra over the saddle and mounted. The horse reared up and he rode off with his quarry.

Chapter Thirty

CHAPTER THIRTY

AOIFE

Aoife knew something went very wrong.

Her parents paced the room like caged wild animals. She didn't understand their discussions of guerrilla warfare, but she knew that Buckhaven knights snuck into the village and set it on fire. That she understood.

She tried not to cry when her mother sat, horrified, and learned that the Buckhaven knights massacred the fire brigade that Maebh and Kieron sent to put out the flames. Every man on the brigade died.

When the Stirling knights went to defend the village the Buckhaven Knights fled into the night.

Aoife wondered what Innesfrees did to bring out such hatred from Buckhaven. Her father angrily vowed revenge.

"How could he do this to innocent people?" her father asked. "How could Ronan slaughter an entire village?"

"He did it to get to you," her mother said. "He knows he can't beat you with Stirling here, so he did what he could to hit you where he knew it would hurt you. He won't stop, not unless someone stops him."

"And that someone needs to be us," her father replied.

***

IAIN

Iain had his hands full. He set up a makeshift sickroom in the Great Hall. There were so many with smoke inhalation that the coughing cacophony wore on his very soul. But the burns worried Iain. So many burns. The traditional healers received those with minor burns, treating them with poultices and salves. Mhari's magical healers treated the more serious burns, working to rejuvenate the skin and repair the deep tissue damage.

Cries of pain mixed with incessant coughing made the noise unimaginably loud. The intense stress took a physical toll on the traditional and magickal healers alike. They fainted from the effort, and villagers were dying.

It would take months before the village would be anywhere near habitable; the damage being so complete. The Wheel kept constantly turning. Yule crept near with its freezing weather and blankets of snow. The villagers needed to be housed out of the elements.

Iain agreed when Maebh ordered the Great Hall into makeshift housing for the remaining villagers. Sanitation became an issue, so she ordered necessaries outside nearby for easy access. They set up cleaning stations to allow villagers to wash off the dirt accumulated from daily life in the castle. The close quarters were risk enough for disease. They didn't need poor sanitation to add to the problem.

While they could only spare very little time for themselves, Iain and Mhari eked out spare moments to share burdens and steal quick kisses. Eventually, Iain invited Mhari to stay with him in his private quarters, so they would have some time together that did not involve burns, coughing, fainting, or human excrement.

***

DUNHARRA

The bounty hunter's furious gallop to outrun them jarred Dunharra awake. Magnus wrenched her in between the saddle and himself so she could not move very much. She could, however, raise a knee and jab him in the kidney. That set him off balance, which set the horse off balance and nearly threw him.

"Hey. None of that, lady," the bounty hunter said and pushed her down, wedging her tighter between himself and the saddle.

"What do you want with me?" Dunharra asked, fear and realization creeping into her voice.

The bounty hunter only glanced at her and said, "You carry a hefty price, lady. That can do a lot for a man like me."

"You don't have to do this. You can let me go, no harm done."

"I let you go, I lost out on five thousand gold," he said, and spurred his horse on.

They were losing ground. They spurred their horses, not sparing them as they galloped behind him. The Wild One bounty hunter turned and saw Anaïs pull out her bow and ready an arrow. She aimed as best she could on a galloping horse and let the arrow fly.

It grazed his ear, and he swore. "By the Mother! Your companions are persistent."

"My friends will go to great lengths for my return," Dunharra warned. "It's best to let me go now."

"Five thousand gold is what's best," the Wild One said. He spurred his horse on to Dunkeld.

Dawn broke over the horizon, and he rode into the closest city; Dunkeld. Dunharra could see some people milling around and that he hoped he could vanish in the growing crowd. He spurred the horse on the rest of the way to Dunkeld and pulled the tired beast to a halt outside The Flaming Gnome and tied the horse to the post.

He hauled Dunharra off the horse and carried her over his shoulder across the street to The Jolly Pecker. She kicked and screamed. Many people watched, but no one intervened.

Zauvadok, Anaïs, Tup, and Iseabail rode at breakneck speed into Dunkeld and spotted Magnus' horse hitched to The Flaming Gnome. They ran inside and found surprised patrons and one unimpressed tavern owner, but no Dunharra.

"Zau!" The sound of Dunharra's voice faded into the background noise of Dunkeld and they couldn't discern where it came from. Upstairs? Outside? They couldn't tell.

"We'll go upstairs, and you go outside," Iseabail said. "She's here somewhere."

Anaïs and Zauvadok flew up the stairs and banged on every door. This elicited annoyed responses from several disturbed, formerly sleeping patrons. Tup, Iseabail, and Calyx ran outside only to hear a muffled shout for help.

"Help!" Dunharra's muffled screams echoed off the storefronts and taverns. Anaïs and Zauvadok exited The Flaming Gnome empty-handed but in time to hear Dun's cry for help.

"She could be in The Jolly Pecker," Tup said.

"Or she could be over at the supply shop," Anaïs said.

"We'll go to the supply shop, you check out The Jolly Pecker," Zauvadok said to Iseabail, Calyx, and Tup.

Anaïs and Zauvadok ran into the supply shop and listened carefully. No Dunharra.

Tup, Iseabail and Calyx entered The Jolly Pecker and heard a scuffle upstairs. They bounded up the stairs to hear the end of a scuffle with a muted, sleepy cry for help. And then silence.

Iseabail looked at Tup and asked, "Which room?"

"I don't know," Tup said. "Let's check all the rooms. You take that side, I'll take this side."

They checked all the rooms. Most were empty, one had two lovers annoyed at being interrupted, and the last room held silence.

Tup banged on the door. No answer came. She immediately knelt and began to pick the lock when they heard the window open. The lock sprung open, and she opened the door to see the Wild One with an unconscious Dunharra over his shoulder.

"Stop!" Tup shouted in their dialect.

The Wild One bounty hunter did indeed stop, but only for a moment before he climbed out the window and down to the ground.

Tup and Iseabail ran down the stairs in time to see him run down an alley with Dunharra over his shoulder. They gave chase. Anaïs and Zauvadok exited the supply shop when Iseabail and Tup chased Magnus into the alley. Anaïs and Zauvadok followed them down the alley.

They turned the corner to find the alley empty.

They were gone.

The bounty hunter found himself at the back of the Jolly Pecker with Dunharra over his shoulder. He turned the corner and stopped when he saw the snarling half orc approach him.

"Dunharra," Zauvadok snarled.

"She's indisposed at the moment. Maybe you should try again some other time?" the bounty hunter teased.

"Give her to me," Zauvadok growled.

"And you get the five thousand gold?" the bounty hunter asked. "I think not."

"Give her back," Zauvadok demanded.

Around the corner at the back of the building came Anaïs, Tup, and Iseabail.

"Give me five thousand gold, and she's yours," the bounty hunter said.

"Give her to me and I'll let you live," Zauvadok said.

The bounty hunter dropped Dunharra like a sack of potatoes and drew his two short swords.

Zauvadok and the bounty hunter seemed evenly suited, and they fought to a stalemate when the bounty hunter got in a lucky slice on Zauvadok's left deltoid. Dark green blood flowed down his arm.

Dunharra woke up in time to smell Zauvadok's blood. "Zau," she murmured, still foggy from the Belleterel.

Zauvadok turned to see Dunharra conscious, and took his attention off the bounty hunter. He took advantage of the opening and sliced his chest from pectoral muscle to navel. Zauvadok roared in pain.

The bounty hunter turned around to see Dunharra guarded by Tup, Anaïs, Iseabail and Calyx. Tup had two ready to throw. Anais had her staff ready, and Iseabail's eyes glowed an icy blue. He knew he had lost this round. The bounty hunter sheathed his swords and ran toward the Aberdeen Trail. He did, however, take one last look at Dunharra's green eyes before he ran. Those entrancing green eyes.

Dunharra immediately ran to Zauvadok, who knelt on the ground. Her eyes already glowing iridescent as she reached him. She touched the gash on his chest. The muscles knit back together, then the skin. With the trace of her finger, the scar vanished. She laid her hand on his left deltoid. Again, the scar vanished beneath her touch.

She stared down the Aberdeen Trail, and the bounty hunter already vanished.

"He'll be back," she said as she wearily stood.

"Let him try," Zauvadok said. "We'll be ready."

Chapter Thirty-One

CHAPTER THIRTY ONE

DUNHARRA

When they returned to camp, Dunharra watched as Anaïs called the wyverns to take their watch over them. Anaïs righted their collapsed tent, and she entered for the night with Zauvadok behind her. Tup, Iseabail, and Calyx headed to their tent, and Dunharra walked over to hers.

Dunharra crouched down, flicked back the flap, and entered the tent. She tried to scream, but the bounty hunter covered her mouth and held a knife to her neck.

"Don't scream," The Wild One bounty hunter whispered in her ear. Dunharra shook her head no. He slowly let go of her mouth but left the knife against her throat. "We can do this easily, or we can do this painfully."

Dunharra's heart pounded in her ears, and her blood ran cold. She had to think; she could not surrender to the panic. But she could only nod.

The bounty hunter grabbed her by the arm and half led and half dragged her from her tent. The wyverns turned their attention to them and alerted, but since they were already in the camp, they did not screech.

Anaïs stuck her head out of the tent but saw no one. She shrugged and climbed back into her tent.

The bounty hunter pulled Dunharra about fifty yards to the south, where he hitched his horse to a tree. He tied her hands and pulled her roughly onto his horse after he mounted. They rode away into the night.

Dunharra, shorter, smaller, and weaker than him, made overpowering her easy. As they rode toward the Great Northern Road, he had ample opportunity to smell her hair. It smelled like Keaau'an honeysuckle. He liked Keaau'an honeysuckle.

Dunharra stayed silent most of the night as they rode under the Triplet Sister Moons. She prayed to the Mother for aid and that she would live to see her friends again. Her heart broke with every gallop.

Morning broke and the bounty hunter made it to the Great Northern Road with Dunharra. He dismounted his horse, pulled Dunharra down less roughly than before, and set her on her feet. They walked into The Dodgy Diplomat and he forced her upstairs to a room. Although sparsely decorated, the room contained a bed and a cot.

"Get a nap in, Dunharra," the bounty hunter said. "We're up again at twilight."

"How can I sleep with my hands tied?" Dunharra asked, hopeful for a reprieve.

"You'll get used to it," he said and got undressed. He usually slept naked.

Dunharra got a good view of the Wild One bounty hunter. Full of muscles, disfigurement, and scars, he turned to face her, thinking to frighten or humiliate her.

Dunharra got a full frontal view of him.

"Do you like your scars?" Dunharra asked.

He saw her unimpressed face, he walked closer to her. "Each scar tells a story."

"But do you like those stories?" Dunharra asked.

"What do you think?"

"I can change that," Dunharra suggested.

"How can you change scars?" Magnus asked. "They're a permanent reminder of something that tried to kill you and failed."

"I can heal," Dunharra said as if it were a confession. "I can make the scars go away."

"Is that so?" he asked.

"Yes."

He reached down and untied her hands. Something in his stomach tingled when he touched her. He pointed to his chest. "My father gave this to me."

"What happened?"

"My father had been drinking, as usual, and took whatever happened that day out on my mother, " the bounty hunter said. "He made her black and blue when he didn't have a good day. And when he didn't have a good day, he drank his day's pay away. He did it that night. My twelve-year-old self found his sword from his days of honor, long since passed, and stood between him and his mother."

The bounty hunter paused. "There I stood, trembling, with a sword pointed at my drunken excuse for a father. Even at that young age, I could slice his chest. When my father roared in pain, I knew I had better run. My father easily relieved me of the sword and gave me a similar slice to remember the day by."

His scar tracked from his right shoulder to his abdomen.

"I don't take away memories," Dunharra warned.

"Can't or don't?" the bounty hunter asked, sharply.

"Don't." Dunharra replied. "I can, I just don't."

Her eyes glowed iridescent. His eyes grew wide as he saw the transformation in his captive. He shivered a little as she reached up and touched his fit, hairless chest. Her finger traced the scar, and it vanished under her touch. Dunharra's gentle healed him completely down to lower layers of skin. She left no trace of the scar behind. The bounty hunter watched with wide eyes and an open mouth. He touched his chest. The scar vanished, and Dunharra's eyes shifted back to green.

"What are you?" the bounty hunter asked as he backed away.

Dunharra sat back on the cot. "You don't want to know."

"Well, get some rest."

"What's your name?"

"Why the fuck do you care?"

"I'd like to know."

The bounty hunter deliberated how much he should tell her. "Magnus."

"Good night, Magnus."

Magnus grunted as he got into bed. Dunharra became confused and scared. He recoiled at her touch, but deep down, it appeared he wanted her to touch him.

Night fell when Dunharra and Magnus got back on the Great Northern Road. They shared the same horse, and he sat behind her, guiding the horse with his arms around her. She found it irritating.

"What are your plans after you deliver me to Ronan?"

"Live very well off of five thousand gold."

"And after that?" Dunharra asked, turning her head to look at him, pressing her shoulder into his chest.

"Find someone else and take them in."

"That's not a life," Dunharra said, leaning back into him.

Magnus allowed her to rest against him. Dunharra couldn't tell if he wanted her doing so, but he didn't stop her.

"Then what is a life? Settling down, have a couple younglings?" He teased her.

"No," Dunharra said, sitting up. "It's different for everyone. Some want younglings. Anaïs and Zau, I imagine will have a youngling. One day I hope to see that."

Magnus found it easier to navigate with her leaning back so he pulled her back against him. Dunharra stiffened, but gradually relaxed.

"So, what do you want?"

"I don't know," Dunharra answered honestly and with a shrug. "No one except my friends has ever been interested in me for me, you know?"

Magnus found that both hard and easy to believe. He found her remarkably beautiful, he knew it before, looking at her wanted poster, even with her hair cut so short. He thought it incredible that no one ever showed more than a passing interest in this woman. Then, he remembered what she had done the night before. Her raw power to heal. No wonder she hid that; everyone would come for her, wanting a piece of her.

They passed the rest of the night in silence.

***

ISEABAIL

The sun rose over the eastern sky, painting it shades of pink and purple. Anaïs, Zauvadok, Tup, Iseabail and Calyx woke refreshed but incomplete.

They filed down to the tavern and showed the innkeeper the wanted poster. Yes, he had seen it before, but yesterday morning he saw her.

"Yah, a Wild One kept her all right," the innkeeper said. "She kept calm, didn't cry or fuss. She didn't seem like he, uh, you know, did anything to her, either."

And indeed, they did. Many bounty hunters used their quarry to satisfy their darker desires, while they ferried them to their destinations. They were instantly relieved, but asked the innkeeper again, "You saw her *yesterday* morning?"

"Yah, sure," he said. "They stayed all day, got up, and left at dark."

"So, they're traveling by night," Zauvadok said. "That's why we are missing them."

"So do we push through for a day to catch up?" Anaïs asked.

"I think that's the only way to find her," Iseabail said.

"I'm up for it," Tup said.

They agreed they would travel all day and night to catch up to the Wild One and Dunharra. They stopped and exchanged their horses for fresh ones and started back on the Great Northern Road toward Buckhaven.

***

DUNHARRA

Magnus and Dunharra stayed on the Great Northern Road toward Buckhaven until the sun rose in the east. They rode until midmorning, when the sun had dried the dew from the grass. They found a room at The Fox's Fang, and Dunharra could see the Temple to the Mother on the island of Valide approaching on the horizon. She could hear the shoebill storks bill clattering. Magnus secured one room with a cot for the day. He brought her upstairs much more gently than yesterday. He shut and locked the door behind them.

Magnus sat her on the cot and undressed to his trousers. "Can you heal another scar?"

"Of course I can," she replied. "I can heal them all."

Magnus scoffed but held his tongue. He pointed to a scar on his face from his right eye that tracked to his upper lip.

"What happened to give you this one?" Dunharra asked.

"A drunk of a father who liked to fight," Magnus said ruefully.

"I'm sorry, Magnus. We all have scars that aren't visible."

Dunharra's eyes turned from green to iridescent. She reached up and touched the scar with her finger. She traced the jagged line from his eye all the way down to his lip. Her fingers lingered on his lip a moment longer after her eyes returned to their normal grass green.

She quickly realized, removed her hand, and sat on the cot.

Magnus strode to the crude mirror hanging on the wall and examined his face. Not a trace of the scar his father gave him remained. She made his skin smooth and intact. Even his lip. He touched his lip and remembered the sensation of Dunharra's fingers.

Magnus turned to Dunharra. "Why do you heal?"

"I...could always so this...," Dunharra began. "As a youngling I could—"

"Not that, woman," Magnus interrupted her. He did not trust himself to say her name. "You have a remarkable ability. Why do you share it?"

Dunharra thought a moment. "I had never thought of it any other way. I do it because I can, and people need it."

"You don't charge?"

"No."

"Why not?"

"Because most people can't pay," Dunharra said, growing frustrated. "They're poor. Most people I heal can barely feed themselves. I refuse to ask for money."

"To the detriment of yourself."

"I get by."

"You are an insane woman."

"Then let me go and be done with me!" Dunharra shouted, standing up face to face with him.

Her words reverberated off the walls. Magnus had never heard her shout before. He didn't know she had it in her.

"No," Magnus said. "Five thousand gold is what you're worth, and that's what I'm going to get."

"Then I am merely a means to an end for you," Dunharra said sadly.

Magnus did not reply, which Dunharra took as an affirmative. She lay down on the cot and turned her back to Magnus. Had she read him wrong?

***

ISEABAIL

Anaïs, Zauvadok, Iseabail, Calyx, and Tup surged onward toward Buckhaven. They had not seen or heard of a black-haired woman with a Wild One for an entire day. They traveled on and had the island of Valide on the horizon. The group had a choice of inns: The Fox's

Fang and The Lie, Drink, and Steel. They chose The Fox's Fang and went inside. Anaïs found a table, they sat down and ordered drinks. Dunharra and the Wild One were here or at The Lie, Drink, and Steel, and they could see the entrance from their vantage point in The Fox's Fang.

The sun sank below the horizon, and the Triplet Sister Moons were dancing, nearly full, in the sky. If Magnus kept to his habit, he would show up with Dunharra in tow within the hour. All they would have to do is wait.

Magnus woke before Dunharra, dressed, and opened the door quietly. He made it halfway down the stairs when he noticed Anaïs, Zauvadok, Iseabail, Calyx, and Tup. He froze and listened to make sure that no one discovered him. Magnus heard them speaking of Dunharra, and why Buckhaven wanted her.

"The only reason I can think of is that she healed Kieron, and Ronan wants revenge," Anaïs said.

"Or maybe he wants her to keep him alive?" Tup asked. "They're at war with Innesfrees and there will be ample opportunities to make attempts on his life."

Magnus crept back up the stairs and entered the room he shared with Dunharra. He found her awake and sitting on the cot. He said, "Your friends are downstairs, watching for you."

Dunharra's face turned instantly hopeful and bright. She stood and tried to run for the door. Magnus grabbed her and threw her onto the bed.

"However, I can't have you tipping them off," Magnus said as he pulled out more Belleterel, wet a rag, and held it to her face.

"Anaïs!" Downstairs, they could barely hear Dunharra's muffled screams. "Zau!" Her scream became more muffled and much quieter. Another moment longer, and she fell unconscious.

Magnus tied her hands and used the bed linens to climb out the window.

Iseabail frowned as Anaïs held up her hand for quiet; she heard something.

"Shit! She's upstairs!" She stood up and ran up the stairs. The rest of them followed and flew up the stairs behind her. They found the door open and ran inside. Once inside they found the window open with the bed linens tied in knots and hanging out the window. Zauvadok looked out the window to see Magnus ride away with an unconscious Dunharra in the saddle with him.

"He's got her and he's riding toward the Disputed Lands!" Zauvadok shouted as he raced down the stairs.

Tup sniffed the air. She searched around and found the wet rag.

"What is it, Tup?" Iseabail asked.

"He's drugging her with Belleterel," Tup said. She pocketed the bottle.

They sprinted down the stairs and ran out of The Fox's Fang. The group unhitched their horses from the post and gave chase. They passed the island of Valide and followed Magnus to the Disputed Lands. He headed to the bridge on the Royal Western Road when he stopped and turned around. He shouted, "Keep following me if you want her dead!"

"Give her back if you want to live!" Zauvadok shouted back.

Magnus turned around and crossed the Royal Western Road Bridge and entered the Disputed Lands. The darkness swallowed them whole, and they vanished.

They followed him over the bridge and into the darkness.

In the complete darkness, all they could only follow the sound of Magnus' horse; they were riding blind.

"Iseabail?" Anaïs asked. "Can you give us some light?"

"Absolutely."

Iseabail's ink on her right shoulder glowed with her heartbeat, and above them formed a foot-wide ball of light that illuminated the dense forest.

They looked ahead of them and saw they were following a riderless horse. They reined in their horses and came to a stop.

"He must have pulled her off somewhere near the entrance to the Disputed Lands," Zauvadok said as he watched the riderless horse fade into the darkness.

"Let's double back and see if we can pick up a trail," Iseabail said.

***

DUNHARRA

Dunharra began to rouse from the Belleterel, but the fall to the ground finished the job. She fully woke up. Magnus covered her mouth to keep her from screaming but the knife to her throat kept her silent.

"They're following the horse in the darkness," he began. "Soon, they'll figure it out and double back to look for us."

"Let me go," Dunharra pleaded. "You don't want me; you want the money."

Magnus drew close to her face. "No. It used to be the money, but now—"

"Now?" Dunharra asked, incredulous.

Magnus put away his knife and untied her wrists. "Come with me," he asked. Not a command. Not an order. "Please."

He held out his hand and Dunharra reluctantly took it. Magnus ran, but in the dense forest, they didn't get far. He tried to find a trail, but it found it impossible in the dark. Magnus pulled her along for a few minutes, but eventually sat on a downed tree to wait the night out. He did not let her hand go.

"Dunharra," Magnus said. He had no other words.

Magnus reached up and caressed her face. He traced her cheekbone with his thumb.

"I don't know what you've done to me," Magnus said. "What are you?"

Magnus did not move his hand. "You make me feel things," Magnus began. Things I haven't felt in years. Your touch gives me tingles."

"Magnus," Dunharra said and reached up to touch his hand.

"Awww, ain't that cute," a voice from behind them said.

They both turned around, shocked that someone came up behind them.

A human male, bulky, burly, and armed with a nasty-looking sword, stood behind them. "I'll be takin da lady now, boy."

"No," Magnus said, pushing Dunharra behind him. "No, you won't." He drew his two swords and stood ready.

The burly man laughed. "Awww, you is cute. Two widdle swords."

"She's mine," Magnus said.

"Not for long," the burly man said.

Their swords clanged in the night, and the sound carried across the Disputed Lands. The noise drew Zauvadok and the others. They turned around and rode toward it.

"Dun, we're coming!" Anaïs shouted.

Dunharra had a tightness in her chest and a sinking feeling in her stomach. Her chance to escape came now, but she doubted she could outrun either of them. She had to try. She broke into a sprint toward what she thought were her friends.

"Dunharra! No!" Magnus shouted, but he tried to warn her too late. She ran straight into the arms of another burly man, who laughed.

"Got her!" he chuckled. "You were right. This required no effort at all."

"Let her go," Magnus threatened. "And you'll live."

"Oh, bounty hunter, worry about yourself," the first burly man said.

"Bring it," Magnus said.

The second burly man picked up a kicking and screaming Dunharra.

Magnus spun and sliced the throat of the first burly man and he fell to the ground, dead. "Let her go!"

The second burly man pulled a dagger from his boot and held it up to Dunharra's neck. Dunharra stopped kicking and froze. She remained perfectly still. The second burly man took two steps backward when Magnus dropped his swords and held his hand out.

"Don't hurt her. Drop the dagger and let her go."

The man pushed the tip of the dagger further into her neck, eliciting a stifled gasp from Dunharra.

"Not giving up on five thousand gold," the second man said. "She's coming with me."

The burly man threw the dagger he formerly held up to Dunharra's neck at Magnus, impaling it in the right side of his chest. He fell to the ground, gurgling and coughing bright purple blood.

"Magnus!" Dunharra squirmed to break free of the burly man but she couldn't. Being bigger and stronger made his job easier. "Let me heal him! Let me go!"

The man laughed and threw her over his shoulder and walked toward Buckhaven.

***

ISEABAIL

Anaïs, Zauvadok, Iseabail, and Tup arrived to find Magnus with a dagger between his chest and shoulder, and bleeding. He breathed but didn't move. Blood trickled from his mouth.

Iseabail climbed down and examined him. "He's got a dagger to the chest."

"Anyone got any healing in them?" Zauvadok asked.

"Why should we heal him?" Anaïs asked as she kicked him. "He's the reason Dunharra's gone."

When Anaïs kicked him he groaned and coughed up more blood.

"He can tell us a lot," Tup said. "Like who has her now and where they're going."

"Fine," Anaïs said with a sour look. "Who has any healing ink?"

"Not me," Tup said, holding up her hands. "Not my line of work."

"I have a little, but not enough for that," Iseabail said, pointing to the dagger in his chest.

"I'm right here," the bounty hunter whispered. "I can hear you."

"Good," Zauvadok said. "That means you're not dead. Yet. What's your name?"

"Magnus."

Zauvadok dismounted his horse and pulled the knife out of his chest. This elicited an agonizing howl from Magnus, and fresh bright purple blood flowed from the wound.. "Iseabail, do what you can."

Iseabail's eyes turned an icy blue as ink on her fingers pulsed in time with her heartbeat. She touched his wound and the flow of purple blood stopped. She could not close the wound or repair any internal damage.

"That's all I have," Iseabail said, sitting Magnus up gently. He coughed more blood.

Zauvadok grabbed Magnus by the armor and hoisted him up to standing.

"Tell me right now where she's gone," Zauvadok growled nose to nose with Magnus.

"I don't know," Magnus replied, pained. "But if I were him, I'd go straight to Buckhaven."

"Alright, let's go," Zauvadok said.

They got up and mounted their horses.

"Take me with you," Magnus pleaded. "I need to find her."

"Why should we, bounty hunter?" Anaïs asked as she punched his wound. It started to ooze blood again, mostly undoing Iseabail's healing work. Magnus cried out and doubled over in pain.

"You have no reason to," Magnus admitted between wheezing gasps. "I've done nothing to make you trust me. But Dunharra. There is something special about her."

"You got that right," Anaïs said. "If you only knew how special she is, you'd never have done this."

She punched him over his wound again, which elicited a cry of pain and sent him back about a yard.

"She healed two of my scars," Magnus said. "Her touch. It's intoxicating."

"Alright, we get it," Zauvadok said, rolling his eyes. "Come on."

"Are you serious right now, Zau?" Anais asked. "We're taking him with us?"

"He saw who took her. He's the best chance we've got to get Dun back. If he steps out of line, he dies."

"This is going to hurt," Zauvadok said.

"Magnus?" Tup asked. "If you still have any Belleterel, you could use it to lessen the pain."

"Good idea, Tup," Zauvadok agreed.

"How did you—?"

"It's my line of work," Tup said. "Or it used to be. Hopefully, my days of killing are over, or soon will be. You left the rag soaked with it in The Fox's Fang in your rush to get away."

"Alright, take the Belleterel," Zauvadok said. "We have hard riding to do."

Chapter Thirty-Two

CHAPTER THIRTY TWO

DUNHARRA

Dunharra kicked and screamed and pounded on the burly man's back. He rewarded her with an annoying slap on the ass. But her elbow to the back of his head made him drop her. She scrambled to her feet and ran in the opposite direction.

"Bitch!" the burly man shouted and ran after her. He ran much slower because of his size and Dunharra easily outpaced him. The burly man picked up rocks and hurled them at the sprinting Dunharra. One hit her in the back, one hit her in the shoulder which knocked her off balance. The third and largest hit the back of her head. Dunharra fell like a sack of potatoes.

He huffed and puffed as he got to where she lay. The burly man nudged her with his foot to see if she responded. He got no response. He turned her over and shook her shoulders and still got no response. A pool of red blood formed underneath her head.

The burly man pulled out the wanted poster and re-read it. The poster clearly stated that she needed to be both alive and well.

He got a good look at Dunharra and backed away, horrified. He dropped the wanted poster on the ground next to her. The burly man wanted to be far away when someone discovered her. He left her lying there in the Disputed Lands alone and ran off.

The Triplet Sister Moons were sliding under the horizon and the sun had not fully breached it when they found her. She lay motionless on the ground. Vultures gathered at the side of the road. They reined their horses to a stop and dismounted as fast as they could. The vultures flapped their black wings and flew up into nearby trees.

Anaïs got there first and looked Dunharra up and down. She didn't look as if she fell from a horse, but Anaïs swore when she noticed her blood-soaked hair and the pool of blood around her head and shoulders. The blood matted her black ringlets and stained her linen shirt.

"Goddammit! Someone bashed her head in!" Anaïs cried. She glared at Magnus as if he allowed this to happen. She stood and punched Magnus in his wound again. He cried out in pain and coughed up more blood.

Zauvadok knelt down and gently shook her shoulders. "Dun, honey, its time to wake up."

Magnus tried to dismount and ended up falling face first onto the ground with a grunt. He coughed up blood into the dirt.

Dunharra scrunched her eyes and wrinkled her nose but did not open her eyes. "My head hurts."

"I know," Anaïs said, her voice soft and soothing. "It's time to get better, sweetie."

"My head hurts," Dunharra whispered again. She breathed deeply and evenly.

Magnus stumbled over to where Dunharra lay on the ground. Zauvadok roughly held him back. "Wait. She'll be fine now."

"But how?" Magnus asked, his voice pained and cracking. "We have to help her!"

Dunharra's eyes opened wide and glowed with iridescent light. She breathed regularly and deeply.

"What the fuck is that?" Magnus asked. "How long will it last?"

"As long as it takes," Iseabail said.

After a minute, Dunharra's eyes turned her normal grass green. She blinked and turned her head to look at Anaïs and Zauvadok. She smiled. "Hi."

"Dunharra!" Magnus exclaimed. He squirmed past Anaïs and Zauvadok and cupped her face in his hands.

Dunharra smiled. "You're alright?" She looked him up and down. "You're not alright."

Before he could argue, she placed her hand upon his chest, and her eyes glowed with the same iridescent light. Dunharra closed the laceration to his lung and drained it of blood, making it easier for him to breathe. She knit the muscles and brought the skin together. She took her finger and traced the scar and it vanished under her touch. Dunharra blinked, and her eyes returned to their normal green.

"That scar's gone too," Dunharra said with a small but satisfied smile.

The sun barely breached the horizon when they left the Disputed Lands and made their way up the Great Northern Road. They stopped at The Fox's Fang to rest the horses, regroup, and plan.

***

RONAN

Ronan fumed. Five thousand gold did not produce the healer. Rumors spread that someone killed her in an attempt to bring her to him. He needed to know the truth.

The healer couldn't be dead.

He could only spare a squad of knights after the war with Innesfrees, so he had new wanted posters doubling the reward for her drawn up and sent two of his spies out get the word on the street.

After hearing she survived an attack in the Disputed Lands, Ronan sent soldiers to bring her in.

***

DUNHARRA

Together, they decided they would try again to go to Ayr. Dunharra liked the idea of diplomatic protection from the Mountain Elves.

They set off on the Great Northern Road and made it past the island of Valide, when they rested the horses. When they got back on the road, they made it halfway to Dunkeld when they needed to rest for the night. They stopped at The Ram.

"Ah! My favorite guests return to me!" Bruno happily shouted from behind the bar. "Come! Sit!" he said and offered the table closest to the bar. "You has a new person. Hello new person!"

The unexpected attention made his face flush. "Magnus," he said shyly.

"Hello, Magnus! Whatcha I get for you?"

They placed their orders and asked about rooms. "I have three rooms only," Bruno said.

"We need four," Anaïs said.

"Three will be fine," Dunharra interrupted. "It'll be alright."

Zauvadok growled at Magnus. "Keep your hands to yourself."

Magnus held up his hands. "Not a problem."

They ate and enjoyed their time with Bruno, who told them stories of his homeland in Manasquan where there were cities built on waterways and people traveled by fancy canoes.

When it came time to call it a night, Zauvadok pulled Magnus aside.

"What are your intentions?" Zauvadok demanded in a hushed tone.

"What do you mean?" Magnus answered. He had a pretty good idea what Zauvadok meant, but wanted him to make him say it.

"With Dunharra, you ridiculous fuck," Zauvadok said, irritation creeping into his voice. "I'll make it real simple for you, Magnus. Don't get any ideas about gaining her trust and then betraying her to the highest bidder."

"I'll be honest; it used to be like that," Magnus began. "I only wanted her for the money."

"You hurt her in any way, I kill you. Understand?"

"Got it," Magnus said, and watched Zauvadok head up to his room with Anaïs.

Tup, Calyx and Iseabail glared at him as they went upstairs together.

Magnus walked up to Dunharra. "You've got protective friends."

"Yes," she said. "They're good people, Magnus."

"Shall we?" Magnus offered his arm for Dunharra to hold. She reluctantly took his arm, and they climbed the stairs together. They entered their room, and he locked the door behind them.

The small room boasted only a bed. One bed.

Magnus and Dunharra looked at each other, and back to the bed.

"You're safe with me," Magnus said holding up his hands. "No funny business, I promise."

"Zauvadok threatens everyone who tries to get close to me," Dunharra said. "His heart is in the right place."

"He's pretty good at it," Magnus said. "I imagine that it's worked, too."

Dunharra suppressed a chuckle. "One hundred percent of the time."

"So, you've never been—?"

"Never. You?"

"I've converted my fair share of virgins," Magnus said.

Dunharra threw her head back and laughed. "I've never heard it put quite in that way! I've always wondered why men think their penis is so important that they think it can change who a woman is."

"I have to tell you that you are exceedingly safe with me in that regard," Magnus said, his face suddenly dark.

"Why does that sadden you?"

"I am broken."

"How?"

"Five years ago, I converted a virgin," Magnus began. "Her parents were long since gone, since younglinghood. She only had her older brother. I took a shine to her. Anneli and I were inseparable. On the morning of Beltane, she surprised me with a gift of a small silver rattle; her way of telling me she became pregnant. We were happy, of course, and made plans to be handfasted. But her brother found out."

"Ooh, that doesn't sound good," Dunharra said.

"No. Her brother never approved of us, but he tolerated me. But when he found out our plans, he erupted in rage. I refused to leave her, so he kidnapped me and held me hostage, then told Anneli that I had left her. That I packed my things and moved away."

"That's horrible," Dunharra said, laying a hand on his arm. He did not take it away.

"When she thought I left her, she took floripon." Magnus collected his composure.

Dunharra knew of floripon. Many people used it as an abortifacient. Dangerous if misused, it needed to be managed closely by a midwife. The results could be devastating.

"But she took too much." He choked back tears. "She lost the baby, and she bled to death. She delivered a girl. In my heart I named the baby Ulla."

When Dunharra looked stunned, Magnus paused for a moment. He drank in her touch when she caressed his cheek with her thumb She wiped away a lone tear.

"When Anneli died, her brother blamed me," Magnus continued. "He had me beaten and tied to a wooden chair. A beating I could take, but what he did next would change me forever."

"What did he do?" Dunharra asked, horrified.

"He stripped me of my pants," Magnus said, and took both of Dunharra's hands in his. "He said he was going to make sure I never did this to anyone else ever again. Then he tied my legs to the legs of the chair. He took two carpenter's nails and a hammer."

Tears fell freely from his eyes as he relived the memory. His face showed the terror of the event.

"He took the hammer and the nails...and nailed my penis to the chair. He left me there to die," Magnus said. "And I gladly would have. I lost Anneli and Ulla, but one of his friends later came back and freed me from that chair. I left Kjalla, and have never been back."

Horror gripped Dunharra. The only words that would come were, "I'm sorry."

"I could never function since," Magnus said. "So, you are safe with me."

Dunharra hugged him and wiped the tears on his cheek away with her thumb. His eyes met Dunharra's, and he said, "I have never told this to anyone before."

"Thank you for trusting me with this," Dunharra said as she held his hand. "Your pain is safe with me."

***

ISEABAIL

The sun silently slipped over the horizon, and rays of golden sunlight beamed through the window. The light illuminated Tup and Iseabail's bare skin as they slept together, entwined in a loving embrace. They nuzzled each other as they resisted waking, and Iseabail kissed Tup's forehead.

"Good morning, darling."

"Good morning," Iseabail whispered. "I don't want to get up."

"Neither do I. I could stay here in your arms forever."

They delayed the start of their day by another hour, cuddling and talking. They lazily got out of bed and dressed, thinking they would delay everyone else, but arrived downstairs in the tavern first. Bruno came up to them with a worried look on his face. "You need to wake them up. All them."

"What's wrong, Bruno?" Iseabail asked.

"Some people came by very early," he began. "Wants know about Dunharra. I send away, but they will come back."

"Oh shit," Tup said as she stood. "I'll get them." Tup ran up the stairs.

"What did they ask you, Bruno?" Iseabail asked.

"They ask about Dunharra and now they offer ten thousand gold," he said. "And Buckhaven soldiers were with them."

"Buckhaven?" Iseabail cried. "By the Mother."

Zauvadok, Anaïs, Dunharra, and Magnus came running down the stairs with Tup close behind them. Zau asked, "What?"

"Ronan's getting serious," Iseabail said. "Buckhaven soldiers came by early this morning, with the promise of coming back. And he doubled the reward."

"Ten thousand gold?" Anaïs spat. "That's a fortune. A literal fortune." She cast a side eye glare at Magnus.

Dunharra's shoulders sagged, and she sighed. Magnus put his arm around her, which she leaned into. Iseabail saw Zauvadok glare at Magnus, but he did not remove his arm.

"We got you," Iseabail said.

"You go," Bruno said. "They'll be back soon. I don't see you."

Dunharra hugged Bruno tightly. "Thank you."

They filed out of The Ram after leaving a hearty tip. They searched around, and seeing no one suspicious and no Buckhaven guards, they headed north toward the Aberdeen Trail.

In formation, a squad of ten soldiers marched; their superior officer dispatched them to search every dive, inn, tavern, brothel, and drug den from Innesfrees to Dundalk, and further, if needed. They had orders to enter the Thunder Hill Forest and search the Aberdeen Trail.

News of the Buckhaven military search spread like wildfire, and the villagers were unhappy. They resisted. People fought back, and authorities made many arrests. Buckhaven knights harassed several diminutive black-haired women, bringing them to Buckhaven, only to release them and leave them stranded in an unfamiliar land after realizing they were not Dunharra. As the knights encroached north, the resentment built to a near fever pitch. Townspeople fought the knights, causing near riots. Some of the townspeople started hunting for Dunharra to get the knights out of their villages and to be left alone.

The doubled reward incentive became too tempting to pass up.

The group acquired fresh horses and rode toward the Aberdeen Trail. They got as far as their previous campsite, when they saw the banners for Buckhaven. They turned around and went back toward the Great Northern Road and saw another set of banners for Buckhaven.

Buckhaven knights encircled them. Iseabail spoke first. "Let us pass. We have no business with Buckhaven."

"We are here to collect one Dunharra Tor," one knight said.

Dunharra stifled a gasp.

"No, you're not," Zauvadok said, drawing his sword.

"Her presence is required by King Ronan," the knight said.

"Where she goes, I go," Iseabail said.

"And where they go, I go," Zauvadok said.

"And I," Magnus said with the others.

"Have it your way," the knight said, rolling his eyes and shaking his head. "You all come with us."

Ten knights surrounded them, and they rode hard all the way to Buckhaven. When they arrived, they were relieved of their horses and weapons. The knights brought them to the receiving parlor to wait. They were morose and silent. Whatever Ronan wanted could not be good. Unlike their last wait in the same receiving parlor, nobody offered them food or drink.

After what seemed like hours, the door opened and Sylvestre slipped in. He said, "Well, well, well...look what the cat dragged in."

"If you want to avoid an international incident, you will let us be on our way," Iseabail began. "You have no right to detain us."

"You are free to go," Sylvestre said dismissively. "Dunharra, however, is a guest of His Majesty."

"What does he want me for?" Dunharra asked, afraid of the answer.

"He wishes to converse with you," Sylvestre said.

"She is not a citizen of Buckhaven," Iseabail said, unfazed. "You can't order her around like this."

"And yet, here we are," Sylvestre said with a smarmy look on his face, full of self-satisfaction.

"When you detained us—" Iseabail started.

"Her. We detained her. You chose to come along," Sylvestre interrupted, pointing at Dunharra for emphasis.

"Regardless, we were on our way to Ayr," Iseabail said. "She has requested asylum from the Mountain Elves."

"Oh my," Sylvestre said as he held a hand to his mouth sarcastically. "And how has Padraig responded?"

"I am the Ambassador to the Southern Nations of Innesfrees, Buckhaven, and Cobh," Iseabail stated, eyes narrowed and mouth snarled. "I have the power to grant asylum, and I have."

"I'll make sure it's noted," Sylvestre said, eyes rolling.

"Good," Iseabail said. "This is not over."

"You may wait here," Sylvestre said. "Dunharra, follow me."

Chapter Thirty-Three

CHAPTER THIRTY THREE

AOIFE

As Iain concentrated on the makeshift infirmary in the great hall, Aoife had ample free time. She accompanied her parents when a squad of ten soldiers from Buckhaven descended on the village and set fire to the repairs.

This time, Innesfrees stood ready. Fifteen Innesfrees knights ambushed Buckhaven, exchanging arrows from behind trees, rocks, and the village ruins. When seven of the Buckhaven soldiers fell, the rest fell back. The battle left six Innesfrees soldiers dead, seven Buckhaven soldiers killed, and three taken hostage. Buckhaven soldiers destroyed the meager repairs to the village, but this time they had soldiers to question.

Aoife watched as her father studied the battle plans intently. Ten of his best knights trained by the Beit Shemesh in guerrilla tactics were ready for his order to begin. They had a new weapon for this raid: a projectile weapon containing caustic chemicals that exploded when mixed. Lithium bombs, the Beit Shemesh called them. They would throw them at the target, and the bombs would explode on contact.

From her father, she understood he planned for his knights to gain entry to Buckhaven, traverse the villages, and make it to the castle proper. They would throw the lithium bombs at the castle door and gain entry. Then, cause as much destruction as possible and get out within ten minutes.

She learned the realities of war, and she didn't like it.

Aoife heard the sad tension in her father's voice as he said, "Send the knights."

***

DUNHARRA

Sylvestre led Dunharra to the throne room and introduced her to King Ronan.

"So, you are the famed Dunharra Tor," Ronan said.

"I don't know about the 'famed' part, Your Majesty, but I am her," she replied.

"I hear you healed Prince Regent Kieron of his injuries."

"That is true," Dunharra replied, careful not to divulge too much information. Answer only the question asked. No more.

"How did you do it?"

"I'm a healer," Dunharra retorted. "It's what I do."

"But how?" Ronan persisted.

"That's like asking, how do you breathe?" Dunharra said. "I do it."

The conversation stalled and he seemed annoyed. "Is there anything you cannot heal?"

Silence.

"I asked you a question!" His words echoed off the marble walls and floor of the throne room.

"There is nothing beyond my scope," Dunharra said. He balled his fist. Her calm demeanor in the face of his interrogation infuriated him.

"Do you know what you are?" Ronan sneered.

Dunharra's blood ran cold. She tried not to show it. She tried to control her heart as it beat against her chest. This was it. She dreaded this all along.

"What am I?"

"An asset," he whispered as he leaned forward.

He stood up and walked down the dais and stood right in front of her. He took his hand and tilted her chin up, so she could look him in the eye. "My asset."

"I am not a toy, Your Majesty," Dunharra protested.

"No," Ronan replied, making Dunharra's skin crawl. "You are much more than that."

Ronan cupped her cheek and ran his thumb over her cheekbone.

She reached up and removed his hand.

"Insolent woman! I am the King!"

"Kings shouldn't need to remind people who they are. Their behavior should speak for itself."

"You will be my guest until further notice," Ronan mocked her. He turned and walked away from her and sat down again on his throne. "Sylvestre!"

Sylvestre stepped out of the shadows. "Yes, Your Majesty?"

"Show Dunharra the utmost kindness," he said. "She will be our guest."

"Of course, Your Majesty,"Sylvestre began. "She has...guests."

"They can do nothing of consequence. If they insist, let them stay," Ronan said, unfazed.

Sylvestre gently took Dunharra's arm and led her back to the receiving parlor, where they waited impatiently for her.

***

DUNHARRA

Sylvestre reentered and said, "If you still insist on remaining with the Lady Tor, King Ronan, out of the kindness of his heart, will allow you to join her in the guest quarters."

"The Lady Tor?" Dunharra asked, incredulous. "My name is Dunharra."

"Yes, of course, Lady Tor. Follow me to the guest quarters."

He led them through cool, dimly lit corridors. They felt as though they were climbing higher into one of the spires, their footsteps echoing off the bare walls. Sconces were lit with short torches with essential oils to give the guest quarters an attractive aroma of cedarwood and lemon.

Sylvestre stopped in front of three rooms, each with wide double doors and arches. He offered Dunharra the first choice of rooms. She chose the right, and invited Magnus to stay with her. Anaïs and Zauvadok chose the center room, and Tup, Iseabail, and Calyx took the room on the left. Knights stood sentry outside the doors.

Dunharra sat on the bed, and Magnus sat on the chair.

"What does Ronan want with you?" Magnus asked.

"He asked how I healed Kieron," Dunharra began. "How I did it. He knows there's something different about me, but he can't put a finger on what."

“Why did you decide not to take me to Ronan?” Dunharra asked.

“When I looked in your eyes, I knew you were different,” Magnus said.

“Flirt,” Dunharra playfully accused.

“Guilty,” Magnus said. “But seriously, what does he want from you?”

“I don’t know,” Dunharra said with a shrug. “He’s obsessed with my healing of Kieron.” Maybe he thinks—”

“Thinks what?” Magnus asked, joining her on the bed.

Dunharra made room for him, feeling butterflies in her stomach. She looked at him and shyly glanced away. “That I’ll keep him alive, like Kieron.”

Dunharra told Magnus how she healed Kieron after three arrows struck him in the chest.

“Why did you change your mind about me?” Dunharra asked, looking up at him.

“Your eyes,” Magnus said. “I couldn’t get your eyes out of my mind. They’re so passionate, but pure and brilliant.”

Dunharra gave him the side eye. “I bet you said that to some virgins you converted.”

Magnus blushed.

Dunharra lay on the bed, and Magnus did the same. She curled up with one of the many pillows.

“You,” Magnus finally said. “Your touch made me shiver in a way I never felt before. The way you healed my scars when you were my captive and never asked for anything in return.”

“Want me to heal another one?” Dunharra asked.

Magnus caressed her face and gazed in her eyes. “Being with you is more than enough.”

Magnus leaned in to kiss Dunharra, but the door banged open against the wall and a Buckhaven knight entered the room. Magnus asked with a growl. "Don't you guys knock?"

"There is a wounded squire," the knight said. "I am to bring the Lady Tor."

"My name is Dunharra. Oh, by the Mother, let's go," she said. "Magnus?"

"Let's do it," Magnus said.

The soldier led them to the practice yard, where the knights trained and occasionally jousted. A jousting match injured a young squire, who bled profusely on the ground.

"What happened?" Dunharra asked as she ran and knelt beside the boy.

"He took a sword to the chest," a knight said. "He should never have entered the fight."

"Whose squire is this?"

"Mine, my lady," a knight came forward. "I take responsibility."

Dunharra immediately knelt down in front of the boy. Her eyes glowed with an iridescent light. She put her hand on the boy's chest. The severity of the injury concerned Dunharra; if she had arrived later, it would have killed him. She repaired the nick in his ascending aorta and stopped the bleeding. He needed some blood volume, so she next concentrated on building that up. After about five minutes, the color came back to the boy's face. She traced her finger over the scar, and it vanished under her touch.

When the scar vanished, the knights, who circled the boy and watched Dunharra work, let out a collective gasp. Dunharra scowled at the knight who bowed his head and stared at the ground.

"You should be ashamed of how you treat your squire. Where are all your healers?" Dunharra then asked, stunned and disgusted that no one attended the boy.

"Gone, my lady," another knight said. "Fled or died on the battlefield."

Dunharra felt saddened but not surprised at the state of healers in Buckhaven.

"Take us back to my room," Dunharra told the knight who brought her here.

"Of course, my lady," the knight said.

Dunharra rolled her eyes. Magnus offered his arm, which she took, and they walked back to their room.

"I suppose Ronan could have put me in a more desolate place," Dunharra said, sitting dejected on the bed. Magnus sat next to her.

"I'm sorry this is happening," he said. He put an arm around her, and she laid her head on his shoulder. "You seem tired."

"When people are near death, like that boy, it can take a little out of me to heal," Dunharra said. "I have a lot in me, and by a lot I mean a lot, but sometimes I need rest."

"Then let's lie down and let you rest," Magnus suggested.

Dunharra and Magnus got comfortable. Now Dunharra blushed. She remembered how close they came to kissing before the knight interrupted them. Magnus smiled. He caressed her face with his hand and peered directly into her grass green eyes.

"Magnus, there's something I think I should tell you," Dunharra said, enjoying his touch.

"What is it, Dunharra?" Magnus asked. He pulled her close to him.

"Up north, by Hijo and Marin, does the Prophecy of the Healer exist there?"

"No, what is that?" Magnus asked. Even during his time in the Southern Kingdoms, he hadn't heard of such a thing.

Dunharra told Magnus the story: hundreds of years ago, Good Witch Eibhlin came to King Ninian the Bold and foretold the coming of a healer who could heal anything. Any injury, any illness, even death could not interfere with her touch.

Magnus listened intently. "That's an intense prophecy, Dunharra."

Dunharra only nodded and avoided his gaze.

"What are you trying to tell me, Dunharra?" Magnus asked gently, getting her to meet his eyes again. "Are you trying to find this healer? Are you sick?"

"No," is all Dunharra could say.

She only said the words out loud once before, to Anaïs and Zauvadok. Her fear of how he would react made her mouth run dry. Dunharra's heart pounded in her chest, and her breathing became shallow and quick. Her stomach fluttered, and she felt as though her entire world would change in that instant.

Because it would.

Do I know him well enough? Would he keep me safe? Would he keep my secret?

"Whatever it is, Dunharra, I'm solid," Magnus said. "I'm not going anywhere if you're sick."

"Magnus, I am that healer," she said. The words rushed out, and before she knew it, she told him.

"You're what?"

Chapter Thirty-Four

CHAPTER THIRTY FOUR

ISEABAIL

Tup and Iseabail lounged on the bed for a good hour before taking up any sort of activity. They began with sultry looks that lingered, then that led to a flirtatious kiss. Dare they in their cute confinement? Yes, they absolutely would.

They lay together in bed, enjoying the afterglow, when Iseabail realized they were in adjoining rooms. She chided herself for only now realizing it.

Tup immediately started looking at the windows, which were nailed in place. She felt the wall for the inevitable draft that comes with secret doors. She felt the walls and then smiled. An easy find, but a hard push. Even with Iseabail helping.

Iseabail could hear Anaïs and Zauvadok searching the room for any way to escape. They examined the windows, which were nailed shut, and felt the walls for latches, secret hinges or anything that would conceal a secret door. When Iseabail and Tup began pushing the door, Anaïs and Zauvadok were silent, and she assumed they were ready to pounce on whoever came through the wall.

They were ready to strike when Iseabail peeked her head inside.

"By the Mother," Zauvadok said. "We searched for an hour!"

"Don't feel bad, Zauvadok," Tup said from behind Iseabail. "It took me a couple of tries to find it too. Comes with the job."

"So, if there's a door between our two rooms, logic would dictate there would be a door between the other room as well," Iseabail speculated.

Tup began the search for the door to Magnus' and Dunharra's room.

***

DUNHARRA

Dunharra sighed. It all came down to this. She expected him to leave.

Magnus sat up, absorbing the news. Dunharra's eyes welled with tears, thinking the worst. Her heart leapt into her throat and her stomach tied itself in knots.

The floor made a harsh, grinding sound and the wall opened. They both looked over at it, surprised. Anaïs and Zauvadok followed by Tup and Iseabail walked through the hidden door. Dunharra and Magnus visibly relaxed but the tension in the room lingered.

"Oh, we interrupted something," Anaïs said.

"Yeah, a murder," Zauvadok said as he got a good look at Dunharra's broken-hearted face. He pushed past Anaïs and flew over to the bed, grabbing Magnus.

"I promised you I would kill you," Zauvadok said as he grabbed his neck and squeezed.

"No," Magnus squeaked. His face turned purple, and he gripped Zauvadok's hand, trying to get him to release the fierce grasp.

"She told me," he rasped. He lost oxygen to his brain fast.

"She told you what?" Zauvadok roared and slammed his head against the marble wall.

"Healer. The Healer," Magnus managed to squeak out before he lost consciousness.

Zauvadok threw him on the bed with a snarl. "What did he do?"

"I told him," Dunharra whispered.

Anaïs sat on the bed with Dunharra and looked at her like she'd lost her mind. "Honey, you what?"

Dunharra leaned forward and touched Magnus' neck to heal the damage Zauvadok's rage inflicted. She repaired the bruised trachea and vocal cords, as well as the large vessels in his neck. She touched his temples with her fingertips and worked to reverse the oxygen deprivation. Dunharra also healed the closed skull fracture and concussion from the impact with the marble wall. When she finished, her eyes returned to their normal grass green.

Magnus woke with a start. He looked around and saw Dunharra and smiled. He lifted his hand and caressed her face.

"I know you said you would kill me, but I didn't think you'd try so soon," Magnus said to Zauvadok.

"I didn't think you'd make her cry so soon, idiot."

"I'm not crying," Dunharra said indignantly.

"Want to talk about it?" Anaïs asked.

"I'd like to talk to Magnus about it," Dunharra said. "Can we get a minute?"

Anaïs, Iseabail, and Tup all went back to Anaïs and Zauvadok's room.

"I've got my eye on you," Zauvadok said, pointing at Magnus. He walked into the adjoining room and shut the door.

A moment went by, and Magnus and Dunharra looked at each other.

"I—" they both began at once.

"You first," Dunharra said, blushing.

Magnus lifted her face to meet his, and he sat down on the bed in front of her. A single tear fell down her face.

"This is where you leave, right?" Dunharra asked as she looked him in the eye.

"Leave?" Magnus asked. "Do you want me to leave?"

"No. I don't."

"Then, at least that's settled," Magnus said, relieved.

"You mean you're staying?"

"If you'll have me, yes." Magnus held out his arms to hold Dunharra and she fell into them.

"I'm the one man Zauvadok can't scare away," Magnus said, and kissed her hair.

Dunharra sat back and looked up. Her eyes met his.

"When I said you were different, I meant it," Magnus said. "I want to be where you are. Zauvadok's approval or not. He and I will come to terms with this."

Dunharra looked up at him. His lips formed a slight smile, and he leaned forward to kiss her. He kissed her lips shyly, but when Dunharra returned it, he grew more confident and gently held her close to him.

"So, are we a thing?" Dunharra asked.

"We're a thing," Magnus said.

"Yay! You're a thing!" Iseabail said through the cracked door.

"Iseabail!"

"Sorry, not sorry," Iseabail said. "Inquiring minds want to know."

Dunharra rolled her eyes, and they all piled into her room.

"But what's up with these doors?" Dunharra asked.

"Tup found them," Iseabail said. "All our rooms connect to each other."

They compared notes about the rooms, and Dunharra told them about the injured squire.

"He put you to a test," Iseabail said. "To see how much you can heal."

"Do you think Ronan knows?" Zauvadok asked, still glowering at Magnus.

"I don't know," Dunharra said. "When we talked, he didn't seem to know much about me or what I can do. He kept asking about how I healed Kieron."

"He's got an inkling, I bet," Anaïs said. "That's why he won't let you go."

"Then we need to get out of here," Dunharra said.

They spent a good part of the evening and night talking about how to make a distraction, so they could spirit away in the confusion. With a knight at each door, that made things more challenging. When the Three Sisters were high in the sky, they called it a night and gathered back together in the morning.

"Keep your hands to yourself, Magnus," Zauvadok glowered.

Magnus held up his hands. "Not a problem. Tonight," he added the last word to irritate Zauvadok. It worked, and he glared at Magnus as Anaïs stood between them.

"Cool it," she said. "You can do your alpha male thing later, after we're out of here. Tonight, sleep."

They each retired to their separate rooms and settled in for the night.

Magnus broke from his norm and slept with his pants on, and Dunharra slept with all her clothes. They spent the night talking, kissing, and snuggling. They fell asleep spooned together.

Morning came too early for everyone. Unexpectedly, someone opened their doors and served them breakfast on simple ceramic plates. They had breakfast together. They needed to talk about a lot of things. After breakfast, Iseabail mentioned something everyone avoided.

"So, there is a knowledge imbalance here that needs to get squared up," Iseabaili began.

"We all know Dunharra is a healer," Iseabail continued. "Why didn't Magnus know?"

"It's not my story to tell," Anaïs said. "It's Dunharra's."

All eyes fell on Dunharra, who swallowed the last of her breakfast hard. Her eyes grew wide, and her lips formed a tight line. She wished she could crawl into a hole and stay there. She couldn't hide the truth anymore. They deserved to know.

Dunharra took a deep breath. "Are you familiar with the Prophecy of the Healer? It's a Southern Nations prophecy; not everyone has heard it."

Tup and Iseabail shook their heads no. They took each other's hands and waited patiently.

"Hundreds of years ago, a witch named Eibhlin, prophesied a healer would come who could heal any injury, illness, or condition," Dunharra continued. "She gave this prediction to Ninian the Bold, who pretty much said that's nice, patted her on the head and said, thank you. He didn't believe such a person could ever exist."

"Are you sick?" Iseabail asked.

“No,” Dunharra answered simply. She took Magnus’ hand and said, “I don’t need a healer. But such a person exists.”

“Are we looking for her?” Tup asked.

Dunharra sighed, as if steeling herself for the truth. “You’re looking at her.”

A hush fell over the room.

“Anaïs and Zauvadok knew first, years ago,” Dunharra said. “Last night I told Magnus. I should have told you before. Fear got to me.”

“What were you afraid of?” Iseabail asked.

“Losing the life I want to live,” Dunharra said. “If this news gets out that the Prophesied Healer has come, my life will never again be my own. I’ll be a pawn of kings.” A single tear fell down her cheek.

“We would never tell,” Tup said. “I thought you would know that about us.”

“I do now,” Dunharra said. “It’s hard when fear has such a grip on you that you can barely breathe. When I didn’t get ink at the celebration, Mhari figured it out. She told Iain, who told Kieron, who told Maebh. It almost got out of control.”

“Now, Ronan is sniffing around,” Zauvadok said. “I bet he has an inkling of what he’s got here, too. If Ronan knows, he’ll tell all of Mantua. And beyond.”

“Or keep me prisoner here as his personal healer,” Dunharra said as her flesh crawled.

“So, what do we do now?” Iseabail asked.

“Proceed as planned,” Anaïs said. “We go to Ayr and get Dunharra the asylum she needs to live her own life.”

“Which is more important now than ever before,” Iseabail said.

“I’m sorry I didn’t tell you before,” Dunharra said.

“You don’t need to be afraid anymore,” Iseabail said. “We’re behind you.”

Chapter Thirty-Five

CHAPTER THIRTY FIVE

DUNHARRA

Dunharra felt the building shake before she heard the rumbling. "What's that shaking?"

Magnus checked out the window and saw chaos everywhere.

"We need to get out of here," Magnus said. The castle is under attack!"

They searched for a way out of the castle while avoiding the battle. They picked through the rubble to the front gate, the only way out. Zauvadok led the way, and they inched their way to the main gate and hid behind pillars and what remained of the walls.

They made a break for it through the main gate. They ran through the gate and down the hill when a lithium bomb exploded right in front of them. Magnus took the brunt of the explosion.

"Keep running," Dunharra shouted. She stopped and knelt by the stunned Magnus, who took shrapnel to his abdomen and pelvis.

Dunharra knelt, grabbed him, and pulled him as far away from the fighting as she could.

"Dunharra, get out of here," Magnus managed.

"Not without you," she replied between drags.

"This is your one chance to escape!"

"Not. Without. You!"

She dragged him as far as she could and then set about healing him. Her eyes glowed the familiar iridescent color and her hands swiftly followed suit. The shrapnel perforated his bowel and bladder. She had to work quickly, since the Innesfrees soldiers were coming back outside, and to make the run back home. They would bring the battle to them.

Anaïs looked back when Zauvadok pulled her along with him. Zauvadok plowed a way through a mass of people, leaving a path behind him Anaïs, Tup, and Iseabail could follow. They ran out of Buckhaven and waited for Dunharra and Magnus to follow.

And waited.

Dunharra breathed deeply and steadily. She needed to be precise and not miss anything. In seconds, shrapnel popped out from under his skin as the skin closed behind it. His bladder leaked urine and blood into his pelvis. She found the offending foreign bodies and removed them. She repaired his bladder and removed the urine and blood from his pelvis. Explosions were coming closer. They needed to move.

Her eyes returned to their normal grass green. Magnus stood and helped Dunharra up, and they started to run out of Buckhaven.

The discovery that Dunharra and her group were missing came soon after the attack started. Following the safe discovery of Ronan and Donal and the end of the attack, the search for those who escaped started.

Magnus and Dunharra ran for their lives toward Anaïs, Zauvadok, Tup, and Iseabail. They were within sight, and thirty yards away promised freedom.

"There she is!" a knight shouted.

Three knights ran directly toward Magnus and Dunharra, gaining quickly. Anaïs, Calyx, and Iseabail threw fire from her hands and took out two of the three guards. They fell dead instantly.

The third knight grabbed Dunharra by her collar and dragged her down. Her shirt tore, and she fell with a shriek, hit her head on the hard, rocky ground. Magnus heard her scream, and he turned around in time to see the knight pick up her limp body and run back toward Buckhaven with it.

"No! Dunharra!" Magnus shouted. He turned around and rushed back toward Buckhaven.

As soon as the others saw Magnus turn around and go back toward Buckhaven, they knew what happened. They sprinted toward Buckhaven in time to see the guard run in with Dunharra, and the gate slam down before Magnus could cross back inside.

Zauvadok reached Magnus with the others not far behind. He grabbed Magnus by the back of the neck and lifted him off the ground. He then shouted, "You lost her. And now she's alone in Buckhaven because you couldn't protect her."

The knight brought Dunharra inside the castle proper and back to her pretty prison to recover. Because of the shortage of healers in Buckhaven, knights occasionally checked on her but did nothing to care for her.

Dunharra woke up in a bed with a terrible headache. She breathed deeply and regularly, and her eyes glowed with an iridescent light. She had a concussion, nothing too terrible, with a mild, closed skull fracture that knit together well. When she finished healing herself, her eyes returned to their usual grass green. She lay on the bed and tried to put the pieces back together of what happened today. Then, she realized the most concerning thing about her predicament.

She was alone.

***

ISEABAIL

After the long trip on foot to Innesfrees, they finally arrived.

Iseabail met Noam at the castle gate. "To what do I owe this honor?" he asked.

"We are here to see Maebh and Kieron," Iseabail said. "We have distressing news."

Noam appeared in Maebh's private chambers while Aoife visited her parents.. Her father read a report of the raid on Buckhaven. When he put the report down, Aoife picked it up. She read about three knights lost in the raid. One tripped and blew himself up with his lithium bombs, and Buckhaven knights slew two. When her father realized she read the report, he took it from her and put it in his pocket.

Noam brought the visitors to a sitting room and escorted them inside. Aoife followed her parents. When her father opened the sitting room door and saw who waited for him, he told Aoife she could go.

Aoife stood outside the door and listened.

"To what do I owe this honor?" Kieron asked them.

"Where's Dunharra?" Maebh asked, concerned.

"That's why we are here, Your Majesty," Iseabail said. "Ronan arrested Dunharra, with no cause and no accusation. He took her into custody."

Iseabail related the information about being held in their cozy cells, and how the raid gave them their chance to escape. However, they recaptured Dunharra. They didn't know her condition.

"She asked for and I granted her asylum," Iseabail continued. "She is being held against her will."

"This is mostly a matter for the Mountain Elves," Maebh said.

"I am requesting both your fastest courier to convey a message to my father, Padraig, regarding her request for asylum and for Stirling to negotiate for Dunharra's return."

"Dunharra has done much for Innesfrees and for you personally," Zauvadok stated, trying to keep his temper. "This is a minor task for you to do for her."

"We concur," Maebh stated. "We shall send for the courier and speak with Lennox, which you may have noticed his troops are still here."

"Thank you, Your Majesties," Iseabail said.

***

DUNHARRA

Ronan summoned Dunharra to his private quarters, where he ordered the repair of the castle walls.

"You summoned your prisoner, Your Majesty?" Dunharra asked.

"You are my guest, my dear."

"Then your guest would like to go home."

"My darling, you have only begun to enjoy the benefits of Buckhaven. Why leave?" Ronan asked, giving his full attention to her.

"I don't want to be here, Your Majesty. And I am not your darling," Dunharra stood before him, trying to suppress her heart beating against her chest.

"You will learn to like it," Ronan said with dark eyes.

"Like it here, or like you?"

"Both. How does Queen Dunharra sound to you, my dear?"

"Queen?" she whispered, stunned. "And if I decline the honor?"

"Then you will experience the... less enjoyable parts of Buckhaven," Ronan threatened.

"I see."

"Come closer," Ronan instructed, motioning her to come nearer to him.

Dunharra came as close as she dared, out of arm's reach.

"You cut your hair."

"Yes, it's shorter."

"All I ask is that you give Buckhaven some time to grow on you," Ronan said with a flourish.

"Please know, Your Majesty, I have requested and received asylum from the Mountain Elves."

Ronan's eyes narrowed and his jaw set, but he said nothing.

"Then until we can get this matter sorted, will you consider Buckhaven, and me, a hospitable replacement?"

He stood up from his desk and approached her. He held out his hand, and she placed hers in his. Ronan kissed her hand gently.

"If you wish it," Dunharra whispered.

"Well then, I will call for you again shortly. I will show you the greenhouse."

Dunharra left that very instant. A knight escorted her to her pretty prison and she lay on the bed. The same bed where she snuggled with Magnus the night before.

Ronan did indeed send for her a few hours later. A knight escorted her to his private residence, where he led her to the greenhouse.

The building consisted entirely of glass and iron. Once they were inside, the internal temperature stunned Dunharra; the warm and humid contrast to the crisp post-Yuletide air surprised her.

"How can this be?"

Ronan explained the absorption of sunlight through the glass by the plants, warming them and the soil inside. The glass traps heat, maintaining a warmer temperature.

Dunharra gazed in awe at the beautiful flowers and vegetables growing at this time of year. "Is this how you feed your people during the winter months?"

"Yes." He picked a bright ruby hibiscus and placed it in Dunharra's hair. "A beautiful flower for a beautiful woman."

"Flatterer," Dunharra said. "I am of average looks, and diminutive at best."

Ronan laughed. "I'll give you the diminutive, but you are anything but average."

"You have no idea."

"Oh, I have some idea," Ronan said, looking into her eyes. "You are the best healer alive; the best in all of Mantua."

Dunharra shrank back.

Ronan noticed a change in her demeanor. "Oh, my darling," he began. "Your secret is safe with me."

Dunharra tried to maintain her composure and steady her furiously beating heart. She absently fiddled with the hibiscus. She must play his game for now. "What secret is that?"

"My Dunharra, you're cute when you're coy," Ronan replied, extending the game.

"You have me at a disadvantage."

"Allow me to bring you to a more comfortable environment," Ronan said, changing the subject.

He brought Dunharra back to his private library where there were thousands of books housed on shelves built into the wall. There were ladders to climb and reach the highest books. Two chairs sat in the middle of the room with a small table between them.

"Do you like what you see?" Ronan asked her.

"This is amazing," Dunharra said, spinning around, looking at the books. "I have never seen so many books in one place."

"We could come here every night, my darling," Ronan cooed. He put his arm around her waist.

Dunharra froze. "Your Majesty, I would like to return to my room," she managed to whisper.

"If you wish," Ronan said. "Until tomorrow, darling."

Chapter Thirty-Six

CHAPTER THIRTY SIX

ISEABAIL

It took six days by Innesfrees' fastest courier to travel to and from Ayr. Padraig gave the Mountain Elf seal of approval to Dunharra's request for asylum.

Iseabail had it in writing, and it made her gleeful. She had four separate, identical copies. She could negotiate Dunharra away from Ronan. With this legal document in hand, Stirling sent envoys to travel to Buckhaven with Iseabail to negotiate the release of Dunharra to the Mountain Elves.

Ronan met them in the throne room, dressed in full Buckhaven regalia. They exchanged pleasantries and introductions.

"This is Bellangere," Iseabail introduced one peer. "And this is Kahedin," motioning to the second envoy. "And I am sure you remember me, Your Majesty."

"That I do."

"We are here to negotiate the release of one Dunharra Tor," Bellangere began, and handed the wax-sealed decree to Ronan.

"And what do you offer me that could compare to the future queen of Buckhaven?" Ronan asked.

Iseabail stifled a gasp. "No, Dunharra would never agree to that," she said.

"The avoidance of Stirling entering the war between Buckhaven and Innesfrees," Kahedin said.

"Hmmm," Ronan dramatically tapped his chin. "What else?"

"What does his excellency want?" Bellangere asked.

"The Rud Eskimiş is a good starting point for negotiations," Ronan said, and winked at Iseabail.

"That is out of the question," Iseabail said, pointing at him.

"Then I suppose round one of the negotiations are over," Ronan said, as he threw the decree in the fireplace.

Iseabail watched it burn as her body tensed. *What an arrogant bastard.*

"This is not over," she said to Ronan.

A knight escorted Iseabail, Bellangere, and Kahedin from the castle with an invitation to return tomorrow. Iseabail accepted and made the arrangements.

***

DUNHARRA

The next morning, Ronan called Dunharra to his quarters again.

"Hello, my darling," Ronan said when the knight brought her in.

"Your Majesty."

"You've worn the same torn clothes for days now," Ronan said. "How about a change?"

"What is His Majesty suggesting?" Dunharra asked.

"Something pretty to bring out your stunning eyes," Ronan flirted.

"His Majesty flirts again," Dunharra retorted. "I am not impressed by pretty things like window dressing."

"What does impress you?" Ronan asked, genuinely interested. He leaned his chin on his hand and studied her.

"Things such as honor and integrity. Fancy clothes are fluff."

"Impressive. Nonetheless, I'll have clothes sent to your room. I would like you to come to dinner tonight."

"What type of affair do you invite me to? Private? Public?"

"Always thinking," Ronan said with admiration in his voice. "I love that about you."

Dunharra's stomach soured. "His Majesty is kind."

"Then, I will see you tonight. There are dignitaries visiting."

Ronan sent an elegant, brilliant emerald green dress with black accents on the chest and sleeves to Dunharra. It fit well, and a young Buckhaven woman helped her into it. She expected to wait for a knight to lead her to the dinner, but Ronan himself knocked on the door.

Dunharra didn't hide her surprise. He dressed in the same shade of emerald green with black accents. When she gave an approving glance, Ronan smiled. She thought he cleaned up well.

Ronan bowed to her and extended his arm to escort her to dinner. She reluctantly took it, but his touch filled her with revulsion. All she thought about were the feelings Magnus evoked when he touched her. That would have to get her through tonight.

They entered the dinner together, her arm on his, to thunderous applause. Dunharra plastered a smile on her face.

"What have you told people?" she asked incredulously. "Do they think we're a couple?"

"Does it matter what other people think?" Ronan asked.

"Do you like the appearance of us together?"

"What man wouldn't want to be seen with a beautiful woman?" Ronan countered, as he smiled at her.

He escorted her to the main table, where he pulled out her chair.

She engaged in polite conversations about Innesfrees, and the weather with Ronan. When Ronan thought she couldn't endure any more, he stood up and stated the dinner had concluded. He extended his arm to Dunharra and escorted her out of the main hall.

"What did you think of this evening?" Ronan asked.

"You put on a delightful party," Dunharra said.

Dunharra could see Ronan's disappointment when she did not continue the conversation.

"Where would you like to go now? The castle is your oyster."

"Home, Your Majesty."

"And where is home?"

"I have a cottage and a cat in the Thunder Hill Forest. It has all that I need and everything I miss," Dunharra said.

"Let me take you to the balcony," Ronan said as he led her there. "The view is quite stunning."

Ronan led her to his private balcony overlooking the fields of winter wheat. She looked up and saw billions of stars. Stars she couldn't see through the trees at her cottage in the Thunder Hill Forest. The beauty of the scene momentarily stole her breath.

"See those lights over to the left?" Ronan asked, pointing toward the night sky. "They are called the Aurora Mantualis. Every now and then, when the conditions are right, we can see those beautiful lights."

"Truly a gift from the Mother," Dunharra said, unable to take her eyes off them.

"All this could be yours," Ronan said, putting an arm around her waist. He drew her close to him, and bought her face close to his. The Triplet Sister moons and the uncountable stars lit Dnharra's face. She shivered in the brisk, post Yuletide cold.

Ronan pulled her closer to him, her body against his. She felt his warmth, and confusion clouded her mind; glad to be warm, but his touch nauseated her. He leaned his head down and gently kissed her lips lightly at first, but then fiercer and more passionate.

When he broke the kiss, Dunharra looked him in the eyes, confused and unsure what to do. No one ever kissed her like that before. She stared at him, open mouthed and wide eyed. Before she could react or could process what happened, Ronan leaned down and kissed her again. His tongue entered her mouth and danced with hers.

Dunharra broke the kiss. "Your Majesty is very forward!"

"Nothing ventured, nothing gained, my Queen."

"I think I should like to retire for the night."

"Of course," he said, and gently led her to her room. "Get used to this, my Queen. This is your future."

Ronan smiled as he shut the door.

***

ISEABAIL

Morning broke over the eastern horizon and the Stirling coalition returned for another day's negotiations. The day proved frigid, but the approaching Imbolc held the promise of an especially cold and snowy early spring. The coalition saw their breath in feather plumes as they entered Castle Buckhaven.

A guide led them to an unusually cozy nook with hot tea, fruited water, and warmed bread, butter, and fruit compotes. Ronan decorated the room in the usual ostentatious Buckhaven style with overstuffed chairs and trimmings of gold accents everywhere.

Ronan entered the room about thirty minutes later, looking rather satisfied with himself. He sat down, and Bellangere gave formal introductions. Iseabail began the negotiation with Innesfrees filing for Buckhaven's unconditional surrender and Stirling not entering the war.

Ronan agreed Stirling would not enter the war but would not concede defeat. He would never surrender, he would sooner die.

"Don't consider it a defeat, Your Majesty," Bellangere said. "Consider it a truce. No winner, no loser."

"I can accept a truce," Ronan said. "Does Innesfrees accept responsibility for the murder of my father?"

"Innesfrees denies accountability for the murder of your father, King Darragh," Kahedin said. "Stirling would endeavor to aid Buckhaven to find the killer."

"Who would decide the killer's fate?" Ronan asked, intrigued.

"We could agree that you would," Bellangere said.

"Then we agree," Ronan said. "A truce, Stirling helps locate my father's murderer, and I decide their fate."

"Huzzah," they said in unison.

"Now to the matter of one Dunharra Tor, Your Majesty," Kahedin said.

"What about her?" Ronan asked.

"We wish to negotiate her release," Kahedin replied. "She is here against her will."

Ronan adopted a posture of 'that's not what she thought last night', and Iseabail saw he reveled in her tension.

"Is she being treated well?" Kahedin inquired. "Is she being cared for?"

"Oh, she is much cared for. I care for her very much."

"Describe her treatment, Your Majesty," Iseabail said. "Is she safe?"

"I gave her a green and black formal gown to attend a state dinner with me last night," Ronan said, rolling his eyes. "I found her company had proved kind"

"Your Majesty, people can interpret that in many ways," Iseabail said.

Ronan sneered and narrowed his eyes at Iseabail. "Would you like to know what she ate as well? How often she used the necessary?"

"As a matter of fact, details would be most reassuring," Iseabail said, and she stood her ground. "The last time you took a guest of Buckhaven, they died. Tortured to death."

"Sins of the father, Ambassador," Ronan said, rolling his eyes again, shrugging.

"You were an accomplice to the coup attempt, if I may remind his Majesty. Buckhaven's track record of caring for its 'guests' is questionable," Iseabail accused him.

"What is it you want, Ambassador?" Ronan asked. His face reddened, and he set his jaw. Iseabail could almost hear his teeth grind.

"I want to see her," Iseabail responded in kind. "I want to speak to her privately to ensure her treatment is not lacking or abusive."

"When?" Ronan asked. Iseabail could see his whole countenance now burning with rage.

"Now."

"No."

"Tomorrow," Iseabail responded immediately. She would not let up.

"Done. If you come back with The Rud Eskimiş, you may have her tomorrow."

"The Mountain Elves granted her asylum. We should have her today."

"This meeting is over. Come back tomorrow, and you will see her."

Ronan leaned back in his chair and rubbed his chin. He didn't like having to show Iseabail Dunharra. His lips pursed into a fine line and he frowned. Ronan hated being told what to do, especially by Iseabail.

Ronan knocked on Dunharra's door and after a moment, she opened a crack. When she saw him, she opened it wider.

"You have guests, darling," Ronan cooed. "Come with me."

Dunharra followed Ronan to the reception room.

When the door to the reception room opened, Dunharra saw Iseabail, Calyx, Tup, Zauvadok, Anaïs, and Magnus. Bellangere and Kahedin were also present, waiting patiently in the back of the room.

"By the Mother!" Dunharra cried. She ran into their waiting arms. "Please tell me you're here to take me home," she pleaded.

"Not yet," Iseabail said.

Iseabail sighed when she saw Dunharra's crestfallen face.

"I'm working on it," Iseabail said. "He wants The Rud Eskimiş in exchange for you."

"So that's his plan," Dunharra said. "He's been trying to woo me. Even kissed me."

"Kissed you!" Magnus said.

"I'm a pawn. He doesn't want me, he wants the Rud Eskimiş," Dunharra reassured him. "He thinks I'm enjoying his banter. Get me out of here."

"We will," Magnus reassured her. "Soon."

"Alright, alright, you've seen her. You see, she's alive, healthy, and well cared for. Time to go, darling."

The knight ushered Dunharra out. She glanced back at Magnus as the knight pulled from the room. Ronan noticed that Magnus' eyes narrowed and his body tensed when he called Dunharra darling. His anger made Ronan smile.

Attendants ushered Zauvadok, Anaïs, Calyx and Tup to a very comfortable waiting area, and brought Iseabail, Bellangere, and Kahedin to the intimate sitting room they visited yesterday.

"So, you see she's well?" Ronan said sarcastically.

"I'd like to see her home," Iseabail retorted.

"I'd like The Rud Eskimiş."

"Is there something else we can offer you?" Bellangere asked.

"No," Ronan replied. "Unless?" Ronan paused for effect. "I can have an exact duplicate made."

"Acceptable," Bellangere said.

"Absolutely not! Do you know what he'll do with it?" Iseabail shouted.

"I find it agreeable as well," Kahedin said.

"Have you two lost your mind?" Iseabail said, standing, challenging them.

"Then it's settled," Ronan said, standing. "When the copy arrives, Dunharra will be free to go, if she chooses."

"What do you mean, *if*?" Iseabail demanded.

"Well, Iseabail, if you must know, we get along rather swimmingly," Ronan teased.

"That's a lie," Iseabail accused him. "Lying does not become you, Your Majesty."

"If I can convince her, is it really a lie?" Ronan teased.

Ronan walked away laughing to himself, leaving Iseabail alone to deal with Bellangere and Kahedin. Iseabail turned to the envoys and said, "Do you know what you've done?"

"We negotiated Dunharra's return, Iseabail," Kahedin said. "We achieved the goal."

"Yes, but at the cost of The Rud Eskimiş?" Iseabail asked. "Do you know what Ronan intends?"

Bellangere and Kahedin's silence answered her question.

"He intends to get the Frozen Crown with the magic in The Rud Eskimiş."

"He'll never succeed," Bellangere said. "Ronan's a king, not a mage."

"He's got himself a mage, Bellangere."

"But you will have Dunharra back." Kahedin tried to sound helpful and failed miserably.

"I hope that will comfort you when we are all forced to bow down to Ronan."

***

AOIFE

Aoife acquired a ladder and could reach the ancient books on the top shelf of the dusty library. If she were not careful, some pages would crumble beneath her fingers. Her reading covered the histories of the Southern Nations, the Mountain Elves, the Wood Elves, the Wild Ones, the Mauu, the Beit Shemesh, the Keaau, and the little that existed concerning the Chernushka. She could find a book on the Island of Artim, and the type of culture they embraced. The one and only book about the Frozen Crown fascinated her the most. She needed to read it like she needed to breathe.

This book needed careful handling, or else the entire page would disintegrate under her touch. She cross-referenced her research. This singular book described the Crown, how it got there, and how to defend against its magical properties. There were very detailed instructions on how and where to apply the ink to use the magick to defend against the weaponization of the Frozen Crown.

She wanted that ink.

The rare and powerful ancient ink mesmerized her. She could show her parents how serious she became. With strong ink came strong authority. Or so she thought.

The next day, after her lessons, she brought Mhari back to her room and asked her to apply the ink. She showed her the details of the application.

"Please? Mhari, it's easy. It's ancient, and look at how cool it looks!"

"Because something looks cool doesn't mean that you should get it," Mhari said. "That will take room from other ink you could get. Despite the numbing, it will still pinch," Mhari warned.

"So, is that a yes?" Aoife asked, with hope shining like the sun in her eyes.

Mhari paused and sighed. "Yes."

"When?" Aoife asked, ready to pop with bottled-up excitement like a champagne cork.

"I'm not busy now," Mhari said. "But I have to gather special ink, and we'll need that book to get it right.

"Aoife!" Maebh stared at her daughter with utter disbelief. "You inked your face!"

"Only next to the hairline, and they are subtle little dots, Mum," Aoife explained. "You can barely see them. Look at behind my neck."

Aoife proudly held up her brilliant red ringlets and showed her mother the spotted ink on the back of her neck. They looked like leopard spots to the untrained eye. “It’s a mix of rare ink that Mhari had to dig deep in her cabinet to get. I found it in one of the very old books in the library.”

“She has been doing very well with her studies, and as a reward, she requested this ink,” Mhari explained.

“Are you sure it’s safe, Mhari?” Maebh asked carefully, looking her in her eyes. “The ink looks rather dangerous.”

“Completely safe, Your Majesty,” Mhari reassured her. People understood the dangers of the crown so well that no one tried to wear it. Aoife would be perfectly safe.

Chapter Thirty-Seven

CHAPTER THIRTY SEVEN

ISEABAIL

Zauvadok and Magnus were sniping at each other again. Iseabail felt sorry for Anaïs, because she had to hear the incessant arguing. "Will you two please knock it off? If Dun were here, she would put a stop to all this foolishness."

"If Dun were here, we would have an entirely different conversation," Zauvadok grumbled.

"Put your coins where your mouth is, big boy," Magnus started again. "Let's go get her."

"What?" Anaïs asked incredulously. "You have finally lost what little sense you had, bounty hunter." Anaïs stood between Magnus and Zauvadok and crossed her arms.

"Let's not wait for The Rud Eskimiş," Magnus suggested. "Let's go get her."

"First off, it's big man," Zauvadok said. "Second, you're very deep in like. Third, you are not thinking things through."

"How so?" Magus asked.

"Iseabail negotiated a truce, and a way to get her back," Anaïs said. "If we go mucking around, it could cause the war to return, and we may never get her back."

"Cool your pants there, Loverboy," Zauvadok said as he poked him.

They were ready to come to blows when Iseabail stepped between them.

"We do this my way, or we may lose her for good," Iseabail said. "Both of you grow up a little and stop this now."

***

DUNHARRA

The rain poured down in Buckhaven, making everything muddy and mucky. Dunharra usually loved rainy days because of the cathartic quality of rinsing the world clean it held for her, but here in her pretty prison, it seemed messy. She gazed out of her window and saw the gray rain clouds that would give snow if the weather turned colder. The rain mirrored the sadness she felt being cooped up.

Dunharra did not have long to wait until Ronan called for her again. He sent a knight to take her to his private quarters.

"Welcome, Dunharra," Ronan said as he stood. He took her hands and kissed them gently. "Please, come in. I have dinner waiting."

On his balcony with the rain as a backdrop, a candlelit setting awaited her. Gold-accented tableware and pure white linens greeted her along with one single red rose. He escorted her to the table and assisted her to sit. He behaved like the perfect gentleman, but Dunharra knew he had ulterior motives, and guarded for whatever lies he threw at her.

"You're looking lovely," Ronan said, as he lingered on her figure.

"My eyes are up here."

"And in a devilish mood as well," Ronan said smiling. "I enjoy a spirited woman."

"Then you will enjoy our dinner banter. So, when can I go home?"

"And leave all this behind?" Ronan asked, gesturing all around him, pretending to be hurt.

"I'm in a pretty prison."

"For your safety, my darling," Ronan said.

"Safety from what? You?" Dunharra asked incredulously.

Ronan sipped some wine. "Maybe," he said. "You are delicate."

"Not delicate like a flower," Dunharra said. "Delicate like a bomb."

Ronan said, "You are fiery. I like that." Ronan smiled widely.

Dinner went on in this way with some small talk sprinkled in. Dunharra indulged in a glass of wine. It made her feel warm and fuzzy.

Dessert arrived, and she sat back in her chair. She didn't recognize it. "What is this?"

"It's called sherbet," Ronan explained. "It's a delicacy from Manasquan. We perfected it. Try it; it's made of shredded ice and fruit."

Dunharra tentatively tried the dessert and found it pleasantly surprising. "It's delicious."

"If you are interested, there is a string quartet setting up in my private chambers where we can dance and talk," Ronan suggested.

"Ronan, you want me for The Rud Eskimiş, and The Rud Eskimiş only," Dunharra challenged him.

"For a time yes," Ronan confessed. "But now I know who you really are."

"And who am I?" Dunharra challenged him again. The wine made her feel bold and brave.

"You, my dear, are the most talented, unparalleled, peerless healer I have ever met," Ronan said. "I believe you are the rumored healer everyone in Innesfrees carries on about."

Dunharra paled and her mouth went dry. "You've got what you want. Let me go."

"I have become quite smitten with you."

"You mean what I can do, or what I can get for you," Dunharra accused him.

"No, not only that, my darling," Ronan continued. "I want you to be my queen."

Dunharra suddenly lost her appetite. Her heart beat hard against her chest. She pursed her lips and swallowed hard against the horror that filled her soul.

"And when you are ready to retire, you will see I have upgraded your arrangements," Ronan informed her. "Fit for a queen."

"You have certainly overwhelmed me, Your Majesty," Dunharra said.

"Ronan," Ronan replied. "You may call me Ronan."

Dunharra's blood ran cold. Her world crashed down around her. Exactly what she feared would happen, happened. She did everything she could to keep control and not give in to fear, but it getting very hard.

"I would very much like to see these new quarters, Ronan," Dunharra asked.

"I know things have taken quite a turn for you, my darling," Ronan said. "You will slowly become accustomed to your new role."

Ronan escorted Dunharra to the Queen's quarters, where Aelwen had lived before her untimely death. Before Dunharra could enter her new prison, Ronan took her by the chin and kissed her forcefully.

"Sweet dreams, my darling," Ronan said, and shut the door.

***

ISEABAIL

Iseabail returned to Buckhaven with Bellangere, Kahedin, and an exact copy of The Rud Eskimiş after several weeks. A knight ushered them into the intimate meeting parlor and waited over two hours.

When Ronan finally arrived, distraction and disinterest clouded him.

"We have The Rud Eskimiş," Iseabail said, nearly choking on her words. "Where is Dunharra?"

"She is not feeling well. She very much wished to see you. However, she can't."

"No, Dunharra, no Rud Eskimiş," Bellangere said.

"No, I am King here," Ronan sneered. "What I say goes. Now give me the book," Ronan said with his hand outstretched.

"No," Iseabail said and clutched it to her chest.

"Knights!" Ronan shouted.

Three strong Buckhaven knights entered the tiny room and pointed swords at Bellangere, Kahedin, and Iseabail. Iseabail reached up and touched the side of the sword pointed at her, and her eyes glowed an icy blue. A shock of electricity flowed up the steel blade and stunned the knight , who fell on the floor, very much alive. The two remaining guards stepped forward and placed their swords directly on the necks of Bellangere and Kahedin.

"Naughty, naughty, Iseabail. It seems we are at an impasse," Ronan shook his finger at her.

"Not an impasse, if you hand over Dunharra."

"I said that you can't see her," Ronan snarled. He leaned forward, nose to nose with Iseabail.

"Make her available." Iseabail didn't flinch.

"Come back tomorrow; she may be well then."

Iseabail looked at the swords on the necks of her companions. With one flick of the wrist, their lives could end. She knew held the disadvantage.

"Fine," Iseabail said, defeated.

"The book," Ronan held out his hand again.

Iseabail handed over the Rud Eskimiş, and the knights sheathed their swords.

A knight ushered them out. And so, each time Iseabail arrived to see Dunharra, and to collect her, she could not see her. Iseabail gathered everyone together to bring them up to speed.

Magnus swore. "What do you think about getting her now?"

"It's becoming a reality," Iseabail said. "Ronan will not give her up."

"Let's make a plan," Anaïs said.

***

RONAN

Ronan casually leafed through The Rud Eskimiş copy when Hagan made his usual entrance and caught Ronan off guard. He leapt up with a start. "Goddammit!"

"My oh my, are you jumpy," Hagan teased.

"Isn't there something you can do to announce your arrival?"

"What? The red tentacles aren't enough?" Hagan asked. "You need to pay attention."

"What is it, Hagan?" Ronan asked, irritated.

"You have a copy of The Rud Eskimiş, I see," Hagan said.

"How do you know it's a copy?" Ronan asked, confused.

"Boy, can you not smell the fresh ink?" Hagan asked, clearly aghast to be dealing with a rank amateur. "Old books have an aroma. Oh, never mind." Hagan shook his head.

"So, what's next?" Ronan asked.

"You give the book to me," Hagan said, holding his hand out.

"No," Ronan said. "What's my guarantee you won't take the book and use the magick on yourself?"

"Oh, fine," he said. "You young ones are way too suspicious. Let me see it."

Ronan turned the book around but kept a solid hold on it. Hagan flipped through the pages, lingering on this one and that. "Ooh, I forgot about that one," he said with delight.

"Will you come on?" Ronan huffed and narrowed his eyes.

"You rush a mage, you get bad magick, boy," Hagan said with a side eye.

"I'm a man," Ronan protested.

"You arrested an innocent woman and are keeping her here against her will," Hagan said, disgusted. "You're a boy. Even I get willing participants."

Ronan's face turned bright red. "Just find the spell."

Hagan flipped the pages more purposefully and found the spell he needed. "Ah! Here it is!" he announced.

Hagan quickly committed the words to memory and smiled grimly.

"I don't need the blood of a virgin, do I?" Ronan asked sarcastically.

"No, but the way things are going, you won't get a virgin either."

Ronan stood nose to nose with Hagan.

"Struck a nerve, did I?" Hagan teased. "The only way you're getting in Dunharra's pants is if you force yourself on her."

"I'll woo her, and she will be my queen. You'll see. Then you'll eat your words."

"That's not a habit of mine, boy," Hagan said, staring directly at Ronan, his eyes shining red. "And not one I'm going to start."

"Get the spell ready, and don't come back until you do," Ronan threatened.

"Or else what? You need me more than I need you. Remember that."

Hagan stepped through his portal and vanished.

***

ISEABAIL

Iseabail made one final visit to Buckhaven to get Dunharra away from Ronan. A knight brought her into the cozy reception room and made her wait. An hour later, Ronan sauntered in and informed Iseabail that Dunharra felt ill and could not see her.

"Where are you keeping her? The jail?" Iseabail asked.

"No, she is in quarters fit for a queen," Ronan sneered. "And my queen she will be."

"Dunharra needs to consent to that," Iseabail said. "She is not some Buckhaven backwater peasant you can have your way with. She has asylum with the Mountain Elves. You are violating international law."

Ronan rolled his eyes and cajoled Iseabail. "She will consent. I'll make it so."

At that, Ronan stood and left Iseabail alone. Iseabail smiled. She had the information she needed.

Iseabail knew the day passed slowly for Magnus. Night meant action, and tonight waiting only made him anxious. She watched him fidget and pace until the sun went down, to the general annoyance of everyone around him, including her. Finally, the time came to move.

Under cover of night, they crept through the Buckhaven castle grounds to the west wing where the queen's quarters were. With luck, Dunharra would still be inside.

A lone stray dog barked at their approach. It garnered no lasting attention, and after a moment's pause, they could continue.

"We should go at this from the completely opposite direction," Magnus whispered. "Ronan will expect us to come for her at the queen's quarters."

Zauvadok growled. "I don't recall this being a joint operation, Magnus. Do you want Dunharra back or not?"

"More than you know," Magnus replied.

That elicited a derisive snort from Zauvadok. "Then keep up, bounty hunter. Don't make us go looking for you."

"Don't make me go looking for you, either," Magnus retorted.

"Will you two shut up?" Tup shushed them. "You're going to get us killed."

They continued to slink through the shadows, slowly making progress toward the west wing of the castle. Tup looked back to tell Magnus to stay close, only to notice he vanished.

"Zauvadok, Magnus is gone."

"Goddammit," Zauvadok said. "He'll get captured, and we'll have to rescue him too."

Iseabil sighed. She wondered what Dunharra even saw in that bounty hunter.

They had to stay confined to the treacherous shadows. Knights roamed the grounds.

There were various nighttime animals to be avoided. Their eyes glowed in the moonlight. Their alarmed chittering threatened to betray their position and encouraged nearby dogs to bark. Eventually, they made it to the west wing window of the room, where they expected Dunharra to be sleeping.

Tup stood on Zauvadok's shoulders and looked into the window. Darkness filled the room. She could see her breath in the cold as she exhaled. She pushed gently on the windowpane, and it moved with a moaning creak. Dunharra sat up in bed and stared at the window. In the dark, she could see nothing. The cold post-Yuletide breeze on her skin gave her goosebumps.

"Hello?" Dunharra tentatively called out.

"Dun?" Tup said from the shoulders of Zauvadok.

"Tup?" Dunharra said as she leapt from the bed and dashed to the window. "Oh, by the Mother, is this my rescue?"

"As long as Magnus doesn't fuck it up, it is," Zauvadok said. "He ran off on his own thinking he's all big and bad. Barney Badass."

Dunharra rubbed her temples. "Why? How? What?"

"Sound the alarm! Intruders! Intruders!" someone started shouting.

Dunharra did not hesitate. She grabbed her cloak and boots, then climbed out the window, into the waiting arms of Zauvadok. His muscular arms grabbed her and gently put her on the ground.

Fires were lit across the castle landscape. The grounds were a mix of dancing shadows and flames licking at the sky. The acrid smell of smoke filled the air. Iseabail watched Magnus as he sat on the thick tree branch, as he watched them pull Dunharra from her room.

"They're going to get her killed, Iseabail,"Magnus said softly.

"How...how did you know...?"

"Stealth is not your strong point," Magnus said without looking at her. His eyes were on Dunharra. "Go back to them and don't wait for me if it gets tight."

"Magnus, wait!" Iseabail hissed into the night.

Magnus jumped down from the tree and overpowered the first knight of about the same build and bodyweight. He stripped the unconscious man of his Buckhaven colors, and donned them himself. Confident he looked the part, he moved to blend in with the other knights moving in on Dunharra and her friends.

He assumed a posture of command and started issuing orders.

Then, in full Buckhaven regalia, he walked up to the shadows where they were crouched.

"You do not belong here," he said in his best commanding voice. "You must leave."

"Not without who we came for," Tup said. "She comes with us."

"Or else what?" Magnus asked. "What will you do?"

Zauvadok stepped out of the darkness. "She'll ask me to clear the way."

"I sent most of the guards on wild goose chases in the castle and doubled the guards on all exits but one," said as he slipped out of the Buckhaven gear. "We have about two minutes before they figure it out. Then you may have to."

"Magnus?" Iseabail asked.

"The one and only," Magnus said with a flourishing bow.

Dunharra sprung out of the shadows and hugged Magnus. He bathed in her loveliness and relished her touch. He drank it in as if it were the only water on Mantua.

"There she is!" a voice shouted from across the courtyard.

"Run!" Magnus ordered.

They all took off running toward the courtyard's only unguarded exit. They all breached the postern when the gate began to close. Dunharra, Iseabail, Calyx, Anaïs, and Tup all got through unscathed. Zauvadok and Magnus had to slide underneath the descending spikes of the gate to make it through.

Zauvadok made it through, but a gate spike impaled Magnus' arm.

Zauvadok turned around. He saw Magnus impaled on the gate and considered leaving him there. He imagined life without Magnus, and while it made him smile, seeing the sadness in Dunharra's eyes wiped that smile from his face. Zauvadok grabbed a bar and lifted the gate far enough to allow Magnus to pull his arm through. Magnus pulled his mangled arm free, and Zauvadok let the gate fall with a thud. Magnus struggled not to scream.

Dunharra stopped in her tracks and ran back to Magnus. She fell on her knees and assessed the damage. She found a gaping three-inch hole in his left forearm that bled profusely.

Dunharra's eyes glowed iridescent and she touched the wound. The veins that were avulsed came together. The muscles knitted together, and tendons reattached. Finally, his skin fused. Dunharra took her finger and traced the scar, which disappeared under her touch. Her eyes then returned to their normal green.

"Dunharra, I—" began Magnus, but Zauvadok interrupted him.

"Not now. Now we go back to Innesfrees," Zauvadok said as he grabbed Magnus' leather armor.

Magnus pushed Zauvadok away and stroked Dunharra's cheek with his thumb. "Dunharra I –"

"Come on, bounty hunter," Zauvadok said. "There's no time to waste."

***

DUNHARRA

They rode hard and fast, barely sparing the horses. They arrived at Innesfrees within a day. Kieron and Maebh welcomed them with open arms. Not much for pomp and circumstance, Dunharra stayed the appropriate amount of time and excused herself for quieter surroundings.

They gave her small guest quarters where she could relax and refresh herself. She spent most of the late afternoon alone. She watched the post-Yule snowfall. It always made her smile. She loved how quiet the snow made the landscape. It made a peaceful contrast to the revelry going on a few yards away.

Dunharra enjoyed the snow for about three hours when she heard a knock on the door. It took her a moment to open it, partly astonished that anyone would miss her and knew where to find her. She would have to find more secretive accommodations next time.

A second rap came on the door before she answered it. She expected Anaïs to be checking on her, but she didn't think she'd be so persistent.

Dunharra opened the door to find not Anaïs but Magnus.

"Magnus? What are you doing here?"

"I care about you. Seriously, I want to know you better."

Dunharra's face heated to an attractive crimson, and she invited him inside. They sat next to each other on comfortable chairs in the bookcase-lined room. Although the chairs were comfortable, they both felt awkward.

Dunharra giggled at the awkwardness, and it broke the ice. "What? You've got no lines to reel me in with?"

"I wouldn't dare," Magnus said. "Personally, I don't like lines. I think they're false and phony."

"So how do you plan to get to know me?"

"Well, you told me an enormous secret of yours. How do you feel about that?"

That stunned Dunharra. Aside from Zauvadok and Anaïs, no one had ever asked her what she thought or how she felt. Only what she could do for them. *Could Magnus be different?*

"How do I feel? I told you the deepest secret of my entire life," Dunharra began. "I am nervous that someone other than they know. I am terrified that this will get out. I am terrified that someone, somewhere, will tell. A careless whisper, or a promise blatantly broken, it haunts me."

"Your secret is safe with me. You are safe with me," Magnus said.

"You told me," Dunharra said. "But what if your injury never happened? Would I be safe with you?"

Magnus sat back and collected his thoughts. "I admit that I find you very attractive. But even if I were whole, you would still be safe with me.

"What if..." Dunharra paused. "You were whole again?"

Magnus froze. "What?" he whispered.

"What if I healed you?" Dunharra asked. "What would you do?"

"I never pictured my life any other way. I have come to terms with a life without sexual activity. And lately, I've been struggling. After all this time, I've met someone who I would like to make love to, and I can't."

"What if I could fix that? Give you back that aspect of your life?"

"You would do that for me? You could do that for me?"

"I can. The question is, do you want it? And would I be safe with you?"

Magnus sat back, stunned. "This is the second time you've left me without words. How can I show gratitude for such a selfless gift?"

"I don't know if I would call it selfless," Dunharra said quietly. She looked him directly in the eye.

"Do you want it? It requires me to touch you whenever you are ready."

"I'm ready," Magnus said, standing.

Dunharra stood and encircled her arms around Magnus' neck. Magnus cupped her face with his hands. He kissed her lips gently at first, and the fire built as he thought about making love with Dunharra. She returned his kiss with equal passion and intensified it herself as her hands explored under his shirt.

Then a knock came on the door. Dunharra and Magnus paused. Dunharra didn't expect anyone. They knocked again, and this time the knock grew insistent.

"Who's there?" Magnus called out.

"Open the door," an angry snarling voice came from the other side of the door.

Magnus put Dunharra protectively behind him as he opened the door a crack. Before him stood a man dressed in black with a wicked scimitar.

Magnus slammed the door shut and placed a chair under the doorknob. The man outside pounded on the door and tried to open it from the outside.

"The word of your escape has gotten out, my love," Magnus said as he looked out the window. There were no knights there, but the abrupt drop to the ground would be painful.

The sound of swords being drawn outside the door and an angry half orc filled the hallway. Dunharra readied magick on her hands for whoever broke through the door. She would not go quietly. They heard a gurgling grunt and a body fell to the stone floor.

"Are you alright, Dun?"

"Fine, Zau," she said, relieved, and shook her hands to let the magick fall away.

Magnus opened the door to find the man in black dead on the floor and a very satisfied half orc standing over him.

"The word of your escape has gotten out, Dun," Zauvadok said.

Dunharra and Magnus followed Zauvadok back to Anaïs, Tup, Calyx, and Iseabail, who were meeting with Kieron and Maebh.

"So, what's the plan now?" Dunharra asked.

"Innesfrees is an ally of the Mountain Elves," Maebh said. "We will protect you while you're here, that goes without saying. But Ronan will not stop his attempts to regain you."

"The better question is how to stay one step ahead of Ronan," Magnus said.

"He has The Rud Eskimiş," Iseabail added. "He can get the Frozen Crown at any time."

"Then let's get in his way," Zauvadok said.

With a plan hammered out, they retired to their guest rooms for the night. The Triple Sister Moons were high in the sky when Dunharra heard a knock on the door. She opened the door a crack and saw Magnus. She swung the door open and invited him to come inside.

"I thought you might have changed your mind," Dunharra said, reaching out and taking his hand.

Magnus kissed her lips with tenderly. "Never."

Dunharra locked the door and wedged a chair under the doorknob before continuing. She stood in front of him and locked eyes with him. "I will heal you completely, as if the injury never happened."

Dunharra helped him out of his trousers and Magnus made himself comfortable on the bed. She examined his penis and the two puncture scars. The puncture wounds showed unusually poor healing. It felt limp, flaccid, and sinewy like a snake.

Her fingers traced the outlines of the scars. Without a word, her eyes glowed iridescent and her hands followed suit. She healed the voluminous scar tissue that at once defaced and deformed him. She worked from the inside out, removing scars and healing the tender tissue that she hoped would soon be fully functional.

A lot of damage needed healing. From the shape and texture of the scarring, infection had set in at one point, with no healing attention. She repaired the veins and tissue where blood would flow freely and allow for the natural function to resume. She repaired his damaged urethra, allowing urine to flow freely. His penis became linear, and at its natural length. She healed him completely.

Dunharra's eyes returned to their normal grass green, and her hands ceased to glow. Magnus gasped.

"You did it," Magnus said, amazed. "You healed me. I never thought I would be whole."

He kissed her with joy and elation.

"So, what now?" Dunharra asked. "We are at a crossroads in our relationship. I don't want to be a passing fling, Magnus."

"You could never be a passing fling for me, Dunharra," Magnus said, caressing her cheek. "Something about you kept me from bringing you to Ronan. Something about you brings out the man in me. There is something special about you I never want to be without. And it's not your healing, although you are a great healer. Hell, you're *the* healer. But it's you I want. You."

Magnus kissed her with a renewed passion; one that he only let himself feel many years ago. One that he believed he had lost forever. A passion that he thought he could never feel again.

Magnus broke the kiss, leaving Dunharra breathless. "Do you want to?"

Dunharra nodded. "Yeah," she whispered and kissed him softly.

He gently lifted her onto the bed and slowly removed her leather pants.

Magnus sank to his knees between her legs and tasted her warm wetness. His tongue explored her until he found her clit, eliciting a surprised gasp from her and a satisfied hum from him.

She arched her back in anticipation and he grasped her hips, alternated licking and sucking her clit until he felt her start to quiver. Dunharra bit back a moan and ran her fingers through his hair.

"Not yet," Magnus said as he teased her stiff nipples with his tongue.

"Magnus," Dunharra begged, as he cupped her breast and ghosted her neck with his lips.

She wrapped her arms around him and pressed her body against his. He could smell the musky aroma of her sweat and tasted the saltiness of it as he flicked her nipples with his tongue.

Dunharra trembled underneath him. He looked her in her eyes and gently buried himself in her. Her breath hitched and she shuddered as he dove inside of her with a rhythm that made them both melt.

Her lips brushed his. Dunharra's tongue swirled around his as he sank into her. She pulled his hips down harder.

Dunharra felt a fire pooling in her abdomen as Magnus drove himself deep inside of her. Time felt like it slowed as waves of fire overtook the both. They both cried out as they climaxed.

Magnus collapsed on her, and she felt him pulse inside her. He ran his hands through her black ringlets and kissed her on her lips.

They celebrated a successful test of cure. They made love for hours that night.

Morning arrived to find Magnus and Dunharra lovingly entwined together. The sun peeked in the window between clouds and lit up their contented faces.

Magnus kissed her lips gently. “Good morning, love.”

She understood why Anaïs always hated to get up so early. She didn’t want this to end.

“Good morning,” Dunharra said.

In what seemed like only minutes, Zauvadok’s heavy knock came on the door.

“Come on, lovebirds!” Zauvadok called through the door. “Time to get up.”

***

RONAN

Ronan slept peacefully, dreaming of the Frozen Crown, having Maebh and Kieron subordinate to him and Dunharra as his queen. He never heard Hagan step through the portal.

Hagan watched him sleep for a few minutes before Ronan felt eyes on him. He woke with a start and swore at Hagan.

“Goddammit, Hagan!” Ronan shouted, sitting up straight in bed.

“I see you’re sleeping alone these days,” Hagan teased.

“Not for long,” Ronan said defensively, and crossed his arms.

“So, where is she?”

“Fuck off, Hagan.”

“Temper, temper, boy,” Hagan said, shaking a finger at him. “I think you should focus on the Crown.”

“You’ll see, she will be my queen.”

“She’s a smart woman, boy,” Hagan countered. “You can’t bully her into anything.”

“Who needs to be a bully when you can woo?”

“Woo?” Hagan asked incredulously. “Who? You? I saw how well that worked for you the first time. Doesn’t she have a man now?”

“What’s that man got to do with me?” Ronan asked, unimpressed. “No sane woman would give up a chance to be a queen. Dunharra is no different.”

“You hope,” Hagan said. “Go get the crown.” He stepped through his portal and vanished.

Chapter Thirty-Eight

CHAPTER THIRTY EIGHT

ISEABAIL

The winter worked out to be as cold as the past summer had been hot. Temperatures dove close to the negative as they set out to beat Ronan to the Frozen Crown. They traveled up the Great Northern Road and stopped to rest the horses near Valide Island. They could hear the shoebilled storks clap their beaks as they gathered on the rocky shore.

They made it halfway to Dunkeld when the Darkness became too thick to travel any further. The group stopped at The Ram for the night.

"Ah! Hello!" Bruno exclaimed with open arms. "You come back! What brings you back?"

"Rooms for the night," Zauvadok said. "We're passing through."

"You come to da right place," Bruno said. "Three rooms or four?

"Four," Zauvadok said.

"Three," Dunharra and Magnus said simultaneously.

"Three," Dunharra said decisively. "Three."

Zauvadok gave Magnus a withering look.

"Three it is," Bruno said as he hurried behind the bar to retrieve the keys to three rooms. "They are next to each other. You'll sleep easily tonight."

Zauvadok pulled Magnus aside, grabbed him by his studded leather armor and stared at him nose to nose. He growled, "Keep her safe."

Iseabail lay awake long after making love with Tup. Her rhythmic breaths were soothing to her and she kissed her on the forehead as she slept. Her swirling thoughts wouldn't let her sleep.

She went downstairs to think things through. She had serious reservations that she didn't know what she needed to know about Tup. This made her anxious. Iseabail knew there must be more to her story.

As she descended the final stairs, she cast a light cantrip to guide her way. She watched Zauvadok sit alone at a table absently playing with a very large dagger, spinning it in his hand with alarming skill. He didn't flinch when she sat down next to him.

"What brings you down here so late at night?" Zauvadok asked. "Why aren't you snuggling with Tup in a warm bed? It's the last night for a while we'll have the luxury."

Iseabail sighed. "I... needed a minute alone. Tup and Calyx are sleeping."

"What's bothering you?" Zauvadok asked.

"I know a lot about Tup. Her thoughts, feelings, wants and needs. But she's never talked about her past. She had a life before me, and she's keeping it close to the vest. I mean, she killed people for a living, and apparently very well judging by her stash of gold. I am wondering how much of it will come back to bite her. Bite us," Iseabail confessed. She absently fidgeted with the light in her hands.

Zauvadok nodded. "I'm having trust issues too. I can't bring myself to trust Magnus with Dun, Iseabail. He kidnapped her to turn her in for the reward, and now he's convinced her of some supposed commitment. He's wormed his way close to her, and we still don't really know if we can trust him."

Iseabail sighed and waved the light cantrip away. She understood his position and empathetically put her hand on his.

"I get it," Iseabail said. " But why does this bother you so much?"

Zauvadok paused. He took a breath, and a chance. "I care for her. She was the only one besides Anaïs who saw through my size and heritage to see who I am inside. She was the only one who would heal Anaïs back in Rhyl, and she was the only one who could save her in the Chamber. I love her. I love her more than I think I should."

"Oh, Zau," Iseabail said, grasping his hand. "This, all of this, stays down here."

"Thank you," Zauvadok replied. "I don't think Anaïs would understand."

Iseabail nodded.

Together they walked back upstairs to their rooms.

Morning came much too early for everyone. Iseabail noticed Zauvadok's irritability and how he only put on a good face for Anaïs.

Eventually, they all made their way downstairs to a cheerful Bruno and breakfast waiting for them.

They set out right after breakfast, after bidding a warm goodbye to Bruno. Once out on the road, they could see the red and blue banners of Buckhaven on the horizon. Buckhaven chased them, behind by half a day, and they knew they needed to pick up the pace.

They rode hard to Dunkeld and rested the horses on the Aberdeen Trail. The tabards of Buckhaven and its banners fluttered in the wind on the horizon. They were making good time and were resting the horses as best they could.

The race to the Frozen Crown began.

And Ronan gained on them.

While they had the advantage of about half a day's ride, the gap narrowed by the hour. When they veered off the Great Northern Road toward the Aberdeen Pass, they could see that Ronan had a full retinue of knights and guards in his entourage. If they met, Ronan would outnumber them three to one. They did not rest until they saw the fires of the Buckhaven campsite.

Once settled in camp themselves, Anaïs cast out her wyverns to watch over the campsite and to help prevent any surprises. They retired to their tents and settled in for a frosty night.

***

RONAN

Ronan made ready with his full armor and flew his colors proudly as he set off to get the Frozen Crown. He took his normal contingency of soldiers, color bearers, and knights, and headed off toward the Great Northern Road.

They needed to travel through the Disputed Lands before they could meet the Great Northern Road. The bright red and blue livery scared off most of the riff raff and kept the hardcore rogues at bay. He made good time and traversed the Disputed Lands with little trouble.

Ronan used his spyglass to get a good look at the group that traveled ahead of him by half a day. He swore profusely when he saw Zauvadok.

They were trying to beat him to the Frozen Crown; if this kept up, they would.

"Let them, Your Majesty," his most senior knight replied. "If they touch it, they'll die. One less problem for you."

"For all but one," Ronan said as his spyglass' gaze fell on Dunharra. She stacked wood for the fire when Tup came over and set it alight. The fire danced and lit up Dunharra's face in shades of orange and yellow. Ronan stared longingly as she smiled, but his countenance turned sour when he saw who she smiled for.

Magnus.

Ronan seethed. Soon she would smile for him. Those kisses would fall on his lips, and those green eyes would dance only for him. He slammed the spyglass shut.

***

ISEABAIL

Late in the night the wyverns screeched out their alarm, jolting a frightened Iseabail awake. A squad of thirteen armed knights approached the camp with torches in their hands. With the ear-piercing shrieks from the wyverns, they all flew out of their tents. When they were out of their tents, the Buckhaven knights set them on fire. Iseabail tried to put out the flames only to have a sword put threateningly at her throat.

Magnus killed two knights making his way to Dunharra before another knight stopped him with a menacing sword at his throat. Zauvadok and Anaïs each killed a knight before being overcome and subdued. Despite wanting to call down lightning, Iseabail and Calyx found the campsite too crowded. The lightning would kill everyone.

The remaining knights marched them back to the Buckhaven encampment, their hands tied but their spirits defiant.

"Well, well, well," Ronan said with a sly grin. "What do we have here?"

"Let us go and avoid an international incident," Iseabail demanded.

"You are obsessed with having an international incident, Iseabail," Ronan teased, laughing at her. "Let me make myself clear. I don't care."

"Keep them contained but alive," Ronan ordered. "I'll take this one with me," he gestured at Dunharra. He turned around and walked away. A knight roughly dragged Dunharra to his tent as she looked back at Magnus and the others.

Iseabail protested being separated from Dunharra. The knights roughly took all of them to the main campfire, and guarded them closely.

***

DUNHARRA

Once they were in the tent, a knight roughly pushed Dunharra into a chair and secured her to it. Ronan waited until they were alone so he could speak freely.

"My dear, the fates have brought us together again," Ronan said.

"This is not the Fates, Ronan. This is kidnapping," Dunharra seethed.

"Oh, my darling," Ronan said as he laid a hand on her arm. "You'll see in time that this is for the best. For both of us."

"I determine what is best for me. Let us go," Dunharra replied.

"Dunharra, dearest Dunharra," Ronan began. "I want you."

Dunharra became sick inside to hear that but kept a straight face. "For what?"

"I want you to be my queen, of course," Ronan said. "To be my wife and lover."

"Ronan, I don't know what to say. Surely you know Magnus and I—"

"A minor indiscretion that is easily overlooked, my dear," Ronan interrupted her. He walked over to her and caressed her face. "I am offering you the chance of a lifetime."

He kept Dunharra in his tent overnight, giving her more creature comforts than the others. She had the luxury of sleeping alone in a warm bedroll and of a night free of ropes. Dunharra and Ronan slept on opposite sides of the tent. If he were to offer her his bed, she would gladly have spent the night out in the elements. She woke to a gentle kiss on her forehead.

"Good morning, love," Ronan said. "How did you sleep?"

"Better than those outside. Have they succumbed to the elements?" Dunharra asked angrily as she got up out of the bedroll.

"No," Ronan sighed heavily, Dunharra surmised that he wished they had. "They had a place by the fire where they could keep warm. Or warm enough to get through the night at least."

"How do you think this is going to entice me to be your queen?"

"You have yet to see the unlimited power of the Frozen Crown, my love. Time to go."

A knight placed Dunharra on her own horse and attached it to Ronan's, and they traveled up the Aberdeen Trail. She gazed longingly at the tiny offshoot trail that would bring her straight home as she passed it by. She fought tears and looked up at the cloudless blue sky, willing none to fall.

"What's troubling you, Dunharra?" Ronan asked.

"Nothing that you could understand. I miss my home," Dunharra replied.

"Buckhaven could be your new home," Ronan said. "All the herbs you could ever want, drying in your own study. Books on any subject your heart desires. You could have all the safety and security to be what you want, when you want. I'll build you an entire wing of the castle, all for your hand, my love."

Dunharra had to admit she felt tempted. Ronan offered her all the things she thought she always wanted, but could never have had otherwise. Everything she ever wanted and more. Temptation haunted her.

But every time Ronan called her his love, she wanted to vomit.

***

ISEABAIL

Iseabail noticed that Magnus became distant and pensive. The pained look on his face made her feel sorry for him. His eyes told her everything. His heart ached.

"What's on your mind, Magnus?" Iseabail asked.

"I can't help but hear what Ronan is offering Dun. Things I never could. I can barely offer her herbs to dry in her cottage, I certainly can't build her her own wing of a castle."

Magnus became quiet for a long moment. "I haven't had the chance to tell her how I really feel. I've tried, but something's always got in the way. Or interrupted me, and then the moment's gone. I'm afraid Ronan's getting to her."

Iseabail nodded. His promises were grandiose. The kind that makes you think twice about what you want in life. Promises that made you think you could do good in the world

"You'll get your chance. She's not one that gives in to that kind of pressure."

"Funny thing," Magnus said. "You always think you have time."

After a moment, Magnus continued. "I am ready to move on with my life. And I want my life to be with Dunharra. But how could I compete with a king?"

Dunharra only got a minute with Magnus before being whisked away to Ronan's tent again. She caressed his face and said, "How do you feel about me? I need to know—"

"Dunharra–" was all Magnus could say before a knight roughly carried her off to Ronan's tent.

"I love you," Magnus whispered.

Iseabail's eyes went wide and she stifled a gasp.

"Wait, what?" Zauvadok asked Magnus incredulously as they watched a knight carry Dunharra away to Ronan's tent.

"What of it?" Magnus sighed, raking his hands through his hair. He became tired of all the fighting with Zauvadok over Dunharra. He loved her, and he didn't care who knew.

"You've known her for what? Ten minutes?" Zauvadok grumbled. "And now you're in love? Sex does not equal love."

"No, it doesn't," Magnus sighed again. His patience with Zauvadok wore thin as he watched Dunharra get not so gently pushed into Ronan's tent. The sight pricked his already tightly strung nerves. "But I do love her."

Iseabail's mind raced back to the conversation she had with Zauvadok in the inn. "Oh, by the Mother," she whispered. She looked at Magnus and then back to Zauvadok.

"You break her heart, I break every bone in your body," Zauvadok growled, and pushed him for good measure.

Iseabail saw that Magnus reached his breaking point. He pushed Zauvadok back, and before he knew it, he landed on the ground fighting with him. Anaïs, Tup, and Iseabail jumped in, and it took all three of them to break them up. They both sported bloody noses and bruised pride. They shook it off and went to separate corners of the tent.

***

RONAN

"Have a seat, my lovely," Ronan crooned as he held out the chair for her.

Dunharra slid into the seat and gave Ronan the side eye. "What's up your sleeve, Ronan?"

"You don't trust that I want to court you honorably?" Ronan asked, feigning offense.

"No," Dunharra shot back.

"Oh, my lady, allow me to show you genuine romance, and not a transactional one," Ronan said.

"What do you mean by that?" Dunharra asked, feeling judged.

"Nothing, my lady," Ronan said. "Others shouldn't define your worth by what you do for them, but by who you are."

Dunharra remained silent. The sting of the truth was strong.

"Your whole life has been transactional, hasn't it?" Ronan continued, digging. "Let me show you what it's like to be loved for who you are and not what you can do for me."

"That's laughable coming from you. How are you going to do that? Captives can't make choices. That's about as transactional as you can get."

Ronan paused. This would not be easy.

"When did you last honestly made a choice for yourself?" Ronan tried another tactic. "Has every choice in your life benefited someone else?"

"You make that sound like it's a bad thing," Dunharra replied.

He could see she tried to keep it together. He hit nerves that were not ready to be plucked.

"My lady," Ronan began. He didn't expect banter. "I see this is taking a toll on you. Would you like to choose? For yourself?"

"I would like to be free to make my own choices." A single tear fell down her cheek.

He kissed the tear and gently wiped it away. "My lady, what would your choice be?"

"To be free to be myself," Dunharra whispered. "Few know who I am."

"I know who you are," Ronan said softly.

"You do not know who I am," Dunharra whispered. She stood to face him and stared him defiantly in the eye.

"I know more than you think," Ronan said as he bent his head down and kissed her gently on the lips.

"And what do you think you know?" Dunharra asked after he kissed her.

"I know you healed Kieron from a certain death," Ronan replied.

"Know that I am no one to trifle with," Dunharra said. "I have killed orcs. I can handle you."

"Fiery," Ronan said, impressed. "I like that."

"Then you'll like this," Dunharra said through gritted teeth. She jammed her knee into his crotch, and he crumpled to the ground in a shivering mess.

***

DUNHARRA

The wind howled outside the tent and it made sleeping difficult at best. Dunharra insisted that they have a blanket to fight off the freezing chill. Ronan gave them three, and the couples all shared them. Magnus' and Zauvadok's truce made her happy. Then a knight took her harshly to Ronan's tent.

"Welcome, my darling," Ronan cooed.

"I trust you've recovered?" Dunharra inquired.

"Entirely," Ronan said as the delicate dance of words began. "Had I known you were so feisty, I would have prepared differently."

"You know so little about me."

"Yet I know so much," Ronan quipped.

"You think you know," Dunharra said.

"Oh, it took me some time, but now I know more than you think," Ronan said, sitting next to her and taking her hand in his.

"Like what?"

"I know you are the Prophesied Healer," Ronan said triumphantly.

Dunharra gasped.

"You don't know that," Dunharra whispered.

"Oh, but I do. It's alright. Your secret is safe with me. As are you."

"What do you want from me?" Dunharra asked.

"An opportunity," Ronan replied simply. "To get to know each other better."

"And if you don't like what you learn?" Dunharra asked.

"To be determined, my lady," Ronan said. "I can't imagine anything about you being a deal breaker. I offer you a chance at what you want most."

"And what is that?" Dunharra asked, still stunned. Her breath came in short bursts.

"To choose," Ronan said. "To choose your life. Healer in high demand or Queen over a peaceful, quiet kingdom with access to anything your heart desires."

"You don't love me," Dunharra accused Ronan. "You love my power and what it can bring you."

"Rarely do royals receive the luxury of love, my lady," Ronan replied, standing to face her. "But in our case, I think we can grow to love each other."

Dunharra's world flipped upside down. He knew what she was, and he made a proposal that would let her be the herbalist and healer she wanted to be. Or thought she wanted to be.

Her entire world upended, and she knew Ronan expected an answer.

Magnus made her hesitate. *How did he feel about her? Did he love her like she loved him? Were the promises Ronan made worth denying Magnus?* Her mind swirled as she took a sip of wine. Uncertainty clogged her throat.

Ronan reached into his pocket and brought out a beautiful, intricate, and well made lace handkerchief and unfolded it on the table before her. Could it be Elven? She had not seen its equal. Inside lay a diamond ring the size of her thumbnail, breathtaking and brilliant. It lay encrusted with smaller but no less brilliant diamonds. Her heart beat against her chest.

"I can't accept this."

"Take it." Ronan put both the kerchief and the ring in her palm and closed her fingers around it. "Take this as a token of my affection and promise of our life together."

Dunharra looked at Ronan, unsure of what to do next. Chills crawled up her spine and her stomach roiled. She glistened with a faint wave of sweat as she held the jewelry in her hand. She shook with the enormity of the situation.

"Wear it on your left ring finger if you accept my proposal," Ronan added.

Ronan knelt before her. His tall stature assured that he looked her in the eye as she sat in the carved, padded chair before him. He kissed her gently at first, and then more passionately. Dunharra's skin crawled and she dropped the ring to the ground.

"Is that your final answer?"

"Final."

"Then you'll freeze with your friends."

Chapter Thirty-Nine

CHAPTER THIRTY NINE

ISEABAIL

The Buckhaven contingency stopped for the night at the narrowest passage between the Copperheart Forest and the Darkness. The knights pitched the captive's tent closest to the Darkness, where the howls and hisses of the night were most easily heard. They pitched the royal tent closest to the relative safety of the Copperheart Forest.

The Darkness was a deep, dark crescent-shaped forest that stood on the east side of the Unnamed City, which lay in ruin. Rumors abounded about the Darkness and the city it surrounded. Some said there were deadly secrets that lay on the land; others thought it the gateway to the damned. Regardless, people should avoid it at all costs.

Iseabail couldn't sleep. She lay awake in the loving arms of Tup, but sleep eluded her. Zauvadok's enormous arms kept Anaïs warm. Iseabail knew she felt none of the swirling drafts that the others shivered through. Magnus wrapped his arms around Dunharra as they slept.

With the frigid cold, the howling of the wind and the Darkness, Iseabail tossed and turned. She didn't want to disturb Tup any more than she already did, so she waited until Tup fell back asleep and slipped out of the captives' tent.

She shivered in the bitterly cold, constant breeze. The icy tentacles of chill would not release her from its grasp regardless of where she put herself. She wandered closer to the trees of the Darkness, seeking cover from the wind.

The Mauu scouts watched carefully as the caravan hugged the Argyll Pass, heading on a direct course to the Royal Eastern Road, which would skirt the Copperheart Forest to the east. Until then, they would dance delicately between the Copperheart Forest and the Darkness. The Mauu hoped that the Buckhaven contingency wanted no part of either.

Iseabail heard a low growl, a warning, for her to stray no closer. She froze in her tracks and searched carefully around her. She saw nothing, but she knew someone or something watched her. Iseabail strayed too far toward the Darkness. The frustration of being Ronan's captive and being dragged along to witness him take the Frozen Crown took its toll on her. The impotent days of waiting while she could do nothing wore on her and rubbed her soul raw. Iseabail feared no hell from the Darkness. She did not move.

Again, a low growl emanated from the Darkness, this time closer but unwilling to crest the edge. Iseabail turned and glared into the Darkness boldly, daring, willing the growler to come forward into the light shed by the Triplet Sister Moons or sit cowardly in the hidden forest.

"Stand down, Mountain Elf," a deep, powerful but feminine voice emanated from the Darkness.

"What do you want?" Iseabail said as she stood her ground.

"We want you to leave," the voice from the Darkness replied. "We want peace and solitude."

"Unfortunately, you'll get neither," Iseabail continued. "We are camping here for the night."

"Then move on," the voice responded, as if it were as simple as that.

"It's not my call. I'm a captive."

"Slave." The voice now carried a sharp, accusatory tone.

"Captive," Iseabail repeated and took a step toward the Darkness.

A muscular, bipedal, humanoid cat stepped out of the Darkness. Armored in dark brown studded leather, thick winter cloak and armed with a massive two-handed sword, the cat moved into the moonlight. Her thick, creamy yellow, jaguar like fur covered her whole body and her thick tail that flicked rapidly. She crossed her arms and regarded Iseabail carefully.

"Who keeps you captive?" the Mauu asked.

"King Ronan of Buckhaven," Iseabail replied.

"King?" the cat asked incredulously. "Ronan is a petulant youngling."

The Mauu's eyes were like a storm coming ashore as Iseabail met her gaze.

"Petulant youngling or not, he's the king now. He means to get the Frozen Crown."

"What is this madness?" The cat crouched to Iseabail's height to look her in the eye. "What do you mean?"

Iseabail explained how King Darragh, working with a mage, sought the Frozen Crown but the assassin Lars poisoned him. The mage thought that King Ronan would make a fine puppet ruler. So he threw his magic behind Ronan.

"Not if the Mauu have anything to say about it," the Mauu answered.

"Who are you?"

"I am Zoya of the Mauu. The Crown is to be untouched."

"You'd better tell Ronan that," Iseabail said. "He aims to have it by any means necessary."

A low rumble emanated from Zoya's throat, then she turned back into the Darkness and vanished.

The Triplet Sister Moons were sliding down the horizon and the sun showed signs of rising. The cold chilled Iseabail to the bone, and wisps of cloud-like breath escaped her mouth. Iseabail trudged to the tent and laid her freezing self next to Tup. She felt warmer, but she also felt something better. She felt home.

***

Iseabail got maybe an hour of sleep next to Tup when the Buckhaven knights woke them for another day's travel. She told them about her walk toward the Darkness and her encounter with Zoya. Then they rode in silence.

To Iseabail's amazement, the Mauu emerged from the Darkness. Four strong, bipedal humanoid cats stepped out into the light and stood in the road, halting the party's progress. They wore studded leather armor, thick winter cloaks, and carried massive two-handed swords. Their jaguar-like fur ruffled in the frigid breeze. They stared with eyes as hard as stone.

The entire caravan came to a stop. Horses stomped and grunted nervously in the biting cold. Fear rattled them, and they refused to go further.

One of Ronan's knights rode forward to see the cause of the commotion. His horse bucked and reared up, never having seen such a creature before. He got control of his horse, but not before inspiring nervousness and disobedience in the other horses.

"What is it you seek?" the knight asked.

"You and your caravan are too close to the Darkness," the Mauu said. "What is it you want?"

"Nothing of your concern; we are passing through," the knight said as he gestured for them to move out of their way.

"You have captives. Set them free," the Mauu demanded.

"Absolutely not!" Ronan, impatient with the delay, rode up to the front of the caravan.

"Your Majesty," the knight bowed.

"I seek to pass by in peace," Ronan said to the Mauu.

"What is the object of your desire?" Zoya asked pointedly, putting a hand on her sword.

"To pass by peaceably."

"Release your captives," Zoya demanded again.

"No," Ronan said simply. Iseabail could see his patience wore thin.

"You treat them worse than slaves. They suffer from exposure. Release them. We will care for them properly.

"No!" Ronan shouted. "They are mine. They will witness me taking the Frozen Crown."

Iseabail watched helplessly as Zoya drew her large and battle scarred two-handed sword. The other three Mauu did the same. Knights in the Buckhaven contingency drew their smaller swords in response. The sound of metal sliding against metal rang out.

"Stand down or you will die here!" Zoya shouted.

"I offer you the same," Ronan sneered.

Without a further word, the Mauu brought on the attack, engaging the first three knights in the caravan. Ronan sat back and watched his knights enter the melee and fall in quick succession to the Mauu. Six more knights engaged the Mauu, and Ronan rode past the fighting and onward toward the Royal Eastern Road flanked by two knights on either side.

The Mauu killed all the remaining knights.

Only Zauvadok, Anaïs, Dunharra, Iseabail, Calyx, Tup, and Magnus remained alive, shivering in the cold. Zoya removed her cloak and put it around Zauvadok, who wrapped it around Anaïs as well. Magnus did the same with Dunharra and Iseabail with Tup and Calyx when the others offered their cloaks to them.

"Follow me," Zoya ordered, and she disappeared into the Darkness.

Iseabail led the way as they followed Zoya as she tracked through the Darkness. She walked slowly, allowing her refugees to keep pace with her as she negotiated a well-disguised trail. Within the hour they were at the edge of a city.

"Cloud Hill," Zoya said. "Here, you will rest and recuperate. Then we will aid you on your way."

Cloud Hill was a city of wood and stone buildings, none over two stories tall. Mauu populated Cloud Hill, and they stood and watched as Zoya led them to a stone dwelling lit by a well-kept fire. The group instantly surrounded the fire, trying to get warm. They held their hands out tentatively, their hands burning from the frostbite as they received the warmth of the fire. Their stomachs growled at the aroma of a thick stew bubbling in a pot near the fire. It had been days since they had eaten.

Once warmed, Dunharra healed each person's frostbite. Iseabail saw what Dunharra did not. Zoya, interested in Dunharra's healing, watched closely as Dunharra's touch restored the skin from ghostly gray and white to its natural color. She healed fingers, toes, tips of ears, and noses.

The Mauu brought them warm clothes and leather armor in the hours after they ate their fill of the bubbling stew, which never seemed to run out. All the clothes and armor fit the wearer, regardless of who put them on. Anaïs, Iseabail and Calyx could see the magick glowing through the stitching.

This is awfully generous for people who want to be left alone, Iseabail. Calyx used their shared mental link to talk with Iseabail.

I know. Iseabail replied. *They want something, but what?*

Zoya provided them with a private room to sleep in, complete with a burning hearth and Mauu-sized bedrolls for each, though half remained unused. They were warm with full bellies for the first time in days. They slept soundly.

They slept until they woke naturally. Deep in the Darkness, Iseabail looked up and saw that the sun penetrated little, and the little light that got through provided no warmth. The trees were thick and old, with a near-impenetrable canopy in which copious birds and other wildlife made their home. This did not resemble the stories told to her about the Mauu.

When they were all awake, Zoya entered the room. She carried with her an assortment of weapons. As each of them made their choice, the weapon seemed to conform to the size of their hand. Tup's choice of short sword immediately balanced with her stature and weight. Iseabail chose a staff with a large clear crystal securely nestled at the top. Once the staff touched her hand, the crystal swirled with magick, and its color changed to an icy blue. Anaïs also chose a staff. The large, clear crystal, secured at the top, swirled and its color changed to a blood red. Magnus chose a fierce-looking two-handed sword. This also adjusted so it fit his hand. Zauvadok's sword felt at home in his hand. He wielded it with ease, as if designed specifically for him.

"This is awfully generous of you, Zoya," Zauvadok began. "What are you looking for in return?"

"Solitude," Zoya replied. "We wish to be undisturbed. Our way of life is peaceful without intervention, human or otherwise. There are many who would come with less than honorable intentions seeking to destroy what we have made here. We wish to be left alone."

"That can't be it," Iseabail said. "You are generous, but is there something else you wish in return for your kindness?"

"King Ronan journeys to Donmus buz Tutmus," Zoya said. "There is only one reason to go to that frozen wasteland. The Frozen Crown. Has he discovered a way around its magick?"

"Yes," Iseabail answered. She retold how he made an alliance with Hagan to subvert the magick using a spell from The Rud Eskimiş.

"This is deeply troubling," Zoya said.

"Indeed," Iseabail said.

"The Frozen Crown has attributes that many people don't know," Zoya began. "Ronan will find this out the hard way. His lust for power and revenge lured him, but the Frozen Crown is dangerous. You must prepare the Southern Kingdoms and stop Ronan. Go with our blessing and then send us good news."

***

DUNHARRA

Zoya escorted them to the edge of the Darkness and wished them good luck. "Bring us good tidings, friends of the Mauu." She put a hand on Dunharra's arm, stopping her. "A moment?"

Could she know? How could she possibly know? She keeps herself to the Darkness. Maybe the tales had not penetrated here.

"How many know about you, Dunharra?"

"Know?" Dunharra's hands shook.

Time seemed to slow to a stop as Dunharra stared back at Zoya. She did not notice that her friends returned to her side. That gave way to numbness and heaviness as Zoya simply held up her hand.

"Us, Ronan," Iseabail replied for Dunharra. "The king and queen of Innesfrees, and two of their healers."

Dunharra sighed. She wanted to find a hole and crawl in it.

"This is not a burden," Zoya said, reading Dunharra's body language.

Dunharra's eyes remained downcast. Zoya lifted her furred hand and held up Dunharra's chin. "This is a gift. You have good friends around you. You will embody this gift with grace."

Dunharra could only nod. "I hope so."

"Protect her," Zoya said. "Not everyone will look kindly on her gift."

Dunharra stepped out of the Darkness first and into the bright light of the noon sun. She covered their eyes against the insult of the light, having become accustomed to darkness and shadow. After all of their affronted eyes adjusted, they got their bearings.

They traveled on a course straight to Innesfrees. It took the better part of the day to make it to Tromso Road and approach the Mirimah River. Zauvadok and Magnus grumbled at each other, but otherwise did not come to blows. Dunharra found a clearing next to a meadow large enough for everyone to camp.

Anaïs' red-eyed wyverns circled the camp on their silent sentry. The night passed without incident. Morning broke in a cloudless sky. One by one they left their tents, their warm breath hanging in the cold air as wispy plumes.

They traveled down the Aberdeen Trail, careful of the pickpockets and petty thieves that grew more frequent the closer they came to the Great Northern Road and Dunkeld. More than once Dunharra swatted away greedy hands from their belts and pockets.

They traveled this way all the way to Dunkeld and to the Ram.

"Zauvadok! You come back," Bruno said, tossing aside the rag he used to wipe down the bar and meeting them at the door. He gave Zauvadok and Magnus hearty claps on the back and kissed the cheeks of the ladies. He led them to a table in the back, big enough to accommodate them. Bruno brought them fine honey mead and bowls of thick stew with large chunks of bread.

"On da house," Bruno said.

"How do you get people to give you things?" Magnus asked.

"It happens when you're not an asshole, Magnus," Zauvadok retorted.

"Which makes it doubly curious how you do it."

Zauvadok growled, and stood when Anaïs laid her hand on his arm. Dunharra did the same with Magnus. They stood down, but the ill will still simmered below the surface.

After an hour of eating and strategizing, they retired upstairs, looking forward to a night in relative safety and in comfortable beds.

Morning broke over the horizon with the promise of spring in the air, much to Dunharra's relief. The intense cold held off for the past few nights. Tiny buds of new life blossomed on the trees. Birds called out the new day, and Dunharra delighted in nature stirring from a long winter's sleep.

The twinkle of Imbolc sparkled in more than one person's eye, making the mood in and around the Ram blissful. Bruno brought candles to light, bay laurel to hang around The Ram, and amethyst stones to display in the common room downstairs to commemorate the return of the light. Although too early to plant, but not too early to plan the coming months' planting. Bruno plotted his garden as they came downstairs for breakfast.

Bruno welcomed them like long-lost friends, as if they had not been there the night before. He placed steaming bowls of oatmeal sweetened with brown maple sugar in front of each of them.

"Imbolc comes soon," he said with a twinkling, knowing eye.

"So, Ronan has the Crown," Dunharra said. "What do we do now?"

"We head to Innesfrees," Iseabail answered. "He'll come down to the Southern Kingdoms hungry for war and retribution. We need to be ready."

"That can't be it," Dunharra said. "There has to be something we can use against him."

"I don't know," Iseabail said. "But if there's anything to use against him, we'll likely find it at Innesfrees."

They stayed with Bruno at The Ram all morning and part of the afternoon planning for Ronan and the Crown.

Chapter Forty

CHAPTER FORTY

RONAN

Ronan rode hard for the rest of the day. He abandoned his knights and Dunharra to the mercies of the Mauu and felt nothing. His heart, to him guiltless, did not ache. He sacrificed them so he could continue to the Frozen Crown. That's all that mattered.

The Frozen Crown. The crown he deserved. He desired it more than anything in this life, and he could almost feel it in his grasp. Now he needed Hagan and he could take it for himself.

The sun hung low on the horizon when he finally rested his exhausted horse. The remaining two knights at his side made camp and a fire that warmed and comforted him. Part of him wished Dunharra would see him grasp the crown in his hands and put it on his head. She would have been the very first witness to his power and authority.

The morning broke, covering the camp with its cleansing light, yet that light brought no warmth. To Ronan, the Wheel could not turn fast enough to bring about the longer and warmer days that came with Imbolc. He wanted those warmer days. Traveling in the bitter cold did not suit him well.

He rode all morning and most of the afternoon, skirting the edge of the Copperheart Forest until he reached the port city of Far Harbor. There he hired a boat to take him straight to Donmus buz Tutmus. It would take the greater part of a day to reach the Arctic island, and the freezing weather, compounded by the season, made the voyage even more dangerous. Small icebergs littered the Great Northern Sea, which made the crossing treacherous. The captain had to emergently maneuver the schooner more than once away from chunks of ice that could tear a gaping hole in the hull and sink his ship.

The sun hung low in the sky and the temperature dropped steadily when the island came into view. The captain sailed as close as he dared, then dropped anchor and sent Ronan off in a rowboat to the rocky shore. When the rowboat hit the shore, it jarred Ronan and elicited a rash of colorful language from him. He stood on the shore, chilled to the bone, looking around for a hint of where to go or what to do.

"Hagan!" Ronan called out. "I'm here! Time to come out."

A swirling, undulating oval of red tentacles appeared about ten feet away from Ronan. Moments later, Hagan stepped through the portal, staff in hand, looking Ronan up and down.

"I normally do not come when called," Hagan said, irritated. "I thought under the circumstances I would make an exception." He leaned on his staff and regarded Ronan.

Ronan rolled his eyes. "Your sacrifice is duly noted," Ronan said sarcastically.

"I should hope so, Ronan," Hagan said pointing at Ronan. "This is above and beyond my call of duty."

"This was your idea, Hagan," Ronan replied.

"No, it was your father's, boy. You are merely a suitable replacement. Let's get moving."

Hagan gripped Ronan's arm and whispered words of magick that made the ink on Hagan's neck glow with a deep blood-red hue. Ronan's world spun. He thought he might fall, be sick, lose control of his bowels, or all three. As suddenly as it started, it came to an abrupt stop. Ronan fell to his knees and vomited up everything he had eaten in the last day.

"Tsk, tsk, Ronan," Hagan said. "You simply must build up your endurance."

"A little warning would have been nice," Ronan snapped as he stood on shaky legs.

"Oh, how dramatic," Hagan sighed.

"Do you have everything you need?" Ronan asked, skeptical of Hagan.

"Yes, now that you're here."

They walked about one hundred feet over icy ground and then saw the Crown. It stopped them both in their tracks. Ronan could not have imagined a more beautiful Crown, encrusted with diamonds that glittered in the setting arctic sun. The Crown, awe inspiring in its simplicity sparkled. Ronan estimated the diamond at the center of the iskender circlet to be at least fifty carats. The Crown sat in a crystal box waiting for someone to come and claim it.

Ronan reached for the Crown when Hagan slapped his hand away. "Patience. You're worse than your father."

Hagan lifted a scroll from inside his cloak and unrolled it. With a few words of magick, the ink on his hands lit with the same deep red glow that Ronan had seen previously. The scroll levitated in the air as Hagan prepared the magick that would save Ronan from being instantly frozen solid when he touched the Crown. Words of magick that Ronan did not understand swirled around him like the wind as Hagan's voice went from a quiet whisper to a great and powerful shout. Red bolts of lightning pierced the sky. Thunder rolled overhead. Nature itself protested this application of magick. Ronan looked down to see the sea churning and roiling. He laughed with satisfaction.

When it seemed as if it were reaching a fever pitch, Hagan clapped his hands once, and all went still. He opened his mouth and out came a deep red plume of smoke. It encircled Ronan and hesitated as if trying to judge his worthiness. Then, in one sudden motion, the plume of red smoke rushed into Ronan's mouth.

"You may now touch the Crown," Hagan said, breathless. It looked to Ronan like Hagan's body felt like it weighed a thousand pounds from the magnitude of magick he employed. He leaned heavily on his staff.

Ronan stepped up and hesitantly opened the glass box that held the Crown. He reached out to touch it. He felt a vibration, a sense of overwhelming power, at his fingertips. Ronan took the Crown in his hands and placed it on his head.

Who disturbs my slumber?

The voice came into Ronan's head, a deep, powerful, gravelly voice. He blinked rapidly and whirled around, and then looked behind him, for the source of the voice. He found no one.

"Oh, did I forget to mention the Frozen Crown is intelligent?" Hagan teased between ragged breaths as he leaned heavily on his staff.

Ronan's eyes bulged. He could not think. He could feel a presence pierce his mind, and he could not stop it. Reflexively, his hands flew to the Crown and tried to remove it.

The Crown did not move. No way existed to remove the Crown manually.

"You bastard!" Ronan shouted. "What have you done?"

"No, what have *you* done?" Hagan said with a cocky smile. "The Crown is now yours. But it comes at a cost."

"What cost?" Ronan asked, breathless and mouth slightly open.

"You'll find out," Hagan said as he slowly limped toward a clearing.

"You son of a bitch!" Ronan snarled and ran to catch up with Hagan. "Get this thing off me!"

"No. It is not easily reversed, and I am in no mood to do so." He laughed, then leaned heavily on his staff again. Ronan thought he lacked the strength to reverse the magick.

"So, what now?" Ronan asked, his voice wavering.

"I take a nap," Hagan said. "You get to know your new friend."

Hagan found a somewhat comfortable spot in the clearing and laid down. Soon, he slept. Ronan heard him snore. This left Ronan alone with the Crown.

Who disturbs my slumber? The voice rang through his head again.

"Ronan O' Dochartaigh, King of Buckhaven," Ronan said aloud, his voice trembling.

Ronan O' Dochartaigh, King of Buckhaven, the voice repeated. *Why have you disturbed my slumber?*

"To get revenge against Innesfrees for assassinating my father," Ronan answered. His mouth went dry. "I want to rule over them and treat them the way they treated my family."

Revenge, the Crown said. *I love it!* Oddly enthused, the Crown vibrated on his head, its voice booming. "Let me tell you how we'll do this."

Ronan sat still and listened as the Crown laid out its plan for domination. A grin began creeping at the corners of his mouth, which before long bloomed into a maniacal smile as the Crown laid out step by step the plan it hatched in its centuries of waiting.

Ronan nudged Hagan awake. "Wake up, it's time to go."

"I don't take orders from you, boy," Hagan grumbled at being awakened early from his much-needed rest.

"You do now," Ronan said, pointing to the Crown. "This says so."

"I got you that Crown, boy," Hagan reminded Ronan as he sat on the frigid ground. "Don't you forget that."

"And I'll be forever grateful," Ronan said with an exaggerated eye roll. "Take me back to the boat."

Hagan grumbled as he heaved his weary body upright. He breathed a heavy sigh and touched Ronan on his shoulder. As before, the world spun, and Ronan felt like he was going to lose every piece of food he ever ate. He had a sensation of flying, swirling, twisting in the wind before he landed with a hard thump on the beach mere feet from the rowboat that would bring him back to the safety of the frigate.

Ronan shook off all the sensations that went along with such teleportation, and the Crown spoke to him. "Hagan is a liability," it said.

"Pushing the limits of my stamina is unwise, boy," Hagan scolded him. "Don't push me again."

He will always tell you what to do, the Crown said. *Always in the shadows, trying to pull your strings and treating you like a youngling. Like a puppet.*

Ronan watched as Hagan walked slowly to the rowboat. His mind swirled as he thought about being beholden to Hagan. He thought Hagan would lord it over him constantly. His heart hardened. Rash, irrational thoughts ran through his mind, inspired by the Crown.

Ronan followed Hagan into the rowboat. He waited patiently as the soldiers rowed out to sea. Once they were halfway to the frigate and fully out at sea, Ronan slowly eased a dagger out of its scabbard.

Yes, the Crown cooed. *Hagan is an obstacle to you. He stands in your way.*

The Crown sparkled in the moonlight as the Triplet Sister Moons danced in the sky. The sea splashed up the sides of the rowboat, and the aroma of salt water flooded their noses.

Kill him, the Crown commanded.

Ronan acted without thinking, doing the bidding of the Crown. Ronan sliced Hagan's neck from behind; the blade briefly glinted in the moonlight before being bathed in fresh blood.

The sailors shouted in shock and surprise as blood spurted from Hagan's neck. With a shove, Ronan pushed Hagan overboard. The rowboat rocked and threatened to capsize. Hagan's blood-soaked, lifeless body fell into the freezing sea.

The two knights looked at each other, eyes wide and staring. They swallowed hard, then continued to row to the frigate in silence.

Chapter Forty-One

CHAPTER FORTY ONE

AOIFE

Aoife walked swiftly to Iain's chambers; now he would teach her lessons she could really use. If she were lucky, she could get ink again soon. She didn't want to risk it, so she picked up the pace.

She knocked on his door as the clock in his room struck seven. Right on time.

They spent the morning studying international relations and diplomacy, thankful for the break from conversational Elvish and harsh Dwarven verbs.

She listened intently to Iain when she felt her ink tingle. All around her face and down her neck tingled, how the sparkling water from Manasquan tingled on her tongue.

"Aoife, your ink is glowing," Iain said tentatively.

"That's the ancient ink Mhari gave me," Aoife replied, confused. "She said I would probably never use it."

"It looks like someone thinks otherwise," Iain said. "We must speak with Mhari and your parents. Now."

Mhari soon joined Iain and Aoife in her mother's private chambers. Her father was already present, enjoying time with his wife. She could tell things got serious right away. She felt a little afraid. Aoife's ink still glowed a deep emerald green and it made her brilliant red hair shine even more. She sat completely still as she watched the ink glow on her face.

"Oh, by the Mother," Mhari gasped as she inspected Aoife's face.

"Mhari? What ink did you give Aoife?" Maebh asked.

Aoife knew trouble brewed because of her glowing ink. All the people she cared about were in one room, and they spoke to each other in harsh tones. It seemed like they were going to have an argument over her, and she didn't like it.

"But what does this mean for Aoife?" Iain asked.

Mhari could not peel her eyes away from Aoife's glowing ink, and her hands trembled. "It was only supposed to be decorative," she said.

"It looks like it's not," Maebh said. "What ink did you give her?"

"Ink to counteract the Frozen Crown," Mhari said, looking at the floor.

"You did what? To a child? My daughter?" Aoife saw her mother's anger intensify. Her mother's eyes narrowed as she stared at Mhari.

"The only thing we have going for us is that Ronan probably doesn't know about Aoife's ink," Kieron said. "We can use that to our advantage."

"She's our child, Kieron. She shouldn't have to," Iain said as he shot a dark look at Kieron.

"If you have a better idea, Iain, we're ready to hear it," her father said, looking Iain directly in the eye.

"Lock down Innesfrees," her mother commanded. "Put the best archers on the turrets and the strongest warriors at the gate. I may not stop this, but I can make it damn hard for Ronan to get at her."

They spent the greater part of the day planning their defense from Ronan and the Frozen Crown. Aoife's heart raced. Images of possible scenarios rushed through her mind. Would she even survive?

Aoife watched as preparations were being made to be ready for Ronan when he arrived. She saw knights set large spikes on triggered wires in the cold, moist ground, covering them with leaves and other natural debris to hide them. Trenches were dug and accommodations were ready to house and hide the townspeople, if Ronan set upon destroying the countryside again.

The inside of Castle Innesfrees bustled with activity. Bandages were being torn and rolled, and herbs, salves, and medications were being prepared for the inevitable wounded. Aoife had the task of taking precious items and storing them deep within the castle to save them if Ronan's raiders breached the walls and entered Innesfrees. She watched as the townspeople stockpiled food and stored away copious amounts of water.

Her mother sent the two fastest couriers Innesfrees had to call for help from Stirling and Cobh. They set out, barely sparing the horses. Aoife knew Stirling would to send aid, but would Cobh? And if they did, would it arrive in time? King Conrad of Cobh was a fickle and unreliable king.

They only had to wait for Ronan to arrive. Their bellweather in Aoife gave them a guide how close Ronan came as the days passed. All the while, Aoife's ink grew in intensity, she could light a darkened room with her presence.

As Ronan crossed the Copperheart Forest by way of the Argyll Pass and Aoife's ink grew brighter, her demeanor darkened. She braced herself for the battle that lay ahead. As Ronan crossed the Mirimah River and traveled Tromso Road toward the Aberdeen Trail, Aoife's mood turned a deep melancholy. During those days, she left her studies and did as she wanted. Iain and Mhari were busy making the infirmary ready, and her mother and father were supervising the preparation of the countryside for war. With each mile Ronan neared, Aoife's ink glowed brighter.

Aoife knew Ronan marched on to Innesfrees.

Seven days after Aoife's ink started glowing, they could see troops amass on the western horizon. With their preparations almost complete, the sighting of the troops sent them into a frenzy, as people ran chaotically around the castle. Aoife spent time at the turrets, watching as more and more troops amassed on the border.

Then she saw him. Ronan. With the Crown. Aoife's ink glowed so brightly, it almost burned to the touch. The nearer Ronan came to her, the Crown also glowed with the same brightness as Aoife's ink. Her ink allowed her to sense the malice that oveflowed from Ronan via the Crown.

She knew what to do. But could she do it?

***

DUNHARRA

Bruno bid them a jovial goodbye as they left The Ram. He reminded them they always had a place there and to visit often. Dunharra had them set off on the Great Northern Road, traveling down to the Southern Kingdoms as quickly as possible. They traveled as far as Valide Island when they saw an army amassed on the horizon. While too far away to discern colors or a faction, Dunharra could easily guess that this was Ronan and the Buckhaven army.

"Ronan moved fast," Magnus observed.

"How are we going to get through that garrison line?" Iseabail asked.

"If we go anywhere near it, we're guests of Ronan again," Dunharra said.

"Our best chance is by boat to the Port of Innesfrees," Zauvadok suggested.

"What if the Buckhaven navy blockaded the port?" Dunharra asked. "Or shut down by the Buckhaven army?"

"I don't think Ronan's had time to organize that yet," Magnus said.

"I don't see where we have much of a choice," Calyx chimed in. "Avoiding certain capture and sailing around the troops to come in from behind sounds like the best thing we could do."

"The Ádh Mor lighthouse is south of Innesfrees," Dunharra said. "We could dock there and come up to Innesfrees, avoiding the Buckhaven troops altogether."

They hired a small boat from Valide Island and sailed down the Bannockburn River. They had little trouble getting through the mouth of the river into the Bay of Charms. Once out on the bay, to their relief, the Buckhaven navy had not yet arrived to blockade the port. However, there were troops close enough to the port that they thought it too risky to try to access it. They sailed down to the Ádh Mór Lighthouse and docked there under the cover of twilight.

They traveled to Stirling as the sun finished its slide under the horizon and the Three Sisters breached the star-filled sky. Taverns and inns dotted the road to Stirling. Within the hour, the purple and black flags of Stirling came into view. The group stopped at the Eye of the Beholder Inn and got three rooms for the night.

Imbolc morning breached the horizon but brought little warmth. The light spilled through the early morning clouds and fell in rays through the windows of The Eye of the Beholder. This illuminated Dunharra's short black ringlets and Magnus could hardly resist running his fingers through it. This woke her from her sleep, so she turned to face him. Magnus rewarded her with a kiss.

Soon they met in the long common room downstairs for breakfast, then set off for Innesfrees. The journey would take until this afternoon, and they spent most of it in quiet, personal conversations.

They arrived in Innesfrees as the Imbolc sun halfway set in the cloudless sky. The celebratory bonfires built before Buckhaven perched on their boundary went unlit and the hearty meals traditionally consumed on this day went unprepared. All of Innesfrees watched the ever-increasing number of knights and soldiers on their northwestern border.

They reached Castle Innesfrees before the knights secured and locked the gate. Upon their arrival, a knight brought them to the war room, where they found Kieron and Maebh locked in battle plans with their strongest, steadfast, and most experienced knights.

"We expect the first volley at daybreak tomorrow," one grizzled knight reported.

A knock at the door broke their concentration. As all eyes fell on Dunharra and the others, an emissary walked through the door holding a scroll covered with the blue and red colors of Buckhaven that captured their full attention.

"Buckhaven sues for Innesfrees' unconditional surrender," the emissary said with a somber and even tone.

"Refused," Maebh said.

"Acknowledged," the emissary replied and promptly exited the room.

Maebh walked to Dunharra. She smiled a weary smile and hugged everyone tightly. "You are welcome here unconditionally."

After the appropriate curtsies, bows, and introduction of Magnus, Dunharra spoke. "We have unfortunate news to give you. Ronan has the Crown."

Maebh nodded. "We suspected as much," she said. She related the news of Aoife's ink and how it glowed when, they supposed, Ronan activated the Crown. She also relayed how the glow grew in intensity as the Crown came closer to Innesfrees.

"Where is Aoife now?" Iseabail asked.

"She watches the forces amassed from the safety of the turrets," Kieron replied, wearily rubbing his eyes. "She has been obsessed since her ink began to glow."

***

AOIFE

Aoife watched as more and more soldiers gathered on the horizon. She didn't know what was happening, but it had to do with her ink and the Crown, and none of it was good. Her mind spun with many possibilities, and her breath caught in her chest. She thought this was what she wanted. To matter and to have a say in decisions that directly affected her. She hadn't envisioned this at all. Questions swirled around her mind like a hurricane, and she wanted to hide.

The cold Imbolc wind blew through her bright red ringlets. She felt an inexplicable pull toward the Crown, and the feeling of inevitable conflict haunted her. The topsy-turvy in her stomach felt like she was in trouble and doing something great at the same time. She fixed her eyes on the shining object on Ronan's head, and her already glowing ink pulsed with her heartbeat. The longer she looked, the louder her heartbeat became. Louder and louder it beat until she could no longer hear the howl of the changing winds. She could only hear her heartbeat.

And the Crown. She could hear the Crown. The Crown feared her.

Aoife's stomach roiled. She leaned into the fear she felt from the Crown, experimenting with exerting her will over it. She could feel her feet leaving the safety of the castle turrets. Slowly, steadily, she rose in the air with her ink pulsating with her heartbeat and glowing brighter than it ever had before. The ink felt hot, like a sunburn on her skin.

She could not tell how high she floated. The wind blew stronger as she floated higher and higher until she floated a full ten feet above the safety of the castle turret. She did not hear or see the geese as they flew toward her. As they banked to avoid the obstacle in the sky, a goose grazed her head with its wing, breaking her concentration, and she plummeted to the ground with a piercing scream. She fell, flailing, and landed crumpled upon the stone turret. Blood trickled from her mouth and nose, and all went black.

***

RONAN

Ronan sat on his horse, which was adorned with the colors of Buckhaven almost to the point of garishness. The Crown spoke to him, telling him where to send which troops and how glorious his reign would be.

And then it stopped. Ronan froze. He listened. The heartbeat in his mind was audible, and it alarmed him that it was not his. The silence of the Crown unsettled him, but the heartbeat was doubly so. It grew louder and louder, blocking out the sound of his army, blocking out the howling Imbolc wind, and blocking out his own connection with the Crown.

But he could still sense the Crown. He sensed its fear. And he was afraid along with it.

Ronan tried to gain control of the Crown and struggled to control his own emotions at the same time. Fear made his blood run cold; the fear he felt from the Crown and his own fear about losing control. His breath quickened, and sweat beaded on his forehead. He felt a blinding, searing pain in his head where the Crown sat. Ronan moaned with pain, and his mouth went dry.

He perceived the Crown's enchantment, and his sole focus became locating the source. He tried to discern where the force that held the Crown in such sway was coming from. His head pounded, and the pain became nearly unbearable and kept him from focusing. The fear, the pain, it all flowed together and became a cacophony that threatened his sanity.

And then the scream; the fierce scream pierced his ears. He held his hands over his ears and screamed himself, alarming his knights, who were growing concerned about him. Then, a sharp pain in his head broke through the reverie, and all went black. He fell from his horse and onto the cold, hard ground.

Yet the Crown remained secure on his head.

His knights whisked Ronan up off the ground and brought him into his tent.

“Your Majesty, can you hear me?” one knight asked.

“Fetch the healers!” another shouted, as squires ran off to find them.

“Is he—?” a third asked.

"Dead? No," Ronan replied, groggy. His eyes remained closed as he tried to process what happened. He rubbed his temple to ease the pounding and dizziness in his head.

We have a powerful enemy in Innesfrees, the Crown said.

Ronan listened carefully, the voice of the Crown rising to the top of the riotous pain that made his head swim.

Nothing less than total annihilation will suffice, the Crown seethed. *That harbinger of doom must die.*

Ronan felt evil and hatred flow from the Crown into his soul. He felt it cloud his judgment and color the way he saw things. Things like how he wanted to rule over Innesfrees and avenge his father.

Vengeance! Yes! Avenge your father, the Crown urged Ronan.

Ronan listened and felt his own desire for vengeance rise. His father knew what was best, and that was absorbing Innesfrees into Buckhaven to form one powerful kingdom. Cobh and Stirling would quake in the face of the new Buckhaven!

Yes, let your rage grow, the Crown suggested. *Feel your anger flow through you.*

The pain in his head ebbed as he let his anger loose. He could feel the satisfaction and approval from the Crown as he let it simmer, slowly coming to a rolling boil.

Ronan sat up and, with the help of his knights, sat in his field chair. Yes, this would mean a change of plans. A change of tactics. He would destroy Innesfrees and all within it. Make it all his own. Every man, woman, and child would fall to the Crown.

Wearing the Crown seemed to work out nicely, he thought.

The Crown laughed. *Nicely indeed.*

***

DUNHARRA

Magnus eyed Dunharra's thin frame. The sun slipped below the horizon, drenching the world with a blue-gray twilight that silhouetted her body. Magnus reached for her hand, which she offered with a shy smile. She gently pulled him close to her and kissed him. She was greatly enthused and highly motivated by his vigorous consent as he laid her on the bed. Magnus eased her out of her clothes, and she helped him with his tunic and trousers.

She kissed him longingly again; the thought of making love with Magnus was keenly on her mind. Magnus nuzzled her neck, kissing it gently, which elicited a sultry purr from her. She knew he loved the happy little noises she made.

Then came a frantic knock at the door.

Dunharra sighed and closed her eyes. Magnus donned his trousers and answered the door to find three young initiates standing awkwardly, trying to look anywhere but at his bare chest.

Dunharra cleared her throat, hoping it would spur one of them to speak.

The youngest initiate spoke from behind the older two. Clumsily, she declared, "The princess sustained an injury. We are to bring Dunharra to the infirmary."

Dunharra sprang from the bed and got dressed quicker than Magnus could speak. She tossed him his tunic with a wink.

"Later," she whispered with a kiss on his cheek.

Dunharra and Magnus followed the three initiates to the infirmary, only to find several healers arguing at the foot of the bed where Aoife lay. She barely breathed, and the blood coming from her mouth and nose gave only the barest hint of what was wrong.

Dunharra knelt next to Aoife and gently laid a hand on her forehead. "How long has she been this way?" she asked.

“We don’t know,” one healer replied. "A guard found her on the turrets and brought her here. "We do not know who injured her," one of the healers replied.

Dunharra drew in a breath and her green eyes glowed iridescent as she healed the injuries to Aoife’s brain, bruised from the Mother only knew what. The concussion was deep and severe but disappeared under Dunharra’s gentle touch. She felt the back of Aoife’s head and found what she expected; broken pieces of bone where a hard-formed skull should be. She took her time to knit the bones back together. Piece by piece, her skull came together and was again one. When Dunharra sufficiently fused the fractures and fissures, and satisfied that she healed all of Aoife’s injuries, her eyes returned to their usual grass green. What happened to Aoife, Dunharra had undone.

Aoife’s eyes fluttered open. It took her a moment to realize that she was no longer on the turrets but in the infirmary. When her eyes fell on her mother, she reached for her.

“Mum!” Aoife cried into her mother’s shoulder. “Ronan has the Crown and it’s evil.”

“I know it’s evil that Ronan has the Crown,” her mother said. “We will—”

“No, Mum,” Aoife interjected. “The Crown is evil. The Crown is alive.”

Dunharra turned to look at Magnus. “Holy shit. How could an inanimate object be alive? How could a thing be evil? It’s a crown.”

Her mother did not seem to understand and hugged her daughter tightly. “It’s alright, Aoife. Rest.”

“But, Mum,” Aoife protested.

The swift attention of the healers bearing down on her drowned Aoife’s protests.

“You must reconvene the war council,” Dunharra said.

***

ISEABAIL

The war council reconvened at dawn. Maebh and Kieron invited Dunharra, Magnus, Zauvadok, Anaïs, Tup, Iseabail, and Calyx. The meeting was contentious, and tempers flared.

Iseabail tried to explain how the Crown controlled Ronan.

"What do you mean, it's intelligent?" Kieron asked, not comprehending that such a thing could exist.

"The Crown has a personality and an intelligence like you and me," Iseabail tried to explain. "It's alive and cognizant in the way you and I are."

"What does that have to do with Aoife?" Maebh asked.

"She bears ink diametrically opposed to the Crown," Iseabail replied. "It could be our only way to survive this."

"No," Kieron said. "I will not send my daughter into war!"

"The choice may not be ours," Iseabail said. "She reacted to its presence. We don't know what her ink will do when confronted with the Crown acting at full power."

"Stirling is coming," Kieron said. "The call for aid went out when Ronan amassed his forces at our borders."

"Find out everything you know about Aoife's ink," Maebh said. "We must know how it works and how much power lies within her now, so we are prepared for the worst-case scenario."

Nods of agreement went around the council.

Mhari brought the texts from which she copied the pattern and infused the ink with its power to Iseabail. The ancient magick was potent; some of it was difficult for Iseabail to read. The Mountain Elves of long ago wrote it in their ancient script.

"How did you read this?" Iseabail asked Mhari.

Mhari demurred. "As a youngling, I apprenticed with an old Mountain Elf. He impressed upon me the power of the ink and the need to use it carefully."

"And what made you think it would be appropriate to put this ink on a youngling?" Iseabail asked Mhari, incredulous.

"Aoife had torn through the ancient tomes of the library," Mhari began. "She had remarkably improved her timeliness and attitude toward her studies. Iain and I thought she deserved a reward. She asked for this ancient ink. Who could have thought that anyone would get the Crown? I mean, even its touch is deadly."

"So, you gave a child ink that counteracted the most powerful object known to Mantua? And possibly the world?" Iseabail asked, growing frustrated with Mhari's impetuousness. "As a prize?"

Mhari set her eyes downcast, fully comprehending the danger she put Aoife in. At last, she said, "But if I hadn't done so, we would be, without a doubt, doomed under the current circumstances."

Iseabail realized that Mhari's impulsivity and thoughtlessness might have saved them all. Her shoulders sank a little as she regarded her. She sighed. "Alright. Tell me all you know about this ink and its magick."

***

AOIFE

Aoife ran around the castle again within an hour of Dunhrra healing her. It would have been sooner if the Innesfrees healers had let her get up. Her ink still glowed and occasionally pulsed, but nothing occurred like the event on the turrets. So, she went back to her room and curled up with an old book. Dubh curled up in her lap and purred loudly.

She read an old story about a Mauu named Zoya who fell in love with a human named Sebes. It was a bittersweet tale of forbidden love; something that Aoife did not understand. Love is love…why can't you be with the one you love?

Aoife made a mental note to ask her mother.

Chapter Forty-Two

CHAPTER FORTY TWO

RONAN

The remaining Buckhaven troops arrived overnight. Ronan's full force was now amassed at Innesfrees' border.

Ronan sat at his war table with his most trusted knights, while other knights and squires stood sentry outside.

"We can attack at any time, Your Majesty," one graying knight reported.

Morning, the Crown commanded. *We attack at dawn.*

"We will attack at dawn," Ronan said, complying word for word with what the Crown instructed.

When dawn came, Ronan led his troops through the village of Innesfrees, only to find empty houses. He cursed under his breath and shook his head, snorting impatiently.

"Burn it," Ronan commanded. "Burn it all!"

Ronan, the Crown, and the Buckhaven army marched up to the field, where the comparatively small Innesfrees forces were waiting. He saw Maebh in her armor and Kieron in his ride up and down the line of troops, calling them to action. Their inspirational words whipped the Innesfrees army into a fighting frenzy, and it made Ronan seethe.

Ronan encountered cheering and screaming warriors. He snorted with derision when he noticed their motivation.

He ordered his archers to send a volley of arrows into the waiting Innesfrees army.

"Shield wall!" Maebh shouted.

Many of the arrows impaled the shields, missing their intended targets. The Innesfrees army marched forward.

Fully under the sway of the Crown, Ronan pointed his sword at Maebh and shouted, "Now!"

The knights on horseback rode toward Innesfrees, while the Innesfrees army held their ground and waited for them to come closer. The horses galloped, and the Buckhaven knights focused intently on attacking the smaller army.

Maebh and Kieron calmed their horses and waited for the Buckhaven cavalry to come closer. Zauvadok, Anaïs, and Magnus manned the hidden spikes while Iseabail and Dunharra prepared to add an element of magick that might catch Ronan off guard. Tup went behind enemy lines.

When the Buckhaven cavalry came within a few yards, Zauvadok, Anaïs, and Magnus triggered the hidden spikes, frightening the horses and throwing their riders onto the spikes. The few riders who controlled their horses retreated to regroup.

Then, Maebh and Kieron rode out, followed by their warriors, leaping the spikes, to meet Ronan's troops head on. Ronan swore when Iseabail and Dunharra sent fire and lightning into the field. He seethed as he watched helplessly as Dunharra's lightning eliminated his archers who were picking off Innesfrees soldiers one by one.

The roar of Iseabail's flames drowned the field, muffling the dying screams of the armies and the sound of metal on metal. Deafening thunder rolled after Dunharra's lightning. The battle lasted until nightfall, when both sides withdrew to their camps to regroup and wait the night out.

"By the Mother! This was supposed to be easy!" Ronan roared.

"Your Majesty," the grayed knight began. His bloodied face frowned. "Innesfrees prepared for us. We still outnumber them."

Kill their mages, the Crown said. *Kill Maebh and Kieron.*

"We must take out their mages," Ronan said. "Then we can eliminate the Prince Regent and the Queen."

"You mean capture them?" the grayed knight suggested.

"Insolence!" The Crown's shout ran inside Ronan's head. "How dare he question me?"

"No, I mean eliminate them," Ronan sneered. He wrinkled his nose and bared his teeth. "They are vermin, and we must treat them as such," Ronan sneered. Don't question me again, Orvyn, or you will join them."

"This goes against the rules of war," Orvyn said as he stood. "Your Highness."

Treason! He will always question your judgment. He will always try to make you look foolish. Especially in front of others.

"Treason!" Ronan shouted. "How dare you question me?"

"I have questioned your judgment since you obtained that vicious Crown, Your Majesty."

"You are relieved as my knight, Orvyn," Ronan spat. "Take him away."

Knights dragged Orvyn from the tent. Once a few yards away, they held him down and slit his throat. They left his body there as a warning to anyone else who might question Ronan's judgment.

Ronan's war council lasted for hours.

Ronan knew the number of warriors still able to fight for Innesfrees was small. Although Innesfrees inflicted heavy casualties, Ronan's forces still outnumbered them. His intelligence told him that the Innesfrees infirmary was bursting at the seams. Burn victims, soldiers, and knights occupied every bed. Every initiate, healer, and herbalist ran getting supplies or working to heal today's injuries.

***

ISEABAIL

Iseabail watched as the war council sat huddled together over a well-worn map. They examined all their options and came to one conclusion. Without Stirling, they faced defeat. Tomorrow. Their oldest and wisest knight concurred. Without Stirling, they would lose the battle.

The Triplet Sister Moons dropped below the horizon and the sun shone in their place, painting the sky in brilliant hues of gold and copper. Ronan met Maebh, Iseabail and Kieron in the center of the blood-soaked field.

Ronan spoke first. "I have decimated you. Surrender and I will not annihilate your people."

"What are your terms?" Maebh asked, her back defiantly straight.

I will strip you of your nobility and annex Innesfrees. Your people may live. Do you yield?

"We do not."

"Have it your way. Their blood is on your hands." Ronan indignantly turned his horse around and rode back to his camp.

Eliminate them, the Crown seethed. *Wipe them from the face of Mantua. Make them an example to anyone who dares to defy you.*

***

AOIFE

From the turrets, Aoife watched the interaction between her parents and Ronan. Her hands gripped the marble ledge so hard her knuckles were white. At this distance, she could not hear the words, but she could get the gist of what happened.

The armies met on the battlefield, Innesfrees significantly outnumbered. Aoife could hear the roar of the battle raging below. The sight churned her stomach, but she remained rooted to the spot on the turrets. Her heart raced as she watched Buckhaven's army slowly but steadily overwhelm the Innesfrees warriors.

It was a rout.

Zauvadok, Magnus, and Anaïs, who were on the battlefield, knew the tide had turned. They battled Buckhaven soldiers until they found themselves surrounded. The Buckhaven soldiers easily overwhelmed and captured them.

Aoife's mouth went dry when she watched her parents ride out onto the battlefield. She didn't understand what was happening, but she knew it could not end well. Aoife leaned over the turret as far as she safely could. She screamed over the roar of the battle, but her cries fell unheard.

Mum!

A Buckhaven knight roughly pulled Maebh from her horse without a word and took her to Ronan's tent. Ronan rode up to Kieron, who was in a posture of suing for peace, but drew his sword upon the rough treatment of Maebh.

"This is for my father, you son of a bitch!" Ronan declared.

Ronan rode up to Kieron and ran him through, twisting the blade as he did so. Kieron fell from his horse into a growing pool of his own blood. What few soldiers who remained gathered around him and carried him back to the castle infirmary, leaving a trail of blood in their wake.

Father!

Aoife felt the ink on the back of her neck. It throbbed and grew warmer with each heartbeat. She fought back tears as she watched her parents separated. With each tear that fell, the ink glowed brighter and brighter.

***

RONAN

Ronan paced in the tent around Maebh, who calmly stood her ground.

"I have defeated your army! Your precious Kieron bleeds out on the battlefield! Will you yet yield?"

"I will not." Maebh's eyes were hard and unyielding.

Foolish woman! the Crown sniped. *She is beneath you.*

Ronan slapped Maebh across her face. Blood flew from her nose, and she stumbled, dizzy.

"Foolish woman! When will you admit defeat?" Ronan shouted, spittle flying from the corners of his mouth.

"I will never capitulate to you, Ronan. You will have to kill me." Maebh said defiantly, hands balled up into fists.

We can accommodate that, the Crown promised.

"That will leave your daughter alone. Pity," Ronan sneered. His eyes narrowed as he regarded Maebh.

"She will build a great kingdom and avenge us. I promise you that," Maebh replied. Maebh stood unmoving in the face of Ronan's fury.

Ronan's hand flew again, knocking Maebh off her feet.

Maebh stumbled but caught herself on the war room table. Blood dripped on the map of Innesfrees, and it smeared when she moved her hand to steady herself.

"She will defeat you in our memory."

Ronan's hand flew a third time, and Maebh fell to the ground. The world spun, and all went black.

Impudent woman! the Crown shouted. *It will be my pleasure to see her die.*

The Crown stopped short. The silence disturbed Ronan, and he searched his mind. He could see only Aoife.

***

AOIFE

Aoife's vision blurred. It was all fuzzy and soft until the center of her vision cleared. She could see what the Crown saw. And she saw her mother on the ground, not moving.

"Mother!" Aoife screamed. Her mind focused on the Crown, everything else forgotten to her. She felt her feet lift off the turret, and she hovered in the air. Her eyes glowed bright green, identical to the color of her pulsating ink.

The youngling, she heard the Crown say.

Aoife could see Ronan walk out of his tent. She could feel that the Crown was in full control of him. He walked through to the center of the battlefield and stood in Kieron's blood.

His eyes grew black as the void of death. Aoife watched as he lifted off the ground and floated in the air, the wind fluttering his clothing and blowing in his hair. He climbed higher, until he was level with Aoife.

No youngling will best me, the Crown threatened.

The Crown screamed inwardly as light burst from Aoife's eyes. Aoife trained it on the Crown.

No youngling will—

A beam of black, devoid of all light, shot from Ronan's eyes, and Aoife saw it on a trajectory straight to her.

The two beams met in the middle. They sizzled and crackled as they fought and counteracted each other. The two hovered in the air, neither beam gaining or giving any ground.

Aoife thought of her mother, roughly whisked away on the whims of Ronan and the Crown. Something clicked inside her. Something came together, and the love she felt for her mother and father shone through.

Aoife's light beat back Ronan's and the Crown's.

Overhead, Aoife was unaware of the thunderheads that gathered, and the sky darkened. The low rumble of thunder rolled through the heavens, and lightning streaked across the sky.

The crackling and sizzling of the clashing beams continued. Foot by foot, Aoife's light pushed harder against the Crown. The Crown gave way. The center diamond of the Crown darkened to black but could gain no ground on Aoife.

No! I will not go back to my icy prison! the Crown shouted.

The Crown redoubled its efforts, momentarily gaining ground. Aoife could hear the Crown cackle in anticipation of its victory, and it echoed in her mind. It was winning.

Scenes of her mother flashed before Aoife's eyes. Each scene evoked emotion in her and gave her strength to continue. She could feel the ink intensify, and it tingled on her skin. Aoife's ink glowed so brightly that all she could see was the light it gave off. She focused on her love for her mother, and Aoife pushed back against the Crown.

The Crown recoiled at the redoubled effort, and its beam of power began to give way. Inch by inch, slowly, Aoife's light pushed back on the Crown.

In one last burst of energy, Aoife's beam of power exploded, encapsulating her and the Crown inside the detonation, and it lit the sky like a firework.

She felt more than saw Ronan fall to the ground, and the Crown fell off his head. It rolled away helplessly and came to a stop a few feet from the insensible man. Roils of blood-red smoke emanated from his mouth and nose, and the magick that kept him safe from the Crown flowed out of his body. Aoife and her ink broke the spell.

Aoife fell from the sky onto the turret. The impact stunned her, she looked around and then it all went black.

***

DUNHARRA

Dunharra saw Aoife and Ronan rise and meet each other in the sky. She watched as they hung in the air, beams of light emanating from them. Dunharra could hardly believe what she saw. She left the battlefield reluctantly when called to tend to Kieron.

He was nearly dead when she arrived in the private section of the infirmary.

He bled so much that there was barely any blood left in his body. She had a lot of work to do and little time to do it if she wanted to save him. Dunharra tore off his armor and ripped his shirt away from the hemorrhaging wound.

She laid her hands on him, and her eyes transformed from her brilliant green to iridescent. In her mind's eye she could see the devastating damage wrought on him. The lacerations included his liver, a slashed inferior vena cava, and a completely sliced-through right kidney.

Dunharra set to work. She worked to knit together his liver, which at one point was bleeding profusely, but with such low blood volume now was little more than a trickle. When Dunharra was sure she fully mended the liver's scarring, she turned her attention to his kidney. The injury cleaved his kidney in two, requiring more time to heal—a luxury she didn't have. The harder she worked, the slower and weaker his heart beat. Until it stopped.

Kieron was dead.

Dunharra swore. She temporarily abandoned her work on his kidney to restart his heart. He would have to do with one kidney for the moment.

Blood. He needed blood, and fast. She drew in a deep breath and poured all her energy into his long bones and pelvis, pulling blood from deep within the marrow. The push and pull of making blood was working, but not fast enough. She had to divide her energy and attention to both making blood and restarting his heart.

Her eyes glowed more intently, and her hands held an ethereal, iridescent glow. Kieron was dead, but as long as she breathed, he would not stay that way.

Finally, she created enough blood to restart his heart and Kieron gasped. It beat weakly at first, irregular and chaotic. Her forehead glistened with effort and concentration. She repaired the inferior vena cava and stemmed the bleeding from there. His heart beat regularly, but it was still weak.

Dunharra, lost in healing Kieron, did not realize she drew a crowd. One by one, the healers stood and stared. The entire room stood still and held its collective breath while Dunharra worked. They could not believe what they were seeing. Kieron should be dead. And yet he breathed.

She returned her attention to his kidney, which was bleeding again with his heart beating. Dunharra worked quickly, and with the kidney healed and reaffixed in its proper place, Kieron's heart beat with renewed strength.

All that remained for Dunharra to do was to close the deep and superficial wounds to his muscle and skin. While Ronan's sword was wickedly sharp, when he twisted the blade in Kieron's abdomen, it avulsed much of the surrounding tissue, making knitting the wound back together a little easier.

Then it was done. Kieron was alive. What Ronan destroyed, she healed. She released her touch and her eyes returned to her normal grass green. She tried to stand and ended up stumbling, caught by Mhari. Her face was the last thing Dunharra saw before it all went black.

***

RONAN

Ronan woke disoriented as the crown fell from his head. Instinctively, he reached for it, his fingers barely touching the iskender. Magick sizzled and sparked at his fingertips, warning him against proceeding. With Hagan gone, there was no one and no magick to protect him from the hazards of the Crown. Undeterred and thinking only of his vengeance, he grabbed the Crown with his hand and placed it back on his head.

No! You fool, this is our undoing! the Crown shouted.

As soon as he removed his hands from the Crown, he could not move. The freezing began in his feet and quickly made its way up his body. He swallowed rapidly against the horror. It was over in a matter of seconds, but for Ronan, those seconds were an eternity. The frozen Ronan toppled over and fell to the ground, shattering into thousands of pieces. The Crown landed on top of the icy pieces, and the inner light slowly faded.

It was over.

Stirling and Cobh arrived on the battlefield in time for the war's end.

With the sudden death of Ronan, young Donal acceded to the throne. Upon the arrival of Stirling and Cobh, Buckhaven went from outnumbering Innesfrees to being outnumbered. Buckhaven petitioned for peace, which Innesfrees readily granted. Buckhaven capitulated and vacated the battlefield after exchanging prisoners.

***

ISEABAIL

Iseabail watched as Magnus searched for Dunharra throughout the castle. He was near panic when she was not where expected her to be.

"Maybe the infirmary?" Iseabail suggested.

There, Iseabail's stomach fell and her mouth went dry as she saw Dunharra laying on the cot. She watched as Magnus knelt next to her. He took her hand and kissed it desperately.

"Dun, honey," he said. "It's time to wake up."

When he received no response, he ran his fingers through her short, curly black ringlets and caressed her cheek with his thumb.

"Dun, wake up. Please. I need you. I can't lose you," he whispered.

Iseabail put a reassuring hand on his shoulder. He leaned into it and sighed.

"Dun, please..."

Iseabail was afraid she wasn't going to wake up. She knew that he feared this too. Had she gone too far? Was there a too far?

"Dun, I love you." After everything that had happened, he finally got to tell her. Iseabail's heart broke for him. He closed his eyes and quietly wept.

A single tear escaped Dunharra's eye. Her eyes opened and they were iridescent.

Iseabail gasped and shook Magnus' shoulder. He peered at Dunharra through wet eyes. Her eyes shifted from iridescent to green and she looked at Magnus.

"I love you too, Magnus."

Iseabail smiled and watched with eyes welled with tears that threatened to spill over as Magnus held her close to him.

***

IAIN

Knights retrieved Aoife from the turrets, bruised and broken. Iain, Mhari, Maebh, and Kieron hovered around her bedside. Iain's body ached and his legs were numb, the mental link between them fully formed. He felt what Aoife felt.

Iain could only watch as Dunharra's eyes transformed from grass green to iridescent, as she healed Aoife's bruises and broken leg, pelvis and vertebrae. She knit the spinal cord together where it was severed, keeping Aoife from feeling and moving her legs. Both Aoife and Iain felt amazed when the numbness vanished. She cleaned up the cuts and scrapes that come with a fall from that height.

It wasn't long before Aoife was up and running around the halls of Castle Innesfrees again.

A few days later, she approached her parents.

"When can I have more ink?"

Chapter Forty-Three

SNEAK PEEK INTO BOOK TWO

ISEABAIL

The night sky was awash with stars and galaxies. The hues of blue and green of the Mantuan Borealis faded in the upcoming sunrise. Tup and Iseabail lay in the thick grass watching the Triplet Sister moons slip under the horizon. Their inked hands clasped; they lay there silently as Jyotsna, Jey, and Jhokomis spun as they danced together with the galaxies. They were almost out of sight when the sun began its rise over the east, bringing the bright light of a new day into the world. It painted the sky in brilliant hues of red, copper, and pink.

"I don't understand what Dun gets from this," Iseabail said. She glanced at Tup. Just like Dunharra, who spent every morning laying in the grass communing with the Mother, watching the exchange of moons and sun, the night sky mesmerized Tup.

Tup laughed. Iseabail loved that sound. She would give almost anything to hear Tup laugh.

Iseabail sat up. Her long bluish-white hair was a mess and littered with pieces of grass. She ran her fingers through it, sending the grass flying away in the warm early morning breeze. Ink covered her long fingers, her left arm, and torso, enabling her use of magick. Her tunic and pants of Elven silk adorned her body also had pieces of grass on them, and she brushed them away.

Calyx, a brownie and Iseabail's familiar, waited inside the Mountain Elf embassy, in their room. She muted their link so Iseabail could be alone with Tup. This provoked mixed feelings in Calyx. Iseabail knew Calyx wanted to give them the privacy they deserved, but she also knew Calyx didn't like the cost. Calyx could still feel their connection, and that comforted her. But Iseabail couldn't help but notice that Calyx grew jealous. Jealous of Iseabail's time and attention.

A year had passed since the war, the assault on Innesfrees and the frozen death of Ronan. The Mauu, with assistance from the Lycaena, had returned the Crown to its frigid resting place in Donmus buz Tutmus. They added magickal wards to make coming near the crown more difficult. Aoife was safe and learning more magick. All seemed right with the world.

It was after Litha, the longest day of the year. The days were slowly growing longer and the nights warmer. The Wheel of the Year inevitably turned as the lovers slowly grew older. It seemed like yesterday when they celebrated Beltane. They wore their daisy flower crowns in their hair and danced with the crowd around a maypole and an enormous bonfire as they celebrated the frivolity of spring.

They spent much of the morning snuggled in each other's arms. Iseabail couldn't stop thinking about her father, Padraig's reaction to them since they had returned to Ayr. Padraig had greeted them warmly as usual with full hugs and kisses on the cheek. But when Iseabail introduced Tup as her lover and fiancé, his reception clearly cooled. He had been distant with Iseabail and avoided Tup ever since.

Iseabail smiled sadly as Tup tried unsuccessfully to console her. Tup said he needed time to process this side of her, since he obviously did not know. Iseabail hoped he would come around. Tup tried to assure her he would see they loved each other, and them being together was a good thing, not something to hide from or disavow.

Crushing emotions overwhelmed Iseabail. She put on a smiling, compliant face as Calyx and Tup reassured her with words of encouragement. That he did indeed still love her. But Iseabail was uncertain. Something inside her gnawed away at her confidence in his affection.

All the things he said and did told her a million things, but none of them was, 'I love you'.

***

PADRAIG

Iseabail had surprised Padraig by putting herself on his schedule, he didn't think she would do that. He made up an excuse about needing to be with the Buckhaven and Innesfrees mediation and left her sitting alone. He needed time, he told himself. Time to think things over. However, he knew that wasn't entirely true.

He cast his unseeing eyes on the breathtaking view outside his window. The snow capped Silver Haven Mountains jutted up in front of him providing him a breathtaking vista, if he only looked. If there ever was a time he needed his wife, it was now. Not a day went by that he didn't miss her terribly, and now it was especially poignant. Saoirse would have known what to say, what to do. She always did. She had been gone for one hundred years, and still the pain was as intense as if it were yesterday.

He couldn't go on this way, avoiding them, Iseabail especially. As the Mountain Elf ambassador and for all the successful, delicate handling of bigger issues than this, he could not bring himself to come to an understanding with his own daughter.

The problem was time. People always thought they had more than they did.

When he asked Iseabail and Tup for a meeting, they readily agreed, hoping for a change in demeanor. He drank his usual lavender lemonade while he waited for them. Tiny, symbolic wheat sheaves, corn dolls and sunflowers decorated the room for the coming Lughnasadh leaving a fragrant aroma.

His hands shook as he waited impatiently for them. He rubbed them together to ebb the shaking. As he refilled his glass, they walked through the door.

"Hello Papa. What can we do for you?" Iseabail asked.

Padraig stood formally and gestured for them to sit across from him, not in her usual spot next to him.

"Have a seat. There is news from the Southern Kingdoms," he said.

Padraig poured aromatic lavender lemonade for them both and made himself comfortable.

"There are rumblings of trouble in Cobh. King Conrad, who usurped the throne after Colm's unexpected death, rules Cobh with an iron fist. Finn Baird, Colm's son, is making a claim to the throne. Now that his grandfather and father have passed on to the Summerlands, he has a legitimate right. My information tells me he is planning a coup any day now."

"With respect, what does that have to do with us? Isn't this a Cobh matter?" Iseabail asked.

"There have been reports of Living Rights violations in Cobh since Conrad seized the throne; rumors of rampant hunger and abuses. The Living Rights Document is clear regarding these matters, and I need those rumors substantiated or refuted."

"Understood. Would you like us to leave today?" Iseabail asked.

"Stay the night if you'd like," Padraig said with open arms. "But be ready to travel in the morning."

Iseabail and Tup nodded in agreement. Padraig knew Iseabail would expect a warm embrace from him as she left. He could not bring himself to do it. He watched her pause hoping for a hug that would not come. Instead of the usual hug, he gave her a light handshake. Padraig could see how it hurt Iseabail. Her eyes never lied; they revealed her devastation, although her mouth remained silent.

Padraig shifted uneasily in his chair. He suspected differences in his daughter for years, but not like this. There had been no struggles with Iseabail being obsessed with boys as she grew up. No dramatic relationships or heartbreaks. There were no tears or slammed doors. He admired that about his daughter, and now it caused him great consternation.

His wife passed away over one hundred years ago when Iseabail was a tiny youngling, barely crawling. Saoirse had younglingbed fever and never fully recuperated. When Iseabail was four months old, she came down with a cold, which in her compromised state, quickly progressed. Bereft and lost without her, he missed her every day.

Saoirse would know what to do. She always knew what to do.

Padraig envisioned a wedding and grandchildren. That image had broken into a thousand tiny pieces, but he had a different reason for his coolness. He had sons who could give him wedding celebrations and grandchildren. If he had a favorite child, Iseabail would be the one. He thought about it for weeks. He could not approve, and he didn't know what that would do to his relationship with his daughter. So, he did his best to avoid her and her lover.

But time did not obey their rules.

***

DUNHARRA

Dunharra and Magnus packed their bags for the trip home. They had gone to Ayr for the Litha celebrations and were ready for the quiet of their cottage in the Thunder Hill Forest, south of the Silver Haven Mountains. Magnus put a loving arm around Dunharra's shoulder and kissed her gently on the cheek. With all the festivities, they had spent a lot of time together, but very little of it alone. Dunharra smiled and gave him the side eye. She couldn't leave it at that.

She stole a kiss, which led to an embrace, which led to them being an hour late setting off for home.

They made their way to the stables and found their horses already saddled, tacked, and waiting for them.

Dunharra and Magnus met Iseabail, Calyx, and Tup in the stables as they were preparing to start their journey to the Southern Kingdoms. Tup, a Wild One, wore a black leather shirt, pants and boots under a cloak with hidden, uncountable pockets. Her short brown hair hung over her undercut shaved head. She also wore one small braid hanging from the left side of her head. Tup wore ink all over her hands, arms, and torso that enhanced her assassin's skills.

"You seem to be off on a long journey. Where are you going?' Dunharra asked. She wore a long sleeved linen top with a black leather stay and black leather pants to hide the fact that she had no ink. She was a skilled healer, but no one could know she could heal and work magick without the ink, so she hid behind comfortable but unseasonable clothes all year long. No one could know who she really was. Only those very close to her could know her secret.

Iseabail told them of the rumblings of trouble in Cobh, and the rumors of Living Rights violations, hunger and abuse since Conrad took the throne. They were to go there, observe and confirm or refute the reports then return to Ayr.

"Sounds like you could use some company on your journey. There is greater safety in numbers," Dunharra said. "Especially with a healer."

"How do you feel about traveling together?" Iseabail asked. Her eyes were not their usual bright blue, but cloudy, like an overcast day when you were expecting sunshine. Iseabail dressed in an icy blue Elven silk tunic with Elven silk pants and leather boots. Iseabail's brownie, which she's bonded with, never leaves her.

"I would love it. Should we get everyone back together? I imagine Anaïs and Zauvadok are restless by now," Magnus answered. Magnus, also a Wild One, former bounty hunter, muscular and strong. He wore studded leather armor. He sported no ink, but his hunting skills more than made up for his lack of it. Magnus pulled his straight brown hair up into a man bun over his undercut shaved head. His steely grey eyes saw only Dunharra.

"I don't see why not," Dunharra said. "They don't live far from us. Let's see if they're up for it."

It took the better part of a day to reach Anaïs and Zauvadok's cottage in Rhyl. They arrived just as the sun slipped below the horizon and the Triplet Sister moons were rising as crescents in the sky, leaving little light to travel by. Their grey cottage, humble and efficient, sat at the base of the Thunder Hill Forest. The windows sparkled in the moonlight, and a warm glow of firelight emanated from inside.

Dunharra knocked on the door and Zauvadok answered with a lively smile when he saw her. He invited them in, and Anaïs also gave them warm hugs and kisses on their cheeks. There were happy tears and hugs. Zauvadok and Magnus gave mutual grunts, then a strong man hug. They spent a good part of the evening catching up over hot teas and cold ales.

Zauvadok a tall half orc, wore a cotton shirt and leather pants. He had red filigree ink on his back which enhanced his strength, and a green dragon on his shoulder. He kept his ink to himself and never took his shirt off for anyone but Anaïs. His skin was the usual orcish greyish-green, but the rest of his features were mostly human except for two orcish teeth, which jutted out of his mouth. Anaïs is Zauvadok's wife and a lithe and thin dark elf. She dressed in supple black leather, a stark contrast to her pure white hair. Her black skin bore much black ink, looking nearly invisible on her soft, supple skin.

Dunharra listened as Iseabail told them about her father and his sudden distancing from her. She could see from her face and from the tone of her voice that it wasn't just taking a toll on her. It broke her heart and crushed her soul. Dunharra knew Iseabail couldn't go on like this.

"I don't know what to do," she said, with tears welling up in her eyes.

"I told her he needs time to adjust," Tup said with Iseabail's fingers entwined in hers. "He obviously didn't know, and it came as a surprise to him."

Tup turned her loving brown eyes to Iseabail. "You need to prepare yourself if he doesn't come around."

Calyx nodded her agreement but did not add to the conversation. Calyx sat by Iseabail's side and wrapped her arm around her.

Dunharra expected Padraig's reaction and warned Iseabail about it. She felt Iseabail should make her own decisions and live her own life out from under the shadow of Padraig. She had made her feelings known, and she would not bring them up again here.

One tear slipped from Iseabail's eye and landed on Tup's fingers.

They talked late into the night.

When morning glittered through the windows, Dunharra lay outside in the grass, watching the sun come up. She felt the damp morning dew covering her as she was in deep communion with the Mother.

Mid-morning came before they were all ready, Anaïs being the last to wake. Zauvadok secured the cottage before they left. They saddled up and were on their way south to Cobh.

Cobh, the southernmost of the Southern Kingdoms, sat on the rugged coastline of the Bay of Charms and about two day's ride from the Ádh Mor lighthouse. Cool ocean breezes blew over the jagged cliffs, and seabirds rode thermals over the waves. They could easily expect a three to four day trip one way to Cobh.

They traveled unbothered for most of the day.

***

ISEABAIL

Iseabail wanted to write notes to her father to chronicle her experiences, but she couldn't help talking about her relationship with Tup and how Padraig's reaction to them affected her.

Before bed, Iseabail wrote a letter to her father.

Papa,

I wish you good tidings and I hope this letter, hopefully the first of many, of the trip finds you well. This is to chronicle our trip in case we do not make it back. We stayed at Zauvadok and Anaïs' cottage last night.

I am concerned because your demeanor changed when I introduced Tup as my fiancé. Does this disappoint you somehow? The change in you is unmistakable.

. We should talk about this; should we return.

While no formal postal service existed in Mantua, there were many official couriers who would deliver letters. There weren't many on the Great Northern Road, but you could get one if you were lucky. The official couriers were reliable, and the cost depended on what you were sending. Tup found a courier and sent the letter to Padraig in Ayr.

They traveled down the Great Northern Road almost to Dunkeld before stopping for the night in The Petty Dragon.

"Three rooms?" Zauvadok asked the innkeeper.

"You're getting my last three. I'm full up for the night. Breakfast in the morning."

Iseabail grasped Tup's hand. The eyes of some curious onlookers focused on them. No doubt they would share a room. Some people lost interest; some stared and watched them walk up the stairs together.

After a long day on the road, they could sleep well.

After breakfast, they were back on the road.

The day passed uneventfully, and they stayed at The Ram that night.

They stayed at the Ram frequently and were on a first name basis with the owner and staff. A rustic building with large, exposed oak beams on the ceiling, ceremonial wheat sheafs, corn dolls and copious amounts of sunflowers decorated the inn for the coming Lughnasadh. The sunflowers left a sweet, satisfying aroma.

"Hey, you guys come back!" Bruno exclaimed. "You my favorite people." He came out from behind the bar and greeted them individually. He hugged and kissed the ladies, and Zauvadok and Magnus received claps on the back and strong man hugs.

They spent the better part of the night catching up. They talked about everything, including Iseabail's father.

"He needs time," Tup lied with a tired sigh. She didn't believe that he needed time. She believed he was firm in his resolve to be cool to Iseabail for the foreseeable future.

"What if he no come around?" Bruno asked.

That question burned in the back of everyone's mind, but no one said it. A pensive silence fell over the group, and they ate the rest of their evening meal in silence.

Later, up in their room, Iseabail's tears burned her face. Tup kissed them away and did her best to be the partner Iseabail needed. Calyx hung back and let Tup do the consoling. When it seemed like Iseabail had cried herself out for the night, they settled in bed. Tup fell asleep quickly, but Calyx and Iseabail used their mental link to talk.

We need to talk about Tup and Padraig, Iseabail.

She dreaded this conversation. She knew Calyx harbored jealousy of her time alone with Tup, but for now it didn't affect their bond. For now.

You need to prepare for the possibility of his not coming around."

You're a ray of sunshine. Where is this coming from?

I love you. Not like Tup loves you, mind you, but I still do. I won't lead you down some primrose path and say everything's going to be alright. Because it might not. I hate what this is doing to you.

"Then what do I do?

You learn to live without him. You don't need his approval to live your life the way you want.

I wish it were that easy.

It is that easy, Iseabail. Just let it go.

Morning broke, and Iseabail woke up last. She, Tup, and Calyx were the last to enjoy Bruno's breakfast of eggs and bacon with toast, butter and jam.

"You come back again. Don't make me wait so long!" Bruno teased, as he hugged each of them.

They promised to return soon and said their goodbyes.

They traveled down the Great Northern Road until it intersected with the Royal Eastern Road and reached Innesfrees. They stopped to pay their respects to Prince Regent Kieron and Queen Maebh.

Innesfrees was halfway rebuilt after the devastating war with Buckhaven, which had destroyed the village and heavily damaged the castle. All the tapestries in the castle had survived the onslaught, including the Prophesied Healer tapestry. The Prophesied Healer tapestry told the story of a healer who would come who could heal any injury or disease, and death itself would cower at their touch. All the Southern Kingdoms watched and waited for the Prophesied Healer to come.

Repairs to the village began. The skeletons of the buildings and houses showed the ongoing progress. Maebh and Kieron wanted to finish the village in time for the Samhain festivities. They were making good time.

Maebh and Kieron were just as Iseabail remembered, although they all could see the barest beginnings of grey at Kieron's temples. Aoife grew into a graceful and beautiful young lady of twelve. She had a full sleeve of filigree and floral ink down her right arm, and she stood at least a foot taller than when they last saw her. She mirrored Iain, her biological father from an affair with Maebh before her marriage to Kieron, at least as far as height was concerned. Otherwise, she resembled her mother in every other way.

They had a quiet, intimate dinner with Kieron and Maebh, during which they caught up. Although this time, Iseabail stayed quiet and kept her problem with her father to herself. She contributed little to the conversation and pushed her food around her plate until someone mentioned Cobh.

“There are rumblings of a coup, Your Majesty,” Iseabail said. “Finn Baird has a legitimate claim to the throne and plans on taking Cobh by force any day now.”

“Regime change would be good for Cobh,” Kieron said. “When Conrad assumed the throne, it benefitted the wealthy, but the people? Not so much. The upper class and royalty are the only ones who are benefiting from Conrad being on the throne.”

“Have you heard of any living rights violations?” Dunharra asked.

“Rumors of unwarranted arrests villagers going hungry while the rich waste enough food to feed them, and he partakes in the practice of the Right of King’s Night.”

“What’s the Right of King’s Night?” Dunharra asked, not sure she wanted to hear the answer.

“When a couple in Cobh marries,” Kieron said, “the King may forcibly take the bride and have the wedding night with her instead of her husband. I'm proud to say that Stirling and Innesfrees never took part in such a practice.”

The mood took a somber turn. The rumors seemed to be true. If so, they had Living Rights violations.

www.ingramcontent.com/pod-product-compliance
Lightning Source LLC
LaVergne TN
LVHW100506110826
845146LV00002B/528

9798992391220